Praise for **C. J. Cherryh** and *Hammerfall*

"One of the finest writers that SF has to offer."

Science Fiction Chronicle

"*Hammerfall* proves that C. J. Cherryh remains at the top of her game in creating worlds and believable characters, as well as telling stories that get the readers' attention from the first sentence."

Tulsa World

"Cherryh introduces the first wholly new world in her fiction in 30 years and makes it memorable with spare, clean, and elegant prose that lends a haunting quality to the story as it intriguingly conjures the desert setting and the close-to-the-bone way of life it entails."

Booklist

"Features her usual blend of gorgeous, slightly knotty prose, deeply conflicted heroes, desperate action and nicely observed cultural details."

Publishers Weekly

Books by
C.J. Cherryh

FORTRESS OF DRAGONS
FORTRESS OF OWLS
FORTRESS OF EAGLES
FORTRESS IN THE EYE OF TIME
HAMMERFALL

Published by HarperCollins*Publishers*

C. J. CHERRYH

HAMMERFALL

An Imprint of HarperCollinsPublishers

This is a work of fiction. Names, characters, places, and incidents are products of the author's imagination or are used fictitiously and are not to be construed as real. Any resemblance to actual events, locales, organizations, or persons, living or dead, is entirely coincidental.

EOS
An Imprint of HarperCollins*Publishers*
10 East 53rd Street
New York, New York 10022-5299

Copyright © 2001 by C.J. Cherryh
Excerpt from *Hammerfall* copyright © 2001 by C. J. Cherryh
Excerpt from *Rebels in Arms* copyright © 2002 by Ben Weaver
Excerpt from *Trapped* copyright © 2002 by James Alan Gardner
Excerpt from *Acorna's Search* copyright © 2001 by Hollywood.Com, Inc.
Excerpt from *The Mystic Rose* copyright © 2001 by Stephen R. Lawhead
ISBN: 0-06-105709-6
www.eosbooks.com

First Eos paperback printing: August 2002
First Eos hardcover printing: July 2001

Eos Trademark Reg. U.S. Pat. Off. and in Other Countries,
Marca Registrada, Hecho en U.S.A.
HarperCollins® is a trademark of HarperCollins Publishers Inc.

Printed in the U.S.A.

10 9 8 7 6 5 4 3 2 1

HAMMERFALL

1

Imagine first a web of stars. Imagine it spread wide and wider. Ships shuttle across it. Information flows.

A star lies at the heart of this web, its center, heart, and mind.

This is the Commonwealth.

Imagine then a single strand of stars in a vast darkness, a beckoning pathway away from the web, a path down which ships can travel.

Beyond lies a treasure, a small lake of G5 suns, a near circle of perfect stars all in reach of one another.

This way, that strand says. After so hard a voyage, reward. Wealth. Resources.

But a whisper comes back down that thread of stars, a ghost of a whisper, an illusion of a whisper.

The web of stars has heard the like before. Others are out there, very far, very faint, irrelevant to our affairs.

Should we have listened?
—The Book of the Landing.

Distance deceived the eye in the Lakht, that wide, red land of the First Descended, where legend said the ships had come down.

At high noon, with the sun reflecting off the plateau, the chimera of a city floated in the haze, appearing as a line of light just below the red, saw-toothed ridge of the Qarain, that upthrust that divided the Lakht from the Anlakht, the true land of death.

The city was both mirage and truth; it appeared always a day before its true self. Marak knew it, walking, walking endlessly beside the beshti, the beasts on which their guards rode.

The long-legged beasts were not deceived. They moved no faster. The guards likewise made no haste.

"The holy city," some of the damned shouted, some in relief, some in fear, knowing it was both the end of their torment and the end of their lives. "Oburan and the Ila's court!"

"Walk faster, walk faster," the guards taunted them lazily, sitting supreme over the column. The lank, curve-necked beasts that carried them plodded at an unchangeable rate. They were patient creatures, splay-footed, towering above most predators of the Lakht, enduring the long trek between wells with scant food and no water. A long, long line of them stretched behind, bringing the tents, the other appurtenances of their journey.

"Oburan!" the fools still cried. "The tower, the tower!"

"Run to it! Run!" the junior guards encouraged their prisoners. "You'll be there before the night, drinking and eating before us."

It was a lie, and some knew better, and warned the rest. The wife of a down-country farmer, walking among them, set up a wail when the word went out that the vision was only the shadow of a city, and that an end was a day and more away.

"It can't be!" she cried. "It's there! I see it! Don't the rest of you see it?"

But the rest had given up both hope and fear of an end to this journey, and walked in the rising sun at the same pace as they had walked all this journey.

Marak was different than the rest. He bore across his heart the tattoo of the abjori, the fighters from rocks and hills. His garments, the long shirt, the trousers, the aifad wrapped about his head against the hellish glare, were all the dye and the weave of Kais Tain, of his own mother's hand. Those patterns alone would have damned him in the days of the war. The tattoos on the backs of his fingers, six, were the number of the Ila's guards he had personally sent down to the shadows. The Ila's men knew it, and watched with special care for any look of rebellion. He had a reputation in the lowlands and on the Lakht itself, a fighter as elusive as the mirage and as fast-moving as the sunrise wind.

He had ridden with his father to this very plain, and for three years had seen the walls of the holy city as a prize for the taking. He and his father had laid their grandiose plans to end the Ila's reign: they had fought. They had had their victories.

Now he stumbled in the ruin of boots made for riding.

His life was thirty summers on this earth and not likely to be longer. His own father had delivered him up to the Ila's men.

"I see the city!" the woman cried to the rest. She was a wife, an honorable woman, among the last to join the march. "Can't you see it? See it rise up and up? We're at the end of this!"

Her name was Norit, and she was soft-skinned and veiled herself against the sun, but she was as mad as the rest of them that walked in this shuffling chain. Like most of them, she had concealed her madness, hidden it successfully all her years, until the visions came thick and fast. Perhaps she had turned to priests, and priests had frightened her into admission. Perhaps guilt had slowly poisoned her spirit. Or perhaps the visions had become too strong and made concealment impossible. She had confessed in tears when the Ila's men came asking for the mad, and her husband had tried to kill her; but the Ila's men said no. She was from the village of Tarsa, at the edge of the Lakht in the west.

Now increasingly the visions overwhelmed her, and she rocked and mourned her former life and poured out her story in her interludes of sanity. Over and over she told the story of her husband, who was the richest man in Tarsa, who had married her when she was thirteen. She wasted her strength crying, when the desert ate up all strength for grief and all water for tears. Her husband might have been relieved to cast her out.

The old man next in line, crookbacked from old injury, had left an aged wife in Modi, a woman who would live, likely, as an unwelcome guest on the charity of her children. The old man talked to spirits, and could not remember his wife's name. He wept about this, and asked others if they knew. "Magin," they would tell him in disgust, but he would forget, and ask again in a few hours. He had hidden his madness longest of all of them. Sometimes he forgot why they walked. But so did the rest of them. The walking had gone on so long it had become ordinary, a condition of existence.

The boy, the young boy, Pogi, who rocked and talked to himself whenever they stopped and sat down . . . he had been the butt of village jokes in Tijanan. Everyone had accounted him harmless, but in what the Ila's men said, the village grew anxious and delivered him to their hands, throwing rocks at him when he tried to go back to their street. He was no one's son. The village had found him one morning by the well, which they said was reason enough for suspicion. A devil might have put him there. So they thought, after the Ila's men asked for the mad: he was the only madman in that village.

The others all had their stories. The caravan was full of the cursed, the doomed, the rejected. Villages had tolerated them as long as they dared. In Kais Tain long before this, Tain had issued a pogrom to cleanse his province of the mad, ten years ago; but the god laughed at him. Now his own son and heir proved tainted. Tain of Kais Tain had successfully rebelled against the Ila and the Lakht, undefeated for ten years, and had all the west under his hand. But his own son had a secret, and betrayed himself in increasing silences, in looks of abstraction, in crying out in his sleep. He had been mad all along. His father had begun to suspect, perhaps, years ago, and denied it; but lately, after their return from the war, the voices had grown too persistent, too consuming to keep the secret any longer. His father had found him out.

And when shortly afterward his father heard the Ila's men were looking for the mad, his father had sent to the Ila's men . . . had given him up, his defiance of the Ila's rule broken by the truth.

His own son, his own son, Tain said over and over. Tain blamed his wife, and sat gloomy and furious in his hall, a man of war finally seeking peace.

For the rest of his life, Tain said in the document he signed, he would not make war. Tain said this aloud to the Ila's men, and signed their book, and they gave him amnesty in exchange for his only son. That was how much sane men feared the mad, who lately, so the rumors said, proliferated in ungodly fashion: the mad appeared all over the land, more and more of them, a plague among the sane, and the sane began to fear a contagion.

"Marak," his mother had called to him as he marched away, *Marak!* like the voices that resounded in his head. *Marak, Marak!* But his sister Patya, who was the soul of laughter, had drawn her striped aifad over her face, casting sand on herself, as if he were already dead. He still saw her sitting there in the street of Kais Tain, a heap of bright cloth and grief.

In his dreams he saw his mother, who had spilled tears for days before his leaving, who walked beside the caravan as it filed out of Kais Tain, and who had walked with him all that afternoon, until sunset.

Then she had agreed to go back to the village, to what fate he was not sure. He had no idea whether she had walked back to Kais Tain at all. She was Haga, out of the lowland tribes, and might have turned aside and gone by paths the Haga knew, and sought wells the Haga knew.

The taint is in your blood, his father had shouted at her when he knew the truth, but he had not struck her. If he had done that, Marak would have struck him down. But his father then looked at him and asked that damning question: "When did it come on you?"

"I don't remember," he had had to confess to Tain, to that strong, scarred face. "From very young."

His father had turned his face away and said not a thing more. So the madness reached back and back to stain all they had ever done together. All the trust they had for each other was a lie. That was the last time they had looked at one another eye to eye.

The sun reached the zenith. The caravan spread its canvas for shelter from the light, the mirage of the city having faded, and the wife of Tarsa, still talking to herself, subsided sobbing into rest.

The others huddled together and averted their eyes from the sun outside their patch of shade, and the boy rocked and talked to himself. The red-bearded man, a middle-aged tanner with the skin on his shoulders peeling yet again from the sun, sat on the heated sand and rocked and prayed to gods the faithful well knew would not heed the mad.

Marak did none of these things. He only sat and stared at the horizon, beneath that shade of an open-sided tent, as sure as his guards and the caravan master that tomorrow, perhaps tomorrow evening, they would reach the end of their journey.

None of the other madmen had ever made the trek across the Lakht. None of the other raving prisoners had ridden to war against the Ila's long-lasting power, and helped the fiercest of the abjori rain fire on those towers.

None of the others had risen so high on a lie. None of the others had been the heir of Kais Tain, or the hope of Tain's long-surviving ambition.

In those days his dreams were secret, mostly at night. A young fighter bent on following his father's path could keep that secret even if he bit his lip bloody, even if the voices distracted him at his father's table or blinded him while he was riding breakneck down a dune face.

But their war had failed before their love did.

Three years had passed since the retreat from the holy city. And in this last year the secrets had multiplied into visions and visions gained voices. Visions that came like threads and sticks of fire wove themselves tighter and tighter until the sights they conjured unpredictably replaced the sight of his eyes.

Come to us, the inner voices said now, more and more insistent. *Come to us. Listen to us.* At such times the whole world swung, repeatedly, violently as if the demons within his eyes attempted to swing the whole body left or right. It was hard to resist the tug when it came. The mad commonly twitched and jerked in the depth of their affliction.

Some houses might not have given up their mad sons. Some houses, even whole villages, might be wholly given over to the taint, and secretive about their shame.

Other houses, other villages, might have killed the afflicted quietly, so as not to have any madmen left to turn over to the Ila. The caravan of the damned had stopped at villages where no one confessed.

The wife of Tarsa wailed and prayed in the grip of her visions. "Look!" she would cry. "The city! The holy tower is here!" and at other times, "Gods bless the Ila," as if the soldiers would have pity if she praised the tyrant.

"The devil is in the east!" the tanner shrieked, and that set off the old man, who asked after his wife, and cried that he had fathered devils who betrayed him.

Sweat trickled down Marak's face and down his neck and under his arms, drying on his ribs. A man's body betrayed him in the heat. It readily gave up its water. In sorrow, it gave up even more.

Somewhere above the sky had been a land rich in life, where all men were born.

Somewhere up there above the burning blue had been a paradise of water, a pool that never stopped flowing.

That place might have been in the heavens, as the priests said, but the heavens during this march hinted nothing of paradise, only a cold light of stars by night and the burning eye of the sun by day.

They said, the priests did, that when the First Descended had come down onto the Lakht, the Ila, undying and eternal, had divided men from beasts, and beasts from vermin: afterward the world and its order was ruled by the god, the single god, and administered by the Ila and her priests.

Marak, like his father, like most of the west, had rejected that belief. There was no help in the heavens, no reliance on priests on earth, or on the god's viceroy. But having fought that authority and having come to this, there was nothing to do with his life on earth except, perhaps, to end it, pouring out the life he owned like water, until the desert drank it dry, until the vermin of the sky swarmed thick. A man died in the day and nothing was left of him by sundown but the bones.

But he had resolved he would see the holy city again. They were within a day's walk. He had come this far out of sheer persistence, knowing he had nothing else to do but die, and seeing what the next day would bring had thus far been better than not seeing it at all.

Now with the illusion of the city in his eyes, he recalled that he might not only see the city, but that the Ila herself had desired to see the mad. And thinking that, he foresaw he might live long enough to find the Ila's throat within his hands. *There* was an ambition.

There was the way to win his father's gratitude, once his father heard that his son had broken the Ila's immortal neck. His father's son was mad and outcast. But he was not helpless.

{East, the world tilted. Tilted and swung like a compass in a bowl.}

The whole plateau heaved and slanted, and the mad, all at once, set their arms to hold themselves from falling.

But the wife suddenly leapt up, shrieked, and began to run. "The city!" she cried. "Oburan! Ila save us!"

Two of the Ila's men laughed at her flight, then got up and pursued as the mad all righted themselves and stared, and the religious babbled about devils.

"The devils are in the Ila's court!" others jeered, being men of the west, abjori at heart. "And the Ila herself the chief of them!"

"Water is there!" the potter cried. "Water free for the drinking."

A few of the mad rose up, cheering the wife on, or decrying blasphemy, but the guards beat them back to the sand. No one else stirred in the heat. The mad watched the wife as she sped, feet kicking up small puffs of the red powder sand.

Might she escape? Marak asked himself in mild curiosity, sitting quietly the while. There were cliffs and falls amid the dunes.

Might she break her neck or burst her heart? Others then

might find the courage to make an effort. He tested his own mind and sought that courage in himself. But now that he had thought of it, now that the city was imminent, the thought of the Ila's throat held him wholly entranced.

The Ila's men ran faster at the last. The contest became foredoomed and most in the caravan lost interest. Most sprawled back on the sand and rested, some with aching heads. But Marak watched in curiosity as the wife eluded the men.

She had wit. And purpose.

He was faintly disappointed as, shortly after that, the Ila's men overhauled the soft-skinned woman and wrestled her, flailing and screaming, to the sand. He had seen it before, the last burst of life from the mad, then a slow descent into despair and apathy, then death.

They wrapped her in her aifad, using it like a rope, and carried her back despite her screaming and struggling. Her braids dragged the ground and whipped in her fury. Bare legs flailed the air. They almost dropped her. She had more courage than most, this wife from Tarsa, and surprising determination.

{East, the demons said again. *East, east, east.}*

But a man sitting might resist the world tilting as it did. He had learned that.

"Lelie!" the wife cried. It was a woman's name. It might be sister or daughter or mother. He had no idea.

They wrapped the wife in more substantial cords, tied her against one of the two strong tent poles that upheld Marak's tent, and left her babbling and shrieking, "Lelie, Lelie."

In the guards' disinterest, in her own helplessness, the wife's struggles grew weaker, but the shouting went on intermittently, until her voice cracked and went hoarse. Her fight lasted until her struggling dwindled to mere twitches against the cords, and her face ran with wasteful tears.

A potter from the lowlands claimed he saw angels on the cliff, claimed it quite calmly, though there was no cliff in sight.

The lad from Tijanan, at the edge of the shade, rocked obsessively for an hour and banged his head bloody against the stony sand.

Toward afternoon the caravan master and his men doled out cold rations; the wife from Tarsa and the boy were both too distraught to eat, but the caravan master beat them with his quirt and the boy ate. The wife they forced to drink, holding her nose until she swallowed, and after a while, the caravanners holding her arms, she swallowed water on her own. It was a sort of kindness. They might have left her to walk thirsty, knowing they would still deliver her to the city by next afternoon, but the sickness came rapidly on the ones who would not drink. Their bodies poured out less and less water, and they died, cheating the Ila of whatever she wished. So the guards assured that they would have no fault in the matter.

Marak made no such rebellion against his fate. He took a little water in his mouth, broke the caked provision with two free hands, and ate, slowly, observing the guards' diminishing battles with the wife, wondering would she yet die before they reached Oburan, and be free.

The mad had proliferated in the west, in the hills, for thirty years, and now rumor said the Ila had had a dream of them, and wished to purify the land once for all of their affliction.

He feared his father might not rule long, and not alone for the shame and the disappointment of his son. Men would not follow the mad, and through him, the taint had come on the house. To cast blame on the woman who had borne him was his father's only salvation with his men, and Marak understood that, but it was likewise his mother's ruin, and there was no refuge for her if she had not gone to the Haga.

Perhaps she had gone there. Perhaps she was there by now. Perhaps she had found some well, and walked on, and told the Haga only that she was divorced from her husband. A Haga wife had that right, absolute and unquestioned. Perhaps she could forget her son.

But he doubted it. She was stubborn, was Kaptai; she was

proud; and she was a devoted mother. Could she lie, regarding her son? Could she leave her daughter, having had her son led away in shame?

Only one thing he could do, one thing he could do to bring an end of questions, one thing he could do to redeem his disgrace: kill the Ila.

One thing he could do to win his father's forgiveness of his mother, and win his sister's honor, and her life, and her chance of happiness and marriage and children.

Marak, Marak, Marak, the voices said. The madness that afflicted the others afflicted him with visions of a tower, of a cave of suns. Thoughts of any purpose or connection went sliding away in sluggish indirection.

Perhaps the cakes they were fed contained some drug that numbed the senses and the will. He thought at times that might be so. They at least contained nettle that numbed the tongue: the potter complained of it. If it was so, if they numbed the mind, if they somewhat numbed the visions and silenced the voices, Marak took the numbness as relief and did not question the food or refuse to eat as the wife had done.

And when the visions left him, when he was free to lie still and dream ordinary dreams, they were of the western lowlands and the stone towers of Kais Tain, the watchmen watching against the sunset, and his father's house between two high towers. It was a house thick-walled against the sun, and dug deep into the cool sand: the village sprawled out on either hand, around the net-covered garden, and the well.

The dream changed. He saw his mother, standing by the golden, dusty roadside, wrapped in dark robes, wrapped and veiled as he had seen her last, enigma.

His father Tain, the warlike, the defiant, the terrible man, simply acquiesced to all the terms, gave him away like a bartered mat, and signed a lasting armistice with the Ila's men. It was only to his family and his officers that Tain Trin Tain revealed his rage and his affront. Before the whole assembly of his men he called his children's mother a whore.

His mother, being Haga, had said not a word in her own

defense, only wrapped her robe about her face, walked out, and refused to meet the stares of her slaves.

Being Haga, she said nothing of her plans. She refused to debate, refused to resist what she could not withstand.

But the desert was no terror to her. Nothing in the world could be a terror to Kaptai, after her husband.

The tilting of the world increased, then stopped as it would do, without warning.

Marak stared, wordless now, watching the world from far, far off. He watched false oases disintegrate and the sun turn the red sand to brass and haze.

A bird flew past, brief shadow, a scout from the holy city, where birds gathered thick and fattened off the refuse. Birds, like other vermin, would eat the dead, if they had dead; but they had none this day. Dissatisfied, it wheeled away.

At last, with the sun well past noon, the order came from the caravan master to strike the tents.

"Hay-up!" the man yelled. He and his family and his slaves came through waving their hands and uttering that *hup-hup-hup* they used on their beasts. *Hup-hup-hup* for the Ila's men. *Hup-hup-hup* for the madmen, too. The wife, exhausted now, could not be roused from her lethargy, and when they loosed her from the pole she lay on the sand and babbled of fire and light and death.

No one cared, not even the other madmen, while they gathered up the tents.

The Ila's men dragged the wife out under the sky, from under the imminent collapse of the last tent. The boy from Tijanan knelt, rhythmically striking his scabbed forehead on the ground, talking to the invisible. Sand stuck to his forehead and grew red with blood.

Today it was the wife who balked. Yesterday it had been the potter, and they had beaten him. The wife they only hit until she brought up her hands to cover her face. Then they knew she would stop fighting them.

Hup, the word was, when the tents were struck and the beasts were laded after their rest. *Hup,* and they took up the wife on one of the beasts, the smallest, packed on and tied on like cargo lest she harm herself. A soldier would walk: the wife was worth a bounty.

Hup, and the sand-colored beasts rose on their long legs, shook out their lofty necks, and began to move, led by the grizzled old white one, their half-lidded eyes deprecating alike the world's folly and the weakness of men.

The Ila's men set their beasts walking, and Marak walked. The sane shepherded the mad.

The Lakht stretched on and on, masking its traps in distance and illusion, the shimmer of false water and the movement of ghostly vermin.

In the passage of hours, again, under a fading sky, Marak saw visions. Towers built themselves in fire and wove themselves in symbols. A cave gaped and glowed with suns equally spaced, marching on forever.

He ignored them and saw the sand through them. He looked at the horizon, where at last the sun sank, where the true holy city might rise before the next day.

Marak, the demons said, having long ago learned his name. *Marak, Marak, Marak.*

The demon voices were sometimes like women's voices, sometimes like men's. He ignored them as he had learned to do all through his thirty years, and gave his attention to the sounds of men and beasts walking ahead of and behind him.

Over it all came the high, thin wail of the wife from Tarsa.

"Damned," the wife cried at the gathering night, "damned, damned, damned, the Ila save us all! We're all damned!"

The sun went down in flame and spread a last illusory glow across the land, like gilded water.

"I am not mad!" the wife cried as she rode. "I am not mad!"

So she said.

And when the night had fallen and cooled the air of the Lakht to a gentler warmth she sang as she rode to a husband who no longer wanted her. "Let us love," she sang, "let us look to the moons for light and make us a house of stone. Let us dig us a well for our lives and plant green vines and melons. Let us make us a child and dance with the children of our children. Let us lie down in our bed and sleep the long sleep and dream the long dream. Let us love."

And so the tune went round again, round and round and round, a litany, as feet grew worn and legs cramped.

"Let us love," the potter cried at the heavens, "let us love, let us love. Oh, mother, mother, mother! Where is my mother?"

And another, an orchardman, "You never had a mother! Be still!"

The boy from Tijanan heard nothing. He walked, hugging himself, waving his arms outward and slapping himself as he walked, complaining about burning fires.

Marak said nothing. The voices sang in his head, too, but nothing of love or dancing or fires. His voices said words to him and his skin went hot and cold while the lines made pictures against the night.

He saw lines of fire making structures. He saw a beacon flashing in the sky, illusion like the rest. He knew that it was illusion, but in the dark the visions easily became more real than the stars above them.

Red light and green alternately flickered, blinded him. At one point he could no longer see to walk, and fell, his trousers ripped at the knee.

Pain followed. He felt about him, blind, his fingers finding only wind-smoothed stones.

He forgot where he was. He had fallen. The world he occupied was mapless. He was on the Lakht. But it might be at the head of his men. It might be in war. They might be raiding a caravan, and he could not remember.

A hand inserted itself into his collar and dragged at him, and after that something passed about his neck, a collar, a rope, he realized, to guide the mad.

They pulled, and he walked, quite, quite blind. He heard his father's voice saying to his mother that she should not speak to the dead.

He heard his father say that she must have gotten him with some no-caste: he could not be Tain's son. Clearly his mother was a whore.

The pain in his knees was dull and distant. Tugs of the rope both pulled him off-balance and reminded him of left and right. He took it meekly, for simple guidance, that he could not walk aside from the column. It was important to stay with the caravan. It was important to be quiet and co-operative. He had something yet to do, a reason to go on walking.

After a passage of time they rested. He was blind, and they gave him bitter beer to drink, the first beer he had had on this trek. It conjured harvest evenings, the yellow, yellow straw, laughter in the fields. It conjured campfires and campaign, and a man lying bandaged and dying of his wounds. They had had such beer in the Lakht, three years ago. They had captured a wagonload of beer and behaved like boys.

Here we are, they had laughed, where the ships came down. Shall we look for ships in the desert?

"Here we are!" they had shouted at the sky, blasphemed, and waved their arms as if they would beckon down heavenly watchers.

They had roused up a band of the Ila's men by mischance and fought them, drunk as they were. His father had hit him when he found out, but not been greatly angry, since none of them had died, and they had killed the Ila's men.

Hup-hup-hup, the word came.

The wife was dully compliant now, having had a double ration of beer, and they set her on her feet and had her walk.

The potter, equally drunk, asked after his mother. "Be still," others of the mad shouted at him, and the Ila's men laughed and rode down on either side of the potter, picked him up by either arm, and carried him far ahead of them, where they dropped him.

The potter sat down until the column overtook him, and then they roused him good-naturedly to his feet. The Ila's men were in high spirits, with the city so near. They gave their sour beer to their prisoners and planned on better in the city that ran with water.

The old man fell down just before dawn and died, so it seemed: no one had touched him. The Ila's men argued

among themselves and decided they needed to bring the
body along, all the same. It might draw vermin, and it was a
danger. They had abandoned the others that had died. But
the Ila would pay them a bounty for each madman, and they
might argue a little gold even out of the body, proving there
was one less of their kind in the world. The city was close. So
was reward.

Marak ate what he was given at dawn, drank what water
he was given. The sun came slipping over the Qarain's saw-
toothed ridge with morning, red fingers lancing across the
powder sand, and the city that spread itself like a seam of
light now was no mirage. Many of the mad cried out, but
some, once fooled, disbelieved it in silence.

In the light and the trickery of the land Marak walked,
walked, walked. The city grew nearer all day, the Lakht never
seeming narrower, or the city nearer. The sun beat down,
blinding, and now, having been generous, the Ila's men
turned impatient. They did not camp at noon, but pressed
onward in the blazing sun.

The boy from Tijanan, whose sight was dimmer than the
rest, at last saw the city the rest of them had seen for hours.
"The holy city!" he shouted, and began to dance about, waving his arms, but the guards, out of humor, beat him, and
shoved him ahead.

The boy, Pogi, walked, striking his head with his hands.

Marak likewise found in the city walls, however distant,
an inspiration. He no longer trudged blindly. He walked as a
man walks toward an encounter with his lifelong enemy, full
of righteous anger.

"Look at him," one of the Ila's men said. "Does he know
where he's going? He's as crazy as the boy."

The boy kept his course when the world tilted. The boy
never had moved to the visions that stirred the rest. His
madness was of a different kind. He was innocent, if their
madness was a crime.

Marak felt the world slide, but he kept his course as well.
He looked at the walls and ignored the pitch.

They reached the stone-paved road. There was no escape at

all, now, and now if never before the dullest must ask themselves what waited for them. But Marak knew. There was comfort in knowing there would be a reason for his dying. There was even a satisfaction in it, when all other purpose had left.

See, Father? I am not that mad. I am not that useless. I lied. All my life was a lie, but it was a rational lie.

What pretenses do the sane make?

What did you pretend, Mother, knowing from my birth that I was not like the rest of you?

And what did you pretend to yourself, Tain Trin Tain, when time after time you believed my lies? You kept asking, but you took all the lies. Why now are you angry?

The sun sank as they walked. The walls of the holy city, slanted and crested with imbedded shards of glass, caught the sunlight and sent light knifing into the eyes as if all the walls were hedged with divine fire. The dome of the Beykaskh, the dome of the Ila's Grace, was wholly tiled with glass, and it blazed like the sun itself. A man could no more look at it by noon than at the burning Eye of Heaven itself.

The mad and the guards alike began to walk with heads lowered, not from shame, but to protect their eyes from the glory of the city.

Birds flew thick about the walls, black spots in the glare. The southern wall was where the gallows were: the city gave the birds its unwanted, its malefactors, and its garbage.

In its wealth it threw out in a day, men said, what whole villages could thrive on for a year. A pool of water stood by the gates, rimmed in stone and overflowing into the sand a good ways out: and out across the sand, on a bed of sandstone, a green-rimmed pond stood always filled.

There vermin of every sort came to water, and to serve as sport for the Ila's archers and her riflemen. That spillage, that pond, was the most profligate consumption of resource possible, and the mad wondered at it, and called that reed-rimmed pool a mirage.

But a pipe ran beside the road, and whereas villages measured and sold every drop, whereas they pressed moisture out of every bit of waste and distilled it in huge stills, it was not the way things were done in Oburan. They sent it out to the pool, to draw vermin.

And as they came up under the shadow of Oburan, they met that rumored wonder greater than the blazing dome and the glass-edged walls. Beside the gate, that fountain known as the Mercy of the Ila gushed from stonework mouths and ran out so profligately that it splashed from the fountain bowl to the troughs and some onto the stones of the street, to be trampled underfoot.

There travelers and traders were free to drink, while the remnant continually overflowed and ran from the trough through tiles until, Marak knew, it reached that distant, reed-rimmed pond.

The beasts had not drunk for ten days. Here, at the long troughs, they crowded one another and pushed and snapped, asserting dominance, while at the upper bowl, the Ila's men wet their hands and wiped their faces at no charge, spilling water as they did. Then the caravanners drank, and here, scrabbling for double handfuls, elbowing one another and frantic with greed and fear and haste, the mad also drank at the bowl.

Marak filled his cupped hands and drank from the troughs the beasts used, having no disdain for a little besha-spit. More, while others were jostling one another and worrying about their share of what was boundless, he filled both hands, first wiped a coating of dust into mud on his face and neck, and then sluiced more up, the cold water running down beneath the shirt.

He was not the common sort of madman, to elbow the others for drink. Here at the lower outflow he had it all to himself. He saw the wife from Tarsa shoved to the ground by the potter, and he seized the man by the collar and held him back until the wife had gotten up, bruised.

"There is no scarcity," he said to the potter. "Are you a man at all, or not?"

The potter's profane answer proved he was a fool, at least, and Marak showed his contempt for the water of the Ila's Mercy by dumping the potter bodily into the beast's trough, perhaps the first water bath the potter had had since his birth. The guards laughed, in far better humor with their bellies full of water, and no one rebuked him for the act.

With that act, he had waked somewhat from the drug in the food they fed him. He felt his heart beating and the blood moving in his veins. Beyond the immediate noise of the beasts, he heard the noise of the curious of the city and the passersby, heard the jeers of a gathering crowd while the potter clawed his way out of more water than he had ever sat in, and dripped onto the pavings. Marak heard young voices squealing as a besha snapped at a tormenting child, and heard the ting and clash of belled harnesses, the sound of a caravan all about them. All the bystanders laughed, having gathered to watch the potter's bath, and had no idea, perhaps, that they were entertained by the mad.

Marak stretched his back and arched it and looked up and up at the threat of the walls, the high barricade that had thwarted Tain's rebellion after all their plans and their ambitions.

He saw from this vantage the glass-edged defenses he and Tain had once tried to breach, and with a soldier's cold eye, too, looked up at the scars he and Tain had left on the limestone walls of the holy city, the jewel of the Lakht. They were no few scars, and lasting ones, but not mortal, no, far from mortal wounds against this city.

They had not known, then, about the guns, or the launchers.

He imagined there were things about the city he did not guess yet. The very reason for this summons was one.

Did the Ila in her power shrug off the war out of the west, and yet seek out the mad on a whim? Was it mere curiosity?

So now the damned and the mad gathered at the Ila's request, to live or to die, and the son of the Ila's enemy was here, one among many, and yet not unknown, he was sure. He was in the records these men had made, and he was sure someone would inform the Ila what a prize her men had gathered in the west. He wondered if the Ila's men would single him out before the Ila knew; would they make his name known in the streets? And he wondered if that happened what the people would do, who had lived through the years of the attack?

Would they resent him?

Attack him, if he shouted out, I am Marak Trin Tain?

He was tempted to do it, if only to die with a name and to make the most trouble possible in his dying. But he had another purpose yet to accomplish.

The guards moved the other prisoners on, and he bowed his head like the rest and walked with them, led like the beasts.

"Walk!" the Ila's men shouted at them. For the first time in a day they used their quirts, set afoot, moving among the mad to set them on their way through the gates.

The journey was over. The caravan masters would seek their pay of the offices, most likely, as in every town, when cargo was off-loaded. The Ila's men had assumed all command now: the beasts and their masters they left behind with the tents and the baggage, all except the beast that carried the old man. The boy, Pogi, stopped to stare at their parting; but the guards whipped him on.

A prudent man might be ready for whatever whim moved the Ila, and the sergeant in charge of the caravan was, over all, a prudent man. He shouted out curses at men who whipped the boy too hard; he shouted encouragement at the mad to walk. "Not so far now," the sergeant said. "You'll sit up there! Move!"

Marak walked behind the beast carrying the dead man, with a view of its legs and underbelly, mostly, as the stone-paved street rose up and up the city's broad terracing, up between the frontages of craft shops and warehouses and the better dwellings.

In a turn more the sunlight dimmed with dusk and colors lost their brilliancy. The day was over. And Marak walked in the wake of the beast, which, watered, stopped a moment to do what beshti rarely did, and moved on. Those afoot got the worst of it.

In their war here, his father's war, not only had they never breached these walls, they had never imagined the teeming mass of people that lived inside the holy city. He walked now within deep shadow of tall buildings and dusk, within a stench of smoke and rot and urine. He felt the slight coolth of perpetually shadowed stone as well as the cooling of the air that followed the sun's descent. Noon could hardly reach this place. He had not appreciated his last view of the sun outside. If he saw it rise again, he was sure now it would be his great misfortune.

High, high up the winding turns of the street they passed now with little curiosity from the people, until the word must have passed, and the residents of the holy city came out to jeer at the madmen, and to pelt them with rotten fruit— with the incredible luxury of the holy city, where there was food discarded, where the middens were richer than villages. Precious moisture ran with common waste down the sides of the streets, and fruit pulp slicked the stones underfoot.

The boy picked up a half-rotten fruit and ate it. The wife fell and soiled her knees in the muddy pulp. Marak pulled her up in the next stride: it was no place to die, in such filth, after so long struggle to come here. She sang to herself as they walked, as water ran between the stones, as better food than many villages ever knew pelted them as common refuse.

"The devils will come down!" the potter yelled at their tormentors. "The devils live on the high hill, in the tower, and they will come down and dance at your funerals!"

At that defiance, the crowd flung more serious missiles. Marak fended a potsherd with his arm, but one of the mad went down: a barber, the man was, and a broken brick struck him in the head, toppling him in his blood.

At that the Ila's men shoved at the crowd and hauled the attacker out, bringing him along, too, beating him with their sticks.

Marak sheltered the wife from Tarsa against his side, away from the more accurate stone-throwers. "Where is love?" she sang unevenly, faintly, as she climbed. "Where is shade in the desert? Where is my love gone?"

They suddenly passed a gate, into a large square, before those who flung stares, not stones; and those were better behaved, but more chilling.

After that they came through a second gate, into the shadow of inner walls, and the reek of asphalt and oil. Steam went up here in rolling clouds. Rumor was true. Such was the wealth of the holy city that they had fuel to spare for furnaces, and gates moved by steam and not the strength of men or beasts. He had heard of it but never seen it.

He bore up the wife, who staggered against him. "Please," she said, "let me rest. Let me rest."

"Soon," he said. He could wish she had died quietly as the old man had died. She was a gentle soul. She had no imagining of the possibilities in this place.

"What is that sound?" she asked when the gates groaned and gave a tortured sound, iron on iron.

"Machines," he said. "The machines of the Beykaskh."

She seemed not to understand him. Perhaps she had never heard how the Beykaskh made gates of iron and boiled water to make them move, or how the Ila, displeased, flung deposed ministers into the works of those machines. The wife from Tarsa wavered in her steps, and looked numb, exhausted as they passed through the last gates, through the heart of the machines.

They were within the inner sanctum, the heart of the holy city. He had come where his father's armies had only hoped to come.

"This is the one," the captain of the Ila's men said suddenly, and seized Marak's arm, and drew him and the wife apart.

The wife fell to her knees, crying out for his help, and for someone named Lelie. No one noticed. She lay on the pavings and the besha that bore the dead old man walked sedately past her defenseless arm, scarcely missing her, stepping delicately over her. Marak saw it, held his breath, but walked obediently where the men bade him go.

This is the one, they said of him, but even now they accounted him no threat.

He would not lose his one chance for the sake of a gesture. He had fixed on one mad act as of some value to his father, as some way in which his father might say, and that the villages might say, *Perhaps he was Tain's, after all.*

If he was Tain's, if he was Tain's, then his mother was no whore, and his sister's honor was safe.

He had one chance. One chance. One chance. He had to be meek and tolerate everything until he found it.

Then the mad would have a name, as far as they told the story. Every name would be remembered, and his father would say, *He was not so mad as the rest, was he?*

2

To every good man the Ila gave the nature of men, and to every good beast the Ila gave the nature of beasts. The Ila named them and divided them one from the other. She appointed them their use and life under the sun.

But even to the beasts of the desert the Ila's Mercy continually pours out her abundance.

Even the destroyers the Ila made for her use.
—The Book of Priests

"In here," the Ila's men said, and made Marak duck, shielding his head from a low doorway. He wiped his eyes as his hair fell across his face, and consequently had grit in them, compounded with the sticky filth that clung to his skin and his hair and his clothes.

Blinking tears, then, he prepared himself for soldiers' rough handling, but saw no authority awaiting him, only four slaves, who stood holding towels and such in a little fountain courtyard dim with twilight.

"The Ila wishes not to be offended," one of the guards said.

So the Ila had indeed heard the news of Tain's misfortune in his son, and become, as he hoped, curious. He would have the audience, and with no need for him to seek it, his most extravagant hopes realized.

The officers of the household, armed and watchful, kept their distance from him, but in an act of leaden, ordinary compliance he began to shed the ruined boots, which brought away shreds of old white skin. New skin had grown, daily, to be worn away in blisters; it was his nature. It was the nature of all the mad, he had learned: they all healed well. Only the greatest injuries, like the boy's, could overwhelm their bodies' defenses.

The slaves took his filthy rags with disgust. With gestures—they did not speak—they wished him to stand beneath a device that poured down water, and pulled a chain. A flood rushed down on him, a chill rush that made his flesh contract. Between his feet, water that had passed over his body stayed not to bathe him, but flowed out a drain so rapidly the puddle never showed soil.

Perhaps that water flowed from the drain out under the wall, and perhaps it flowed down the streets to carry the waste of the holy city, or perhaps, again, it passed down clay pipes, to join the Mercy of the Ila, the drink of unknowing passersby.

{*Marak, Marak, Marak,* his voices said, chiding him . . . or beckoning him to folly: he never knew.}

Meanwhile the slaves washed his body with soft clothes, scrubbing in their ignorance at his tattoos, at the mark he wore, the abjori emblem, in blue above his heart, scrubbed at the killing-marks on his right hand.

"They will not come off," he said to them after enduring their efforts. Perhaps the slaves had never been outside the Beykaskh: at least they desisted when told. They loosed his hair and scrubbed it, and combed it with gentle fingers. The last of twilight was going. A slave brought out lamps and hung them in the open courtyard, providing a golden light.

They had him sit down, next, and by that light carefully shaved his face clean, a luxury he had not had in all the time of walking. They used a straight razor which if he had seized it would have been a fearsome weapon. But he waited. They were deft and quick, and even followed the shave with a soothing herbal, while he sat with his hands on his knees, the object of the guards' indolent stares.

There was no reason for shame. The long walk had worn him, but he had healed. He was thinner than he had been, but he was still strong. He was still Tain's son, no matter Tain had rejected him. He was still himself.

He expected clean clothes of some sort. It hardly made sense to waste so much water and clothe him again in garments foul with refuse. And indeed, they unfolded clothing from the protection of thick towels. They gave him a shirt of cloth as fine as a bride's gown, shirt and trousers that felt strangely old and worn to comfort as they slid over his skin. There was a belt, which was foolish to give a prisoner, but they gave it, all the same. They carefully combed his hair, and bound it with soft leather. Instead of the galling rope about his neck, they wished to place a light chain of ornate links, common brass, such as common folk wore. That alone he refused, wishing no Lakhtani chain on his neck, no matter their custom.

"He wants one of gold," the chief guard said to the slaves, mocking him, and added: "Let it be. It's no matter of importance."

That *was* the importance. But it was not important in the guards' thinking, and he said nothing.

All these proceedings, he was sure, readied him to come into the heart of the Beykaskh, and near the Ila. It had fallen dark now, except their lamp. The slaves brought boots for his feet which fit amazingly well . . . so much care they took for his comfort. They must have measured his ruined ones, split seams and all. And where did one find an array of boots simply waiting?

And would he see the Ila tonight, and have his chance at this late hour? Or must he wait?

{*Marak, Marak,* the voices said, damnably ill timed.}

He shut his eyes, pretending weariness to conceal his distraction. But worse than the voices, that swinging sense came over him, the one that could take a man's balance.

"Come along," his guards said.

{*Marak,* the voices said. *Marak. Get up. Walk.*}

He made a careful, practiced effort against that swinging feeling. He gained his balance. Above all things else he wished no restraint, no impediment to the one chance he might have at the Ila, and he had no need, for a moment, to pretend helplessness for his guards' sake. The structures of fire blinded him, and the world swung violently, always toward the east.

They led him by either arm, the captain and the guard, out that low fountain-court door and into the hallway.

More guards stood on duty here, men in the gilt-trimmed uniform of the elite of the Ila's men. Now it was certain where he was going. Now his palms sweated and his heart beat hard. *Be silent!* he chided his voices, attempting to govern them, as he rarely could.

He succeeded. He faced stairs, and he climbed doggedly, at his guards' orders. He knew how he wished to die.

3

The Ila descended to the Lakht and established the center of the earth. Outside was the wasteland. Until that time there were no villages anywhere and there was no cultivated field.

The Ila established the Holy City and from it went out appointed authorities to establish other centers throughout the land, to widen the habitable lands, to drive back the vermin, and to enrich the earth with gardens.
—The Book of Oburan, ch. 1, v. 1.

He hoped for single audience. In his wildest hopes he wished to come very near the Ila, and to have her guards far away.

But to his disappointment he was not alone. A group gathered in an upper hall outside a set of massive doors, a motley group of old and young, men and women, all dressed in the ordinary white and brown of the holy city. All the company had a haggard look. Some bore recent wounds. Were they the local harvest of the streets, Marak wondered?

But among them, along the edge, he saw the wife from Tarsa, the potter, the barber, and the rest that had come with him. Then he knew that he was not alone in this audience, only better dressed.

They must be all mad, the scourings of the Ila's search, not only from the villages of the west, but from all the land. There were that many more of them, filling the hallway as far as the corner.

The metal doors sighed heavily and opened, no hand touching them.

Beyond them was a narrow, pillared hall. At the end of the hall was a dais and a high seat, and on that seat was a figure robed in red.

The Ila. The source of all authority . . . deathless, immortal, so some said. A god on earth, priests maintained, and the Ila did not refuse their worship.

If she was a god, Marak proposed to find out. Under his brow, head bowed among the herd, he measured the length he must go to reach that figure. He imagined to himself dealing one, just one strong blow to that fragile-seeming neck before they cut him down.

Orders passed in gestures, the permissive lifting of the Ila's hand, and the guards brought them forward as a group, for the Ila's examination.

Marak's heart beat fast. He had seen men and beasts run, even shot through the heart. He could perhaps reach her before the guards even organized an objection.

But until they offered to prevent him from a peaceful, even requested, advance, he made himself as obedient as the rest of the madmen.

Marak, the voices said suddenly, and the mad twitched and turned and spun for the Ila's amusement. He restrained himself desperately from moving to that urge: it was his one breach from the rest, the one indignity he had refused all his life.

There were drawn blades all around them, guards stationed among the pillars. The Ila's men were justifiably anxious in this viewing of the mad. They waited for the afflicted to do something more extravagant to prove their madness, and now a guard prodded him in the side, curious about his difference.

Pride would not allow him. He had run into the desert as a boy. He had hidden his fits in storerooms, in privacy, in long rides into the waste. He had learned that the fits had had a rhythm: they came at certain hours of the day, at certain times in the night, regular as the calendar, regular as the moons in waxing and waning. He had learned to live with them, to pretend, to conceal the twitches and the urges.

But lately the fits had gone out of rhythm, out of the ordinary.

This manifestation now was out of rhythm, as if the Ila's very presence had provoked it.

{*Marak,* the voices said. *Turn. Walk. Come.*} And quietly, biting his lip until the blood came, he would not.

The mad, within the room, became agitated. The Ila sat observing them. An au'it sat nearby, writing, writing. One by one the records went down, as the guards separated each madman from the herd in turn for the au'it to record his name, his origin, his behavior, turning each back when they were done. The Ila seemed bored, impatient.

Then a signal passed, a motion of the Ila's hand, and the guards held back the latest madman they had cut out of the herd.

"Tain's son," the Ila said, and the guards, letting go the one, prodded at Marak instead and moved him forward.

Now, Marak thought, anticipating the next few moments, and became steady as any hunter. Hate fueled his patience. Desire kept his head down and held his gait to an ordinary shamble, all to come as close as he could.

They stopped him just short of the distance inside which he might move and not be stopped. The guards brought chains and put them on his hands. He bore that meekly, too: the chains were a weapon, brass chains, solid and capable of shielding a fist, of looping a throat, of cracking a skull. Then they put a spear backwards through the ring attached, and two men held it, but that was not enough. The spear, too, was a weapon within his reach.

With those precautions they moved him to the very foot of the Ila's seat.

A great calm came on him, even a sense of leisure in which he could satisfy his curiosity before he used his last chance. He looked up at the Ila, the tyrant, the ruler of all the world, as if he owned her.

"Marak Trin," the captain said, and the au'it wrote.

Then the traitor voices started in his skull, dinning: *Marak Trin. Marak Trin. Marak Trin,* a foolish, mindless echo, hindering him from clear thought.

In the desert, on the wide plains of the Lakht, in constant company with the mad, aware of the rest, the voices had grown louder and more insistent. He fought them down. He looked up at the red robes, the blood red robes, up to the Ila's face, and found it very aptly time to die, before the voices were all he heard. But he had never seen the like of her.

White, white skin, and gloved hands, and booted feet. On the Lakht, they valued white skin, skin the sun had not touched. They whitened the skins of brides and grooms with creams. They valued slender bodies that clearly had never lifted burdens or carried water, or scratched a living from the desert.

All these marks of beauty the Ila had. She wore a close cap of red silk, and inner robes of silk shaded like flame. She exuded wealth, and power, and, some said, holiness.

Yet she seemed frail, in size and strength so like his young sister, he was dismayed.

"Are you truly mad?" she asked him directly, as his sister might have asked, a question, an entangling snare of question that caught his mind and his heart. He had killed enemies. He had never killed a girl.

But he had never failed an intended target, either. He would; he would not; and in desperation he leapt at the steps. He dragged his guards with him. He hauled at the chains and had three men stumbling at his feet. He seized the spear and lifted his hands, aiming it at that slight figure.

A thunderbolt struck him, sizzled through bone and nerve and flung him back in a sliding course down the steps. The guards smothered him with their bodies, wrenched at the chains, and hit him, but that impact of bone on flesh was nothing, nothing to the thunderbolt.

"No, no, no," the Ila said, a light voice, like chimes. "Don't harm him. You knew Tain's son would have tried it."

Marak could not get his breath past his tongue or move his chest beneath the living weight of the guards pressing down on him. He lay half-buried, on the hard edge of the steps, the object of every eye, and had time to realize the failure of his ambition, the shame of his father, and to know he had once and for all lost his mother's life.

The gods struck down the hand that touched the Ila. Had he not heard that warning all his life? He had no gods, and the Tain had none . . . but he had incontrovertibly met a wall of force, and it had stolen all his breath, shaken his heart in his chest, made his limbs twitch. To make it even worse, the voices roared wildly in his ears, a deafening rush like the sound of waters.

The guards raised him up to his knees. He could not even manage to hold that position, once released, and slumped down onto his face on the floor, under the curious stares of the mad, in the spite of the Ila's men.

"Marak Trin," the Ila said.

He could lift his head, that much, enough to stare up at her. He moved an arm and, discovering that unthought movement under his command, attempted to draw it beneath him. It moved. He drew one and then the other knee across the cold, polished stone and heaved himself up, laughably like the beasts, rump first, then the forearms. The hands still would not move. He felt nothing but a tingling in his feet.

"Marak Trin Tain."

The roaring in his ears went on, a torment in itself, making her voice distant. He had succeeded only in kneeling at this tyrant's feet. There were deaths and deaths in the holy city. Men were impaled on hooks and flung from the walls or hung alive for the vermin of the air. He wondered which death was his, or if the lightning of her fingers would suffice, and burn him to a crisp.

"Are you mad?" the Ila asked. The room spun like the direction of the voices. The pain gathered in his bones and seemed to have found a home there, and in his silence an angry guard brought a length of chain down across his back. "Are you mad?" the Ila asked again, in that soft voice. "Or is this one of your father's tricks?"

"As mad as they are," he said. He was dismayed to discover sudden cowardice in himself, that he feared another of those blows, and he despised himself that his mouth found it bet-

HAMMERFALL   33

ter to answer. He no longer knew for what he hoped. He told himself that his hope was to get to his feet again, and to try again, but his limbs would not, could not, and his heart had discovered a fear to equal fear of his father. "Mad as all the rest," he mumbled.

"And your father gave you up."

He failed to answer. The chain came down across his back.

"Yes," he said.

"And when did you know you had the madness?"

"Years," he said. "For years."

"As a boy?"

It admitted a time of helplessness. It opened the door to his father's house, his mother's shame, his father's disowning him after all these years. He said nothing, and knew the blow of the chain would come. Damn them, he thought, and then discovered the limit of his fear, right at the boundary of stubborn, foolish pride.

The chain crashed across his back.

But the lift of a gloved hand had prevented its full force and forestalled another blow.

"Tain knew?" the Ila asked. "Or is Tain Trin Tain mad, too?"

"No," he said, and caught a breath. "No to both."

"How many others are mad in your household?"

"None that I know." It was the question she had asked the others. They were into the safe litany of the others' questions, and he could let go his breath and cease to expect the blows. He could gather his strength.

"How did it come?"

"As lights. As voices." The red-robed au'it wrote each answer, sitting on the steps by the Ila's feet, her book on her lap and her pen moving busily between ink-cake and page.

"And Tain did not at any time know."

"No," he said. "Not until the last. I kept it secret."

"And what betrayed you?" The Ila moved, a whisper of silk like the creeping of a serpent as she leaned her pale chin on a red-gloved, jeweled fist. "Did you fall in a fit?"

"I did," he said. Shame heated his face. He had fallen at his father's feet, in front of all the chiefs. He spared himself confessing that part, that moment, all the shocked faces.

"What did your father do?"

"He asked me the truth, and I stopped lying." The silence hung there, filled with only that. He wanted to move on. "He had heard your men were gathering up the mad. He sent for them."

"He was glad to let you go."

"If glad is true," he said. His father's life was blunted, now, turned sharply back on itself: no heir, no wife, and now a diminished reputation, either in laughter or in pity. Was that gladness in Tain Trin Tain? Was Tain in any wise relieved to have signed that armistice with the Ila?

He thought not. But he thought little else. The pain in his body diminished, but the roaring in his ears reached a numbing pitch, and persisted, as if all the voices were bottled up in him, trying to find expression. Death began again to seem friendly. He asked himself how much more before his brain scrambled, before he had to scream. He bit his lip, bit it bloody.

"Do you see lights and hear voices?" the Ila asked.

"Yes."

"And what do these voices say?"

"Nothing of sense." Could it *be* worse? He doubted he could keep his feet if he could gain them.

"And the pictures? The images? The visions?"

He fixed his sight on the Ila's face, one stable point in a swinging world. It spun, and tilted, and stopped, over and over again. "Buildings," he said. "Buildings. A tower."

"This tower? The Beykaskh?"

He shook his head to clear it. She might take that headshake for no, and it was the truth. He focused on her, only on her. Past the whiteness, she had a classic Lakhtanin face, thin and bow-nosed. Her lids were black-rimmed. The iris was dark. The eyes became pits into which sense could fall, and, no, she was not a child: the eyes alone said she was not a child.

A gloved finger raised, forbidding, then curled itself across the lips, convenient resting place. "The son of my enemy. The one who burns my towns, steals from my treasury, robs my caravans, despoils my priests. What shall I make of you?"

The pain had spread out of the joints and migrated to soft places. The noise in his ears roared and made her voice distant.

"Tain has given his son away," the Ila mocked him, "so *I* take him. What shall I make of you, Marak Trin Tain? What shall I name you instead?"

Mockery he would not endure. "General of your armies," he said, courting their violence. "Captain of your guard."

She leaned back, lifted a hand, perhaps to forestall her officers. The au'it, who had written it all, ceased writing, poised the pen above the page of her book.

The Ila's hand described a circle in the air. The au'it shut the book and put down her pen.

"Now without record," the Ila said, "I ask you . . . where *is* this madness?"

"In the east," he said without thinking, and astonished himself. It was in the east. Everything was in the east. It had no reason to be, but he knew it was, and it disturbed him to the heart.

"You wish to be a captain of my guard," the Ila said. "I have a one that suffices. But a captain of explorers, perhaps, as there used to be, before there were the tribes. So you are. I name you to ride out for me and find the source of the madness. I name you to go where the mad go when they wander out, and find out why they turn to the east. I name you to return to me and to report whatever you learn. And *if* you return to me and report the truth, I will give you a gift. *You* will rule Kais Tain."

A stir of utter dismay went through the captains.

He himself did not believe it.

"I have set my seal on Kais Tain," the Ila said, "and have all persons therein under that seal. Write it!" she said, and the au'it wet her pen and wrote. "They live or they die as you please me, and after you do my will, they live or they die as they please you. What other reward do you wish for your service?"

Was he not to die? He searched all the crevices of that utterance, looking for the reason in what he heard.

Was he not to die? And did the Ila make a barbed joke, and had the au'it written it in the book as if it were the truth, and the law?

The pain made it difficult to think. The roaring made it difficult to hear anything sensible.

"Is that enough?" the Ila asked him, as if she bargained in a market. "Do you agree to my terms?"

He could not think on his knees. He struggled to his feet. Fire shot up and down the bones. Defying it, he straightened his back, and fire ran there, too.

"My mother," he said. "Now. My sister. I want them safe from Tain."

The Ila moved a vertical finger against her lips and gazed at him.

"Is there a dispute within Tain's house?"

"He's threatened them. Keep them safe. Provide for them. And I'll get your answer."

"I don't bargain."

"I do." His effrontery stung the guards. They began to move; they laid hands on him; and desisted, perhaps in fear of lightning.

"I shall provide you all you need," the Ila said mildly, "and appoint you a captain as you ask, and give you all the resources you ask. And I shall set my seal on your mother and your sister and have them safe. Do you agree?"

It was surely a trap, a trick, a mockery. But the roaring burst like a dam in his ears, and the madmen turned and twitched together, some falling on the floor.

"Leave," the Ila said, motioning toward the doors. "And take them out!" She pointed at Marak. "*You stay!*"

Her guards slowly, with backward glances, gathered the mad, some of them standing, some on the floor, and cleared the room even of themselves. The au'it hesitated, last, but even to her the Ila made a sign, and the au'it gathered her ink and her book and slunk away to a door behind the pillars.

Then the Ila rose from her chair and descended three

steps, silk whispering, falling like old blood about her movements.

Then she sat down, like some marketwife, midway on those steps. She was that close, as fragile as temple porcelain. But pain ran through Marak's joints like knives and reminded him at every breath what those gloved hands could do.

Those hands joined, made a bridge against her lips. Highborn women might whiten their faces with cosmetic to show their lack of exposure to the sun, and come outdoors only by night. Her skin left no mark on the gloves. It was translucent white, alive. The eyes were deep as wells.

"I wish your loyalty in this," she said. "Will I have it?"

He asked himself what other choice he had, compared to life, and being given power to rescue those two on earth he loved. The opposite was implicit in the Ila's gift: that all he loved were still under her seal.

"I see no recourse," he said. "No choice."

"When I heard you were among the mad I gathered, I knew I had a resource above the others. What coin will truly win you, Marak Trin? A province? A great house?"

She mocked him. And he searched his soul and knew to his distress that in company with her offer, life itself interested him, and her proposition interested him. He had lived with death all the way to the holy city. She gave him tomorrow instead and offered him the lives of his mother and sister into the bargain. All his principles ebbed away, gone like the strength in his limbs.

She had sat down like a marketwife. In deliberate mockery of the fear he felt he sank down and sat like a field hand, cross-legged, at the last in a hard collapse against the stone. All she offered might be a lie, but from a posture like hers he answered and he listened, having been caught and corrupted by this idea of hers. Everything in him longed for answers, longed for reason, for purpose, for some logic to his life.

"What if I do this?" he said. "What do you expect me to find out there?"

"If I knew," she said, "would I have to send anyone?"

"If I'm that mad, how shall I remember to come back?"

"If you are that mad," she said, "will you care? And if you are not mad, will you serve my needs? I think not. I think only the mad can find this answer."

"It may be," he said.

"You attacked my city."

"So I did."

"And failed."

"And failed," he said.

"Why?" she asked, as if she had no idea at all. "To take? Or to destroy?"

A wise question, an incisive question. It told her everything of his wishes in a word.

He made a move of his hand, about them, thinking of the machines. "If the machines would work for us," he said, "I would be very content to sit in this hall."

"And would you do better than I, sitting here?"

"I would not pour water into the desert," he said. In this mad give-and-take, the memory of such waste still galled him. "I would build a stone cistern, and put it next to the walls, and let whoever wished settle around it and grow fruit."

It might be a foolish answer, as the holy city saw it. The Ila listened to him, listened very gravely. "You think we waste it."

"What else is it, when it pours out under the sun? You feed the vermin. They multiply out there."

Her lips quirked. It might have been a smile. "You would turn us into a village."

"It's not likely," he said.

"Not likely that you would ever have taken Oburan? No. Far from likely. It was far from likely when you and your father came up onto the Lakht. Surely you knew that."

He shrugged, having no wish to discuss his father's plans or their misguided strategy, or the failed aim of his thirty years of life. The world might turn again, and, meanwhile, he was alive, and he had eyes, and he had seen the inside of this place. No, it was not likely that he or his father would have sat in this hall, rulers of all the world, but fortunes shifted. If she willed, his were changing; he was not dead yet. He managed not to meet her eyes, and asked himself why he cared for her respect, or what he suddenly had to fear in this debate.

Did he believe in her proposal? He was not sure, that was the thing. And the voices still cried, screamed, roared, all their words confounded in the depths of his hearing.

"You have never renounced your ambition," she said.

He shrugged, and did look up, discovered, pinned for the moment to the truth. "No," he said. "But it's not likely."

"The voices have always spoken to you?"

"Does it matter?"

"You are to investigate, Marak Trin. You are my eyes and my ears in this matter. I ask, and you've promised me answers. How long have the voices spoken to you?"

"Since about my sixth year. Since then."

"And the visions?"

"They've always been there."

"Did a stranger come to Kais Tain when you were a baby?"

"I have no way to know," he said. "Why do you ask?"

"It's a common part of the story. A mysterious stranger. A visitation. A baby that grows up mad."

He found that idea sinister beyond belief. No stranger had touched him that he knew, but his mother had never said, one way or the other.

"It wouldn't be easy to come into our household."

"Among the lords of Kais Tain? Perhaps not. But very easy, in most peasant houses. Perhaps it's why mad lords are so rare, and mad farmers are so common. Farmers are generally more hospitable."

"I've no idea." They sat so easily, so madly companionable. "Who are these strangers? What do they do, and why?"

"I have some ideas. I know, for instance, that the madness that afflicts you is a specific madness, and that all that have it are under thirty years of age. How old are you?"

"Thirty." He thought of the old man, and doubted what she said. But had it been the same madness? Was there more than one kind?

"Do you hear the voices now?"

"I hear a roaring." What she asked was an intimate confession, one he had never made except to his father and his mother. "I sometimes hear my name."

"That seems common," she said, leaning forward, as if they gossiped together. "What else do you hear?"

He shook his head. "Nothing."

"Yet you know this thing is in the east."

"The world tilts that way."

"Does it?"

"To us it does. It does it morning and evening, regular as you like it. Watch the madmen. Most will fall down."

She neither laughed nor grew angry. "If I had your ears, if I had your eyes, I could know what I wish to know. If I had your strength, I might walk to the east and know what I wish to know. So I purchase them. I purchase *you*. Is the price enough?"

"I can't bargain with you."

"Ah, but you can. Ask me."

"I have nothing to ask."

"If you betray me, I promise you Kais Tain will smoke for days. I promise your mother and your sister will die very unhappily. Does that excite your interest? I thought so. I give you this one year of their safety for free, and all the resources you may need, a regiment of my guard if you wish it. Gold? Gold is sand under my feet. But knowledge? That, you can bring me. Then you and I will talk again. Name what you need to accomplish what I ask."

He saw she was utterly in earnest. "Keep your regiment," he said. "Give me my freedom. The safety of my house and its villages for this year. And my father's life, even if he's offended your officers."

"What do you care for him?"

"He's my father. He's signed your armistice."

"Done. What else?"

What else was there? It was the last chance to amend their bargain. "Give me the madmen," he said. He saw little use for them in the holy city, where they would die, hanged or stoned, the common fate of the mad once discovered. They had walked together, he and the wife of Tarsa, and the potter, and he could not walk away alive and forget their fate. "If you mean all you say, you have no need for them, and I might learn from them."

A red-gloved hand waved away inconsequences. "Take them. Do as you please with them. A caravan and its hire. Riding beasts. All these things."

"Weapons." His were gone. "Tents enough for all of us."

She laughed like a child, as if, together, she on the steps, he on the ground, they were two children planning a delicious prank. "An au'it to write things down."

"I can write," he said in offended pride.

"I write," she said with a wave of her hand, "but I find it tedious. An au'it, I say."

"What if the au'it runs mad? Shall I be blamed?"

"You will not be blamed." The red-gloved hands clasped silken knees. The eyes deep as wells stared at him. "The east is full of strange things. So is the Lakht. Take the regiment."

"I never needed one. I rode all about these hills and your regiments couldn't find us. The sand and the stones are no threat to me."

"The vermin are. Bandits are."

"Only when you feed them on corpses and fat caravans! The holy city is their source of food. Pour out water, and vermin and bandits alike fight among themselves." He shrugged. "A regiment will take more time than an ordinary caravan. I know the Lakht. I don't need them. Give me a good caravan master. Good sound canvas."

"And the mad."

"And the mad."

"Better than a regiment?"

"We've learned the desert, have we not? We walked here."

A long, long moment that dark gaze continued, intimate and close.

"I shall be very disappointed if you fail. Is there anything you might ask of me, any favor for yourself alone."

"Only what I've asked," he said.

Perhaps it disquieted her to find a man who wanted so little. But there was nothing at all he wanted. There was absolutely nothing she could give, except his freedom, and the lives of his mother and sister and his father.

"I dreamed of the east," she said in a low voice. "As the mad do. I will have an answer, Marak Trin. I *will* have an answer."

"If I'm alive to come back, I will come back. Let my mother and my sister go where they choose and you'll have your answer and all my effort. I've lied in my life. But I've never broken a promise."

The Ila drew off a glove, finger by finger, as they did in the market, as they did in a court of law. Her hand was long and white, blue-veined marble, and she offered him her fingers to touch, concluding a bargain, flesh to flesh, with no au'it to write it. Her flesh was warm as his own. She smelled of fruit and rain, smelled of wealth and water.

"Your household keeps its word," she said. "It always has. Its one virtue. Go outside. Bring my captain in."

He rose with difficulty. The joints of his knees felt assaulted, still aching with the fire she had loosed. A roaring was in his ears, making him dizzy. He was not fit to ride, not today; but he would. If her promise brought him the means to leave this place and walk out under the sky again, he would do that. He made out the voices past the roaring in his ears. *East*, they cried, *east!* and he realized he was set free, to do what the voices had wanted all his life. Freedom racketed about his whole being, demanding a test, demanding immediate action.

East. East. East.

He backed away, wobbling. The Ila rose and mounted the steps, and sat down in her chair, composed and still.

But reaching the door he realized it had no latch, and he had no knowledge how to open it. She made a fool of him, consciously, perhaps. He gazed at it in dismay, reminded in such small detail how far the holy city was beyond his expectation.

She opened the door, perhaps. At least it sighed a steamy breath and admitted one of her chief captains, a man scowling, hand on dagger, ready to kill.

"Here are my orders," the Ila said from her chair high at the end of the room. "Give him the madmen, an au'it, and a master caravanner, and whatever canvas and goods and beasts he requires. Marak Trin Tain is under my seal. When he goes out from this hall, respect him. When he comes back to these doors, admit him. Write it!"

The au'it, Marak saw from the doorway, had slunk back to sit at the Ila's feet. Quickly she spread out her book, and the au'it wrote whatever seemed good to write.

"I have sent for the wife and daughter of Tain Trin Tain, and spared Tain his fate. Write it!"

What would they cry through the holy city and through the market? Marak Trin is the Ila's man?

His father would hear it, sooner or later. His father would be appalled, outraged, and, yes, shamed a second time.

But could he refuse to yield up to the Ila's demand his cast-off wife and daughter, where he had sent his son?

And could his son have done otherwise, when Tain Trin Tain had once bowed to the Ila and signed their armistice?

In that sense it was not his decision. It became the Ila's. And Tain would have known, when he threw down the damnation against his wife, that he had cleaved the two of them one from the other and thrown conscience after, a casual piece of baggage. He only hoped the Ila's men reached Kais Tain in time for his mother's safety.

Love of his father? Loyalty? He no longer knew where to find that in himself. In the Ila's promise, he had lost one direction and found another. He did not resent the pain of the Ila's blow: lords struck when offended. It was an element, like heat, like thirst, to be endured. She had met the price, and he *was* bought. Had his father done as much, for all his blows through the years?

He walked out with the captain, sure as he did so that here was a man, like his father, who had sooner see him dead. But the captain said not a word against the Ila's wishes, took him directly to the armory and let him equip himself with good, serviceable weapons: a dagger, a boot-knife, even considering that rarest of weapons, a pistol, difficult to keep in desert dust, and hungry for metal.

"Sand will impair it," the captain said, plainly not in favor of him having it. "And aim is a matter of training."

"I have no time for that," he said, and put aside that piece that, itself, could have hired a regiment.

A bow—there were numerous good ones—might give him both range and rapidity of fire, but nothing to defeat a mobbing among the vermin, and it was a lowland weapon. In the summer heat of the Lakht the laminations outright melted and gave way.

In the end he settled for the *machai*, a light, thin blade, as much tool as weapon, that he hung from his belt, and a good harness-knife.

The captain looked at him oddly, and honestly tried to press at least a spear on him.

"An encumbrance," Marak said. It was the same reason he wished none of the Ila's regiments, which encumbered themselves with all these things and baked in hardened leather besides, in the desert heat. "I want only this. For the rest of us, good boots. We'll ride. We'll all ride. But good boots. One never knows."

"As you wish," the captain said, but after that the captain seemed worried, as if he had failed somehow in his duty, in sending him out short of equipment with an army of well-shod madmen, of which he was chief. The captain tried to make up for it in other offerings, silver heating-mirrors, a burning-glass, two fine blankets, and a personal, leather-bound kit of salves and medicines, all of which Marak did take.

Then the captain walked him out to the pens, a fair distance, and pulled a riding beast from the reserve pens, a creature of a quality Kais Tain rarely saw.

That, he prized, and found that he and the captain had reached an accommodation of practical cooperation. Under other circumstances they would have been aiming weapons at one another. But now the captain seemed to understand he was not there to steal away goods, but to carry out the Ila's wishes, economically, and asking no great show about it.

In that understanding they became almost amiable, and the captain chided sergeants who hid back the better harness. They laid out the best. The captain's name, he learned, was Memnanan. He had spent all his life in the Ila's service as he had spent his in Tain's.

They walked companionably through areas of the Beykaskh that Marak knew his father would spend a hundred men's lives to see. He looked up against the night sky at the high defenses, the strong walls and observed a series of latchless gates that sighed with steam.

They had never even come close to piercing these defenses. Only their raids on caravans had gained notice, and that, likely, for its inconvenience, unless they should have threatened the flow of goods for a full year.

The storerooms they visited and those they passed were immense. All the wealth in the world was here. They passed the kitchens. The vermin of the city ignored morsels of bread cast in a drainway. It lay and rotted. He found that as much a wonder as the steam-driven doors.

"We have sent for a caravan master," Memnanan said. "We count forty-one who will make the whole journey, including yourself. Getting them outfitted will take hours, at the quickest."

The captain ordered a midnight supper and shared it with him under an awning near the kitchens, the two of them drinking beer that finally numbed the pain, both getting a small degree drunk, and debating seriously about the merits of the western forges and the balance of their blades. In pride of opinion, they each cast at a target, the back of a strongroom door.

They were within a finger of each other and the center of the target. Another beer and they might have sworn themselves brothers. And in that thought, Marak recoiled from the notion, and sobered, as the captain must surely do.

A sergeant reported that the caravan master had come into the outer courtyard. This arrival turned out to be a one-eyed man with his three sons, who together owned fifty beasts, six slaves, and five tents, with two freedmen as assistants. This caravan master had served the Ila's particular needs for ten years, so he said, and took her pay and feared her as he feared the summer wind.

"There are not enough beasts to carry us," Marak said to the man. "If the party numbers over forty, we're short, and it needs more supply than that."

"To Pori," the caravan master said, which might be his understanding of the mission.

"Off the edge of the Lakht. Beyond Pori." There was no lying to the caravan master, above all else. This was the man on whose judgment and preparation all their lives depended.

"There is nothing beyond Pori," the caravan master said.

"That's why we need more beasts and more supply," Marak said, and appealed to the captain with a glance. "I need more tents, more beshti, first-quality, far more than the weapons."

The captain snapped his fingers and called over the aide who had brought the caravan master; and the aide went in and called out an au'it, who sat down on a bench in the courtyard and prepared to write on loose sheets. A slave brought a lamp close to her, and set it down on a bare wooden table, while small insects died and sparked in the flame.

"How many beasts?" the captain asked Marak.

"Ask the caravan master," Marak said. "He knows that, or he knows nothing."

"Ask wide, but prudently," the captain said sternly to the master. "This is the Ila's charge."

The master, whose name was Obidhen, looked down and counted, a rapid movement of fingers, the desert way, that took the place of the au'it's scribing. "Sixty-nine beasts," Obidhen said. "The tents are enough, ten to a tent. More will mean more beasts, more food, more pack beasts, more work, more risk. I have slaves enough, my grown sons, and the two freedmen."

"The tents are enough," Marak agreed.

"This is a modest man," the captain said to Obidhen. "The Ila finds merit in him, the god knows why."

Obidhen looked at Marak askance, not having been told, perhaps, that his party consisted entirely of madmen.

But after that, the supplies must be gotten and loaded, and the caravan master went out with orders to gather what he needed immediately, on the Ila's charge, and form his caravan outside the walls by the fountain immediately. Obidhen promised three hours by the clepsydra in the courtyard, having his beasts within the pens to the north of the city, and his gear and his tents, he said, well-ordered and waiting in the warehouses by the northern gate. He could find the rest, with the Ila's seal on the order, within the allotted time.

"We will need for each man or woman a change of clothing," Marak said. "Waterskins. Mending for their boots and clothing. And salves and medicines for the lot."

"Done," the captain said then, and appointed aides to bring it, and a corporal to rouse out a detail to carry it down past the fountain gate, to be parceled out as Obidhen directed, every man and woman a packet to keep in personal charge . . . not so much water as might be a calamity to lose, but enough to augment their water-storage by one full day and their food by a week.

"Sergeant Magin will escort you as far as your first camp out from the walls," the captain said, when the au'it had written down the details for whoever read such records. "I know," Memnanan said. "You wish no escort. This is not an escort."

"I take the warning," Marak said.

Memnanan, looked at him as if there was far, far more he wanted to ask, and to say, and to know, before he turned an abjori lowlander and a caravan of good size loose in his jurisdiction.

"You will carry a letter and water-seal," Memnanan said, "for the lord of Pori."

It would speed their journey, if they might water to the limit of their capacity before descending the rim. Marak approved. For the rest, he trusted Obidhen knew the wells, and the hazards.

It was approaching dawn by the time he was satisfied about the rest of the baggage, and by the time the Ila's men reported the mad were delivered to the bottom of the hill. He had thought it might take longer, and saw now that there would be no rest, not even an hour, but that was well enough. His back ached, his ears roared, his joints ached, and his eyes blurred with exhaustion, but the expectation of life and freedom had become bedrock, underlying all actions, the urgency of the departure as overwhelming as the direction, and the Ila's officers were inclined to take her orders as like the god's, instantly to be fulfilled. *East,* his voices said, persistent, though the Ila's blast had deafened him. *East. Now. Haste.*

"I will come back," he said, if Memnanan had doubted it.

Memnanan eyed him at a certain remove, as if still trying to sum him up. He likewise fixed Memnanan in his mind, a man not remarkable to look at, but distinguished by honesty, by wit, by intelligence. Someday they might be bitter enemies. In this hour they were close allies, and he meant to remember this name, this face, for good, whatever fell between them.

Then still haunted by his voices, half-deafened and aching in his bones, he turned and left, to walk down the hill like any common traveler. Memnanan sent the sergeant and his men down with him, and the au'it that the Ila had instructed to go with him walked with him, too, down the streets he had walked up mere hours ago as a prisoner.

The city rested neither by day nor by night . . . only changed its traffic. As folk did in the downland villages, people in Oburan did their major business by day; but the city being also of the Lakht, there were still plenty of curious onlookers abroad even in the depth of the night. They wondered at him, perhaps, not having had the rumor from the day people what he was. But they seemed to wonder more at the au'it, red-robed, the visible presence of the Ila, where they crossed the occasional circle of bug-besieged, oil-wasteful lamplight. Omi, they said. *Lord. Lady.* They bowed, or covered their faces, fearing her more than weapons.

When they reached the gates, gates that stood open by night in these times of peace, they had only to walk outside, there by the Mercy of the Ila, where Obidhen had arranged his beasts and their burdens. The pack beasts all sat saddled. Their burdens, which seemed all apportioned, sat ready to be bound to the saddles just before they set themselves under way. The riding beasts, too, were saddled, awaiting their riders. Obidhen had been a busy man.

"We are ready," Obidhen reported, bowing.

"The au'it will ride with us," Marak said. "I doubt she knows how. I doubt many of the others do."

"We have been advised," Obidhen said. It was still a question of how much Obidhen had been advised, but Marak thought likely Obidhen had by now heard the nature of his party.

The sergeant commanding the Ila's men, too, gave the necessary commands to the caravan master, and went off to secure their own riding beasts from somewhere near, while Obidhen began to appoint his party of madmen to their beasts.

That was the orderly beginning of the matter. Then Obidhen's slaves, strong men, each, roused each of the forty-some riding beasts up, beginning with the au'it, and hoisted their passengers up, like children.

"Sit still!" Marak shouted out. "Let them settle!"

It was appalling confusion. The beasts, in the uncertainty of so many new riders, lost patience and moved away from nudging knees and elbows, adding to the bawling confusion. Two and three of the novice riders toppled hard onto the sand. Marak seized stray reins, and so did the freedmen and the sons and Obidhen himself; while onlookers gathered from the city gate to add to the confusion. The soldiers, riding up with shouts and derision, had to gather in reins to hold other bawling beasts.

Meanwhile no few riders let their beasts escape their inexpert reining, and those animals set to circling, ignoring tugs on their reins by the simple trick of laying their heads around. It was no surprise that several novices had their feet bitten, which brought howls and panic anew, and catcalls from the gate despite the presence of the au'it and the soldiers.

The madmen were mostly villagers, but they had walked the desert, not ridden it. Save a few desert-bred folk and two others who were clearly expert, the most of the madmen had never ridden in their lives, and the slaves had a great deal to do to convince any of the beasts thus mounted to keep a line.

Marak approached his own well-bred besha and took his quirt from the saddle. After the recent confusion his beast rolled a wary eye back, sizing him up.

Marak took the rein and stepped smoothly into the higher mounting loop. The besha, perhaps relieved to sense a rider who knew the fast way aboard, half straightened his forelegs and came up under him as he landed.

There was no need for *hup-hup-hup!* Marak sized the beast up, too, braced both hands against the double horn, one high, one low, as the back legs shifted.

The pitch forward reversed in the next breath as the forelegs straightened.

And just when an inexperienced rider would least expect it, the hind legs drove in one long shove, propelling the rider forward and all but upside down for an instant, testing the strength of the girth around the beast's broad, deep chest.

That was what the double horn and straight-armed brace of the hands was for, and *that* was why children and old folk mounted a besha only with assistance, while it was standing.

A fourth, a minor jolt, almost a hop, straightened the forelegs entirely, and at that, the rider's whole body snapped back to view the world from twice a man's height, poised on a stilt-limbed body four times his size. It all proceeded in a few blinks of the eye; and weary as he was, trembling as he held the rein, and surrounded by a band of madmen apt to fall in the dust or lose toes to vexed mounts, Marak still found a breath of freedom.

The beast under him, no common run of the herd, wanted to move. He held it back. The besha swayed back and forth under him, grumbling in its chest, as beshti would do when they were full of spirit and impatient with the lowly pack beasts. Marak allowed no nonsense, settled his right foot possessively on the besha's curved neck, and heaved a deep and shaken sigh. The besha under him did the same.

They all were up. No one had been killed. Obidhen's sons linked the animals that would move under halter, to loud complaints and the occasional outright squall of indignation from riding beasts unaccustomed to such treatment when they were under saddle.

The packs, meanwhile, all had their specific places, hung over the packsaddles, tied down with a few short turns of rope. The caravan slaves hastened, sometimes running from one beast to the other, beshti patience notoriously scant with imbalance or hesitation. Everything was packed, every packet balanced for the two sides of the saddle, everything apportioned to the individual beast's capacity to carry: *there* was the mark of a veteran caravanner. Every pack went on the first time, and every beast responded to the light snap, not the impact, of a quirt.

A last few madmen, desert-bred, mounted up on their own, and rode back and forth, free of the detested lead, restless, as anxious as the beasts.

Certainly the caravan master's three sons had no need of help when the time came. "Bas!" the order was, making a standing beast simply put out one foreleg. That served as a footbridge to an unseen mounting loop and, by a quick turn, to the saddle. To the unknowing eye, in the dim light of dawn, the master's eldest son had leapt to his besha's back.

It was the trick of the young, the lithe, the desert-bred, and Marak doubted he could still do it himself. He had softened considerably in village life, since their retreat from the Lakht, and he knew now he had watched his father, too, grow soft, and angry, and settle in for the life of a village lord. There had been the start of the bitterness, a man always mourning the chance that had never come, the vengeance that had never fallen into his hands.

Thoughts muddled. Sounds became distant, and the weariness weighed down and down, numbing senses. The foot-braced attitude Marak held, keeping his beast at rest, was one in which he had slept many a ride, and of all things else he had left behind with his youthful confidence, his body had not forgotten how to keep centered on a swaying back. He shivered in the dawn, but at least no one noticed his weakness. The shivering was lack of sleep; it was the unaccountable shift of his fortunes. It was the roaring in his ears, that the Ila's retaliation had brought on him, and now that he had done everything, now that there was nothing more for him to do but sleep, it was beyond him to fight his exhaustion. Body heat fled. He drew his robes close about him, even covering his fingers within that warmth and taking in the heat of the huge body under him.

The roaring increased within his ears. Pain had invaded his joints, down to his fingers and his toes, and reasserted itself, after so long ignoring it. But it was only exhaustion, so he argued with himself. It all would pass. The trembling would pass. Surely the roaring in his ears would pass with sleep.

"Are we going home?" one confused madman asked another in his hearing, as the line filed past, and the caravan set itself in motion. "Where shall we go?"

One madman answered another: "East, man. We go east. Everything is east. And then we go back and tell the Ila what we find. That's the crazy part. Tain's son is one of us. He claims he'll figure it out."

4

The law of the caravans is this: that the master of the caravan has the power of life and death over all who travel under his rule, except over a priest, except over an au'it, except over the Ila's man. These lives belong to the Ila. The master of the caravan must preserve them at the cost of all others.
—The Book of Oburan

The sun rose as a vast, expanded disk and climbed above the Lakht in an unforgiving sky. The day's heat grew and grew, and built toward that hour when prudent travelers pitched their tents. Marak had indeed slept in the saddle, an uneasy sleep, a sleep with a watchful eye on the mad and on the soldiers and the caravan master and his sons alike; but no greater disturbance demanded his attention than the passage of birds, shadows on the sand, and the track of a solitary belly-creeper headed for the reed-rimmed Mercy.

Past midday, with the pond behind them, the heat only increased. The caravan master ordered a halt until the heat of the day had passed, and Marak, among the rest, was glad to bid his beast kneel and to step down from the saddle.

In the jolt of the beast's kneeling down, his own knees and elbows ached with remembered fire. He sat down on the burning sand against his beast's broad side while the caravan master and the servants pitched the tents.

The au'it settled near him, book and kit in her lap.

There would be nothing remarkable in this camp to record. He was determined on that point.

He said to her, instead, "Write the names of the mad." It seemed a harmless question. "Write the names of their cities. Write what they look for." It might keep her from hovering near him.

The au'it bowed her head and went on her mission, visiting the rest, who disposed themselves in a tight, sweaty huddle under the first canvas stretched . . . forty madmen, all in a space for ten.

Marak cared little for what she did or reported. The holy city had gone below the horizon, but it would appear many times during the next night and day, and for that sight he no longer roused himself. He only cared that he hear no loud sounds and that nothing require him to stir, and where he would find the strength in his legs to mount the beast again this afternoon he could not imagine. Now the pain had set in. Now the weakness swept over him. The caravan master's sons would heave him up as they did the wife of Tarsa and the potter.

He would burn with shame, he, Marak Trin, once Trin Tain, his father's heir.

Terror of the Lakht, the men had called him. Not lately.

He rested foolishly in the sun, not even seeking shelter in the first canvas spread: at this pitch of disgust with himself he could not abide the looks and the questions of his fellow travelers, the recipients of his charity, the models of his fortune. It was the latter truth that galled him most, that in point of fact, as far as the Ila cared and as far as the soldiers cared, he had become no different than the rest of them. He brooded on his situation, his aifad pulled about his face, shading him from what was now, though he had invited every one of them, an unwelcome company.

But when all five tents were all up, all open-sided to let the air flow through, the mad had somewhat spread out and settled down on their mats. Then he stirred himself.

"Omi," Obidhen accosted him. *My lord.* "I'll have the

number one tent, with my freedmen and the slaves. My second son Landhi will have the next, Rom, my eldest, the third and Tofi, my youngest, can manage the fourth. I can place two freedmen with the first and manage the fifth myself, unless, omi, you will take charge there. You know the Lakht. You clearly know the necessities. If you will take the au'it in your care and be master there, it might be best."

He understood the delicate position the master was in. The Ila's soldiers had camped in that fifth tent, men over whom the master had little authority.

"I will deal with it," he said to the master, "and I *do* know the Lakht."

The master bowed, clearly relieved. He was relieved. He had a tent where his word was law. As for the soldiers, they would leave after their noon rest, and good riddance, Marak thought. He took his waterskin, took his mat, almost last of the pile, and went to that shade, sure that the au'it, still pursuing her questions, would come back to him in due time.

Meanwhile he spread his mat near the edge of the shade, where the breeze moved beneath the shelter, and went and got his rations. As master of the fifth tent, he was the arbiter of disputes, the dispenser of stores on days when they chose not to share a common meal. There were no disputes, no questions, and peacefully he unwrapped what he had to eat, the common fare on days when the travel was too hard and the press of that work too fast and furious to spread out the sun-ovens and cook. The cake was the sort of dry ration common to the Lakht, where water was too precious to let into food. Water stayed in the canteen, and one mixed the two in the mouth, to sustain life and make it possible to swallow. That was the usual fare of the desert tribes on the move, and the mad had learned it on the march. They might know nothing about riding beasts; but they knew by now how to eat and drink in the desert. These were the survivors, toughest, most adaptable of the lot. He had nothing to tell them regarding the preciousness of water and the apportionment of supplies . . . given they were in their sane minds.

The Ila's men, meanwhile, unwrapped their supper and ate fruit from the market, dripped juice wantonly on the sand, and pitched the pits away still having flesh on them. Marak glowered, resting, nursing the recurrence of pain the Ila had given him.

The au'it came back. "Two have left," she said.

"Have they taken beasts?" Marak asked.

"No," the au'it said. "When we stopped to rest, they simply walked away."

"They're dead," he said.

Those who also had walked the Lakht to the holy city had not prevented them or reported them, and there was a certain logic in that. If they would walk away today, they would walk away tomorrow, having eaten and drunk a day's rations in the meanwhile. The desert killed the wasteful and the extravagant quickly, surely, and covered them over. He had given them their chance and spent a day's food on them. Effectively they were dead, and he could not fault their choice.

It might be the better choice, who could know? He had asked for their lives in a moment in which he fought for his own life. Now he had no notion what he had done to these madmen, whether it was good or not. He had no idea whether he had rescued these people or damned them to a lingering death.

But he knew why he shuddered at the reasonless, wasteful actions of the men and women that surrounded him. The soldiers swilled water. One of the mad at the moment had wandered out and turned in circles, looking up at the sky and staring at the sun. Because he had asked for this man's life, was he responsible? Could he advise the man against his visions? Could he do better in leading this band of fools?

Could he say he would not, himself, sooner or later, be that crazed?

The au'it, in the soft, rarely used voice of her profession, reported the two names of the lost among the others from her book, and listed the rest as he had wished, with their origins. None of the names of the mad meant much to him, except that the wife from Tarsa had a name: Norit; and the potter had a name, Kosul. He took account of those and of others, despite the roaring that had begun in his ears, and meant to remember them.

It proved, too, that there were tribesmen among the mad. He had thought so. That was good news, in this land . . . only granted they were not the ones who had walked away.

He lay down to sleep after eating. It seemed to him this afternoon that the air was either hotter than the rule, or he might be fevered. He had been in pain, and his wounds always went fevered: it was his weakness from childhood.

When the fever came, however, he always healed.

And he waked after a sleep of a few hours in less pain, which put him in a better frame of mind. To his relief, too, there was less of the intermittent buzzing and roaring behind the voices in his ears, so he began to hope that, too, might abate. He heard one of his voices calling him, distinctly so: *Marak, Marak, Marak,* that idle repetition clear for the first time since the Ila's fire had run through his bones.

He had never thought he would be relieved to hear that voice, but he was. A voice was better than the roaring sound, and far better than dulled ears and diminished senses.

But less welcome, this afternoon, his eyes flashed with inner light, as the images once had done when he was a child, when he first remembered them building shapes in his eyes. It was as if they were building back again.

He healed. He always healed. Even the madness healed itself to its old terms, as if it were an inescapable condition of his good health.

He lay on his mat and listened to his voices until the sun sank and the caravan master and his sons began to strike tents. Then it was time to move. The soldiers gathered their water-plump flesh up onto riding beasts and rode back the way they had come, returning to the city. No one was sorry for that.

And the mad, once rested, wandered about with more energy than before, carrying their own mats, some even helping with the tents now that the soldiers were gone, now that they were sure they were no longer prisoners.

Everyone was out and about, finally, except the wife from Tarsa, Norit, who sat and rocked, rocked, rocked, as the boy had used to.

The caravan master came cautiously to inform him they must strike this tent, too, if they were to move, and asking him would he persuade the madwoman to get up.

Marak saw from the tail of his eye that the au'it made a note in her book. He wondered what she wrote, and for whom she wrote it.

He went and assisted the wife, Norit, to her feet. And the au'it made another note.

Marak, Marak, Marak. The sound went on, maddening. The lights within his skull outshone the sun, a long, long tunnel of suns.

The slaves had saddled his riding beast. In this gathering bout of madness he thought it was Osan, the name of his very first, when he was a boy; and as he settled himself in the saddle and endured the neck-snapping jolts of the beast rising, he decided that that was its name. His life had come to a new beginning. He had cast away responsibility to his father, and taken up responsibility for madmen . . . he knew he could not cure them, no more than he could heal himself. But here he was. He had achieved the command for which his affliction fitted him.

A breeze rose with the lowering of the sun, the first breath of air, a reminder of life in the midst of the great flat, and it roused Osan's spirits, too. Marak took in the rein and walked Osan in a circle until all the mad were up and until the caravan masters had mounted their own beasts. Then he let Osan go, riding first with the master's sons, and then alone, striking a good traveling pace.

He had used to ride into the western desert for days. Where have you been? his father would ask, and he would lie and call it hunting, when his hunting was voices and the visions. He would kill something at the last, and bring it back, and his father would believe him.

He recalled killing a bird, and remembered how he had stroked its head and thought if he were not mad it would not be dead, because there was precious little good to him in killing it. He had stamped it into the sand. He had thrown rocks at it. Then, in cowardice, he had killed another, to have something to show his father for his day in the wilderness.

Osan, his companion of prior lies and deceptions about his madness, was bone and dust now. The shoulder on which he used to lean was gone. There was no more help from that quarter. There was this beast, which would live or die with him. So with all these men. He need not go anywhere to explain himself this night. No more. No more lies. He was what he was, and the soldiers, their last tie to the city, had left them. Only the caravan master could dispute his word, and Obidhen, set under his orders, called him lord.

They were well equipped, like the best of caravans. There were no walkers to slow them. There were no wagons. Out away from the wells as a fast, well-equipped caravan could travel, there was less chance of bandits. It was water that drew predators.

Marak, the voices said, past the roaring in his ears. *Marak. This way.*

East where the sun rose. East where the world slid. East, east, east, and an end of questions, for men and women in universal agreement, a handful of souls all set desperately toward the identical, desperate, crazed obsession.

So his jagged reasoning went as they traveled on into the night, when every man was isolate and when the dark cooled the land to shadow and starlight.

At times he slept in the saddle. At times he waked to look at the stars and realize that nothing known lay in front of him.

In the enduring dark this new Osan called up emotions in him that he thought the drugs and the march had killed. Osan made his hands remember love and his body remember freedom, and those two things stirred other feelings.

Marak, Marak, Marak, his voices said. His body fell into a rhythm it had known from before he could remember, a rhythm he had learned in his father's arms, when that had been the safe place, the shaded place, the secure place.

Now that of all things was the deadliest place, the most painful place for memory to go.

There was only Osan.

Freedom was all he had ever asked of his father.

A cave of suns beckoned him, blinding bright: he squinted his eyes even in the dark, and it made no more sense than it ever had.

A tower rose up against the stars, a black shape, a vacancy of light. *Marak,* the voices said.

He had fought the voices' advice, smothered the images, hidden them all his life, and now he had nothing to learn of the world but the truth of what they meant. It was as if they, he and the madmen, all shed their clothes and ran naked in the dark. The au'it had told him all their names, and he knew now he was not alone. He had sisters. He had brothers. The truly mad had walked away to die and now he was left with those who, like him, had wit enough to dominate the visions, and will enough to live.

They were going to find the answers. Together, in the east, they would find the answers.

5

In the wisdom of the Ila, the Holy City first sent out the tribes to discover the land, and to them the Holy City appointed the skill to rule the high Lakht. The next to go out from the Holy City were the lords of villages, with their households, and they went to the wells of sweet water that the tribes had found and occupied them. For that reason no village may deny water to the tribes. To the caravans it may sell water, but the tribes may take what they need.
—The Book of Goson

Day came. The world might resume its sanity, but the mad continued in their course, and the beasts continued their patient, easy stride.

So, so, so, Marak thought, as the sun warmed the tense muscles of his shoulders: so, after all, the sun came up, and he, who had thought himself above the mad, was after all no different, no more and no less fit to survive.

He was reconciled. He began to look at faces. He learned them. He matched them with names.

The sun came up and rose higher and they camped at greater leisure, cooking, eating, and sleeping, a close row of five tents. When the air cooled, they rode on again. A few of the mad even attempted to mount as the more experienced riders did. One, the potter, fell. But he had courage, and the others felt the impact in their bones. They laughed only when he laughed.

A few riders continually caused their beasts more trouble than guidance with the rein. The wife from Tarsa, Norit, kept hers too tight, perhaps afraid that the beast would bolt and carry her away into the deep desert.

"No," Marak said, having seen the caravan master's vain effort to change her habit. "No. Hold the rein this way, over your hand. A simple turn of the wrist signals the beast. If you always twitch, he stops hearing you, like a child who shouts too much. Let your back give. Let the rein flow unless you have an order. I assure you, you haven't strength enough in your arm to pull him back if he wanted to run. He doesn't want to. It's much too hot."

She gripped the rein, all the same. Her hands must ache.

"If you annoy him like that," Marak said, "he simply grows worse. But he will always turn his head to a gentle tug, like that, yes, that's enough. And if he hesitates to turn, use the quirt on the opposite shoulder, just a touch."

"What if I make him angry?" Clearly this was an abiding fear.

"Does a midge annoy you? Your pulling on his jaw annoys him, I say. It makes his mouth sore. Touch lightly. Pull lightly. But *only* when you want him to turn. Perhaps twice a day, when we camp and when we start out."

She did try, and loosened the amount of rein, but the knuckles were still white in their grip on the loose rein.

"All right. Let the rein fall to your lap," he said. "Let it drop." He saw now how it was, that this was a woman for whom the whole world had run away in chaos, and she was given one rein, and this one rein managed her course toward the edge of the world. She managed it with an iron grip. "Listen to me. Trust me. Let it drop."

It was as if he asked her to leap over a cliff.

"Drop it, I say."

She carefully let the rein lie in her lap, and sat like a rock precariously balanced, awaiting disaster.

"Foot up," he said, while their beasts walked side by side, "in the crook of his neck. That stops you leaning forward and him pitching you over his head. Shoulders behind the small of your back. That prevents you sliding back over his rump. Your hips move as he moves."

She sat like a rock.

"You've made love," he said. "You were a wife. *Follow him.*"

She gave him a shocked glance. Her eyes were wide and frightened.

"There are worse things than falling off," he said while that silence persisted. "Let your back sway. Don't forget how."

She gathered up the rein, having proved the beast would not bolt. He had robbed her, perhaps, of one sense of dominance over the world. Now he told her to make love to what she feared, and her spine was still stiff, her carriage eloquent of offense. But her spine began to give. She listened.

"If you wish to live," he said, "make this beast your ally. If you should become separated from the rest, if you can stay with the besha, she'll shade you from the sun, she'll shelter you from the wind, and she'll inevitably carry you to water if you don't touch the rein. She's your greatest help. She might be your life."

She did not want to hear that either, he thought. But she listened. Her besha was a good deal happier with the partnership.

She was not the only offender. He showed the same lesson to an orchardman from Goson, whose name was Korin, to the potter, Kosul, from his own group, and to a woman from the west, Maol, a farmwife who blushed redder than sunburn, but who understood what he wished to say.

There were five among the forty-odd that he had no need to show. These were riders. Two were traders, two had been soldiers: on them Obidhen had come to rely for help.

And one was a Lakhtani woman, of the desert tribes, a dark-skinned woman named Hati, who was one of the nine others in his tent, with the au'it, the potter, and the orchardman, three farmers, a weaver, and the wife from Tarsa.

Hati's mastery over the beasts was sure as instinct, and she had a seat a western lowlander admired. She occasionally assisted Obidhen when the beasts grew fractious, and he had seen her rouse the beasts and settle them again by voice alone, that strange call that the desert-bred beasts knew. She was a gift, among them, one whose knowledge Obidhen's sons attempted to gain, attempting to engage her in conversation . . . with intent of gaining more than knowledge, it might be.

But she went veiled, and disconsolate, and brooded. Marak shared a tent with her and never had seen her face.

They camped, and slept, and broke camp. The day seemed cooler than the last. The beasts were willing to move, throwing their heads and switching their tails with pent-up energy.

They crossed a wide pan, where a memory of water had made a crust, and leached up alkali. The beasts' feet grew white to the knee, and the caravan trail across this place was distinct, a track through the crust.

They crossed it, and the dark came down again, the stars brightening. Everyone had forgotten their instruction during the evening ride, with the beasts in a fractious mood, and made themselves increasing trouble. Marak peevishly reminded a few, and included the soldiers, who caused a disturbance in the pace.

But now they had entered a quieter time, pleasant, even cool air under the gathering dusk, and he found himself looking respectfully at Hati, and looking longer and longer. The hands were long and beautiful. The body beneath the veils seemed young. She was a puzzle, unique among those the Ila had gathered. The tribes stoned their madmen. Hati was here, alive. When he thought about that fact he could only be the more intrigued.

"The beast is yours," he said, riding close to her. "Go with us or go your way. No one will prevent you."

Hati said nothing, nor quite looked at him. In the deep dusk her dark hands showed lighter bands about the fingers and wrists. A tribeswoman's silver, her respectability, had doubtless banded her wrists, lifelong, and now left only the paler flesh.

Her tribe had cast her out, he decided. They had kept what they wished, as they did the dead, from whom they stripped all ornament—silver being a useless distinction for the scavengers.

"Or will you stay?" he asked her, persisting in his attempt to draw her out. "I need your help. You know the Lakht better than any of us. Do you understand at all?"

The move of her head said yes.

"Then teach the rest of these villagers good sense. I see how you ride. Teach them."

"Why?"

Why was a good question. "Because I asked the Ila for their lives. Because hanging in the holy city is easier than breaking a leg out here."

She looked straight at him, hearing him, at least. All he could see was her eyes. She might be anything, think anything, beneath the veils. And she was as mad as he was. There was that.

"I'm Hati," she said.

"Marak. Marak Trin."

"I know." She said not a thing more, nor did she encourage conversation. He left her, finally, and gave up on the attempt.

But during that night, by starlight, she rode by one and the other of the women, even the au'it, speaking in low tones, correcting posture, correcting a grip on the reins. The sun rose, and she spoke to men, more animated and more assured, even forceful in her corrections, even correcting the better riders. By midmorning the downland men feared her direct reproof—never a loud reproof, but correct, and stinging, if she repeated it.

When they stopped to spread the tents at noon, Hati encouraged the wife, Norit, to ride the beast down to his sitting rest, and not to be handed off like baggage. Norit stayed in the saddle, and stepped off without help, and when the men still mounted saw that, they all did the same, though the orchardman was pitched off at the very last and sprawled gently flat on the sand.

Hati went and stood over the unfortunate man, hands on her hips, flung back her veil, and offered her sober opinion that he was learning, but should not have moved his hand from the saddlebow just yet.

Marak, just having slid down from his own beast, began to laugh then, a dazed, unanticipated laughter that seeped upward like water from the ground.

And once he laughed, others of the mad laughed. The orchardman got up and dusted himself off, taking the taunts of the potter in glowering good humor, and finally with a grin.

Then seeing the orchardman in better humor, madmen sat down on the burning hot sand and laughed until they rolled.

They were free. He had freed them all. Even the two who had walked off to die . . . they were free.

And once they had laughed, and wiped their eyes, then after all these days they began to talk to one another, except, always, the au'it.

More, the tribeswoman, Hati, having let down her veil, did not put it back. She had acquired authority despite the lack of bracelets on her arms and rings on her fingers. And her whole being expanded. Her eyes flashed. Her walk became a stride.

That woman was his lieutenant, Marak decided. If he was omi, in the mind of Obidhen and his sons, and if this was the company he led, he had now seen the one he would rely on to back him in an emergency. She had the wits and the courage. The two ex-soldiers that he might have chosen were both duller men, good fighters, perhaps, but if they had no clear objective to gain and no one to provide the idea, or to shout orders moment by moment, they sat inert. They watched the women, however, with predatory eyes . . . and then bent wary glances in his direction, and in the master's, clearly sizing up their will to prevent them. It was clear where their source of initiative rested. He would not trust them with food, water, or women.

Most damning regarding any reliance on them in extremity, when the voices came, they twitched violently and stared at the east, the worst afflicted of all the party, following that lead when many of the others sat, still resolute and possessed of their dignity.

Hati was indeed the one. He had watched her move,

watched her gestures expand and her strides become confident. He saw, in those expanded movements, the natural grace and shape of the woman. Today he saw her face, and it was a darkly beautiful face, which his eyes dwelt on and followed with thoughts. He was not dead. If he had doubted his manhood had survived the desert, he did not now.

6

Or if any tree shall be deformed of its nature, the fruit of that tree shall not be eaten. It must be rooted up and given to a priest.
—The Book of the Priests

The mad shall be searched out. Everyone that bears the affliction shall be saved alive and shall not be hidden, but given to the Ila's messengers. No man shall conceal madness in his wife, or his son, or his daughter, or his father. Every one must be delivered up. Also if any beast should have the madness, it shall be kept from harm and delivered alive to the Ila's messengers, or if dead, its flesh shall not be eaten: it shall be saved intact and delivered to the Ila's messengers.
—The Book of the Ila's Au'it

After the camp they left the pans, and if it was flat and featureless before, the Lakht began to take on a red sameness, the very heart of the midland plateau, endless low ridges of dunes that stood as obstacles to their progress, red, powdery sand that was almost dust. They walked the ridges, a maze that led them generally east.

There was not a bird, not a track on the sand in this region. They were far from any well, any source of water. Wind turned up bones along the route, the bones of beshti, three of them together with no trace of harness, proving even wild beshti met their match in the storms of the Lakht.

The voices came louder, as the days went. *Marak,* they said, *Marak, do you hear us?*

Or again, mindless noise, *Marak, Marak, Marak.*

The voices were back, clearer than they had ever been. There seemed a satisfaction in them, finally. In a sense Marak felt safer than he had ever felt, truer to what had made demands all his life, and more settled on his course. He no longer thought of bolting. But he had equally dismissed thought of the journey ever coming to an end. It had become its own world. It enveloped all purpose, all planning.

The beasts went single file on the dunes, but on the crusted pan they tended to spread out and to go by twos and threes, and to sort that order by a kind of slow drifting in pace, a tendency of one beast to move a little faster than the next, or one rider to grow tired of the backside of the next beast, and to seek another view.

In that way, on a certain day, Hati drifted up close to him and said nothing, only cast eyes on him as they rode, at fairly close range, unveiled.

He knew suddenly by those looks what she bid for. And now that it was offered, he drew back, asking himself how it would be, and what they would set loose. There were no partners within their company. There never had been. Dealings between them had assumed a quiet sameness, her own rule, and she violated it.

In the economy of the desert he had grown averse to changing anything that worked. He found nothing to say, pretending not to see, while his thoughts raced in a kind of panic. They rode together a time, and then Hati fell back again.

What stopped him, he decided, lying on his mat at noon, arms under his head, might be the notion of sharing a mat with a madness as great and as quiet as his own.

And there was the question of doing it by broad daylight and under the eyes of all the rest. There was no place but the tent he shared with her and Norit, with the au'it, the potter and the orchardman and the other men. Going aside into the dunes for privacy was complete foolishness, a good way to meet the desert's lethal surprises. The most privacy they had was a curtain at one corner of each tent, which was the latrine, and no one went farther, or expected to be unobserved elsewhere. Clearly, others would observe them.

He turned his head and found her, as he feared she would be, lying on her side, watching him.

That evening, as they rode across a red, rippled flat, she rode next to him, not even using the excuse of the beasts' wandering in line.

"Why do you look away?" she asked him. Those eyes could melt brass. And they were not dark. They were clear brown. He found himself noticing that fact for the first time, in the light of evening, and admiring what he saw. His blood was moving faster. He found he was in increasing difficulty in refusing her, and had to decide now . . . to send her away with a firm rebuff.

Or not.

"I don't look away," he said, and then committed himself. Halfway. "But not here."

"Where?" she asked. She passed a dark hand about her, at all the Lakht, and seemed to laugh at him. "If not here, where? The latrine? I think not."

"We'll come to a village," he said. "Under a roof."

"A roof," she said in wonder, as if that were the least necessary thing he could have named.

"I'm from the villages."

"You don't ride like it," she said. "Under a roof." It still seemed to amaze her.

"Or if we find some safe place."

She laughed at his foolishness, the notion of finding anywhere alone in the desert a safe place, and he knew she was right. Rocks held predators: the empty sand held predators. Beyond a dune was an invitation to disaster. There was no place, and now he wanted one, badly.

"Hati is my name. Hati Makri an'i Keran."

From Keran, that was, Makri her mother-name and Keran her tribe-name. Hearing it, he was surprised, and not surprised: he knew the customs of the Keran, who refused all outsider wars and as often as not refused the Ila's taxes and levies. They were wild people, fierce, apt to fight singly, if not as a tribe.

And had the madness that afflicted the villages crept even there, to the wildest, least sociable people in the world?

"Peace," he said. That was the first thing strangers said when they met in the desert.

"Peace," she said. Her eyes shone with satisfaction, having won him. "Under a roof, then." Then she added: "The woman from Tarsa also."

In the Keran a woman could demand a second wife or a second husband, or an agreement of spouses could demand a third or a fourth, for that matter. He had seen how Hati had taken to Norit, to the soft-handed wife from Tarsa, and instructed her, until now Norit could mount and dismount and ride far better than he had ever thought. Norit was surely a puzzle to Hati, and she had become a friend, of sorts.

He saw how he had committed himself. He was not a coward, to back away. He was not in Kais Tain, where marriage was singular and women, but not men, could die for a mere suspicion of infidelity.

To what, then, had he agreed? To a night under a roof? To a lifetime, and two women? And a breach with all the customs of the west? His father would be appalled.

"I am not an'i Keran," he said.

"Once we sleep together, you are," Hati said, and added a confidence which sent a warmth through him that was by no means the sinking sun: "I am initiate."

Did they not say, for a proverb of the unfindable, *a Kerani virgin*? The women of that tribe took care there were none. But she had not called herself wife, or widow. She had not had a man before him.

No one but the au'it had slept near him. But when next they pitched the tents Hati unrolled her mat next to his. Without a word, assuming the right, she lay down in her robes and her veil.

Not until a roof, he had said, but he had given her a certain right by the agreement they had made together, and he had no notion quite what to do to prevent this steady, purposeful assault on his senses.

With the furnace-warm air blowing through the open sides of the tent, she turned on her side facing him. He turned on his back and stared at the canvas above them.

Above it the noon sun was a light shining through the heavy fabric, and the sideless tent billowed and bucked in occasional gusts. A rope needed tightening. But that was the slaves' job, not his. It was the master's job to see to it.

It was better to be here, lying at ease, than riding against the furnace-hot wind.

It was better to have a woman than to be alone.

He had no wish to drive her away. He had no wish to end this proposal in a quarrel before they had even shared a bed.

A hand touched his. Her fingers ran from his open palm to his arm and his shoulder. He lay still and ignored her enticement, finding it on the one hand pleasant and on the other vexing, an assault on his mind, as well as his body.

Suddenly, subtly, the voices spoke. He heard them and knew what stopped her hand wandering, what made her rest a moment, too, eyes shut ... every line of her expression said she hated that intrusion, resented it, detested its timing.

He observed the strong cast of her unveiled face, the long, slim hand that rested on a breast breathing hard, the offended pride of a woman who had been cast out, humiliated, but not broken.

The voices dinned in his own ears, *Marak, Marak, Marak.*

He had never taken the chance to talk directly to another of the afflicted on the one fact of their lives they all knew.

"They call my name," he said to that closed, taut face. "Do they call yours?"

Her eyes opened, searched his. None of the mad was willing to speak about their affliction. It was all but rude to breach that silence.

"Yes," she said. "They called my child-name and now they call my woman-name."

"The same," he confessed, which he had only admitted to his father. "Day and night."

"If we walk east forever, what will we meet? The bitter water?"

"If we walk that far." No one lived near the bitter water. No bird flew. The water-edge there was a land of white crusts and death. The toughest men in the world lived at the edge of the bitter plain and hammered out salt and breathed it and tasted it until they died. Everywhere in the world, men somehow found a way to live. Those men were free, at least. They traded with the Ila. They did not obey her.

The lines of fire built within his eyes. They made a form, rising up and up.

"Do you see a tower?" he asked the an'i Keran.

"Yes," she said.

"Do you see it now?"

"Yes," she said. Two mad visions touched one another. Two were the same. He suspected they all were, and that every man heard his own name.

"I called it a spire," she said, "before I saw the holy city. Could it be the Beykaskh?"

"Not the Beykaskh," he said. He was as sure of that as he was sure the direction was east. "No tower that I know, so tall and thin. A spire. A rock spire?"

"So," she said.

"I wonder what the others call it." He stared at the sun through the coarse canvas, felt the heat of the wind touch the sweat on his throat and arms like a lover's breath. "Ask the others what they see. Let the au'it write it for the Ila's curiosity. And tell me what you learn. Gather all the visions."

The au'it stirred on the mat nearby. She was uncannily alert to her duty, but he had no further orders for her.

"Hati will ask the others. You write it. But rest now. Sleep."

The woman eased back to her rest.

In the evening when they waked, Hati took the au'it and went about from one man to the other, asking the same question.

The au'it wrote in her book until dark made it too hard, and when the sun rose again, Hati moved her beast about among the company, taking the au'it with her. The au'it, bracing her book on the saddlebow, holding her ink-cake in one hand, wrote and wrote, at every encounter, as happy as Marak had ever seen that thin, sober face. Despite the sun, despite the heat, despite the wind that riffled the pages, the au'it listened and wrote, and satisfied her reason for going with them.

The demons brought the tower vision to the surface so easily now. There was the tower, there was the star, there was the cave of suns, always in the east. He felt that pitch toward it, morning and evening, always the same sense that the world had tipped precariously.

But the voices that called his name evidently called others. Clearly they called Hati's.

There had been a time he had believed in the god, believing the god spoke to him, in those years when the young so readily formed belief; and in one small part of his heart he found he resented discovering the voices were not his alone. He knew now that he was not the center and focus of their desire, and he began to know that his severance from his father was no greater a calamity than the potter's, say, or Hati's. A common potter had lost his family and trade to the same visions, the same urging.

So the potter was found out in his difference, and either he turned himself in to the Ila's men or his community had done it. Was that not worth as much regret, as much bitterness? Was it not as great a betrayal, one's lifelong neighbors and customers, against an honest craftsman?

He waited to hear what Hati would find out, and yet he guessed the answer. Had not the mad all moved together, all twitched at once, when they were gathered together?

One wished one's life-changing affliction to be unique. And after Hati reported to him, all of them knew it was not.

Of common visions there was the high place, so Hati reported and so the au'it wrote. There was the light, the sun, the star, multiple moons aloft and in a row. These were all the second vision. There was the cave, the hall, the hollow place, that was the third, though for Marak the cave had always held the lights. He did not have that vision independently, but combined with another common theme.

Of forty-some madmen, regarding most of the visions, they all agreed.

They agreed that the pitch when it came was always to the east, though some had thought it was toward the rising sun.

And the voices indeed called them each by name, from childhood.

From childhood they had had the lines of fire building structures in their vision, as if lines were engraved on their eyes like patterns on a pot: the same lines repeated and repeated, sometimes enlivened with fire, sometimes not. And the vision when it came was in red.

From childhood they had heard a noise in their ears, and that noise sooner or later had become a voice calling their names.

So it was not their madness that made them unique. In fact, their affliction was a leveler, and it made them much the same.

Sometimes, they confessed, their hands and bodies moved involuntarily, in small twitches. In some it had affected their trade or their craft. One, the farmwife, Maol, had learned to draw strange symbols, the same that he saw behind his eyelids.

Marak had had the twitching affliction, to some minor degree, when he was resting; he had labored from boyhood to conceal it, tucking his arms tightly as he slept, blaming it on nightmares.

Sometimes his head ached; that was so for the lot of them. His had ached fiercely in his early years, blinding headaches, but so did his mother's.

Was she mad? He had never thought so.

There was a gift, too, to being mad. All the mad, when they suffered small wounds, healed without a scar, and they all suffered brief, sometimes quite high, fever when they did so.

Ontori, a stonemason, said he had broken both legs falling as a boy. He walked demonstrably without a limp.

Hati showed him her hand at their next setting-forth. "I cut this badly when I was a child. Across the palm. I was trimming gola root and the knife slipped. There is no scar."

He had taken sword cuts, too, one egregious one, which his father had dealt him in practice. He has good skin, his mother had said defensively, when all trace of it vanished in

a month. He always heals, his mother had said, and said it
fiercely: she knew it was not right.

He had healed of everything but the clan mark, which was
dye. High fever had followed the tattooing, however, and a
great deal of swelling had ensued. It had healed and come out
faded within the month, as if it were decades old. Some men
had always thought him older than he was because of it. His
mother had said maybe the fever had broken up the color. His
father thought the dye had been weak, and blamed the artist.

"Some say we can't die," Hati said. "But I know we can.
Three in my group died on the march. I'm sure those who
left us the first night both died."

"We die," Marak said, with no doubt at all. "Some died on
our march. Of accident. Of age, maybe. There was a boy, too.
He wasn't the same as us, I never thought so. But he was a
good boy." He wished he could have asked the boy if his vision, too, was different. He thought of the old man who had
died. His vision had seemed different. He had not twitched
when the rest of them did.

The Ila had begun the questions. All under thirty, she
said. He himself was as old as the oldest of the most of the
madmen. Only the old man who had died, whose madness
had seemed different, too—the old man and the boy had not
moved when the mad moved, had never seemed to feel the
pitch eastward.

The affliction itself wove a web that had tied the true
madmen all together: he had never known how much so,
until he asked himself what the Ila had asked.

But more, the mad themselves were amazed to hear such
accurate questions from one like them, and began to ask and
answer questions they had hidden all their lives. Yes, yes, and
yes, the answers were. It *is* like that. I see that, too.

It brought a strange elation. Even delighted laughter.

But it brought anxiousness, too. There was one question
none of them could answer, and that was why the east, and
why the madness should exist at all.

"The gods are leading us," the stonemason said, without a
doubt in the world.

Marak wished he had that simple faith. He disliked thinking about the tower. He had no notion why.

Voices whispered quietly, the while he thought about it, *Marak, Marak, Marak.*

These seemed to warned him of danger, as sometimes the voices did.

But he could not tell where it was.

In Hati? He thought not.

East, the voices whispered to him, and the skin tightened on his arms.

East, east, east. Go faster.

7

No man may foul a well. The defiler of a well shall be cast out with no provision and no tent, and no tribe and no village may shelter him.
—The Book of Priests

The night of that day came hazy and hot as a furnace, the stars shimmering in the heavens. The beshti, water-short, were ill-tempered. One slave had an arm bitten for no worse offense than walking past a pack beast in the dark. The caravan master took great pains to attend the wound, and to cover the bite with salves to keep away insects, and worse. It was not only the act of a reasonable master. Wind carried the smell of blood into the desert, and blood drew vermin.

West, west, west, the voices said, contrary, but with a smell of danger, not allure.

"The wind is coming," Hati said, with a twitch of her shoulders, and at last Marak put a name to what had been prickling at his senses all day.

Wind. Weather-sense had served him once before in the campaign on the Lakht. He had refused to lead his men out on a certain day. The enemy, the Ila's men, had perished.

It was like that now.

"How soon?" he asked Hati, and Hati shrugged.

"A day, perhaps as much as two. Sunset may show it."

He had not spoken much to Obidhen. The master and his sons, the freedmen and the slaves, all kept to their own company, ruling over separate tents, riding together, the freedmen riding last, to be sure no one fell behind unnoticed. They doled out water and supplies to him for his tent without much converse. They were not pleased today: the bitter well they hoped to find for the beasts' use had failed them.

He decided he should say something to the caravan master, a warning, however Obidhen might receive it. "I have a bad feeling about the weather," was the only shape he could put to it. "So does the an'i Keran."

They rested. And toward the evening, when they ordinarily should ride out again, Obidhen called out to his sons and his helpers:

"Drive in the deep-stakes."

Then, walking over to Marak with his hands tucked in his belt-band, he said, "I agree. There will come a blow. We won't budge tonight."

"So," Marak said. "We understand."

There were expressions of relief throughout his tent when they heard the news, and that relief pervaded the camp, tent to tent. The nameless fear had taken a shape, and he heard others claim they felt bad weather, even vying with one another as to how early they had known. The subterfuges they had used, the lies they had told, the discipline they had exerted not to betray their affliction were all cast away. They had begun to compete with one another in their madness. The desert was the collective enemy, and their inner demons had become guides, protectors, allies.

The slaves had the deep-stakes out, and more cordage, and Marak turned the men out to help sort cordage as the caravan master's son and the slaves drove the long anchoring stakes down and down into the sand. They anchored to them with more cord, and ran cordage up and over the canvas with laced hitches, so that when the wind blew there would be a good webwork of rope to hold the canvas from tearing.

The sun lowered in fire, a glow all along the west: Hati was right.

Last, they unbundled the side flaps and lashed them into place along the sides of the tent, ready to unfurl when the wind came, as come it would.

This will be one to remember, some said, in their new weather-wisdom.

It will be bad, Hati said, and her estimation, Marak readily believed. Obidhen ordered two water packs given to the beshti, the sweet water they carried for themselves, carefully measured.

Fear was still there. Any man, lowlander or Lakhtanin, feared the west wind in summer, but they were as ready as they could be. Some joked. The jokes rang hollow in the storm-sense that all but smothered cheer, yet they laughed.

It was coming, and there was nothing they could do more than they had done.

Marak, for one, decided to rest and take advantage of a night without traveling, and sleep another few hours. The air was stiflingly still; men talked in low voices off across the shelter of the open-sided tent. The au'it, who had written their preparations, wrote something else now, while the dim light lasted.

Hati lay down to sleep by him, as she had slept for days.

But now in the sense of storm that quieted the whole tent, Norit, too, moved her mat closer, and whispered, "I'm afraid."

"Settle," Marak said. "The tents will be safe. The tribes survive these winds many times a year."

Hati shifted against him to make room for Norit. It was hot, and still at the moment.

It was not that Norit particularly chose him, he thought, but that Hati had formed a friendship. Norit had become her lieutenant as Hati had become his, and took to that responsibility. In Tarsa a cast-off wife was no one's and nothing, of no honor, no estate, no support at all. In Hati, Norit had found anchor against a different kind of storm.

And in the process he had acquired unlooked-for obligations. Hati co-opted him, placing herself between him and all others. Now Norit added herself, and he found, as in the vision, the random pieces made unexpected structure, not one he would have chosen.

Norit suffered from her madness. She no longer sang to herself aloud, but made small sounds as she talked to her visions. No one dressed her hair: by day, as she rode, she combed her black mane obsessively with her fingers, until it straggled in some order over her shoulders. She combed it now as she rested on her back, staring at the visions that came. She plucked at her fingers as if taking off rings. She talked to the unseen. She was not the most wholesome of their company.

But if Norit had a virtue, it was persistence, even in living, and he respected that, and tolerated her strangeness. Of all the marches the mad had made on their way to the holy city, theirs had been the harshest, under the worst of the Ila's men, in provinces once hostile to the Ila, where rebellion was still recent in memory. The common run of the Ila's men had treated the mad as enemies, and devils, and had no mercy. They had driven the fragile sense from some before they died. Love, Norit had sung. Let us find love.

And having been launched on another long march without her will, Norit spoke to no one but Hati at any length at all, but if Hati waved a hand, Norit carried this or that and if the baggage wanted moving, Norit moved it. Sometimes her eyes stared at things not even another madman could guess. She had learned the besha, and rode from sitting start to kneeling. All that Hati did, Norit did. If Hati groomed her beast, Norit did. If Hati went to interfere in the slaves' cooking, Norit went and listened.

"It builds," Norit said to the gathering dark. "It builds. It carries away villages."

Elsewhere he heard men talking. There was little movement in the tent. They had worked hard getting the deep-stakes in. There was a thin sandstone under the sand beneath this tent. They had worn the skin from their hands weaving the web of cordage and snugging it down. Now they lay, nursed their blisters, and listened to a slight stir and flap of the canvas.

"Perhaps it won't come," the potter said.

The orchardman said, "Shut up. At least we get to sleep a few more hours."

The time dragged by.

Little gusts stirred the tent against the web of cordage. The beasts complained and moaned, and moved behind the tents, where they would take shelter for the duration.

Marak got up and went out from under the tent to see what was coming, in the murky last of the light. A red wall of dust spread over half the sky, deceptive in its very size.

Hati had come out, and Norit did, and the rest came after her, with the wind stirring their garments.

The boys and the slaves had turned out from the other four tents, too, with the onset of the wind. They set to tightening the web of rope, which had stretched out in the heat.

"Put down the sides!" they shouted. It was time. They unrolled the sides of the tents, and made those fast by their rings and by cords.

Then they all went inside their smothering dark tents and settled down to wait. The storm light came, a sickly twilight outside the single opening they had left. At his order, each of them piled his own waterskin with the common stores, some reluctantly, but they obeyed. Then they lay ready to seal the tent entirely once the blow started. The light fell on the edges of faces and bodies: they looked toward the light as a precious commodity about to vanish.

The beasts moaned outside as the wind set up its own complaint, thumping at the canvas in a sudden violence.

"We can have rations every morning and every evening," Marak said so all could hear him. "Look at where your mat is, and where the water and food is. The au'it will sleep by the water. There will be water at the same times each day, no other, so don't plan otherwise. It may be days, and it will be dark, so get your bearings before the light goes."

There was no complaint. They had had their midday supper. They would take their rations cold, no luxury of cooking at all in the utter lack of sunlight, and short water for drinking. Even the villages knew the lowland storms, and feared these as they feared the god himself.

The gust carried sand, the wind turning redder and redder outside, veiling all detail between themselves and the world. The light slowly diminished both by sunset and by storm until the dark outside was deep and violent, leaving the merest hint of a doorway to good eyes.

Marak went and drew the flap shut and laced it down by feel. The wind howled, and the canvas thumped and strained. Some man inside wailed, a frightened human voice appealing to the god, and others joined it in querulous chatter.

"It's nothing but the wind," Marak said, walking the carefully memorized track back to his mat. "The poles are set and the stakes are deep. Be quiet. You from the villages, the Lakht throws storms such as you've not seen. This may last all through tomorrow and the day after that, and perhaps a third. Storms often come in the summer, on the Lakht, but the stakes will hold, and we will last it out. Go to sleep. Sleep as much as you can."

The wind all but drowned his voice at the last. His eyes could find no light at all. If he had not known where his mat was, he never could have found it.

He sat down. The wind acquired the voices that resounded in his head: *Marak, Marak, Marak,* endlessly. He felt Hati's touch, and lay down on his back, listening to the voices and to the thumping of the canvas. He had the waterskins at his back, and all the rations for the tent positioned there, with the au'it, the impartial, the incorruptible witness, sitting directly against them.

He hoped the master's sons and the slaves had done their work well. He had seen nothing to fault in their work. But now they knew they were very small, and the desert wind was a towering devil, thumping and battering all about the edges of their shelter, trying to get fingers within the lacings.

For about a half an hour he rested and listened to the fury build.

An arm came about him, and a warm body shaped itself
to him on his left, and he knew the culprit as he moved an
arm to send her back to her own mat.

A knee intruded, however, and lips found his bare neck.

Hati whispered something, interrupted breath against his
neck. Perhaps she told him they were going nowhere. Perhaps she said no one could see or hear what they did, and
that this answered to a roof. He rolled over, seized a slender
arm, drew the offender close by the neck until he had a fist-
ful of long braids and knew for certain it was Hati.

Then he took a deep breath and brought his lips where he
judged hers waited. His guess was right.

The intruder's arms came about him, and lips drew
breath at last in the moment he allowed, then renewed the
kiss before he was ready.

In the same moment a lithe body shed robes and wriggled
beneath him.

"This is no roof," he said, vexed at her breach of their
agreement. People at rest all around them could not be that
deaf, even if they were blind.

But the dark was so absolute and the howl of the wind
and the thump of canvas so enveloped them he was not sure
even she heard him. She came around him, having loosened
her clothes, and his push at her met bare breasts, a skin as
smooth, as fine, as sweet and soft as he had thought. Her
warmth settled about him and the canvas beat and thumped
around them with the flutter of a heart that had been running a long, long race.

Why object, the storm said, why refuse, why should anyone care? We are cast out there, but not yet dead.

He found his way through her clothes, and she found
hers. He felt the force of her let loose in the dark, saw the
burning lines of his delusions, and he heard above the wind
the voices that made them both mad. *Marak,* they said,
Marak. Hati. Hati.

Others might witness, if the madness of together-seeing
pierced the dark. They two held no secrets, held nothing
back, all the way to a long thunderous battering of the wind

above them, then an ebb into dark and sound and over-heated flesh.

He was through, then, but she found ways: she breathed into his sound-deafened ear and intruded a tongue, which drew his attention amazingly. Dutifully he returned the effort with a languid hand, but meanwhile she found places to touch no woman had tried with him and found places to be that no woman ever had managed.

Initiate: she was that; an'i Keran, and he, being no virgin, either, found places to touch and hold that from moment to moment sent long, long shivers through the body he embraced.

She had her satisfaction, he thought: a man might burn quicker, but for her there was no end yet, and certainly no lack of invention ... did they not say it of the an'i Keran, that they could last the whole night?

Came more hands then than he had counted, and a second, softer presence. He was dismayed, thinking Norit had grown afraid in the storm. She sought comfort and clearly found something more than she had bargained for: she drew back at once.

But Hati ... he was sure it was Hati ... flung arms about them both, so Norit stayed, shivering and holding him fiercely.

He had no intention of forcing himself on an honest wife. He comforted her with a one-armed though naked embrace, and found her shoulder, as he thought, half-clothed, too. He did not know who was to blame, Hati or Norit, but the leg that lay across him was bare, and then one arrived from the other side, tangled with cloth. Bare breasts too ample to be Hati's moved against his skin and pressed urgently.

More than one woman was not his custom. But it was Hati's custom, the custom of the an'i Keran, and whether she shoved Norit at him, or whether Norit had her own plan, Norit's clothes went the way of the others.

If Norit spoke, he could not hear it, but Norit's body moved about him. Her demands were, in her way, as fierce as Hati's. He thought to make his hands and his lips her satisfaction . . . so he thought, but the hot wind battering against the tent and the twisting fever-warmth of bodies set the whole night to throbbing. The fever was on him, as it came on him after wounds. He found his way into her body, or perhaps into Hati's; and then gave himself over to both of them, while the fever burned and throbbed in his brain. It would not abate, not for life, not for breath. He began to fear for himself, that it was a new dimension to the madness, that it would burst his heart. He feared the others might share it, and set on all of them in a frenzy like the beasts in heat; but what the others did with each other or to themselves around about, he had no clear idea.

No one troubled them, not for hours, and as the hours passed without a dawn they joined whenever the urge came on one of them. The others obliged, himself with Hati and Norit, the lean an'i Keran and the soft village wife with him in turn. He broke all the moral laws in the roaring dark, but found himself taken between times into quiet rest between them, a sweet haven. There, though voices spoke their names and the vision-objects came and went, tower and star and cave, he was sheltered from the storm. The whole world whirled away toward the east. The wind outraced them, sweeping them along in its wake; but he was safe. He was safe and protected as he had never been, no secrets, no guilt, no regret, no fear.

They slept, one naked, fevered lump, sweating precious moisture toward each other's bodies, until came someone, a consensus of several of the tent's occupants, came pleading for water, and asking, in a shout above the storm, when the storm should end and whether it had already been dawn.

"I am no prophet," he shouted back, holding the man's shoulder to make himself heard clearly. "Probably it's dawn. This is a bad storm. Drink as little as you possibly can. Eat even more sparingly. You may be hungry, but if it goes on for five *days* you will not starve, do you hear me?" His madness informed him he could guess the duration of the storm and with abandon he leaned on that understanding. "Two more days and it will be past us," he promised them. He was uncommonly sure of it, and: "Two days," one shouted to the next, until they all agreed, and asked for their drink.

They numbered ten in this tent. There were five tents. The beasts took care of themselves, outside, bred to the storm and capable of surviving: they neither ate nor drank nor required attention while the wind blew, nor would stir from the shadow of the tents. There they would sit, nostrils mostly shut, eyes shut, ears folded, legs folded, to all useful purposes asleep, but capable of rousing whenever the wind shifted.

He wrapped his blanket about him and doled out from the personal waterskins a little water for each into the measured copper cap, in which he felt the level with his finger, and spilled not a drop. He likewise gave out small measures of dry cake, and instructed the villagers to eat it very, very slowly. "Where is the au'it?" he asked, and Hati found her, and he saw she, too, silent in the dark, had her ration. They had been days on the Lakht, had measured their water to reach Pori without resort to the wells, and now faced a lengthy delay that could become a serious matter if they were stalled here too long. They had divided all the water, placed a certain portion of it with each tent for safety, and he knew they were down on their supply, that they were not desperate, but that they were going to be scant on rations when they reached Pori.

After the others had gone back to their places, he shared the same measures of food and water with Norit and Hati, then slept. By now they made one bundle, their hands resting comfortably on one another, while the storm continued outside.

There were needs of nature: there was the latrine in the tent, the sand pit in the back left corner. Since the flaps were down; it was not possible to go outside, and the utter dark, more than the curtain, gave a general modesty.

At one point the potter told a bawdy story, and the orchardman told another.

He listened, and Hati jabbed him in the ribs, laughing, and began to trouble him again, which he did not refuse. Norit settled against him, soft and gentle, as different from

Hati as night from dark; and in time Norit had her pleasure, too ... no difference to her, it seemed, how it came, only that it came, and she kissed him and proved her gratitude.

He feared the other men in the tent might think he had too much of a good thing, and they had nothing but the potter's stories. What they had started, the others had to know, and must be jealous. Still, he was omi, lord, and it was the nature of the world that lords had, and common men lacked.

Was it not the Ila's law? Was it not the world the Ila had made, since the First Descended?

"Is it not evening?" one asked, wanting water, and he said no until three and four came asking. He thought he was right about the time, and held to it, and no one defied him.

After that, Norit claimed her turn first.

He came to know for certain in the dark that there was every virtue in Norit, except sanity. She sang against his ear. She spoke of a star to guide them east, when there was nothing but dark outside.

Finally she slept a true, sweet sleep, and after she slept he was very glad to have Hati's safe arms about him and Hati's strong body against his. Into Norit's madness a man could sink and lose himself, bit by bit. Hati was the storm wind itself, a force, a demand for movement and resourcefulness. But in Norit the demons lived and had full possession.

Both of them still drew from him the best of his nature, Norit, that patience and compassion he had had only for what he protected, and Hati, that sense of life and challenge for its own sake that he had lost somewhere on the Lakht, in his father's wars. He felt sorry for Norit; but he felt wholly alive when he held Hati. She was a match for him, completely unlike any match the ambitious villages had tried to send him when he was Tain's son. No, he had said, rejecting some, and no, his father had said, never suspecting that any of those very sane girls would think him a bad bargain, never suspecting he said no for fear of discovery.

But now he owned himself met, matched, mated with a creature that would never give back a step from his most outrageous actions, never fear his madness, never hesitate.

Hati, he said to himself, but there was no speech in the howling thunder above them.

On the next day, that day he had been so sure the storm would pass, a pole tore loose and they had to go out, the four or five among them who understood how to pitch a tent, and secure the ropes. The air had chilled. The sun had been cut off from the sand so long the air and the sand itself had turned bitter cold. With fingernails broken to the quick by the dry sand they dug for the eye of the deep-stake bolt and found it by the ragged scrap of rope left to it, still warm from the heat of days ago. They dug down to it and rigged a new line.

Then they retreated, shivering and coughing and wiping grit from their eyes and their noses and the edges of their mouths.

The storm continued to batter them, and his two days bid now to be a lie. He was ashamed of having promised those who trusted him a relief he could not deliver; but at least they had saved the tent.

Within hours, however, the wind was quieter. A look out the flap proved there was something like light beyond the walls, a transparent red promising the storm had indeed eased, but there was no view of anything farther than the tent stake nearest the door, and a man dared not expose the eyes or any more of the skin than he must.

Marak ducked his head back inside, and answered anxious questions with, "It's a little quieter."

One could hear it. The thunder of the canvas was muted: it had boomed and racketed so he thought he would lose what he had left of his reason, and now it was an occasional spate of wind.

But, chilled, he was doubly glad to find his mat and his comfort again, and find Hati's arms and Norit's to comfort him and to brush the dust from his hair and his clothing.

His throat was dry as the dust he had breathed. He was keeper of the food and water and could have had more; he could have given more to the men who had helped with the rope, but he honestly had no notion who they were and wished to open no doors to dispute. He simply advised himself and all of them to the same ration.

He slept, exhausted, the whole world seeming to spin about and fall to the east.

And after that short sleep, he waked to a near silence in the wind.

He stirred, drew on his robe against the chill, and pulled up his aifad against the dust that must still be moving. He unlaced the flap as others of their tentmates stirred, and he peered out at the other tents through the reddened, dust-choked air.

There had been four tents in his field of view when the storm began. Now there were only three. He tried to figure their positions, thinking one might still be veiled in dust. But there was a gap, right next to them.

Ropes had failed. The tent nearest them had gone.

He took a lap of the aifad about his head to shield his eyes from the grit and dust, went out and scanned nearer the ground, looking for any lump of canvas where survivors might have secured a secondary hold against the wind.

Hati had come out behind him, so had the au'it, and so had the several who had helped him save their own tent.

"Stay here!" he said to Hati, not wishing to leave the water and food to chance or the desires of villagers, and most of all wanting someone sensible who could shout him back to his own tent if the wind rose up again, as it might, in the few moments he meant to be away from shelter.

Hati raised no objection, well understanding. "Stay here," she said to the others. "The wind may come up. Stay close!"

The beasts had survived. Rare the storm that could wear them down. They were lumps of sand, tucked noses to the wind, in the lee of their own tent and the other, and roused as they saw movement, standing up to stretch cramped limbs.

Obidhen's tent was still standing, past the place where the other had stood. He went to that tent, and shouted outside it until, within, someone unlaced the flap.

Two slaves were there. No one else. Not Obidhen, not his son Rom, not the freedmen or the four other slaves.

"Where is master Obidhen?" Marak asked.

"Give us water," the slaves there begged, and he knew that tale instantly: without the caravan master to govern the water, these two fools had fallen to the whole tent's water stores and consumed them. Their suffering was deserved, and far from fatal.

"Out and dig!" he said. "Or die!" He threatened a blow of his fist to the foremost, and the pair moved, ducking after gear.

Marak, Marak, the voices cried, and the whole world was threat and danger.

He left them immediately, went to the fourth tent in the blowing dust, careful not to lose his bearings, for intermittently the fifth and farther tent vanished in the sand red haze.

There, too, he got a man to unlace the flap, and expected Obidhen's son Rom, but the two ex-soldiers roused out to do the job, and light poured past them onto stark, frightened faces . . . among the rest, he saw three women disheveled, half-clothed, terrified. He began to form a notion of utter disaster. He imagined someone from the tent in difficulty making it as far as the caravan master, who attempted to help, and then engaged his other sons.

"Ontari." Marak ignored the disheveled soldiers and addressed the man he knew best, the stonecutter, who had good sense. "Take charge here." What had gone on for three days between these women and the soldiers and perhaps several others, he suspected and deplored, but there were still their lives to lose if this was only an abatement of the storm. "Turn out and dig, all of you. We have to recover the supplies. The fool slaves have eaten and drunk for three days!"

"Omi," Ontari said, and rallied the rest. Ontari was a big man. Marak gave the three women a long look that told them he knew, while he asked himself what he could possibly do about their difficulty. He found no answer except to set Hati to find out the truth. In the meanwhile all their lives were at risk.

"The storm may have force left," he said to the women.

"Whatever happened here, we don't know how much time we have and we've lost a good portion of our water, buried in that tent. Out and dig! Everyone!"

Marak! The voices assumed a tone of panic, and his heart beat like something trapped.

He went to the fifth tent, and there found the youngest of Obidhen's sons, Tofi, alive, and a company larger by two than he had left it.

"Your father and your brothers are gone," Marak said, rendered blunt in the hammering of the voices and the threat of the wind. "Get out and direct the slaves! We've lost them, and we've lost a tent!"

That a tent might be gone was no news to the boy. Two had escaped the ruined tent, and come here, and the boy might hope that his father and brothers had gotten to some other shelter. The report that dashed that hope was clearly a shock.

"Have you looked in the other tents?" the boy asked.

"Gone, I say! We need hands to dig. Turn out!"

There was no time for grief, none for assessing what had happened. They took shovels such as they had and used bare hands. Obidhen's son.

It was the old, old story on the Lakht. Someone from the missing tent, Landhi's tent, had straggled across to Obidhen during a lull to request help with an increasing problem. Obidhen, the slaves, and the two traders who had been in his tent had gone out to help, and whether or not they had ever even reached Landhi's tent in time, or been carried away by the next gust when it blew loose, they had run a high risk in a storm and lost their wager. Perhaps some survivor had gone over to Rom in the fourth tent, fatal mistake, and now he was gone. Meanwhile two complete novices from Landhi's tent, having made it clear and having lost their bearings, had run into Tofi's tent downwind and told him as much as he knew, but by then the storm was fierce, making it folly to go out looking, and Tofi had wisely stayed put, refusing to go when he could not see.

As for the others, there was no question where survivors might be, if there were to be any survivors. When that tent had gone, it had become a mass of half-anchored canvas and cordage in the blinding sand, a lethal monster of canvas and whipping rope, and unless one side of the tent had remained anchored and unless that heap of sand concealed a canvas shelter between elements of the baggage and water stores, there was no hope for the rest at all.

Deep as the sand had accumulated where the tent had been, Marak had doubted from the beginning that anyone could survive, and nine men had been in that tent with Landhi, not counting Obidhen, the freedmen, his older son Rom, and the four slaves who had come to their aid.

Obidhen's tent had had its share of their remaining water and its share of their supplies, most of it gone, and Marak had no mercy, no more than Tofi, who railed on the well-fed slaves, beating them when they lagged.

"The storm may have force left," Tofi shouted, flinging sand with a shovel. "Dig faster. All of you."

They abandoned shovels and dug with their bare hands as they came near the supplies, and found the first of the dead, Tofi sobbing and swearing the while. The fifteen beasts that had belonged to the lost tent had sought shelter behind another tent, and they had survived. The supplies, bundled in canvas, turned up knee deep under sand. One corner of the bundle, wrapped solidly, had abraded to threads, but had not spoiled. The water, buried deepest in the stack, had survived, and that was a relief.

They found the bodies of most of the lost up against those bundles, the caravan master and his sons among the rest, a lump of sand and cloth, where all in the tent who had not wandered to safety or to their deaths had attempted to protect themselves. The sand had come over and smothered them, in the outermost bodies blasting skin from flesh and flesh from bone.

Tofi was beside himself with grief. "Murderers!" he cried when they found his brothers and his father. He ran and took a rope's end to the slaves. They ran screaming, with Tofi chasing them through the remnant of the storm. He caught the slowest, and beat him with his fists; but Marak ran after and pulled him off the slave.

"They are slaves," he reasoned with the boy. "They had no orders. They had no idea what to do!"

"They're fools!" the boy wept.

"Take charge of them. Take charge, or lose all that you have from your father. What can your father pass to you, but this caravan, and these two slaves? They are your skilled workers! We need their work! Don't kill them!"

The strength went out of the boy, and his hand fell, and he kicked the slave at his feet. "Get up! Get to work!"

The slave gathered himself up, still protecting his head, and backed away, preferring to run away into the desert, while the wind battered at all of them, while the voices insisted, *Marak, Marak, Marak*, and a tower built, and built and built.

The sand still blew so that farther figures were shadows, and invaded the eyes so a man only dared look out and breathe through the gauze headcloth. It was no time to be beating those who knew how to rig the tents and tend the beasts.

"You are your father's heir," Marak shouted at the boy, above the flap and thunder of the nearby tent, the wind momentarily gusting. He held the boy's arm in a tight grip, compelling his attention. "Take charge of the caravan. The an'i Keran and I can ride on alone, and likely survive, but these other lives are all in your hand. Your father's legacy is yours to keep or lose! What did he teach you?"

There still were sobs, but dry ones.

"Come back," Marak shouted at the distant shadows that were the two slaves. "He will not kill you. You'll die out there!"

Cautiously, shadows still, the slaves came closer.

"Get to work!" Tofi shouted in a broken voice still boyish in its pitch. "Get to work, you water-fat layabouts, or I'll have the hide off you! I have all the water, now, you sons of devils! I have all the food, I have the tents, and damn your lazy souls, you'll work for food and shelter!"

They came slinking back, avoiding the boy, but setting to work at the digging with might and main. The boy continued his sobs as he worked, and his headcloth was soaked with sweat and tears that gathered dust and blinded him. The only recourse was to tug the cloth and shift it about and try to stop the tears and the exertion that left a mouth taking in the raw, dry wind. Marak knew. He felt the boy's grief with the memory of his own, every sting of frustration and self-blame: but in no wise was it Tofi's fault. The Lakht killed, and it killed for small mistakes, which even Obidhen had made.

Some of the dead they could not find. They might have run for shelter in another tent and not been as lucky as the two who had reached Tofi, or they might simply have gotten turned around from the men they were trying to help. The battering of sand-laden wind disoriented even the experienced traveler. There was all the desert around them to search, and they had no resources to risk.

The entire toll, they found by counting heads, was twenty-one dead, and the water and supplies the two slaves had gorged themselves on.

Of resources, they had the two slaves, four tents secure, the irons and snarled cordage from the fifth, and all the beasts.

By the evening the storm blew past, so that the stars began to appear in the heavens, the brightest first, then a wealth of them, like jewels scattered through the heavens. It was never so clear as after a blow.

The twenty-one dead meant that number would not be eating and drinking. That meant they were not short of water or food. Amid other pieces of good news, the boy Tofi thought he knew the way to Pori village, and recited the stars that guided them, Kop and Luta, which were clear and cold above them. He had been there. He thought he could go back accurately, and they would have no shortage of food or water, or canvas, which was well: Hati avowed Pori was within the range of the Keran, but she had never been there.

But of skilled hands . . . there was a marked shortage.

"Give the order," Marak said to the boy, and Tofi said, "Break camp." Tofi said it louder, for the slaves. "Get up! Strike the tents!"

It was no small labor, when the deep-irons were driven. They had to be dug out; and it was brutal work. In the absence of the freedmen and the other, more senior slaves, near their freedom, all of them, men and women, dug with whatever they could, all of them anxious to be on their way out of this ill-omened place. The slaves who had eaten and drunk so well were obedient, now, and by no means weak from hunger. One might hope those two had grown wiser and learned from all their mistakes, but Marak doubted it. Once the wind blew, and men began thinking that other men were going to take more than their share, the impulses that governed were not always wise. In the case of the slaves who, alone of the work party, had gotten back to their tent alive, they had thought they were dead anyway. So they grabbed and consumed in panic, vying with each other for the last scrap and thought nothing about the next day.

They learned now or both of them were dead, in Marak's reckoning. The boy could think of mercy, once he realized the slaves had likely had nothing to do with his father's death, and were guilty of nothing but surviving. But the Lakht was merciless even to the skilled, like Obidhen, let alone to fools who drank their water up for fear of dying, and there were few second chances.

The dead they had laid out decently, covering them under with the sand they dug out from around their supplies. They spent no extra labor at it, however. It was a burial only for the boy's comfort, and the boy knew as a matter of course that vermin of the sand, like the vermin of the air, were clever and persistent. The company simply said the names of the lost a last time, and were done with ceremony.

One seemed apt to be the next casualty, Proffa the tailor. Until the storm he had been strong enough, but when they had packed, and the time came, in the mid of the night, to get up on a beast and ride, Proffa was scarcely able to sit the saddle.

So they set him on like baggage, well padded with their mats, and cared for him on the march. It seemed to Marak that the tailor's heart had failed him, perhaps as he understood the cost it was simply to go on living. The mad healed, but Proffa did not.

All these things the au'it wrote in her book the next day.

The caravan master, though rich by the desert's standards, had never been written down in his life, and now an au'it from the holy city had written down his death.

"Have you written his name?" the boy asked earnestly. "It's Obidhen Anfatin."

The au'it wrote, and the boy gave her one of his treasures, one of his father's bracelets.

Common folk had become uncommon, Marak thought, as they set up camp. Even the slaves had begun to grudge their own deaths, and now they had names: Mogar was the one Tofi had beaten, the least agile, but the strongest. The other slave was Bosginde.

They had begun to take note of one another. Friendships and enmities had formed. Certain ones rode together, like sisters, like brothers. Two women of the last tent, having suffered from rough men in their last camp, had armed themselves with knives and clung to Hati and Norit.

More, there had been a lengthy, angry conversation among the women the nature of which Marak did not inquire.

But once they camped, in consideration of possible violence, he suggested to Tofi they pitch only two tents for shade, and close to one another. The women who had suffered were out of the northwest lowlands and certainly had no idea how to manage in the desert. He suggested the women join Tofi and the two slaves, and keep Tofi comforted, while the two ex-soldiers went to Ontori's tent.

The Lakht brought out the best or the worst in men, and men who had abused their tentmates for three days while they all were in danger of dying were fools. Likewise the women, who had lived through it all and still were on their feet, were not fools, and had gathered the means to defend themselves.

"If these women complain after this," Marak said to Kassan, senior of the two ex-soldiers, the most likely instigators, in his opinion. "If they complain, you'll never see the east."

A suitable fear went across the man's face. "It wasn't me," Kassan said. "It was Foragi."

"Then change his mind," Marak said, "or kill him. I've set the stonemason over you: Ontari. If either of you ever offends these women, I've given him authority to kill you both."

"Omi," Kassan said. Kassan was the one of the two soldiers with the wit to understand the proposition; and he hoped Kassan had the wit to be afraid. Kassan went away, doubtless to warn the other man they were in danger, and if his threat produced mutiny in the ex-soldiers, he was sure their looks would show it: they were not men for deep intrigue.

After noon, they broke camp, and the two soldiers avoided his gaze and ducked their heads.

It was, over all, the women who looked different. Hati had been talking to them, and one of them, Maol the farmwife, glowered and fingered something beneath her belt when she looked at those men.

As for Tofi, still mourning his father and his brothers, Maol and her friend among the three women took him as their special charge, a handsome, quick young lad, and in need of comfort. The third woman, whose name was Malin, seemed to have had a falling-out with the other two. She approached the soldiers, who tried to have nothing to do with her.

They broke camp at sunset and moved on, following the stars Tofi named.

Marak, the voices said, *Marak, Marak,* but they did not seem displeased. The voices still whispered—hourly now—and the visions still came, and he knew that Tofi's guide stars were the same stars they had followed, the bright ones, to the east.

And if the morning and the evening pitched him east so reliably he never could have lost his way, so with all of them: they were not lost, nor dissuaded, and needed not have worried about knowing the way. The boy Tofi, who owned the beasts and the tents, was increasingly confident of their direction.

So was Hati, who with Norit shared his mat at night. Since the storm, he had no shame left in that regard, only hung a robe for a curtain, and so he heard two of the three women did, with Tofi, and together they got along.

But one of the three, on the outs with the women from the start, had set up to content various other men, and had them, two and three an evening, outside near the beasts, before they would get under way for the night, so he wondered whether the soldiers had been entirely at fault in the tent and who had started the business during the storm.

"Malin takes pay," Hati said when he asked her opinion.

"What do they pay?" Marak asked, feeling like an innocent. There was none of the men rich in coin or bracelets.

"Food," Hati said.

"They will not." He was outraged. Taking part of a man's ration weakened the man and strengthened a woman who by now had made her choice, and who, if prostitution was not her trade, might have revenge on her mind . . . or who, if it was, might become the object of revenge from the other women. "The hell! Tell them they may not use force. But they can't use their rations, either. Let Malin choose what to do. Tell her let them win her favors."

Marak, Marak, Marak, his inner voice said, impatient with him. He had more and greater worries than Malin.

But after Hati had a talk with them, the men who courted Malin, the prostitute, vied with small favors, helping her down from her beast, carrying her mat, unrolling it as if she ruled the camp. Malin flourished, better served than many a wife, and Norit and Maol and the other woman, Jurid, frowned daggers at her, but Hati shrugged and carried her own mat and hauled her own saddle with a wry and amused look.

They had cooked meals with the sun-mirrors in clear weather. But they had lost their cook, among the dead slaves, give or take Hati's occasional merciful intervention, and now the cooking changed: it was Tofi's two women, Maol and Jurid, who provided the skill. They were profligate with the spices; and Marak thought it a great improvement.

He found leisure for such thoughts. In Hati's arms and in

Norit's he was happy, and that, too, was a new thought. He discovered he had seldom been happy, in his life. He had never been free in his life. But now . . . he had no idea whether he was, or not.

He found himself looking at Hati during their rides simply for the pleasure the sight gave him. Norit was a fine woman, and a comfortable one, and he liked her despite her other qualities: if he had met her alone, in such circumstances, he might have declared he loved her. But Hati stirred something in him that had never waked to anyone. He found all her movements a fascination. He found every expression memorable, and she had so many. If Hati should leave their journey, he thought he would follow Hati rather than the visions . . . it was that potent a lure.

But because they shared the visions, they went together, and wondered together what they might come to.

"Do you suppose there is a tower?" Hati asked. "Or is it a spire of rock?"

"If it's a tower, men built it," he said. "And the stars are clearly the stars we follow. And what shall we find?"

"Great treasure," Hati said expansively, with the wave of a hand toward the dark, "and we won't go back to the Ila. We'll be rich, and have fifty white beshti and lie on dyed cloth, under tents with gold fittings. We'll have a hundred slaves to do the work, and we'll eat melons twice a day."

The au'it slept, gently snoring. It was safe to talk treason.

"We'll grow fat," he said, and asked Norit, who lay at his other side, "What would you have if you were rich?"

"A house with a vineyard," Norit said, "and a fine bed with a mattress."

"No slaves?" asked Hati.

"Oh, four. They can work in the vineyard," Norit said, "and every one of them will have a house and a good soft bed and wine with supper."

"You're too kind," Hati said. "They'll cut your throat if you don't beat them."

"I was wishing," Norit defended herself. "If I'm wishing, I can wish them to be honest workers."

"If we're wishing," Marak said, entranced with this folly, "we can wish for peace between the Lakht and the lowlands, and sane minds for all of us."

"Perhaps the visions will stop when we see this high place," Hati said, putting an arm over him and snuggling close. "Most of us hope so. Those of us who have hope. And I do."

"I hope so," Marak said. He had not put it in words before, but that was the promise in the madness, that there was something to find, something to do, something to see that they must see, and once they had found it and done it and seen it they would be sane, and at peace, and free forever.

There was a flaw in this notion, of which he was keenly aware. He had promised the Ila his return, and a report. More, on the Lakht and around it for as far as the lands stretched, he knew nowhere else to go to postpone that report, especially since he had the au'it in his care.

Live as an'i Keran? He could, but he would reject the tribal life. He had no wish to fight their battles, when he had had his belly full of his father's.

Besides, he had made a pledge, and still kept it, and knew that this freedom of his lasted as long as the journey . . . at least, he had had it clear in his mind until there was Hati; and now his pledge left him a tangled maze of choices.

The Ila had promised him his mother's life, and his sister's, and he had bargained for that.

What had he bargained?

"And what would you have?" Norit asked him. "What would you have if you could have anything in the world?"

"My freedom," he said.

"Nothing else?" Norit asked, disappointed. Her father had owned her; then a husband did. He supposed now he owned, in some measure, in Norit's sight. He tried to set her free, but freedom was not even within her imagination. When she was free to do what she wished, she sang to herself, and looked at no one, and was maddest of the mad.

But Hati, he thought, well understood what he meant. They understood each other; and were both free; and that was what he loved in her.

"If I were rich," he said, "I think I would be Tofi, with a good number of beasts and tents, and the whole desert in front of me."

"A good wish," Hati said, with her fingers laced in his, and gave a sigh, and clearly intended to sleep.

He shut his eyes. They had three days to go before the village, so Tofi thought, and the concern they had lest they miss their trail, at least, was done. They would not die of the storm, and it had taken them seven days since to be sure of it.

The sick man, Proffa the tailor, died on the next day, and they laid him out on the sand where he had fallen from his beast. He had been dead before he hit the ground, so Marak judged, two days short of Pori village, where they all might rest.

The Lakht had no mercy on the weak. That was always the truth. The vermin of the air were already circling, waiting for them to leave the body. After they left, the larger vermin would come, and when they gave up, the insects would move in, and the creepers that preyed on those.

Still they laid out Proffa and gave him that small respect. It was a hot day, and most stood in the shadow of their beasts. But some made it a chance to walk about and stretch their legs, and others to take a rationed drink. The prostitute, Malin, moistened her scarf from her waterskin and wiped the dust from her face and neck.

Two days to the village, and some thought their arrival was that sure . . . or perhaps, contrary to his orders, she thought her water supply was that sure.

Tofi walked to his side, grimacing in the sun reflecting off the alkali of a crusted pan. "We should camp farther on," Tofi said, although it was about the time they should have stopped. It begged trouble to stay near the dead, however, and the distance they ought to keep meant another hour or two of riding. It was in the high heat of the day, but Marak himself raised no objection.

"We should do that," he agreed, and passed the order. "We'll move on. Two hours."

There were complaints, a general murmur from the inexperienced, loudest from Malin.

He mounted up; Hati did; and likewise Norit. He saw Malin demanding the ex-soldiers lift her up to her saddle.

In her he saw a woman grown reckless and demanding of her two chief debtors.

He saw a sign of death in her extravagance, too, but did not know whether it was Malin's.

8

In the beginning of days the Ila gave the tribes the secrets of water, where it might lie and how they might render bitter water into sweet. Likewise she appointed them their districts and their wells, which they maintain as their own, provided only that caravans may pass through their territories without hindrance and provided that only villages may levy a water-charge.
—The Book of Priests

In the conduct of a caravan there is one master, and the word of the master when he is in the desert is like the word of a priest. The Ila has given the master this authority.
—The Book of the Ila

In the next night they arrived on a road of sorts: and by dawn even a villager could see it. The caravans had traveled this way so often and so long they had worn a depression on the earth, a trench that the great storms both covered and uncovered. At times they rode in this depressed line for hours.

On the next afternoon they went over deep dunes, but Tofi found the road again, and it led east.

Other roads converged with it at a low spot, a small pile of stones that marked where, if one dug, one might find water . . . for it was not villages that determined the route of the caravans: it was water, trickles of it too small to sustain a village, but enough for a caravan. Wherever a highland loomed up, whenever the land generally tended down from that, springs might exist, often hidden in sand like this one, or making mere wet spots in the rocks, or again, crusts of white on the sand, where minerals had leached. The caravan roads met at such places. At such places the beshti could drink. So could the vermin, and there was some danger in approaching the center of the place, but they went, the beshti's feet cracking the white crust, the beshti's voices making a loud threat, clearing the vicinity.

There they gathered, sucking up the water that might kill a man, drinking so fast and so deep they drained the shallow pool and waited for more.

This water they might distill if they were desperate, using the sun ovens. They were at a place that could save them if they were out of resources. But the stale remnant of sweet water in their skins would last long enough, so Tofi said, by all he knew: this well was the marker, and the village was indeed that close.

That was the ninth day since the storm, and some of the mad felt of their diminished waterskins and uncertainly looked at the muddy soup, wondering whether they ought, perhaps, to pour their good water together in a few skins and take what bitter water they could.

Tofi said not, and there was worry and recrimination in the camp when they rested. They were at the end of their food and their water: only the beshti, well watered, bringing up their cuds, appeared content.

But when on the tenth day the trail went down beside a great wide shelf of layered rock, all broken and rubbled, and when they began generally, if scarcely perceptibly, to descend, then Hati said they were surely nearing an end; then Marak recognized in the high rocks and the presence of the bitter spring higher up the source of water that might sustain a village, and he was encouraged. By all visible evidence, Tofi was not wrong in his estimations.

By the third day Tofi was certain enough that, after they had ridden all morning, and as an uncommonly hot sun beat down like a hammer, he gave no order to pitch the tents.

The caravan track, already broad, joined with two others and made a wide, wind-scoured depression as high as the beasts' shoulders.

Now their course veered a little south, following that line. All of them, all the mad, grew anxious, just by that veering off their eastward course, knowing better, as they did.

East, their voices said.

And the voices clamored at Marak, too: *Haste, haste, haste. Move on. Don't stop.*

Patience, Marak told his demons. Be patient. The dead are no use to anyone. Rest and water. Rest and water. We can't be cheated of that.

East, they argued. *Marak, Marak, Marak. Move on. There is no time.*

The collective roads made a centuries-used trail down beside another ragged shelf of crumbling rock.

And from that trail they rode along a rocky ridge, and they began to descend again.

They came between two tall rocks and saw below them a broad double circle of dune-choked buildings and bright awnings, and a black netting that stretched over a garden the equal in size of the village itself.

"Pori," Tofi said, as if he himself had doubted. A smile spread over his face and cracked the dust, and it spread to other faces. "Pori," they said. "*Pori!*"

It was the end or the beginning of the Lakht, however one came to it, and for a Lakht village it was rich in water, if not in trade of caravans seeking water and rest. The caravans that came were out of the south: Marak remotely knew of it as a navigation point, one of several in the Lakht; and knew that the few caravans out of the remote south lowlands used this place, climbing the Lakht toward Oburan, and bending then toward Keish-an-Dei. There the tribes of the Lakht declared twice-annual peace, and met to trade and marry and plan their mischief on their brothers of the western Lakht, Hati's tribe among them.

But the tribes of the eastern Lakht were fallible allies, so Tain had learned, and Marak remembered. We cannot come this year: the wells have failed. We cannot meet you; the westerners have offended us. We cannot send reinforcements: our priest is uneasy.

As for Pori, like any entity on the Lakht, it valued commerce and took it where it could, barring feuds or weather. And it kept its neutrality. Promising everything, it had not joined Tain, either.

Clearly the village had suffered from the recent storm, and was still digging out. Tall dunes stood against walls, rising up to the eaves of some houses. Sand choked the streets. Roofs were missing patches of tile. But the black netting was intact. That said everything. Pori would safeguard that so long as the village lived.

And as they rode down among the rocks, they at last saw villagers, tiles or shovels in hand, who stopped their work on the far side of a house, and at the first sight of them, shouted: "A caravan, a caravan!" so that the whole village poured out to see.

Tofi brought his caravan to a halt at the well, at the opening of the double crescent of houses, where they surrounded a wide, sandy commons.

Here stood a stone-covered well, with troughs for animals. Even water as abundant as fed a village could not be allowed to stand under the sun and be half–drunk up by the heat: it was too precious for that. Pori—in the lowlands it would have been Kais Pori—had built a fine stone vault above ground for its well, with walls thicker than the stretch of a man's arms. That well house protected the water, and likely fed a great amount into a deep cistern. It ran out into troughs for the beasts only when a strong man pulled a lever and let it flow out.

Already there was no holding the beasts, who knew what was their due and who liked sweet water better than foul. They crowded up to the trough, where as yet there was no water, and pushed and shoved for dominance.

Meanwhile the authorities of the village had come out from a house nearest the well, many-walled and rich.

"I have a letter!" Tofi said, having gotten down with the agility of his years, and waved it for all to see, a crumpled paper they had saved from Obidhen's death, bearing the Ila's red seal.

The lord of the village came to Tofi, took the offered letter, and read it.

"A caravan from Oburan! The Ila's charge!" the village lord cried with a wave of his hand. "The Ila's charge, all they desire in water or in supplies! Open up the pipes!"

The water master had moved to his post, either to guard or to loose the precious commodity, and at that word, turned and hammered the tap open, letting the water flow from the stone mouth. It ran along the dry stone troughs. The stronger beasts, shouldering one another, trailing and treading on the reins that should have held them, moved in.

They drank with grunts of satisfaction and a great deal of jostling side to side to bully lesser animals, who tried to reach their long necks past. There was no charity among them, no more than among men on the Lakht: the strongest drank first.

The well continued to pour out water, abundant enough for all the beasts, and young girls came bringing cups full of water for them in the caravan, water they could drink freely, sweet water, cool from its underground cistern, in good brass cups.

In the end every beast had its fill, and Tofi's slaves recovered their charges by the trailing leads.

Kais Tain, Marak thought, looking around him, was such a village as this . . . more prosperous by far; but the wonder was that any village survived here on the edge of the caravan routes, while the village spread an awning and they sat at their ease to enjoy the air from the veiled garden leaves.

At Kais Tain, beside the water house, was such a garden as stood here; in every village with a well there was such a garden. The remaining water from the troughs went out by a drain hole, and into a stone-lined pit where waste and wastewater of the whole village collected.

Nothing was wasted.

And from that rich, moist pit the gardeners hauled up a treasure that, gathered over centuries, enriched the pit of sand and carefully hoarded earth, deep pit floored and walled about with stone, roofed with wide-meshed woven nets against the vermin of the air.

In Pori the garden was so old and so deep it stretched on behind the best houses, a source of wealth and pride. Twenty-four tall palms ringed that stone wall on the side nearest the well, drinking with their slighter need any moisture that reached through cracks in the stone floor of the garden, and returning the gift in the form of fruits in their season and fiber for weaving.

Ruling all, even the official who governed the flow, a water-au'it sat guard by the drain, an old woman with a knotted cord in her hands, not a pen such as the Ila's au'it used. She told the charge for the water. She chanted and counted the knots as they flowed through the fingers. It was so many knots of flow by a chant as old as the Lakht. It was so many dippers of water for the men. The caravan must pay, even at the Ila's charge, and the water-au'it's eyes missed nothing in the milling confusion.

More, with a caravan to feed and the Ila's charge, the sellers spread out their wares under the palms. It might take them a season to collect their goods in pay, but they would be city goods, and the haste to show what they had to trade became a frenzy of voices.

"Come help our guide," Marak said, and Hati and Norit and the au'it came with him, and walked beside their young caravan master, for even at the Ila's charge, they were not anxious to be cheated. When a merchant proposed an outrageous price for palm-fiber cord, Hati sniffed, examined it minutely, and the price came down. Norit sniffed when the price of salve seemed high; and the word flowed by scarcely perceptible signals: the prices revised themselves to reason.

At the Ila's charge Tofi bought a few dried fruits for the journey, per head, and dry-bread, and salt, and all these things were bundled up to stores.

But Marak, at the Ila's charge, asked four silver rings from the trade master and gave them two each to Norit and to Hati, his one indiscretion. He was not surprised when Norit, exchanging them, came back with a fine striped aifad of the eastern Lakht pattern and a pot of cinnabar rouge.

Hati bought two silver bracelets, redemption for her

honor. It was the bracelets he had intended, jewelry for Hati; but out of fairness he asked a gift for Norit as well. And Tofi, once he heard, bought bracelets each for his women, for Maol and Jurid. Then the ex-soldiers had grief from Malin, and Malin turned up with two bracelets. How had that happened? Marak asked himself with suspicion, and set the au'it to finding out where the money had come from, but to no avail. Even fear of the Ila could not unravel that mystery.

At such a spreading of coin and charges about, however, the whole of Kais Pori laid out a feast, dried and fresh fruit, and delicately spiced peas, with baked roots swimming in rare grease, a delicacy which some of the poor of the northwest had never sampled.

They all sat on the ground, farmer-style, and sucked grease from their fingers and dipped them in salt until they had had enough of both. Their au'it and the water-au'it had put their heads together, and talked, and talked, all through the meal. The villagers danced. Even they, the madmen, danced, and the prostitute and the women with Tofi danced, while the antheiri hummed their notes and the drums thumped a rapid rhythm.

The drums became a voice, however, and the voices called out of the east. They drank beer while the voices dinned names into their ears. The vision of the tower built itself out of the dung fire.

Afterward, shamelessly, in the open-sided tent, their own, and ignoring the roofs of the village, Marak lay down with two women of very different kind. Hati, with new bracelets shining in the dim light, silver against dark skin, let her skilled hands go wandering, and drew his where she wished them. Norit was shy, but cried out scandalously until Hati stopped her with her hand across her mouth, laughing, with embarrassed glances toward the nearby houses.

Norit's eyes remained eloquent, and her whole body trembled and sweated with passion. Norit made love amid her madness, and said she saw a shining hall, and lights, and people walked there.

Marak himself saw the cave of suns; and Hati swore the

same. The voices cried at them together, each in their own names, and the visions were the same vision and the whole world slid away toward the east under their backs.

They lay in each other's arms all night.

Malin and a certain woman of the village, the au'it reported, obliged various of the men, and the soldiers were out of sorts, so perhaps the mystery of Malin's bracelets was solved; but Marak let it go.

There was this to surviving the desert together, that life was worth celebrating, and those who had been wise could turn foolish and those who had been fools came out wise men; and if that was the source of Malin's bracelets, Marak decided that was Malin's business.

But in the night the visions increased, and the two ex-soldiers who had survived the Lakht, Malin's lovers, walked away from the village toward the east, simply walking.

Marak found it out in the morning, when they gathered for a generous breakfast of flatbread and milk. They were two men short, Malin was smug in her collection of bracelets, and those two, once he knew the tale, he could all but feel, walking, walking, walking, waterless and foolish, put out with Malin, having had far too much drink last night, and having perhaps grown fonder of Malin than she of them.

"We should break camp and overtake them," Marak said. The visions and voices troubled him more by the moment.

"Let them go," Malin said: she had mistaken popularity for authority, and spoke out her opinions as she pleased.

"We have another day here," Tofi protested.

"The men will die of thirst out there," Marak said. He saw the hall and figures, as Norit had said. He saw men walking, and he had lost two men to those visions: Hati had said all visions were the same, and had they not seen what he had been seeing all night? "Unless we break camp now, they're dead men. They have the visions we have. The calling is east. For once, Kassan and Foragi are right."

Tofi looked unhappy, but even Maol murmured, "East," and the look was in their eyes.

So they struck the tents, the slaves both moping through

their task, mourning the rich tables of the village, and bundled up the gear a day ahead of their plan. They roused out the beasts, who were no more ready to leave than the slaves, and who put up a great protest of lamenting and moaning. The beasts fled the reach of the slaves, and predictably the whole village of Pori turned out to watch and laugh.

Hati frowned, but Norit thought it funny, and laughed, too. "A'ip!" Hati said sharply, the command to halt, and stalked out into the circling pursuit, seized her own reluctant beast by the halter lead, and brought him back. Then she snagged Marak's, and brought him back, to the cheers of the onlookers, who mocked the slaves and cheered the other beasts on.

The au'it solemnly wrote her account, perched primly on a pile of their baggage awaiting beasts to carry it.

The beasts tired, the slaves put out a great effort, and caught one after another of the rebel animals. They had traded two of the beasts to the lord of Pori, and by refitting the saddles with side poles, made their other excess animals into pack beasts, but those complained about the loading, and hated the poles. It was all a swirl of bawling beasts and complaints and calls for this and that item in the most possible confusion.

The water-au'it meanwhile measured out the flow by which they filled all the waterskins, theirs and those large ones the beasts carried, to the brim. They favored themselves, at the Ila's charge, with a last, full drink from the sweet water, and the lord of the village, not disparaging madmen who paid well, gave each of them a fresh fruit, even the slaves.

It was a welcome surprise. Tofi was ready, however, and gave the lord a token, one of their fine bronze heating-mirrors, wrapped in soft leather.

"Count this, too, from the Ila," Marak said in all honesty.

"We look forward to your return," the lord of Pori said, bowed deeply and cherished the big mirror against his heart.

Would they? Marak asked himself. He had not asked himself that question in their stay here. It was their mission. But would they?

The lord's wife presented a bundle of dried fruit, which was a fine gift, too, one which Marak did not intend to hoard to himself; but by now he feared he was not as expressive as he wished. *Marak, Marak,* the voices were saying and in his head he saw the cave of suns and imagined Kassan and Foragi descending rocks, afoot, in danger. In his blood was a fever to be moving he had not felt since the Ila's hall. Structures of fire shot through his vision, and the sweet-sour taste of the living fruit, dripping with juices, provided its own distraction. He bid farewell with juice-wet fingers and kept the pit in his mouth, too distracted for conversation or wit.

Haste, the voices seemed to say now. *Haste,* as if someone were waiting and impatient. Was the vision of Kassan and Foragi added to the rest? Or did ordinary men see such things? He had never understood, having been mad all his life.

There was still loud complaint from the beasts, from the village edge to the caravan track outside, and onto the flat that stretched before them. But, *Marak!* the voices said, over and over and over, and the fire was in the rest of them. Water and fresh fruit and willing flesh had no power like what seethed in the mad now. It had overpowered the soldiers. Now it overpowered even Malin, who might have wanted to stay in Pori. She wept. She ran off among the buildings. And she crept back again, and sought her riding beast, catching its rein. But she had no one to help her mount. She tried to make it kneel, and it only circled and bawled.

"Damn you!" she shouted. It made some of the villagers laugh, but none of the mad was amused.

"Do we want her?" Hati asked, in the haze of images and the din of voices.

Malin had gotten two village men to lift her up, and suffered indignities of their hands on the way. But she landed astride, her clothes utterly in disarray, and took the rein in both hands, and kicked the recalcitrant beast as fiercely as she could. It threw back its head and complained, but she had the rein in her hands, and turned him, to the howling mirth of the villagers.

"Let us go," Marak said to Tofi, who was already out of countenance with the sudden departure, and with Malin, and the missing soldiers.

"This isn't wise," Tofi said. "This isn't a race, omi."

Marak was sure it was not. But it satisfied the voices. And not even Malin could slither out of their grip.

9

The stars in heaven are numbered and the Ila knows the names of them.
—The Book of Oburan

They found their missing pair staggering along toward noon, glassy-eyed and confused, on a steep shale. Alive. That was the wonder.

"Where are you going, fools?" Marak asked.

"To the tower," Foragi said, and the other, Kassan:

"The cave."

"Give them water," Marak said. "They seem alive enough to save."

"Things are growing in our eyes," the one cried, and it was all too true: Marak knew; all the mad knew: there were times that the lines of fire seemed to proliferate, to demand attention, to build and build and build.

They had brought beasts saddled for their fellow fools, but it was too steep to mount, and they were big men, too heavy to lift up at the disadvantage of the slope. The ex-soldiers had to walk down.

"These men we can do without," Tofi said in a low voice as they rode. "The woman we can do without, most of all.

They're the troublemakers. There always are, in a caravan, and these are ours."

"There always are," Marak agreed. "Without their bad example, someone else would have to be the fool. Would they not?"

Tofi gave an uncertain laugh, and thought about it on the way down the shale.

By the time they got down it was noon, and Foragi had cut his boot on a rock, and bloodied his foot. That was not good. Tofi was out of sorts, and Marak this time agreed with him.

"We shouldn't camp near this accident," Tofi said. "We should bind that up, and get him on his beast, and be another hour away before we rest."

"We'll do that," Marak said, well knowing the reasons. He himself got the kit and bound up the wound and dried it with powders, and scoured the boot out with sand and liniment. The au'it recorded the men's recovery, and their treatment.

In the meanwhile they all baked in the sun, and the beasts grew ill-tempered before they set themselves under way, several of the pack beasts having sat down, then refusing to rise until they were completely unpacked and allowed to stand. Then they had to be packed up again, all to grumbling and complaint and bawling up and down the line.

They were at the edge of a stony plain, lower than the highlands of the Lakht, a region littered with fragments of shale. The persistent wind moved the sand always in the same direction, in great red ripples flecked with black, and there was no easy way across. The beasts complained. Men complained.

Tofi avowed he had no idea, beyond Pori, where they were bound, except the star Kop still would provide their easterly direction.

"East is all we have," Marak confessed to Hati, to Norit, to the au'it, and necessarily to the men who shared his tent, two hours later, in the hellish heat of a still afternoon on the pan. "East. I don't know what else to do, now."

Since the debacle at noon, he had regretted leaving Pori.

His haste to put them on the road seemed foolish to him now that they had found the soldiers alive, even if another night might have lost them. They had lost others. Proffa the tailor had been a fine man, worth ten of those two. But an underlying urgency gnawed at his reason. He saw it working in the soldiers. He saw it building in others. There was no more economy and no more common sense where that impulse took over. Structures built within his eyes. They shaped letters. *Hurry,* they said. *No delay.*

They burned there, overlying the world.

"I see words," he admitted to Hati.

"How can you see words?"

"I see them," he said. "Like the au'it. I read. We're late for something. We have to hurry. I don't know why that's so. The soldiers knew it. Maybe they can read, though I'd have doubted it."

The au'it wrote all they said, for the Ila's record.

"I see people walking," one of the others said, Kosul the potter, who sat nearby, and that, it struck him, was exactly what Norit had said. "They want us all."

"The people there in the tower want us," Norit said in this council of equals they had made in their tent. "I don't know why."

Heads generally nodded agreement.

And who had said there were people in the tower? But now they all believed it, and everyone agreed. Whether or not the soldiers could read, he had no idea. They had chosen the shade of the other tent, preferring the company of Maol and Tofi and the slaves, who detested them . . . most of all preferring Malin, who would not come near Hati, and there were only two tents in which to shelter.

Marak's skin crawled. He wanted to rise up and deny all relationship with the rest of them.

And yet he increasingly formed a notion in his head not only of a threat sweeping down on them from every quarter of the earth, but of a refuge toward which they walked, one at the very heart of all the mystery they pursued, one they must reach soon, or die.

He shivered, and Norit caught the shiver, and so did Hati, then no few of the others.

All at once, for no reason whatsoever, he—all of them, perhaps—saw a hall of suns; and figures moving shadowlike among them. Structures traced fire across his vision.

He shouted. He clenched his hands and saw a door before him, and that door moved with no hand touching it, like the Ila's doors, but what was behind that door he could not answer and did not want to know.

A man cried out near him, and fell down in a fit. "I see spirits!" he cried. "The god! The god! Ila save us and intercede! I see the god!"

Fever rushed over Marak's skin, making his heart beat hard and his ears roar with sound.

Marak, a single voice said, wishing his attention, and he tried to give it, but the images came pouring through. From the other tent, at greater remove, there were shrieks and shouts.

Tower and cave and star, and each opened, and divulged a heart of structures and shapes and forms and light, all jumbled together. Walls were built of light and fire. Structures had tastes. Sounds had texture like rough sand.

He shouted. He leapt up and found something to lean on, the smooth strength of a tent pole, proving where he was. He rested his head against it, and stayed there long, long, not daring move until the visions stopped.

The fever had come back, as if he had taken a wound; and when his vision cleared he saw Norit had clenched her arms across her stomach and Hati had her hands braced before her mouth, gazing at nothing at all.

They had rushed out into the wilderness like novices, they had found their lost, and now they suffered for it.

Tofi came over to find them in that condition. Men were lying in fits and others lying tranquilly staring at the ceiling. "What's this?" Tofi cried, and then began to back out from under the shade of the tent, as if he feared for his life. They all might be in that condition, in both tents, all but the sane.

Marak roused himself so far as to lift his head. "Resting," Marak said. "Only resting. Is it time to move?"

Marak! The voices screamed at him, shook him, raged at him with lights. *Hurry, hurry, hurry!*

"It's time," Tofi said fearfully, doubtless longing for Pori, and safety, and sane men.

Marak pulled Hati up, saw the vacancy in her eyes, and shook her. "Wake," he said. "Wake. Sleep in the saddle."

No father, no mother, no sister, no wife, no lover could divert them. Lifelong, one purpose, one need. East. East. East, where the sun begins.

Norit, too, he pulled to her feet. The au'it and Tofi woke the others, and they began to pull the stakes and collapse the tents.

Malin and the soldiers, it turned out, had gone, simply walked ahead of them when the madness had taken hold, and no one had noticed until they all mounted up, and there were two beasts too many. So all their haste to leave Pori was wasted, and no one much cared about three fools madder than the rest of them.

But Marak cared. The land descended, beyond the dunes, in more dry, broken shale, black rock that heated enough in the afternoon to blister a human foot, and the beasts hated the footing . . . the heat hurt even through their pads, and their long, thin legs had trouble dealing with a skid.

More, there began to be blood on the shale, and off toward the shadowing east, an ominous gathering of vermin dotted the sky.

They were following three fools. What could they expect?

Yet *haste! haste! haste!* the voices railed, and the tower built itself, and fire ran across the horizon.

"They're leaving blood," Hati said, on the slide above him. "This is not safe."

"What is safe?" Tofi asked with an anxious laugh, from below them. They were on the steep part of the shale, now, and every step the beasts made cracked into a thousand sliding fragments. "What has been safe?"

He no more than said it than there came a loud slippage

and dark rush of dust and shale past them, and beasts bawled and shied in a cascade of fragments.

One of the pack beasts had fallen, and took his burden with him, sliding all the way down to the bottom. It flailed and bawled and could not rise from its burden, and it remained a sobering example of a misstep until they could make the long descent and deal with it.

The beast when they reached it had broken bones, and had to be killed: Bosginde did that with a quick stroke and covered the blood-soaked shale with shovelfuls of dry sand, where he could scrape enough together for the purpose.

The water bags had not broken. None of the supplies was lost, except a tent's deep-irons, which lay far up on the unstable slope, in plain sight, but Tofi ruled against sending anyone up, no matter the value.

"We can cut the beast up for meat," the potter said. "We can take the best."

"No," Hati said fiercely. "Leave it all. Leave all the gear. Let us move. We may have saved those three fools, but we may lose ourselves if we stand staring!"

There was that feeling in the wind. There was disaster about the whole day, and Tofi gave the order to the slaves to apportion out the packs and get them all moving.

Even so, the first crawling vermin appeared among the rocks before they had gotten the packs redistributed.

"What is that?" Norit asked, looking around her. There was a scrabbling in the rocks, a snarl of combat. "What's that?"

"A feast in the desert gains too many guests," Marak said. They had followed a blood trail. With the letting of the blood from the beast's wounds, they had the raw meat smell about them. It carried far on the desert wind: even a man could smell it. Carrying pack items that might have blood on them had risk, once the carrion-eaters gathered.

Haste, the voices said to him, *no delay. No waiting.*

The storm would have driven the vermin to cover, and to hunger, and the rearrangement of the land would drive some of the smallest out of their ranges. The whole path of the storm might be unsettled, and that storm track took shape in the back of Marak's mind the way the shape of the storm had appeared in the images. He sensed desperation in the circling predators. He cursed himself for a fool not having anticipated that Foragi might have been already past reason.

One need not fear the strongest beast on the Lakht, that was the proverb. The strongest would take the carcass. But the weak were gathering, too, and they might follow the second choice. He saw the sky over them gathering with ten and twenty and thirty of the vermin.

"Hurry," Tofi said to the slaves, as they went about the work with the packs. "You'll be first and afoot if the vermin come on us! *Move*, you sons of damnation!"

The first of the flying and the crawling vermin arrived and began worrying at the carcass with them only a stone's throw away. Another few sent down a shower of shale fragments, coming down the slide.

The quick and the desperate came first. They were not the strongest, only the earliest, the most opportunistic, harbinger of what else would come. They growled and tore into the carcass and the scent of blood and then entrails grew in the air.

"Hurry!" Hati said.

"A'ip!" Tofi yelled. "Ya! *a'ip!*" The beast the slaves were loading stood trembling, and without complaint, when she gave a jerk on its lead.

More of the flying vermin had landed.

And a glance off across the land showed a furtive, eye-deceiving movement as if the land itself had come to life.

Marak saw Norit into the saddle, delayed to assist Tofi's women while Tofi railed on his slaves. Osan had gotten up onto his feet.

He did not delay then to make Osan kneel again. He seized the rein, jumped, and seized the saddle, hauling himself up by brute strength until he put a foot in the mounting loop, a move he had doubted he could do. Osan was moving before he could land in the saddle and tuck his leading foot into place. Tofi scrambled up, and the slaves mounted in des-

perate haste, the pack beasts tethered in line and each trying
to move at once.

Osan quickened his pace, flicking his ears in distress, laying them back at what he smelled. The beasts knew what the
nomads of the Lakht knew, what Hati had foretold. Marak
himself had never seen a mobbing . . . few in the Lakht had
seen it and lived.

The beasts picked up their pace, treading heedlessly,
crushing small vermin that chanced underfoot, creatures
hardly more than a hand's length. The mobbing started on
that scale, other creatures turning toward the smell of death
near at hand, already beginning to gorge and being bitten
and clawed by other creatures nearby.

In an instant what had begun as a flattened multipede became a fist-sized ball of struggling eaters that grew larger by
the moment.

All that hunger, Marak thought, only a day or so out from
the rich oasis of Pori. And the storm had churned it to madness of a different kind, a natural frenzy.

The beshti hit a traveling run, a difficult pace for the un-
habituated, and next to a flat-out bolt, which might fling the
weak riders from the saddle. Marak held Osan back, and
crossed him in front of Tofi's men, who were about to break
ahead.

"Don't wear them down," he said sharply. Hati pulled in
front with the same advice, and they slowed the impulse
toward outright flight. At a moderate pace they reached sand
that no longer moved.

Then they counted themselves truly escaped, and fortunate.

They did not overtake Malin and the ex-soldiers.

They did not camp at noon, either. They kept going with
minor rests, taking a little of the dried fruit for their meal,
and a little water, enduring the heat of the sun, and even the
beasts did not complain. The distance between them and the
disturbance still seemed perilously scant, the beasts still were
skittish, and they rode until they had put the whole afternoon behind them.

Then they settled down for a shortened rest, with no tents pitched, lying on their mats until the stars came out.

In the distance a hunter howled, and most all the still bodies in the camp roused and turned and looked toward that horizon.

So did the beasts, lifting their heads in perfect unison.

Marak saw nothing but a flat, endless, wind-scoured land.

He let his head back and trusted the beasts to raise a fuss if danger came close. The voices urged him, pleaded with him, *Hurry, hurry, hurry!* even now, and rest came hard.

Fear was on the wind tonight. The tower built itself, and the cave of suns was in it, and he heard voices multiplying.

Then he gained the strangest notion that he should get up, and take his beast and keep traveling.

Certain of the sleeping madmen sat up, too. Hati had gotten to her feet, and then Norit, who plunged her head into her hands and shook her head, refusing the vision, perhaps, or perhaps only weary beyond words.

The beasts themselves, not being mad, could not sustain such a pace. But after all the fright and terror of the day, still, the mad rose up, not listening, locked in that intensity of purpose that drove men to walk to their deaths.

Malin and the soldiers had been the first.

"No," Marak said. He went to them, seized one arm and the other, and shook at them. "Wake up. Don't follow it afoot like Malin and Kassan. You saw what happened with the beast. You know what happened to those that walked out. In a few hours we will go. But not straggling off by twos and threes like fools! Listen to me!"

Two heard him. The orchardman began to walk, and the potter followed.

He caught the orchardman and hit him hard with his fist, pitching the man down. He overtook the potter, a slighter man, and hit him, the same. The man went down unconscious, and that was the end of his walking off in the night.

The orchardman sat nursing a bloody lip and muttering to himself, but sane enough with the pain of a chipped tooth to know he had been a fool.

Marak went back with a sore hand and sat down to suck at a cut knuckle.

"Let them go," Hati said.

"Why should you care?" Norit asked. "Why should any of us care?"

The erosion was reaching the rest of them, a slippage of what kept their company together, a bleeding of reason and sanity.

"Because we *should* care," he said. "Because when they brought us from the villages we became beasts. I don't wish to be a beast again. And I *won't* be a beast. Damn the visions! I may not go to the tower, and damn them all. It's my choice! *It's become my choice, and I may not choose what they want me to choose!*"

Hati thought about that. And in his mind, at least, the visions had become quiet.

Sanity seemed to have settled over them all for the while.

"It's our choice," Hati echoed him. "I can make it. I decide."

Norit said, "There's no use dying before we know what it is we're looking for, is there?"

"No," he said. "There is not." He gathered them both against him, Hati against his side, Norit against his knees. They were beyond passion, since Pori. The intervening days they had had no strength to spare. Things had assumed a haste that had no reason, and now he reminded himself he had company, and had lives in his hand, and could not make Kassan's choices.

Within the hour, all the same, they saddled up the beasts again and rode on, but sensibly so, to use the cool of the night while they had it and to stop again close to their ordinary schedule. They rode on into the day and by then, though the chipped tooth stayed chipped, the orchardman's lip showed healed. More, the orchardman and the potter were quarreling again and calling one another fools, and the whole company seemed in better humor.

The sun went to noon, and they pitched the tents precisely as they needed to, on a sandy flat. They were still on the storm track: the recent debris of oasis fiber-palms where no trees grew showed how very far the winds had carried debris. It had likely come from the palms at Pori. Usually the sun heated their tea; they lit the fiber for fuel, and it brewed up a fine spiced porridge with the added flavor of smoke.

In the afternoon, however, and before they could break camp and have the tents safely folded, the wind began to blow. The breeze was a relief from the heat, but it gusted and battered at them and made more work with the tents.

The wind grew worse with the evening. Dry and hot, it wearied the bones, blew up the dust, and made the deep-irons a serious consideration by the next noonday, if they were to pitch the tents.

"It's only a small blow," Marak said, when Tofi hesitated, and feared they might misjudge the weather. The urge to move was so strong his skin itched. "Wrap up in mats. We can do without the tents."

"No, omi. If we misjudge, it's the death of us. We have to pitch the tents."

He knew better. As he had known the storm's limit, he knew the limit of this, and so Hati argued his point, and so many of the mad joined him, all grumbling: no one wanted the delay. The visions came and went; but *east, east, east!* the madness shrieked, and there was anger, and there were sulking faces. Tofi flung wide his arms and shouted at them all, "All right, all right, we will not use the deep irons, at least, and may the god have mercy on our lives!"

They pitched the two tents, which billowed and bucked as if they had a life of their own, in the lee of a low ridge, which they had somewhat between them and the wind. The animals settled peacefully to their noontime meal, and the lot of them, mad and sane, had dried fruit and a little grain-cake.

Marak, the voices said. Every noontime they spoke. They spoke to Maol, Tofi's woman, who stood in the dusty noon sun, battered and shaken by the wind. She had forgotten Tofi, forgotten who she was. Norit watched her, singing to herself, her fingers measuring all along the hem of her robe, as if this were somehow important.

Every man, every woman, seemed numb. There was no strength, no time amid the visions: passion ebbed and evaporated with every trace of moisture shed into the wind.

Norit sang of water, of a stream and a lost love, and her voice, childlike at times, haunted the wind. The woman, Maol, swayed, as if dancing to that music.

Marak!

He looked up, his heart beating hard. All at once he wished more than life to rise up and walk toward that summons.

Instead he doggedly lowered his chin into the muffling, protective aifad and fingered the stitching on his boot, losing himself in the patterns. Hati, likewise veiled, was against his side. Norit was with him, sitting, swaying. The au'it slept nearby, the Ila's eyes and ears, in company with madmen who thought of nothing more than losing themselves in the desert and becoming food for the hunters.

Marak!

Now he rose to his feet without even thinking. So had Hati, and Norit, and all the mad. Only Tofi slept, only the slaves, and the au'it.

Marak's heart sped. No, he said to himself. No! But the voices said yes.

Hati began to walk. He reached out to stop her, and shook at her, and seized Norit by the arm as Norit began to walk past him. The dust had begun to rise. It obscured all the horizon.

And in the blowing dust, a ghost, a spirit, a mirage without the sun, a figure stood.

It seemed to be a man in thick gauzy robes, in the colors of the sand.

No tribesman. The vision of the tower rose up, built itself in Marak's eyes where the man stood.

And vanished.

Marak blinked the blowing dust into tears, resisted the impulse to wipe, that would abrade his eyes. The slack of the gust showed him the shape again.

Hati pointed. She saw the same. Norit stood close to him, held to him, pressed against his side, and all the while this vision came walking down the slope, and became clearer and clearer to their eyes.

"He is no tribe I know," Hati said.

In an an'i Keran, that was remarkable enough. The Keran were masters of the Lakht, and there were means to tell one tribe from the other: to know those differences was life and death.

The stranger came ahead with confidence, and that also was remarkable, and ominous.

"We might be bandits," Marak said. "We have no prosperous look. And we are no tribe." The man was trusting . . . or there were more of them beyond that hill.

But as the man came, the voices clamored. *East, east, east,* became *here. Now. This place. This man.* Marak's heart beat like a smith's hammer.

Marak dropped his veil, a villager's friendliness, despite the choking dust; he lifted a hand in token of peace, and the vision, or the man, whatever it might be, likewise lifted his right hand and walked into their camp.

The mad were all on their feet, and drew back from this visitor, not far back, but far enough.

"Togin, Kosul, Kofan, Ontori, Edan." The visitor named their names for them, as if he had always known them. "Marak, Hati, Norit." The incantation went on, inexplicable, accurate, and complete, as the veiled man faced them one by one.

"Tofi," the man said, among the last. He even named the slaves. "Bosginde, and Mogar. Not least, the au'it."

It was the only name that remained secret among them, as the au'it had never confessed one. She had waked, and reached for her kit, and her book, and, shocked out of her rest in a gale of sand by this vision, spat onto her ink-cake and began to write.

"Who are *you*?" Marak asked. Their visitor showed his power and his knowledge of them, but gave them nothing of his own nature. This was not necessarily the indication of a friend. "Where do you come from?"

"Ian is my name." The visitor reached up and took down his veil. "As for where I come from, from the wind and the air is where I come from, and from the empty place behind the wind."

That was to say, the land of ghosts, by the priests' way of saying. No few of the villagers blessed themselves in fear, and nothing the man said comforted any of them, but Marak had no inclination to fall on his face to save his life, or to believe this man because he quoted the writings. He had come to the east, after so much, and so long, and was *this* his answer, Marak asked himself, this arrogant man with clever riddles and an appeal to superstition?

And if he was the god himself, Marak asked himself, beyond that, then would he flinch from the dust and the blasts of wind?

And if he were a ghost or a god, would he have watering eyes?

Marak thought not.

And was this *Ian* the end of his visions, and all the madness?

Was this *all*?

Marak drew in a deep breath and folded his arms, feet braced against any inclination to move. "What do you want?" he asked this Ian bluntly.

Not welcomely so, he thought, since Ian looked at him, looked at him long and hard, not pleased. He might have been a curiosity, a momentary obstacle, a piece of some passing and despised interest.

"*You*," Ian said. "*You*. Marak Trin Tain." Ian walked a little past him, and looked at him, and then looked curiously at Norit, and at Hati, one by one. "They are with you."

"Yes," Marak said.

"You three," Ian said. "Come with me. The others, stay in camp. You'll be supplied whatever you need."

No, was Marak's first impulse, defiantly no.

Marak, Marak, Marak, the voices cried, pleading with him. *Come.*

His madness acquired a direction, and leaned toward this man, this stranger. He could have run screaming at the sun, turned circles like Maol. *Marak, Marak, Marak,* they said, deafening him, showing him memories of riding in the hills, confronting his father, walking away from all he knew . . . recalling for him the acclamation of an army, and the straggling, ragged line of the mad.

Marak!

He would do nothing, *nothing* to conform to his madness. Pride prevented him. He trembled, he gathered his strength, knowing he could not walk away in disdain and resist the eastward tilting without falling down.

"Come," Ian said to him more civilly. "Come."

The tilting made him stagger, finally, rarely, it swayed him off his balance, and he feared it would fling him down in the dirt if he resisted. Besides, this *Ian* offered him answers, offered him the courtesy of asking repeatedly. Reluctantly, grudgingly, he followed, Hati and Norit walking with him: at least he had them where he could watch over them.

But then he was aware of another presence, another soft tread on the sand. Ian turned and said, harshly, *"I said the three."*

Marak turned, too, and saw the au'it, who clutched her book to her chest and wide-eyed, thin-lipped, resisted the dismissal.

"She is the Ila's au'it," Marak said. "She has orders to go where I go."

"Whose orders?"

"The Ila's."

"The Ila's orders have no weight here," Ian said.

"They have with me." They had stopped on the exposed hill, where the wind battered them and the heavier sand stung bare skin. Ian's scent came to them on that wind, too, a curious scent, like sun-heated cloth, like living plants. "We're all mad here except the young master, the two slaves, and the au'it. We see visions and hear voices.—Do you?"

Ian gazed at him a long, long moment, seeming to measure him twice and three times and perhaps not to like the sum he arrived at. He was a strange sort of man, strange in his smell, tanned, with wisps of pale hair blowing out from under the headcloth, and with narrow, close-lidded eyes. Marak had never seen such sun-bleached hair, and never seen green eyes, green like stagnant water. The cloth of the sand-colored robes was fine as that in the Ila's court, cloth of gauze of many lengths and layers, so that they blew and whipped in the wind, individually as light as the dust itself.

Wealth, such cloth said. Power, that wealth said.

And that the Ila's orders did not reach here did not persuade him to trust this Ian, no matter how the voices dinned into his ears and no matter how the feelings in his heart said this was, after all his trials, the place. The Ila ruled everything. In Kais Tain they might have said that the Ila's rule did not extend there, but they did not disrespect an au'it.

"Come," Ian said then, shrugging off the matter of the au'it, ignoring her presence, and led them farther, over the low dune. After that they walked along Ian's back trail—he left tracks like a man—on for some little distance toward a sandstone ridge, and along that for a considerable distance south.

Go with Ian, the voices said. *Believe him. This is the place. This at last is the right place.*

The desire and the voices grew, overwhelming better sense, and heat, and thirst. But limbs grew weary in walking. Feet ached, and rubbed raw in boots. The au'it lagged, carrying her heavy book, and Norit stumbled.

Still Ian walked at the same pace.

"If we were to trek all afternoon to get where we're going, we might have saddled the beasts," Marak said, vexed, helping Norit.

Ian turned and confronted him for another lengthy stare, a test of wills, perhaps.

Or perhaps Ian heard voices of his own. It occurred to Marak at that moment that such might be the case.

"Not far, now," Ian said, and led them, at a slower pace, up another rise.

In the great distance and through the blowing dust a slope-walled spire rose up ahead of them, rising out of the flat desert as the land rose. It was an anomalous thing, and yet familiar, so very familiar it sent chills down Marak's spine.

Hati touched his arm, for a moment stopped still, and half whispered, "The spire."

"The tower," Norit said.

Closer, the voices whispered. *Closer, Marak Trin Tain.*

"Come," Ian said again.

They struggled to keep Ian's pace, and it was hard to ignore the clamor of voices, now, urging *Faster, faster, faster.*

Hard, but possible. They were not fools, and he was not a slave to his madness. Marak deliberately slowed his pace, walking at a rate he thought Norit and the au'it could sustain. Hati slowed. So they all fell behind. Ian looked back, displeased, but none of them walked faster, so Ian fell to their pace.

Slower still, as the tower grew clearer out of the air, and clearer. They came close enough to see the stony ground around about it, a strange depression atop a hill of cindery rocks, with bits of glass catching the light.

Marak paused for rest, to Ian's great annoyance, as the sun was setting, as those bits of glass were catching the red light.

It was a tower as great as any in the holy city, and not a structure of air and fire. Its sand-colored walls, casting back the sunset glow in the west, might be stone, but if so, there was no joint of masonry.

"It has no windows," Norit said, "nor doors."

And what use was it in itself, Marak asked himself, and why had it haunted the mad, and what did it mean to any of them? As a dream it had seemed to mean things on its own, a high place, a landmark to guide the mad.

If it was a real place it had to have uses, and occupants, and a reason for being there.

For that reason, too, he sat down where he stood, and Hati and Norit and the au'it settled by him.

"It's not that far," Ian said, standing as if ready to walk again.

"Why should we trust you?" Marak said. "Why should we go any farther? We've seen what it is."

"Have you?" Ian asked. "You haven't seen everything. And you know *nothing*. Get up."

Up, up, up, the voices echoed in Marak's head. He saw the cave of suns, and now Norit's figures moving within that cave. Norit and Hati each had his hands, and Norit's was cold. Hati's sweated; and the au'it wrote, hunched over to protect her book from the wind.

"Stubborn," Ian said. "Your reputation has reached us. But I won't stand out here all night. You can sit here as long as you like, and go back and make up lies to tell the rest, for all I care. The au'it may be the only one of you with courage to investigate what this place is. Will you come, au'it?"

The au'it stopped her writing, and lifted her head, and considered the proposition.

Marak found the proposition as impossible to ignore. The truth was he could not walk away from it without answers. But he was not inclined to meet a fortified position without looking it over and thinking it through, if nothing more than the evident fact that it had no weak points, and it had no evident communication with the outside, and it gave every evidence of being like the Beykaskh in its defenses.

The au'it looked at him, however, instead of folding her book. Everyone looked at him, as if he should know the risks. He did not, and knew he could only guess what they were venturing into.

But he got up. "Go back to the others," he said to Hati. "Take Norit with you." The au'it was doomed as he was, to carry out the Ila's orders: in that matter he had no authority over her.

Hati, however, refused to do as he asked. "I came to see this place," she said, and brought home to him the simple truth that he was not alone in his obsession and his visions: Hati's were as strong; and maybe neither of them stronger than Norit's. She had stood up and moved toward Ian.

Marak gave an exasperated sigh and stood up, and Hati and the au'it with him, and the three of them walked where Ian led, subtly uphill for a long walk toward the tower's base. Hot glass, as if from some army of glassworkers, seemed to have fallen on the sand all about, cooling, including grains and holes and bubbles in its convolutions. If they had had to walk over that in the dark, they might have had hard going. But there was a broad walkway of safe, plain sand as the sun sank and lengthened shadows to their greatest extent, even the shadows of bits of glass that studded the sand.

"I've seen this," Hati said under her breath. "I have seen this kind of glass."

So had he, long ago, with the army. "At Oburan," he said. "At Oburan, when the wind blew clear the western plain."

"There's nothing like this in the lowlands," Norit said, clinging to Marak's hand. "Nothing at all like this in the lowlands."

Ian, meanwhile, walked steadily before them. The open sand was a tablet slowly erased, revised every time the wind blew, but the walkway through the plain of glass showed the passage of feet both coming and going: Marak did not miss it, and he had not, as they entered that pathway and added their prints to the rest, the fact there had been a traffic going around the depression of glass, and beyond the dune.

He doubted that Hati had missed that fact, either, but he said nothing, only stored it up as an indication there might be more than one destination hereabouts, perhaps another one beyond the hill that obscured their vision of all the land beyond, and perhaps more to this place than the tower. The prints he saw went around the scattered glass, and up on the other side, and out of sight, as the land either stretched on in a broad flat or fell away in a depression. There was no place round about higher than the base of the tower.

At this range it filled all their vision, and those footprints went confidently toward a bare wall at its base, where a subtle jointing showed where a door might be.

So there were mundane accommodations like doorways, Marak said to himself. Ian did not walk through walls, or expect it of them.

That seam cracked before they reached it, and let out a warm bright light, welcoming rather than threatening: as a door, like the Ila's doors, a large square dropped back and slid to one side, rapidly, and with no hand to move it.

Inside, a series of lighted globes marched along the ceiling of a long, long hall.

It was the cave of suns. Marak recognized it, and his heart skipped a beat. They were within the vision. Hati and Norit must realize it.

Ian walked ahead of them, booted feet echoing sharply on a floor like glass, under blinding suns that now assumed a mortal scale, floating globes of brilliant, fireless light.

"This is the place," Norit whispered as she walked. Her voice trembled. "This is what I always see."

Marak pressed her hand, and Hati's, and the au'it hovered close by. He trembled. He was ashamed to acknowledge it to himself and twice ashamed to have Hati and Norit know it, but he trembled. He was here, within his lifelong vision, and he could not but think of all the hours of misery, all the days and nights he had fled his father's house, trying not to be discovered in his madness; of nights on the Lakht, on campaign, trying to conceal from the men he led that he heard voices and saw this place, over and over and over again.

All these things . . . all the years, all the losses of self and pride . . . came to this hallway, and proved, not madness, but prophecy. And for what, he asked himself angrily. For what?

He freed his hand of Hati's and pulled down the lap of his aifad to have a better look, to breathe the cold, strange air of this place. The air smelled faintly of water and herbs and things like asphalt.

There were doors, countless doors in this hall of light, if those seams meant anything; and there were doors at the end of the hall.

"Ian," someone said, behind them.

Marak stopped; they all stopped, and turned.

A woman stood behind them, in the same sand-colored robes.

"Is this Marak?" she asked, and an unanticipated flood of heat rushed through Marak's head, filling his face, his neck, his whole body with fever warmth. His pulse hammered in his temples, for no reason, none. The heat came from inside him, but what caused it was here, this place, this woman.

Marak, the voices said, echoed in his head, *Marak Trin Tain, Hati Makri an'i Keran, Norit Tath, and a nameless au'it belonging to the Ila.*

The words went round and round and echoed from up above the suns.

All at once the hall went blank. The hard glass floor met Marak's right knee. Norit and then Hati tumbled past his arms, and he tried to save them from the hard floor. They tumbled through his hands. Numb, he reached for his knife—toppled, simply toppled, hit the cold glassy floor with his shoulder and then with his head.

This was foolish, he thought in dismay. He had fallen over like a child that had forgotten how to walk. There was no cause for this weakness. Nothing had happened to him. There was no pain. He should not have fallen.

Marak, Marak, Marak, the voices said. Visions poured through his head. Voices numbed his ears with nonsense, roaring like the storm wind.

Of course he had weapons. Following Ian, coming in here, he had had at least that confidence.

But he knew now he had carried his defeat inside him, the same enslavement that had drawn him across the desert.

His father won this argument. Worthless, his father had said, and the suns burned and blinded his eyes, each with a curious white-hot pattern at its heart.

"Marak," Ian said, and reached down a hand. He could no longer move. In jagged red lines the visions built towers, then letters beneath them, but he could make no sense of them. The letters streamed into the dark of the towers, and down twisting corridors, deep, and deeper and deeper by the moment.

"Fool," his father said.

He had fallen at practice, in the dust of the courtyard. If he did not get up, his father would hit him. He tried. He kept trying.

10

All metal belongs to the Ila. When it is broken its reshaping must be written down and its weight accounted, whether it be iron or silver or gold or copper. All metal the Ila gives for the good of villages. The earth will not grow it. It will not spring up like water. If a village or a tribe finds any metal, they must make it known to a priest. If it is traded, an au'it must write it. If it is sold, an au'it must write it. If it is lost in a well, that well must be drained. So also if it is lost in sand or carried off by a beast, an au'it must write it, and it must be hunted out.
—The Book of Oburan

Fever burned in Marak's skin, ran in veins of fire through his body. His bones ached. Strange smells assaulted his nostrils. The place reeked like the lye pits, or a tanner's vat at noonday.

He lay in a bed of sorts, unable to move his arms. "Hati," he said, and then, scrupulously, dutifully, to be fair: "Norit?"

He had no sense of living presence near him. He wondered where they were.

He wondered where *he* was.

Very faintly and remote from his immediate concern, too, he thought of the au'it, and the rest of the madmen the Ila had sent with him, at his word.

He thought of Tofi, who had lost everything on this journey. Of Malin and Kassan and Foragi, the fools who had walked into the desert.

A man in sand-colored robes had lured him from the safety of a camp where he at least had allies. He had been a fool to leave, and a greater fool to walk into the tower. He had thought so much of following the vision at the last he had forgotten good sense.

Mad, Tain had said. *Not my son. Not my blood. Living in my house, taking my food.*

When he failed Tain's expectations Tain had had no love for him. But when he exceeded them he had Tain's bitter jealousy. The army had cheered for him, and Tain had sulked in his tent, full of resentment.

Was there nowhere any right course?

He saw his sister sitting in the dust, his mother falling behind, left sonless.

He saw the faces of his father's men, all staring, all grim and betraying nothing while Tain accused him. *Not my son.*

After an interval he heard footsteps moving around him. He smelled strange, pungent things. The roaring in his ears built and built to a sickening headache.

Perhaps he was dying. The possibility failed to alarm him. There was no particular pain, except the headache, and he had had no few of those in his life.

But if he was dying, it was without answers, and *that* was not fair.

If he was dying, he had led Hati and Norit here, and they needed him awake, not lying here half-witted. Their absence was a grievance and a worry, and when he thought of them, that worry increased and the headache became less.

"Hati," he said aloud, and tried to move.

Voices spoke to him, or around him. He felt small, vexing pains. He grew ill with the smells, and he grew angrier and angrier at his helplessness. If he fought, he could open his eyes. If he fought, he could think. If he fought, he could remember why he was here and where Hati had gone.

The voices went away. There was utter quiet for a time. It was hard to maintain the struggle. It slipped away from him, just slipped away.

And with no sense of connection to that dark place, he simply waked up, in a brown, smooth-walled room.

He lay under a light cover, on a bed that stank of lye or

some such thing, under a glowing sun that lit the whole room, and he had not a stitch on.

He sat up, on cloth fine and smooth as any he had ever felt, and as clean to look at, though it stank. He was clean, he was shaven, his hair was washed and reeked of alcohol and lye. The sunburn on his hands and the new blisters on his feet had diminished to a little peeling skin, and that told him, given the way he healed, that it had been more than a few hours he had lain here, and that the dark dream might be no dream at all.

He swung his legs off the bed.

Sand-colored clothing lay on a shining metal chair at the foot of the bed. It made him remember Ian and the guidance that had brought him here.

"Ian!" he shouted out, damning him for his betrayal. "Ian!"

He expected no response. He doubted Ian would want to be near him at the moment.

But if the clothes were here, they were surely for him, who had none, and they were cleaner than the rest, smelling at least of nothing worse than herbs.

He put on the breeches and shirt and belt, sat down to put on the boots . . . in every particular like the boots he had come in, but new, as if they had been re-created down to the last stitch.

He hesitated at the gauzy robe, robes indicating tribe and tribe indicating allegiance; but he was not accustomed to go about in half undress, either; and when he picked it up, he saw how a shoulder stitch of strong twill bound the layers into a garment that could be shrugged on with its folds in place.

The aifad, too, was doubled gauze. He had no doubt how to put it up and wrap it if he chose. Clever, he thought, more than clever. He let the aifad lie on his shoulders, seeing no need of its protection in this sterile place.

Fine cloth, strange smells, burning lights . . . it was not sun that shone through the ceiling. It had several sources behind the translucent panels. This windowless smooth box of a room was beyond doubt a part of the cave of suns, within the tower. He was not far from where he had fallen and not far, he hoped, from Hati and Norit . . . not forgetting the au'it, either, who was little suited to indignities like this.

The door was shut, a plain brown panel, showing no more feature than the wall and no means to open it. It was cold like iron. He thought of the Ila's metal doors, the power of them, and refused to be daunted. He had met this riddle before, and looked for a plate to touch.

"Ian!" he shouted at the door, and struck it with his hand.

The door opened. But it was Norit who appeared, Norit, dressed as he was, in the sand-colored gauze.

She simply stood there.

"Are you all right?" he asked. Her silence, her lack of joy, sent a chill through him. He embraced her as a man ought to greet his wife, and she acted as if he had never touched her before. Then she pushed away and went and sat down on the rumpled bed.

He found nothing right. His ears suddenly roared. His balance went uncertain, and Norit for a moment looked like an utter stranger to him.

The door was still open. He looked outside, down a metal hall like the vision of the cave.

But it was not the same hall: in small points, the number of suns and the number of doors, it was different than where they had been. They were about halfway down it, in a room to the side.

"It's a hallway," Norit whispered. "It's just a hallway. That's all it ever was, the cave of suns."

"Have you seen all of this place? Have you met anyone? Who is the woman?"

"Luz." Norit, who was a simple woman and a villager, never experienced in the outside, let alone the heart of mysteries. "Her name is Luz."

"Where's Hati?"

"I think she's somewhere near."

"Have you talked to them?"

"They talk to *me*," Norit said, and shuddered. "I can hear them."

He could not. There was only the roaring. "What is this place?"

A second shudder. Norit drew in a deep breath. "The woman named Luz. She told me her name is Luz. She wants me to be still, now, and let her talk."

If he were not a madman all his life he might have shaken his head and refused to understand. But they were both mad. This room was mad. The things they had seen and heard for years were mad.

Now a woman named Luz wished to speak to him through Norit's lips, and Norit was starkly terrified.

"What does she want?"

That seemed a more than difficult question. Norit seemed to wrestle with it, and put her hands to her temples as if her head ached unbearably.

"I don't know," Norit said. "She wants to talk. She wants to talk!"

"Then let her," he said, thinking only that Norit was in pain, but the second after he said it he regretted the advice.

Norit winced, and set her eyes on him, her back straightening.

"Marak."

Someone else was there. Someone *else* framed that word through Norit's lips.

"I see you," the stranger said.

"Don't hurt her," Marak warned the stranger, not remotely knowing how he might separate this stranger from Norit. "Don't hurt her."

For an instant there was a break, a less rigid backbone. "She isn't hurting me," Norit said. "But she scares me. She wants me to say . . . she wants me to say exactly the words, and not to think about them. All these things. I'm scared. But she says I'm safe if I don't get up. She wants to talk to you."

"Then, damn her, why doesn't she come talk to me herself?"

"She says you'll believe it if it comes through me. She says she wants *you*. She wants you, most of all, to listen to her."

He was not well-disposed to anyone in this place. "To do what?"

"I think—" Norit began. "I think—I don't know. I don't know what she wants."

"What do any of them want?" he retorted in anger at the powers behind the walls. Norit squeezed her eyes shut and held her hands to her ears. "Damn it, where is Hati?"

Marak! Marak! Marak!

The roaring grew and grew, and deafened him, and he flung himself down onto the bed, took Norit in his arms, and held her and rocked her against him, both of them rocking to the tides in the sound and the light and the noise. He would not surrender her to them, he would not surrender Hati, or himself.

"Don't!" Norit cried, pushing at him. "Don't, don't, don't!"

He began to understand it was at him Norit shouted. He relaxed his hold, letting her pull away, and tried to still the voices in his head. *Marak,* they said. *Be calm*—when his being calm was only to their advantage, none of his.

"We are mad," Norit said, having captured half a breath, "we are mad because we have these creatures in our blood. And they have them inside, too. Luz has them, very, very tiny, so tiny no eye can see; but they move through our blood and through our ears and our eyes and they make us have the visions. They make the fever. They heal us. They make the sound and the pain and they build the lines we see in our eyes: they trace them on our eyes, and they whisper them into our ears. They take words out of the air, from the tower, to a place in the sky, to us, wherever we are."

"Why?"

"They're our gift."

"A *gift,* is it?" He pushed Norit back to look at her, to see within her eyes whether he could see any trace of these engravings on her eyes. "Is it a *gift,* to be outcast from every civilized village? Is it a *gift,* to be whipped across the desert and die within a day of a village?"

"I am Luz," she whispered, this woman almost within his arms, this body he had held tenderly at night and held now at arm's length, like some venomous animal. "I say it is a gift. A gift we give, Marak Trin Tain, risking our lives!"

"Damn your gift!" he said, and shook her, and then was appalled, because it was Norit he had hurt. "*Damn your gift. We're the ones who die for it. My mother and my sister will die because of your gift! I've sworn my life to the Ila because of your gift!* Take it back! Let us go!"

"You need it."

"For *what*?"

"Life," Norit's lips said, whispered. "Life, if you'll take it. Life for more than the ones you've brought if you'll listen."

There had been a time he had chased the truth. He was not willing to find it in what this *Luz* dictated things to be. He would not take her word for the truth, not her desires, not her rules, not her half promises like some seller in the bazaar. None of it. He rose up off the bed, or began to, but Norit reached for his wrist.

He would have rejected the effort. It was the fumbling, desperate character of the grip that restrained him and reminded him that Norit, too, was there to suffer for what he said and did.

"She wants you to listen," Norit said. "Please listen."

There were many, many hostages, in the Ila's hands, in Luz's hands.

And where could he go? What could he do, to find Hati, and to rescue Norit?

"Listen to what?" he answered not Norit, but Luz.

"She wants *you*," Norit said. "She wants *you*, because you're Marak Trin Tain, because she knows your name, she knows who you are, she knows what you did in the war, and she knows the Ila sent you."

"Yes the Ila sent me. The Ila gathered all the mad together and chose me to find her answer, to find out what we see and why we walk off into the desert to die like damned fools." Temper rose up, the temper that was Tain's curse, and his, and he choked it back, because it was only Norit he could hurt if he let it fly. "So what is this great truth? Why have we been tormented all our lives, and what good is it to anyone, and why should this Luz *or* the Ila care about a handful of madmen?"

"She's given us a gift," Norit's lips repeated, trembling at every word. Her eyes were immense, dark and haunted. She drew a deep breath, shut her eyes, and the tremor went away. "We have had our thirty years. Thirty years to gather in those that will listen, thirty years to store away your knowledge, so what you know . . . will not . . . will not perish." She spoke. Then terror overwhelmed Norit. Her lips trembled into silence, as if she denied all that had flowed through her mouth.

Pity moved Marak's hand to her cheek, gently, gently, and wiped a tear. "You are not to blame," he said. "Norit. You are *not* to blame."

"I love you," Norit said. "You were kind to me, and I love you. Remember it if I can't."

It was like a good-bye. It haunted him. And there was nothing he could do to help her. He brushed her cheek, straightened her hair.

"Let her speak to me," he said. "Let her speak. Let's see if we can make sense of this. And damn this Luz, she'll give you back your right mind again when she's done."

"I hear," Norit's lips said. And Norit's eyes were in torment.

"Then tell the truth! Why do you do this to her? Why not come in here and speak to me yourself?"

Marak! roared in his head. *Marak, Marak, Marak!* so loudly that he flinched.

"Speak to me, damn you, don't shout!"

"I've spoken to you," Norit's lips said, "for nearly thirty years, and you won't hear me. You hear what you want to hear." Norit hesitated, trembling. "You recast everything the way you want to hear it. You're very stubborn."

"It's my father's inheritance," he said. He caressed Norit's cheek and found his own hand trembling. "I'm here. Tell me whatever she wishes, Norit. I love you. For your sake, I'll listen."

"I can't think!" Norit said in a faint voice. "I see things and I can't think about them, and I hear words and they don't make sense. She hates me; she says she doesn't, but I know she does!"

"Let her be!" he said to whoever possessed Norit. "Talk to *me,* and let her be!"

"Norit is far easier." Of a sudden Norit's head drooped, and her whole body sank into his arms, so that for a moment he feared Norit was dead . . . but Norit lay in his embrace, aware, and breathing as if she had run for her life.

"Luz wants you to listen," Norit whispered against him, teeth chattering. "Luz wants you to listen and not to fight her."

"Hush," he said. "Hush. I'll try." He did try. He shut his eyes and tried to make sense of the whisper in his skull.

"She thinks things," Norit said, at the limit of her expression, trembling. "She wants things. My ears buzz. She's angry because you won't listen to her."

"I'm trying! Let her give us Hati back. Let her make sense and come into this room and talk to us face-to-face. It was she I saw in the metal hall, wasn't it? She's flesh and blood like the rest of us. Why won't she come here to talk?"

"Will she be safe, she asks."

"I swear she'll be safe. Just let her leave you alone." He wiped a strand of hair from Norit's cheek. "Luz! Do you hear me?"

Somewhere a door opened. Theirs closed. He looked up from over Norit's head.

"We're locked in," Norit said in a faint voice.

"We've *been* locked in," he said. "This whole damned place locks us in." He thought of Hati, who never but in the Beykaskh itself had experienced a roof. He thought of Hati shut in a little room, with no way out.

"She says . . ." Norit whispered. "She says . . . I should say exactly these words, and you have to listen."

"I'm listening."

"We have to go back. You promised the Ila to go back, and we have to. We have to tell the Ila . . . we have to tell the Ila . . ."

Suddenly the walls of the room went black, and the vision of the stars spread itself all across them. Norit cried out. Marak held to her; and suffered a vision of stars lit with lightning.

The tower rode that blue-glowing fire to the ground, and reached out arms and dug into the earth, substantial as a mountain, on a plain of glass.

And they still sat on a pale, foreign bed, clinging to one another.

"*The beginning,*" a voice said from above them. "*Your beginning. The First Descended.*"

Marak leapt up, but all around him was the desert, limned square, on the walls, a moving image with neither wind nor smell, and square-cornered.

From the tower, walkers went out across the desert.

Vision blurred, and caravans plied their trade, and all seemed ordinary.

"Do you see it?" he asked Norit, who had stayed seated on the bed. Her face said yes before she nodded and half hid her face in her hands.

"*The tower of the Beykaskh,*" the voice said.

He turned slowly and Norit turned, until they saw the tower again, set against the red, saw-toothed upthrust of the Qarain.

Had they come a circle? Was that where they had come, after all their journey? Were they within the Beykaskh?

That tower stood, and the vision rose up on wings like the birds of the air and turned until he swayed on his feet and Norit leapt up and held to him for her own balance.

The tower became domed, and they swooped down at the level of the sand, dizzied, and powerless to stop the rush of vision.

The tower put forth walls, and the walls rose up, and the dome rose, and the walls shone with the sun.

"*From this,*" their voice said, Luz said, "*all else comes.*"

The Beykaskh suddenly poured out the Mercy of the Ila, and the Mercy of the Ila formed the reed-rimmed pool as he had seen it, but subtly changed.

Creatures like the beshti, but not, drank there, and he saw into the water, and saw moving creatures, and saw spirals and dots and chains, and them composed of smaller and smaller chains, and finally of small structures, not like the structures he had seen built of fire.

These structures were dots, only dots of colors, and they changed and multiplied, and faded into larger things, and larger, and larger, and larger, threatening, and enveloping, until he saw the dots become small packets, and those packets become rows, and those rows become sheets, and those sheets become the skin of a man, and his ear, and his face, and his head and his body. He had no idea why this vision so terrified him, but the rapid shifts had made him both dizzy and afraid.

"These are the makers," Luz said. *"The Ila understands. Now you know what she knows. The makers flowed out into the pool and the beasts she had brought drank, and bred, and changed as the Ila directed. The beasts changed, and men changed to fit this land. Doesn't your scripture say that she divided the beasts from the vermin?"*

"I know nothing about it," Marak retorted, because none of it made sense at all, and he cared nothing about it, only for escaping this place and taking Norit and Hati with him. It was not the act of friends to try to awe him with such a show. "I don't believe in the scriptures or the priests. And if you want anything from us, open the doors. Bring the walls back. Give us Hati back. And the au'it."

"This was five hundred thirty-eight years ago," Luz said, *"when she created the pool and sent out this new breed of men, under priests she instructed. This was five hundred thirty-eight years ago when the First Descended took this world and hid from their enemies."*

There was a new thread. "What enemies?" he asked.

"Enemies her predecessors made. She found a desert and transformed it. She sent out the makers and by them she fitted her creation to survive. She set up the priests to teach a history she wrote. As far as the priests' god exists, she is that god, and the devil of your belief is her enemy. Both are false. But we're

not here to argue philosophy. We're here to save as much as we can save, before her enemy destroys this creation of hers. You are a resource to us, a threat to them, and we've won a reprieve: we've won this world, we've won the chance to save you, if you'll only listen. That's why we've called you here . . . to save your lives."

It was too much to swallow at one taking. All around him, within his arms, was the evidence of intentions not as benign as the promise. And all his knowledge a lie? He refused to fall down and worship their truth, either.

"What do you think of us, Marak Trin Tain? Do you want to listen?"

"I'll listen," he said. "You keep your damned hands off us. And bring Hati here!"

The sunlight grew on the walls, and whitened, and the vision was done. He found Norit's trembling had spread to his own limbs. Nothing he knew was true? Where did lies start and stop?

The door whisked open. He expected a monster. He saw instead a perfectly ordinary woman, in house clothes, without a robe, like a prostitute. She had no definite age. With robes, she might have been a baker, a potter, a weaver. But she was very, very pale. Only the Ila had such skin.

The Ila, and, he guessed, Luz.

"Marak," Luz said in her own voice, and with an accent neither westerly nor easterly, only mildly strange. "Norit." This with a nod to his companion, who clung trembling to his arms.

"So what do you want?" Marak asked. He held Norit close, and then on a second thought, put her apart from him. He had drawn the Ila's lightning. He might draw this woman's: he expected it, because he was not in a mood to bow down, with Hati unaccounted for. "One thief calls the other a liar. What does it mean to the man who's lost his silver?"

"Bad news," Luz said. "The Ila could tell you, but she erased all the records five hundred years ago. The Ila settled here, where she had no right to settle. Her enemies have found her, they've set about to wipe this earth clean of life, and we've argued that we can unmake her makers and create benign ones. There, do you understand it?"

"I understand you want something from us, and I doubt you're telling more truth than the Ila does."

"Are you willing to die for her sake?"

"No, I'm not willing to die. No more than the rest of us."

"Yet you promised to go back to her."

"I've reason."

"So you will go."

"I may."

"You might save no few lives if you did. But I warn you that you may lose your own. There's safety here, and if you leave it, you run a risk of not getting back in time. It's moments before the destruction."

"And this is a safe place?"

"It will remain safe. Her enemies have agreed. They let us be here, to work out this problem."

"Problem," he scoffed.

"Not that we don't share it, Ian and I. We've agreed to be down here. We've agreed not to leave this place, ever. That's no small thing."

"Down here. Where is *here*?"

"On this world, so to speak. This earth. This patch of land. You're on a round world circling a star, Marak Trin Tain. That's knowledge she took from your grandfather's grandfathers."

"Does it matter?" He disbelieved anything she offered. "Does it matter, except that I get out of here with the people I walked in with?"

"Direct and to the point. I know your reputation. I can see why you got here. Dare I believe you're one who might get back?"

"I'm supposed to tell the Ila what I find here."

"Tell her. Perhaps she'll want to come here."

The Ila, travel across the desert? Join madmen?

"She won't."

"Don't be so sure. I'll send you with a message. She may hear it."

"What message?"

"The same she sent to me."

There was a flaw in the woman's omniscience. Slight as it seemed, he leapt on it, took perverse satisfaction in that flaw. "She sent you nothing. She doesn't even know you exist."

"Oh, but she did send, all the same. She doesn't know *what* I am, but she sent you to find that out. Her message is that she understands what we've done, she understands it's challenged her creation, she understands her makers have failed against ours, and take it for granted that she's tried to cure the mad. But she can't. She's gathered all the visions. She knows their meaning. She knows someone is here, and by the fact we've beaten her makers, she has an idea who we are. But she wants to know what we mean to do, and why, and that's what you're to tell her."

"What do you mean to do?"

"Gather survivors. Keep them alive. And when the *ondat* change this world so that nothing she's loosed will survive, we'll set new makers loose, ones the *ondat* will approve."

"The *ondat*."

"Her enemies."

"And our lives?"

Luz was silent a breath or two, then: "I regret risking them again. But if there's one power that can call the rest to shelter, it won't be a handful of madmen urging the village lord to come here. She can call them. Her priests can. We couldn't make war on her: her hold is too secure. But we can use her influence over her own creation. The god of this world can bring us the people and save their lives. But you're almost too late . . . if you're not too late already. I can direct you. I can talk to you and I can talk to the *ondat* and I may secure you a safe course, but not if they know I'm bringing the Ila herself to safety. It's a risk."

"Then why do you take such a risk?"

"She's not as innocent as the rest of you—she wasn't the one who poured out makers on an *ondat* world, not one of that company, but she was part of it. Her worst sin was to save lives . . . your lives. She took this place for a refuge. But politics—" Luz shook her head. "Five hundred years of argument about your fate, and you've threatened no one. She's threatened no one. She can't leave. We've persuaded the *ondat* to this compromise: that they may change this world so the makers are forced to change, but we may moderate that change: we can remove the threat and assure the *ondat* we can stop it. Her cooperation would make our work easier. Say that. Tell her I'll make her welcome. Tell her there is an escape, a narrow one, and the window may close before she can take it, even as it is. We were given thirty years, and those years were up when the Ila sent us this unexpected gift. She knows that we've loosed new makers. Tell her to listen to you, and listen to me, and come to the tower while there's still time."

"With the mad? The Ila of Oburan, to live with the mad?"

"Oh, very much so," Luz said. "One needs not erase history. One needs only fail to teach one generation of children. Fail with two, and the destruction widens. She may deserve her damnation for what she has done, but it was done, perhaps, to keep you content with what limited things she could give. To make you her good servants. And keep you alive, for company."

The land circling a star and wars with some tribe named the *ondat,* and dots and creatures let loose in their very blood. He had had nature to explain the world that was, but he had never understood why nature was what it was, either. He had never understood the vermin, or where men came from, except what the priests said, that the First Descended dropped down from the heavens and divided beasts from vermin.

"Where are the *ondat*?" he asked.

"Up above, where you can't reach them. Believe this: that you threaten the peace. It's not the land you have. The enemy doesn't care about that. It's that *you* exist according to the Ila's plan, and that the Mercy of the Ila continues to pour out makers; useless, we say, since you've overburdened the land as it is, and never will be more than you are, but it's your existence, all the same, that prolongs the war. You loosed makers on *their* world. They don't forget that. They wish you dead."

He understood everything down to *their world*. He had no idea where that was. But he understood revenge. He understood it was useless to plead against it, and he knew that survival required allies.

"They gave us thirty years," Luz said, "to loose our own makers, and to gather our people and our goods and our records, before this world changes into what it will be. Thirty years ago we set to work. Thirty years ago we went out across the Lakht and into the villages, such as we could reach. We loosed new makers, in your blood, and they set to work, and enabled you to hear us, and brought a great many to us. Then the Ila, as you call her, gave us this final gift, in you. So we send you back to her with a message. A last chance. That's all you need to know."

"To come here. Because you ask her to."

"I'll give you a word: *nanocele*. There. Does that tell you all you need?"

He was stung. He knew when he was being mocked. And when someone he could not fight was waiting for that admission. "It tells me nothing."

"So I can't tell you more than that, can I? I don't force you to go back. But if you do go, tell her the answers are all here, and refuge is here, for anyone she can bring. We never planned for her to come. But if we had her records, her knowledge, her memory, we could do very much more."

As if the Ila should come here, and lift one manicured finger to bargain. Norit had put her arms about him. He put his about her.

"You made us mad," he said to Luz. "You did this. Why should we believe anything? What do we care about nanoceles?"

Darkness flooded his sight, and an object spinning out of darkness toward a shining distant globe. That object went falling, and falling, in fire, and suddenly he was looking up at that fall, across the blue heavens, and toward the Qarain. Norit cried out. He flinched.

A star. Was that a falling star?

"Say that I give you a new vision," Luz said. "And there will be more. The thirty years are up. I would have said there was no hope. That we had gathered all who could survive to reach us. But since you were ours, and since at the last moment we knew you had gone to the Ila, we had far more hope."

"Who told you?"

"Your own voice. The things you heard. Oh, we didn't know who Marak Trin was, not until you made war on the Ila. We doubted from the beginning you would succeed. We feared on the other hand you might disrupt everything. We lent you our advantages, still; the makers assured you would heal, and live. We can call in those who hear our voice: but you refused to hear us. So we thought we wouldn't have you, after all. Thanks to her, we do, and we have all of those you brought. But *she* can send out messengers to the tribes and the villages. She can bring all of Oburan with her, if you can persuade her and bring her here—her, and her records. Bring those."

He still was shaken, dizzied by the feeling of falling with the star. The things Luz said involved a simple act, but the reason behind it defied understanding, and his suspicion, old as his understanding of the world, said not to trust this.

"The world's going to end, Marak Trin. But this place will survive." Luz walked to the door. "It's this simple: you can stay here, or you can go back and rescue all you can."

"To what good?"

"To all the good there is," Luz said. "Or will ever be. If you choose to go, if the danger becomes too great, you can turn back. We won't refuse you. Understand: you come very late. I'm not sure you'll get there at all, or that you'll get back with anything more than yourselves—if you're very lucky. The *ondat* have waited thirty passes of this world around its star. I expected the attack to begin twenty days ago."

"Have we weapons?"

"No weapons. No fighting. Only a safe place. When people run for their lives, a few more may run here. Pori might make it here, by accident. For the rest . . . they'll die. And as for the Ila, oh, I assure you your Ila understands what we are. That's why she's sent you. She wants to know what the terms are, whether she can defeat our makers, and by that, whether she has a hope. If you choose to go, tell her we've reached an agreement with the *ondat*: we may reshape what the hammer fails to break. The world will so change that her design will not survive. But I can save her. She established this as a camp on the way to the *ondat* world, but she never attacked them. There is forgiveness. We can arrange it."

It was too vast to understand. There was no reason that this ordinary woman could stand here and convince him of these things. But what was there to believe?

"Can we save the people with me?"

"They're already safe, camped outside. We will protect them."

"And Kais Tain? And the villages?"

"I've told you. The time is already up. The time you have is what you can steal. Every hour you stand arguing is an hour taken from their survival. If she calls in the villages, can't she call more in her name, than you in yours?"

It was true.

But there was no fairness about this attack. There was no logic, no reason, no justice in anything she said about the world.

Yet she said this was the appointed refuge from what was coming, whatever it was.

"Where's Hati?" he asked her.

"Nearby. She can go where she wishes. Anyone here can go where he wishes."

"And the au'it?"

"May also choose." Luz had her hand on the door, and the door opened. "It's not all darkness. If nothing kills you outright, the makers will help you live long enough to have a fair chance. Go tell the Ila, or stay here while the hammer falls. Take the au'it, or send her alone. It's all your choice."

"The au'it would never get there by herself."

"Likely not," Luz said, and walked out, leaving the door open.

He left Norit and went to the door. Luz was halfway down the metal hall of suns. He knew nothing to say. In just that long, Luz had turned everything upside down, and then begun to reiterate everything she said, so he knew they were at an end.

"Hati!" he shouted to that vacancy. His temper had risen. Now his fear did.

There were other doors all along the hall, all closed.

Luz opened the door at the end of the hall and went out. "Hati!"

A door opened on its own, far down the hall.

Hati came through it, clothed in fine cloth as they were. She saw them, and began to run. Marak caught her in his arms, crushed her lean, hard body against him, smelling what was incontrovertibly Hati, and having in his arms all he needed in the world.

"Where have you been?" he asked.

"In this place," Hati said. "In this room. The air never moved. And I saw dark, I saw one thing falling into another. I thought *I* was falling. I met a woman named Luz. She said the world would die, but we could be safe, or we could go back to Oburan and bring the rest here."

"So she said."

"You saw her?"

"Do you trust her?" he asked Hati. Not, Do you believe her? That was one question. But, Do you trust her? That was another. Staying in this claimed safety more than tempted him: it seemed the only sane answer in a mad, death-bound world, the only just answer for Hati, and Norit, and Tofi.

But not for him. He had a mother, a sister, a father, all resting on his promise to come back. He had the memory of villages, and the people he had known, and no few he had grown up with. And he had the word of a stranger and the promise of an enemy, and he was mad as the rest, but he knew what he could live with, and what he could not, right or wrong or fair to Hati, he could not stay.

"I don't *trust* strangers," Hati said. "I don't trust *her.*"

"I have to go back. I'm supposed to rescue the god-cursed

Ila." He had no clear notion in his mind what he would do, or how he would do it, except to retrace their steps, walk into the Ila's hall, and say a woman crazier than he was had sent a message that would not make her happy. Mad as it was, the urgency loomed taller and taller, like the vision of the tower. "I have to. I have to. I said I would come back. She said she'd save my mother and my sister for a year. I don't know if she'll keep her word. But I know I have to."

Hati's embrace tightened, hard, harder. "Do you know a way out of this place?" she asked.

He thought he knew. It was a sense of direction, like knowing where north was, if he wondered about it. There was a door in the other direction, and he turned toward it, one arm around Hati, the other about Norit. He thought about the au'it, and whether she might join them on their way out, and at a crossing of the next hall, the au'it came out, in her own red robes, but clean, head to toe. She held her book and her writing kit as she joined them, and walked with them quickly as far as the end of the hallway, and another door.

That door opened without warning. Ian was behind it.

"Are you looking for the door?" Ian asked. "Follow me."

It was not a welcome presence. But Ian led them to the next door, and touched it to make it open.

Outside was the world and the sunlight, a pale blue sky, and red dunes and sandstone, going on forever.

Outside was a camp of white tents at the foot of the glass-strewn hill on which the tower stood.

Marak paid no attention to Ian as they left, and Ian said no further word to them. Marak heard the door shut behind them, and he felt the hot familiar wind in their faces as they walked down to the tents, faster and faster, with mounting desire to be there, and not at the tower.

"It's Tofi," Marak said. He knew the beasts that sat comfortably by those strange white tents: he knew the baggage piled up there. Two tents were pitched, white and looking as if they could have nothing to do with the red rock and the dust.

And from under those open-sided tents the mad came out to welcome them, all the madmen clothed in gauze robes the same as they were, waving, happy, cheering their safe return.

"Malin," Hati said in astonishment as they came down the hill. "That's Malin." Kassan and Foragi were there, too, the ex-soldiers. They had made it here, against all expectation.

Tofi came, running. His robe was green-striped brown, a blue aifad, his own, as every stitch about him was his own: the others, destitute, took gifts, but Tofi put on his best, and Marak was glad at the sight of him.

"They said you were well," Tofi said, as they met and clasped hands. "But I said they should let you go. This strange man came to us. There's plenty of water here, and people, people from all over . . ."

The others clustered around them as they came downhill. "Where have you been?" the questions ran. "What have you seen?"

"Lights," Marak found to say to them. "A woman." There were the new visions, and if the other madmen shared them there was no hint of it. The faces were happy, and their enthusiasm carried them along, all talking at once.

"We have these clothes, and no end of food and water."

"We can wash. We can even wash in it."

"And fruits," the orchardman put in, "with not a blemish on them."

"The tents cool the air," the stonemason said. "This is the god's paradise."

They went down among those tents, in this babble of strangers and new clothes, and out from the shade under the white tents flowed an unnaturally cool air. Tables stood within the shade of one tent, the tent wholly devoted to that purpose, and on those tables sat a ravaged wealth of food.

Wealth and water had poured out on the madmen, the rejected of the world. *Their* visions had brought them only good, that Marak saw. He looked back and up at the foot of the tower, which was so large, and which to his own observation held only Ian and Luz.

So much wealth to give away.

Paradise, the stonemason said.

But was it? Where was the orchard to provide this? There must be far more to all that tower than they had been allowed to see. There must be answers they had never had, questions they had not had the least idea how to ask.

And there were the visions, and the explanations that roused more questions. *Death,* was Luz's message.

"They gave us food and water at no cost," Tofi exalted their hosts, "and these clothes, and as much food as we want, they give. Eat. Take anything." Tofi took bread from the table to show them. "Whatever we eat, they give us more. It never spoils. No vermin come here."

"How many of these strangers have you seen?" he asked Tofi.

"That bring the food and visit us? People like us. They come from all over, from Pori, too, and from the tribes. Malin and Kassan and Foragi are here, did you see them? They don't remember how they found this place. They waked up here, under a white tent."

All the mad. All those that wandered away from the villages, fed, and clothed, and kept in safety—if they survived the desert.

He was overwhelmed, surfeited with this babble of good fortune. Hati and Norit were beset with questions and details of the wealth here, the au'it sat down and opened her book to record these wonders, and in a sudden need for escape, Marak walked out into the heat of the sun, where their beasts sat, well fed and supplied, by a pool of water that had no right to be where it was.

The sun warmed his shoulders. He walked where a multitude of feet had tracked the sand, and he climbed the sandstone slant to gain a vantage and a breath of the world's own sun-heated wind.

He had to ask himself and his demons what he ought to do with Luz's warning, what was truth, what was safe, what was a mirage that killed the fools that believed it . . . that was what he sought, simple solitude, on the safety of an often-used trail.

But as he climbed he saw a gleam of white, and a wider and a wider gleam, the other side of the rise on which the tower sat. A city of white canvas spread across the sand.

White tents. Shelter. People. A green-bordered river of water, shaded by palms.

He sat down. He did not even remember doing it. He simply sat and stared at that sight with shock spreading through him like the cold out of the tents.

Steps sounded behind them, so ordinary he failed to question them. Hati came and sat down, and after that Norit, and then the au'it, too, came and sat down by him. None of them spoke for a long time, looking at that sight, that clear evidence that Luz at least had told a part of the truth.

He could not leave this vision untested. He got up and began walking down the slant of the sand that rose up against the sandstone, down a well-trodden path that led him down to the level of those orderly white tents. Hati followed, and Norit and the au'it trailed them both, all the way to the edge of the encampment, where a green-banked pool stood. Beshti wandered at liberty at some distance around the pool, halterless, seeming to belong to no one. Children ran and played, and splashed in the water.

The children stopped and stared. In their gift-robes, they looked like everyone else in sight, but the au'it with them did not. When they walked by and into the rows of tents, people stopped their work and stared.

The people were like the people of any village. There was a potter at work, a weaver. There were all these ordinary activities.

"Where are you from?" Marak asked a potter, and with a clay-caked hand the potter indicated himself and several adults around him.

"From La Oshai," the potter said with an anxious glance at the au'it. It was a village in the northwest. "My wife is from Elgi." That was on the western edge of the Lakht. "We met here.—Where are you from?"

"Kais Tain," Marak said. He walked farther, with Hati and Norit, and the au'it trailing them. He asked names. He asked origins. The whole place was a mingling, and as far as he could tell it went on and on.

"The hammer will fall," one weaver said suddenly, after naming his village. "This is the only safe place. This is the only place."

"Are you happy here?" Norit asked, and the man's overly anxious smile faded.

"I wish my wife would come. I wish I could go out there and tell her."

"Can't you?" Marak asked.

"I don't know the way," the man said.

It was the only unhappiness they had met face-to-face; and it was too painful, and brought back what Luz had said, that everyone who was not here would be under attack, and no one could save them.

Marak turned and walked away, out under the heat of the sun, and walked back to the pool and up toward the ridge, Hati and Norit and the au'it in his tracks.

He had become a void, a sheet of sand on which nothing at all was written.

The unfortunate man down among the tents, a weaver, had no idea of directions. Perhaps he had followed a vision to get here. He had none to take him home to his wife.

Marak climbed the steep sand to the ridge and looked back on wealth greater than he had ever imagined, on green-edged water, on the white, cooling tents, hundreds of them, and hundreds of individuals ripped up from their lives and set down in paradise . . . but it was a paradise without loved ones. All the villages, all the city, all the tribes had no warning, no knowledge of Luz and this place.

The hammer will fall, he heard in his head, and all at once the vision came, the rock and the shining sphere.

Marak, it said. *Marak, Marak,* the old refrain, the old restlessness. Peace here had no comfort.

"I have to go back," he said to Hati and to Norit and the au'it. "The madness won't stop for me. I have to go. I have to report what's here. My mother and sister, that man's wife . . . who's to tell *them,* if I don't go?"

He walked away down the slope, recklessly downhill toward their own camp, and under the white tent, Hati and Norit with him, still trying to follow: he could not shake them with a declaration of madness. The au'it, too, fell in with them as they went, a small force that knifed straight to the heart of their small camp. He expected to be alone. He *wanted* to be alone in his folly.

Tofi was there, with a costly cup in his hand, and lifted it cheerfully. "So you've seen the sight from the ridge. They say we'll join the rest. Perhaps we were waiting for you. Sit, sit down and drink."

"I need two beasts," Marak said, "mine, and two pack beasts, irons, and canvas." He was more and more sure of his choice, however much it hurt. He had led the mad and the lost to safety; and with the alarm Luz had set seething inside him, and the voices dinning in his ears, he could not stay here, grazing on provided fodder like the beasts. He was never made to sit and fold his hands and ask for sweet fruit to land on the table.

But going? Luz wanted his unquestioning acceptance, his absolute belief; and his own father had never gotten that from him. Who were Ian and Luz to ask it?

The cup had stopped in its course from Tofi's lips, and hesitated: Tofi lowered it to his knee, immediately sober. "Where are you going?"

"Back," he said, and Tofi looked dismayed. "Back to Oburan."

"With no guide?"

"I know the stars," he said. "I can find my way." He was aware of Hati and Norit, standing near him, but they said nothing. He left Tofi, having informed him what he was taking, and went out to find Osan among the idle beasts.

He led him back toward the place where the saddles were stacked, supported on their untouched baggage.

Hati walked from that place, as he was arriving. She carried her saddle in one arm and hauled Norit's in the other hand. Norit walked behind.

"Where do you intend to go?" he asked.

"To Oburan," Hati said. "Norit, too. Where are *you* going?"

He stood wordless for a moment. Then he shrugged, with a tightness in his throat. "I suppose to Oburan."

Hati went to find her beast and Norit's. That was that.

He found his saddle, and set out three of the pack saddles, and chose a bundled tent he knew was their own, and water-skins, still filled with Pori's water.

Tofi came and brought the slaves.

"One tent," Marak said to him. It was Tofi's property he proposed to take, but he saw no reason for Tofi to deny him the use of what lay for the most part unused, unnecessary in paradise.

"You're going to Oburan, you say."

"Yes," Marak said. "Hati and Norit, too, and the au'it will go. One tent. Five, six beasts."

Tofi frowned and looked at the horizon and at him as if he prepared to bargain. "I'm a fool," Tofi said with a sigh. "But my father told the Ila he would come back. He won't give me peace otherwise. He's a cursed stubborn old man. So are my brothers."

Tofi spoke of them as if they were still alive, and gazed into an empty horizon, but perhaps saw something in it. There was more than one kind of madness.

"The people in the tower say world is ending," Marak said. "And we have to warn everyone else."

"We've heard that," Tofi said.

"I see it," Marak said. "Hati, and Norit, and I, we all three see it."

Tofi shrugged. "I don't. But *I'm* not mad."

"Then stay here. This place will be safe. They say so, at least." This with a glance toward the tower. "They'll let you stay. You don't have to be one of us."

"Maybe not," Tofi said, "but I'm not one of this batch, either. I'm scared. I don't say I'm not. But there's nothing here for me until I finish this trek. I keep hearing the old man . . . like your voices. He says, 'Get up, get up, get up, boy. You're not done here.' He's ashamed of me. If there's anyone going back to finish the contract, and I don't, I know him: he'll give me no peace."

Rock hit shining sphere, again, and again, and again.

Marak blinked, feeling an inward chill. "You may die. The people in the tower say there's some calamity already on its way, whatever it is. We may not make it to the city, let alone back again."

"That's all right," Tofi said. "Everyone else is dead." He was still grieving, and the grief broke through for a moment in a tremor of his chin. "I'll do it, I say. Then my father will shut up."

"Five of us, then," Marak said.

"Seven," Tofi said. "The slaves are my father's. Now they're mine. I won't ride off and leave them. They owe me. They owe me their wretched *lives*. They'll damned well pay their debt, wherever we end up."

11

The Ila neither ages nor suffers illness: from her all life flows, and life and health is her gift to those who keep her law.
—The Book of Priests

Tofi argued with the slaves. He cajoled, he raised a quirt, he threatened

"Pack up," Tofi said. "You're fools here. You haven't a trade, you don't have relatives." That availed nothing. "I'll free you when we get to Oburan," Tofi said. "You'll be freedmen when you come back."

There was no movement.

"Damn you, I'll pay you wages when you're free!"

The slaves looked at one another, then began to get up, one and the other. "Move!" Tofi said, and they moved, and went to work.

They took all the beshti, all Tofi's goods. The beasts complained about being roused out for service, but not beyond the ordinary. They were well rested and well watered, and had eaten all they wished for the several days of their sojourn here. Gorging to their bellies' contentment and moving on was the sum of what they did all their lives, and now the packs were lighter, the gear distributed out over those beasts that had no riders, by the simple change of running two deep-irons through saddle rings and lashing them down. The loads they made were so light that for a besha's strength, it was as if they carried no weight at all.

The mad turned out to stare at the process. Some of them, understanding where they were going, even professed a thought of going with them.

But after all was said and settled, to a man, they chose the rich tables and the promise of safety. Only as the seven of them rode away, their former companions lined the cool edge of the tent, waving, calling out well-wishes to them. One, Maol, one of Tofi's two women, ran out to offer them fresh fruit for their journey and to shed tears at the parting. "Thank you," she said. "Thank you for our lives."

But the rest simply stood back to watch them go, as much as if to say that of all the mad, they counted their former guides the most afflicted.

Beyond the tents the beasts stretched out fully into that natural walk that could eat up so much ground a day. The slaves rode hindmost, loaded with food, which they ate with abandon, no one forbidding it. They had more than enough water to reach Pori, they had food enough for their whole journey: they had all Tofi's wealth of tents.

The weather held fair.

That noon when they camped, they pitched only a single tent, heated water for tea and a good supper, and left the rest of the baggage packed and ready to put up on the beasts. The au'it wrote and wrote, seldom looking up, such was her haste and her concentration.

The sky was the brightest of blues, clear of dust. The wind was gentle, but enough to move beneath the canvas. If the world threatened to end, still, the day seemed uncommonly good, and peaceful, and lacking all desperation.

The time was already up, Luz had said, and Norit had heard it. Yet perhaps the tower-dwellers were fallible in their knowledge, or simply lying, to trap all the others in this paradise.

If there was anyone who might know, Marak said to himself, the Ila might know what the truth of things was. There *should* be an answer, beyond folding the hands and sitting down under the white tents.

The world to be snuffed out? Extinguished by some nameless enemy? This *ondat*? And they should give it up with no more than Luz's saying so?

He did not accept it. He refused to accept it. But try to save it, that he would.

He lay beside Hati and Norit and found his eyes shutting. He had not truly slept, not a natural sleep, and now it came on him irresistibly, like a drug.

Then he heard the voices, saying, *Marak, hurry. Hurry, Marak.* He had no strength to open his eyes. The vision came like nightmare.

Objects struck one another, impact repeated itself over and over and over. He rode the falling object down and down, and the sphere became land, and desert, and the desert plumed up like a fountain of sand and billowed up like a cloud that raced over the land, over dunes and villages.

Came a new vision: water flowed in the desert, over rocks burned black. A stream coursed, cascaded. He could hear it dripping, flowing, gurgling down the rocks and into a broad expanse of water that swelled, swelled, swelled.

He could see his father's house, in Kais Tain, all of mud brick, sprawling around deep-floored gardens and wells that made that sound, that wonderful, rich sound of water that the dream made fearsome.

He visited his own rooms, and heard the women laughing as they prepared food for the house: there was always plenty laid out. There were always children.

He could see the stable yard, and the beasts he loved; and his little sister Patya fed Osan with her hand. She had to learn to flatten her hand, or lose fingers. She laughed at Osan's questing lip. That laughter haunted him, and reminded him not all was well with that house, these days.

He could not see his mother, or his father. He searched the house for them.

The rocks above the house spilled down a dependable amount of water in every season, and the spring flowed from there down to a second well house. From there it went to the garden, which all the village tended. Each house had its own tree and its own vines, and everyone knew which was which, and whose grew best. The householders shared such secrets, and were generous with their surplus, beyond what they needed. The village was fed before it sold the excess. It was the custom.

The great house, too, had its vines and its bushes in a garden apart, and a few slaves tended them, freedmen on the house records, but they liked their work in the garden too well and their freedom was to do the work they loved. He learned that lesson from those men and women, that so long as they could not own the garden, their best way to be happy was to work in it for reasonable reward and a share of the fruit. They were richer than the Ila in her palace, wise in their own domain, respected throughout the village for their advice and their competence.

But they had no governance beyond their garden . . . and no power over its fate.

Tain, on the other hand, was born to power. Tain had to keep his holdings by force, fighting against those who wished to take the food from people's mouths, fighting against bandits and the Ila's taxmen; and so he fought, and so the villagers and people of the district fought at his command. Some died, and left widows and children who, but for Tain's upkeep, were helpless. And in the end Tain cast out his wife and his son.

Perhaps after all it was better to be those freed slaves, content with the vines and each other's company. They enjoyed as much as they wished of the fruit . . . and that was better than many had as daily fare. They were assured of beds, and knew every day what they had to do, which was to prune the vines and tend the trees. Every year of their lives was like the last.

That was the life of the mad at the tower, to have tables spread with every good thing, and to work only at need. The inhabitants of the white tents carried the names of villages with them. They brought their crafts and practiced them. They married and begat and might see their children grow.

But whence came the laws, and who made the food, and how long would it come so easily, if destruction came?

At the pleasure of Luz and Ian, how long would they eat as well and have everything their hearts desired?

He waked with a hard-beating heart and a remote, guilty regret for not urging more of the mad to come with them. Paradise was not enough for him. Not enough for Norit and Hati, not enough for Tofi, either, as it seemed. Least of all for the au'it, whose whole devotion was to the Ila.

But what was enough? What would be enough to give him peace of these dreams, these voices, this driving necessity to do, and escape, and move?

In the late afternoon they packed up in a very little time and rode on through the night at that same ground-devouring pace. By noon they camped.

Marak, Marak, Marak, the voices said, as if discontent at his stopping. The voices he heard during the day all sounded like Luz, until while they were setting up the tent he put his hands over his ears, trying not to hear; and squeezed his eyes until they flashed with red, trying not to see.

We have to sleep, he raged at Luz. He wished her to understand, to have some comprehension she was driving him beyond endurance, but Luz gave no sign of hearing him.

Water will fall from heaven, Luz told him, as he tossed and turned, attempting to sleep.

Hati waked and put an arm about him, and after that he tried not to move, but the voices kept up.

"Do you hear voices?" he asked Hati.

"Yes," Hati whispered back. "I hear promises. And threats. I think it's Luz. What kind of place has just two people, and it so huge? It never made sense."

Norit, meanwhile, slept. Marak hugged Hati against him and tried to sleep, but he rose early, while the sun was still hot, and roused Tofi and the slaves out to get under way.

The beasts grumbled. Tofi grumbled not having had all their sleep. *Haste, haste, haste,* the voices said. Luz tormented them with threats, with visions, with promises: Norit suffered, too, and her eyes looked weary and worried.

They came to that rising of the land that led up to the Lakht, and to the path on the slope where they had lost the one beast.

"That's where the besha fell," Tofi said, pointing. "That's our trail."

They looked up, but nothing remained up on the shale where it had fallen, not a bone, not a scrap of cloth or a remnant of the saddle. Of vermin there was no other sign. They ate, and they dispersed . . . might have fought among themselves. The survivors would be sated. The crumbling rock gave no hint of past violence, only a single trail of bright reflection on the slope where broken shale marked the fatal slide.

They had arrived on the ascent by midmorning, as they hoped. They dismounted and led their beasts up, and climbed with caution: whoever had made the fragile path down off the Lakht, likely Pori's hunters, had somewhat compacted the fragile rock, and their own passage had compacted it further, but it was steep and narrow, no place for a misstep, and one beast tended to rush up behind the beast higher up.

The slaves below, hindmost, were not helping. "Fools!" Tofi called out, looking back, and risked his life, descending the trail side to hold back one beast until the one ahead had vacated a foothold for it.

They made the crest. They were on the Lakht. Tofi, bedraggled and dusty, came up last. "I said get before them!" Tofi shouted at the slaves. "I said hold the line back! I said be a *gateway*, not an open door! Shall I free fools? How will you make a living in the world?"

The slaves were chagrined, and hung their heads; but it came to Marak with sudden force that Tofi believed the world would go on, and that he himself went on believing it, at heart . . . while if Luz was right there would be no continuation, no order of life such as they knew—

If Luz was right. If she was, then Tofi's promises were a mirage, Tofi's promises, his beliefs . . . all mirage, all blind faith. After a rest full of nightmares and visions it came to him like a blow to the heart, and for an instant the question devastated him: *How will you make a living in the world?*

How would they deal with a changed desert, and this enemy, and Luz's protection.

What would he say to the Ila if he could reach her?

Is Luz telling the truth? That would be the first thing.

To find his mother and get her into his hands . . . that was where he was going.

But for what? For what better life?

He sat down on a convenient flat shelf of rock, and tried not to find deeper answers. He had to rest; they all had to rest. The beasts were weak-legged from the climb, and sat down under their burdens. It was no time for prolonged thinking. It could only lead to despair.

"We should pitch the tent," Tofi came to him to say. "We have plenty of water, no lack of food. The sun is not quite at noon, but it makes sense to stop."

Did it? Did it, when Luz said it might already be too late to carry their message? Despair and urgency wavered back and forth in his brain like chill and fever, an approaching panic.

There was no reason to lame the beasts or drive themselves to collapse: that was no help to them.

"Pitch the tent," Marak said, and resolved on less desperate speed and a steady progress for the days ahead. They would reach Pori in the night, and then expect no more diversions until Oburan, not diverting or stopping for any wells, since they still had sufficient water and a wealth of supplies. They were making good time, having cut two days off their trek already.

They had their supper while the burning light of noon came in under the tent edges. They ate well, even extravagantly, and lay down to sleep.

But in early afternoon, Norit sat up, waking both of them with her sharp gasp.

"We should not go to Pori," she said.

"Not go to Pori," Hati said in amazement, when it was their chief watering stop on the way to the holy city. Marak was half-asleep, having achieved rest, and cudgeled his brain toward coherent action.

"We should not go there," Norit said in a whisper, and seemed to look into the distance, at something not evident to them. "When we bring the rest, we need Pori, but not now. Go north."

Norit was not the one to give them orders. Norit had expressed few opinions, until now. Marak got to one knee and put out a hand and turned her head gently until she did look at him.

"There's no time," she said. "We can't wait. Take the northern trail. Tofi will know."

When did Norit know any trails on the Lakht? "Luz!" he said, and Norit blinked, and took a deep breath.

"Take my advice," Norit said as if she were god-on-earth, and with a lift of her chin. She drew her shoulder from under his hand as if he polluted her with his touch.

Hati had laid a hand on her knife, alarmed; but Marak seized Norit's hand, hard.

"Wake up," he said, and Norit blinked twice, and looked astonished at herself, on the edge of tears.

"Luz spoke through you," Hati said.

"I heard," Norit said, and shivered and ran her fingers into her hair, clenching it, pulling it, self-distraction. "I hear her. I don't want to hear her."

"Damn Luz," he said. "We'll go on to Pori. Never mind what Luz wants."

Norit flashed him a look of terror. "No," Norit said, and pain rushed through him, and through Hati, and through Norit, until pain was all there was, and he was descended to mere creature, wallowing on the ground where he had fallen. Lights flashed in his eyes and pain roared in his ears.

"Listen to advice," Luz said fiercely in that sound, Norit leaning above him with unwonted fierceness. "It's already begun! I can't stop it! Do what I say!"

Pain racked him. He dragged himself up, appalled and angry. He strode out from under the tent, into the sun, and began kicking loose the tent stakes, blindly, even before the slaves had gathered up their goods.

"Wait, wait!" Tofi cried, waving his arms. "What's wrong with her? What's wrong with any of you?"

Marak knew his act was as mad as Norit's. The pain reached his ears and his skull and hammered at him. He spun about, arms wide, looking up at the eye of heaven as if he flew, as if he were bound to nothing but the blue-white air, as if he were caught between the hammer of the sun and the anvil of the earth. He would fling himself down and die before he became utterly mad. He would cast himself off the cliffs before he became a mindless slave to the voices.

"You'll have nothing!" he shouted at the heavens. "*You'll have nothing from me!*"

The pain in his head became pain in his chest and in his spine and in his gut, and the noise in his ears became a light like the sun. He spun and he spun and he spun until he fell.

He lay on the sun-scorched sand, whole, and unbroken.

Luz said, into his ears: *Listen to me. Lives are at risk. It's already begun. Someone will see to Pori. Go north, away from danger.*

Hati dragged his head into her lap, shading him with her body, touching his face with precious water. "Marak. Marak. Wake up. Wake up! Don't leave us."

Don't leave us, don't leave us, don't leave us.

"Marak," Hati said, and fear was in her voice, where fear was a stranger. "Marak, wake up. Do you hear me?"

He could not leave Hati lost. He could not leave Norit possessed of devils, with no one to understand her.

He drew several great breaths and slowly blinked at Hati's shadowed face, against the sunglare. He saw Norit beyond her shoulder, a plain, sweet, woman's face dim to his eyes, wild-haired and bareheaded, haloed by the sun.

He reached back with his hands and pushed himself up, gathered a knee under him with Hati's help and then Tofi's.

He looked dazedly at Norit, wondering if he was looking at the same time at Luz.

But if it was not also Norit within that body, he reasoned, then Norit had no other place to be, and whatever she carried within her, he could not turn on her. He had no power to drive out his own vision. He certainly had no power to condemn hers.

"We will pass by Pori," he said, to Tofi, to Hati, to whoever cared. In that promise, the pressure in his head eased, and Luz grew silent. Tofi had a frightened look.

He staggered upright, staggered as he walked toward the tent to continue ripping up the stakes, still dizzied by his looking at the sun. He was not accustomed to defeat. He burned from the shame of his actions.

And for what, he asked himself, for what reason?

Tofi yelled at the slaves to help, and lent a hand. Together, with Hati and with Norit, all of them helping, they folded the tent and packed it. They loaded the beasts, and roused them to their feet, ready to move.

"This northern way," Marak said to Tofi. "Do you know it?"

"There is a shorter way across the highland," Tofi said. "My father never used it. I can *try* to find it."

Try, in an unforgiving waste. But it seemed to him he knew.

And Luz knew. Luz knew exactly where they were, and where she wanted them to go.

Tofi had a worried look and clearly waited for him to say, No, no, let us go the sane and reasonable passage, but he waited in vain.

"We have guidance," Marak said. He had never been more angry in his life, but never in his life had any man more deserved a plain answer from him than young Tofi. "The woman in the tower speaks to Norit. I don't trust it, but she wants us to go to Oburan. At least we're agreed in that."

"I suppose we have water enough to make mistakes," Tofi said faintly, and shook his head and walked off to mount up.

They set the au'it into the saddle; and helped Norit, who seemed dazed and hesitant: Luz or Norit, it would be Norit's bones that broke, and they roused her besha up and set her securely on it.

The rest of them got up, and Tofi turned them north. Beasts that had anticipated one road and now were turned onto another bellowed their frustration to the skies, as much as to say that they remembered Pori, and fools forgot where the water was.

The complaints gradually faded. The sun sank and vanished in a brassy dusk.

"Look!" Hati said, as a star fell.

They looked aloft for falling stars, then, that sign of overthrow and change, and saw another, and a third and a fourth.

Then a fifth blazed bright, and stuttered a trail of fire across the sky. The beasts saw it in alarm, and their heads swung up.

A seventh and an eighth, as bright, traced a path from horizon to horizon.

Marak had viewed the first falling stars as a curiosity, but now he saw a ninth fall, bright and leaving a trail behind it.

A tenth, and thunder cracked among the stars, making everyone jump, and then laugh, caught in foolish fear.

Everyone had seen falling stars. They happened in the sixth and the eighth month, very many a night, but, Marak said to himself, this was the fourth month, no more than early in the fourth month, at that, and the heavens lit up in bright trails, one after another, interspersed with bright interrupted ones.

Another star fell, this one in a crack of thunder, and shattered in a cloud that blotted out the stars along its track.

"This will continue," Norit said in a tone both cold and assured, and yet trembling with Norit's chin. "This will continue. It will likely miss Pori. But the plain beyond isn't safe."

Now the heavens showed streaks of a star-fall denser than anything Marak had ever seen. At every moment the sky showed another, and another, and another, then five, ten at once, and more and more and more, faster than a man could count.

"Is this the world ending?" Tofi asked. He had his arms folded over his head as he rode, as if that could make him safe from plummeting stars. The slaves cried out in alarm as another of the bright ones came down, and burst in a long trail of fire.

"Keep moving," Norit said, and that new vision came, overwhelming, of rock hurtling into sphere, then a swarm of rocks, again and again and again. "This is the lightest of the fall. This is what will happen, here, and across the world, far worse."

Marak all but lost his balance riding as his eyes revised the scale of those rocks of the vision as equal to the stars above them, careening down in dizzying succession.

And what was the sphere?

"The falling rocks," he said: those were the only words he could find for what he saw, and the import of them he could not measure by any attack he had ever seen. "The spheres."

"The death of all of us," Tofi moaned, hiding his head, and the slaves rode up close to them, pointing at the largest, waiting to die. "Look!" they cried. "Look!" until they ran out of astonishment.

It went on for hours: at times there seemed thousands at once, until the whole heavens were streaked with light, even while the sun was coming up. Norit hugged her arms against herself like a beaten child as she rode, rocking to the besha's gait.

And the sun rose and reached its height.

They reached a flat, and spread the tent, but kept looking toward the white-hot heavens as they hammered home the stakes. They had lost confidence in the sky. It was long before they slept, and waked and exited the tent to break camp as the sky began to shadow.

Another star fell, herald of another such night.

The slaves cried out. The au'it opened her book and recorded the fall. But a second and a third followed.

"Let us be on our way," Marak said to Tofi. "If the heavens fall, what can we do? Let's go."

But now the slaves went about their work with fearful looks at the sky, while the beasts, often reluctant, put up a mindful resistance and bawled and circled away from attempts to load them.

At a great boom out of the sky, the beasts bolted.

"They know they're going to die," the slaves cried. "We're all going to die!"

"I will free you *now!*" Tofi cried. "I will pay you wages *now!* Catch them!"

The slaves took out, running. Hati raced out, caught her own beast, managed to get into the saddle, and rode out and got ahead of the most of the strays, driving them back with blows of her quirt, to Tofi's effusive gratitude. The slaves caught the others and led them back, panting and staggering, too exhausted and too frightened, perhaps, to attempt to ride.

Meanwhile the rain of fire continued in the heavens, and a strange cloud hung where the star had burst.

Marak put Norit up on her beast, and the au'it onto hers. He mounted up on Osan as the slaves struggled with the packs and, with Hati, kept the frightened younger animals in place while the slaves made the older of the pack beasts kneel, and loaded up such of the baggage as waited ready.

Seeing the other beasts sitting calmly under their packs, then, the skittish ones began to kneel on their own, the habit of their kind.

They struck the tent. The rest of the baggage went on.

Then they set themselves under way, under the overthrow of heaven, making all possible speed.

12

In the afternoon sky in the third day of the third cycle of the first season a strange pale light appeared and the sun seemed to set in the east in daylight. The light endured as a sunset and faded as a sunset fades, but pale throughout. The lord of the tribe asked the grandmothers whether the tribe should go to know the source of this light, but it was near calving time and the grandmothers said it was far away and the walk would risk the calves and mothers. The lord of the tribe asked whether they should tell a village, and the grandmothers said the village priest would make trouble for the tribe.
—The Spoken Traditions of the Andesar

The sky whitened into day, and they reached an alkali pan. They had no need to drink, and would not drink of the well that they could dig in this place, not at the most desperate. They simply used the stony flat for a noontime camp, just off the clinging white powder, and the au'it sat and wrote in her book, flicking now and again at windblown white dust that fell on her pages.

The two slaves bickered with Tofi, who swore he had never freed them, that he had only said he might free them if they caught all the beasts, but Marak, seeing unhappiness and surly workers, took the slaves' side. "You did say it. They're free men. Now they have to earn their food."

Neither side liked that completely, and the beasts sat bawling and complaining while Tofi and the slaves, now freedmen, bartered over wages in the hot sun.

"Pay them what you pay any hireling!" Marak said, to end the dispute. "And no more!" He pointed at the au'it and made such a gesture as the Ila herself might make. "Write it! Besides, the world is ending. What does a little extravagance matter?"

The au'it wrote.

It was the first time he had said it in those terms. The slaves fell into silence. Tofi did, and after the beasts were unladed and the tent was up, Tofi on the spot untied a wrapped string and counted out gold rings. "If you have any sense," Tofi muttered to the new freedmen as he did so, "don't spend anything on drink. Buy goods when we get to Oburan and sell them where we're going. You know how it's done. If the world is ending, one can still make a profit. Think of what the white tents *don't* have, buy it cheap as you can and sell *that.*"

"Master," they still called him, when they were happy with him. They went away and compared the rings they had, content, as if the world might, after all, go on.

Marak settled down with Hati and Norit, and, taking some cheer from Tofi's pragmatic wisdom, he stretched himself out to sleep. Meanwhile the au'it, tucked up with her book, settled against the tent pole and unwrapped a new cake of ink: she had written up the old one until there was nothing left but the corners. She sharpened a new pen.

They all were exhausted, after chasing panicked beshti and watching the heavens come down in fragments: they had used deep-irons to tether the beasts this time, and they slept more deeply in that confidence.

Marak, the voices began; and Norit shook at him, and waked him.

There was still ample light. He looked at the angle of the shadows and grimaced, incoherent with sleep, but Norit had waked Hati, too, and then Tofi.

Haste, the voices said, too disquieting for rest. Tofi looked like the risen dead. Hati scowled, and the slaves-now-freedmen moaned and resisted. But they were awake. There was reason, so Marak said to himself, and gathered himself up to his feet, out under a sun only a quarter down the sky and a heat still shimmering on the sand.

It was no good to curse. Norit did as Luz did, and was, herself, exhausted. They struck their sole tent, loaded the beasts, and dug up the stakes, sweating.

Then they began their daily trek to the west, under a sky still too bright for stars. Marak slept, nodding. So Hati did, and Tofi, from time to time, until they acquired a better mood and had some sense of rest. Norit managed: at least her head drooped, and Marak kept an eye on her for fear she might fall off; but she stayed, and waked, and rubbed her eyes, adjusting the aifad to shade them. There was little talk, little to distract them in a monotony of riding.

Hati pointed after a time to something Marak's eye had begun to pick out far to the west, in the sunset, a particularly bright seam of light. But they had no notion, any of them, what that was. The au'it wrote, clutching her book and her pen and her ink-cake despite the lurch of the beast under her, in the absolutely last of the light.

As the sun faded and the stars showed, that glow persisted.

"Like fire," one of the freedmen said. "What's out there to burn?"

None of them knew. In the dark, stars began to fall again, none of the noisy sort, only a steady, gentle, remorseless fall.

"Will they all fall?" Hati asked at last in distress, scanning the heavens as they rode. She pointed at bright Almar. "See, Almar is still up there."

"They are not stars that fall," Norit said. "Almar won't be among them."

"What are they, then?" Marak asked, angry not at Norit, but at Luz. "What are they? Are they the vision?"

"Water," Norit said. "Water, iron . . . stone and metals. A wealth of iron."

Perhaps it was Norit that answered him, out of her madness. Or Luz told them the unlikely truth.

They never knew what the burning was. That next day, when they pitched the tent and lay down on their mats, Norit turned her back to both of them and lay apart.

Marak looked at Hati, questioning, and Hati at him, but

neither of them knew what to do for her. He knew that within Luz's will, Norit suffered, and that knowledge left him sleepless as they rested.

He thought about it. He tried to think what to do.

The au'it slept. Tofi and the men slept. There were no witnesses. He gave Hati's hand a squeeze, one comrade asking leave of another, and moved to Norit's side, stroked Norit's arm, and after a time moved her hair aside from her ear to whisper into it: "Norit. Do you want to make love?"

Norit flinched and covered her eyes, turning away.

He was given a no, but not, he thought, from Norit, who had no choice about Luz, or the visions. He had never forced himself on a woman. But he knew the ravages of the madness, how it ate up sleep and gave no rest, and wore out the body without giving it any useful ease. He saw it happening to Norit, and he gathered Norit up in his arms and kissed her on the lips.

"Let me go!" Luz cried. She struck him with the heel of her hand, trying to break free.

"Let Norit go," he retorted, and did not abate his attentions, not though Norit's body struggled and her mouth cursed as Norit never had, with words that made no sense in any dialect.

Her struggles, her outcries, waked Tofi and the slaves and the au'it, who stared in dismay. Had he not disapproved the soldiers for the very same act?

He spent no time explaining his actions. He swept Norit up and carried her out of the tent kicking and struggling. Gently, for Norit's sake, he set her down on the shaded sand outside and proceeded to what he intended.

"Damn you!" Luz cried.

Only when Norit pounded him with her fists and began to gasp after breath did he turn gentle with her, and then Norit simply lay in his arms and cried and sobbed. He had least of all intended to hurt her.

"You hate me," she wept. "You hate me!"

"Never, Norit," he said, and added honestly: "I'm not that sure about Luz."

She struck at him, and he caught her fist easily within his, she was so small and her violence so slight. He lifted her face and tried to make her look at him, but she shut her eyes.

"Tell me the truth, Norit. Tell me the truth. Do you hear me? Look at me and tell me the truth. What do you want, and what does Luz want?"

Her eyes squeezed shut. She made no other struggle, no other response, either, as he tucked her clothing back to rights and smoothed her hair gently into place. He had no idea what he had won, or if he had won any relief for Norit— he had hoped if he could bring her back for an hour, Norit might have a chance, and he knew by what seethed in his own mind that she had less of a chance if Luz was always there.

But now he regretted doing what he had done. He had tried to help Norit. He had no idea now whether he had scared her instead of Luz, or offended her, or what vengeance he might have brought down on them all.

He led her back into the tent and let her go, and she sat down on her own mat. She sat staring at the wall for a long while before she lay down again and tucked her clothing tightly about her.

Tofi and the men likely were awake with all the commotion, but they were pretending otherwise. The au'it certainly had waked, and wrote, silent in her preoccupation.

Hati lay with one arm beneath her head, gazing at the sun through the canvas as he lay down beside her.

"Luz has her all the time," he said. "I don't know which I dealt with. I tried to help. I don't think I did."

"Norit knows what you do," Hati said. "Norit wants help."

"I think she does. But she can't push Luz out."

"Norit can't say no to anyone, least of all to Luz. But she wants you. She wants you more than anything."

"What can I do? What cure is there for her?"

"None," Hati said, "until Norit says no to Luz." Hati rolled over and opened her arms to him, and drew him in despite the heat.

At that small move, Norit moved, and leapt up, and

shoved the au'it out of the way and sent the au'it's pen into the sand in her rush out of the tent.

Marak leapt up, and Hati did, dodging the au'it, half-stumbling over Tofi and his helpers, hurrying to stop her as she raced out of the shade of the tent.

Norit ran past the resting beasts, wasting strength and sweat in the heat, and Marak ran foremost after her. Hati ran behind him. There was a rock shelf beyond, where a careless foot might slip, and Norit sent herself straight for it, maybe knowing what was there, maybe forgetting that hazard.

Before she could reach that edge Marak caught her, and barely so. They fell down on the stony ground, full length.

Her clothing had saved her skin, except her hands bled. His arm bled. But the madness was in possession of her. She struck at him as he got up and dragged her to her feet, struck him hard, and then only halfheartedly. "I want to die," Norit cried, as he held her, but Luz said, in the next breath, trying to stand erect: "She won't succeed. I won't let her come to harm."

He still had possession of Norit's wrist. Hati arrived at a walk, now, ahead of Tofi and his two men. To their appalled looks, he shook his head and walked toward the camp, leading Norit by a firm grip.

Norit said not a thing, nor objected when he set her down on her mat and harshly told her to stay there. The blood on her hands was still fresh, but the wounds were already dry as if hours old.

The au'it had not ventured far from the tent. She had watched their return. She sat and wrote, now, a dry, persistent scratching, recording Norit's desperate rush toward death.

Marak, Marak, Marak was in his head, then. He expected vengeance, pain, he had no idea what, but what he received was a dinning urgency to move on. *Haste,* the voices said. *Haste. Enough.* The vision of the falling star began again.

He went out and began kicking furiously at the tent stakes.

Then Tofi and Hati, outside, began to help him. He ripped his own hand bloody, pulling up a stake, and the pain scarcely reached him.

"Damn them!" he shouted at the white-hot sky. "Damn them all!"

But no one answered, no one came to offer reason. Hati went to bring out Norit and the au'it and their mats before the tent went down.

It billowed flat, the former slaves folded it, packed it, and loaded it in rare, fearful silence. The sun was still high as they mounted up and rode on, and the beasts, ignorant of all the mistakes they had made, grumbled, disturbed early from their cud-chewing.

The whole afternoon long seemed to pass in numb, para- lytic silence, inside and out, as if even the madness stood back from him and from Norit. Perhaps Luz was aghast at the violence.

His hand healed. By nightfall the flesh was sealed over. Norit showed no lasting injury. The stars began to fall and fell until the dawn.

Over the next several days the voices were silent, ex- hausted, perhaps, or Luz, distant in her tower, plotted some revenge. She gave no hint. Perhaps on her bed she thought about him. Perhaps she and Ian made love. Marak cared nothing for that, either. Perhaps they could hear him as he heard the visions. He wished only for their continued si- lence. Norit was more herself, fearful of the star-fall, tender in her dealings with everyone, lacking prophecies.

They reached the very heart of the Lakht, within sight of the Qarain itself, and the border of the Anlakht, and every night the stars still fell, stitching small streaks across the dusk and across the night, occasionally exploding into fire. Every day the au'it wrote, and wrote copiously, but what she might have to say Marak had no idea.

The days became hot, the hottest any of them remem- bered. The sky was a brazen dome above their heads, and, having no shortage of water, they let the wind blow over the sweat that ran on their limbs. The beasts, however, grew irri- table in the heat, and the heat wore on them all: when they rested it was a numb sort of rest, more desperate uncon- sciousness than sleep. The open-sided tent offered shade, but gave far less relief when the wind failed. Heat rose shimmering from the sand. Light glared off the rocks, and hot air gathered under the canvas.

Marak found to his chagrin that he had lost all count of the days, but more worrisome, he had ceased to care. Habits on which life itself depended faded from importance in the oppressive air. The au'it never spoke, in all these days. Norit had grown increasingly quiet and hard to rouse. Hati moped in the weather. Tofi looked ten years older from sunburn and dirt, while the ex-slaves recalled the white tents, and safety, and sat listless in the shade. They found a bitter spring, and the beshti, well watered, disdained it. But their water supply had become, at least marginally, a concern, and after this they determined to reserve the good water and let the beshti go in want. Tofi harbored a secret worry, and still claimed he knew the way, but Marak began to suspect otherwise.

The silence of the voices began to seem not freedom, but abandonment, stemming from the assault on Norit, as best Marak reckoned. He asked himself whether Luz would damn all the world for his crime against her, and began to think every day of dying, not that dying held any attraction for him, only that it seemed the likely outcome.

And every night as they rode the sky was streaked with falling stars, sometimes so violent in their fall they flew apart in pieces, and sometimes so near them they screamed on their way down.

He had seen very many strange things, he decided, enough strange things that he ought to be satisfied. But he was not. On the way to the tower, when they had known nothing, he and Hati had shared a passion for life. Now he and Hati looked at each other through identical visions, made love sometimes, but more often laced fingertips, only fingertips, lying near and not against one another: the heat around them was stifling, sapping all strength. Together they cared for Norit, and were concerned for her, both of them helpless to rescue her.

They traveled and put up their tent, and had grain-cake to eat. To do more asked strength they hoarded. They sat. They ate.

"The sky," Norit said suddenly.

Brisk movement came back to her limbs, and awareness to her eyes, and she rose to her feet, staring toward the end of the tent, toward the west.

Hati's fingers knotted into his sleeve, a demand, a claim, when Norit's distress distracted him.

"She may kill herself," he said, and a sense of omen dawned on him, a sudden conviction that time had slipped away from him, and the vision was imminent.

"She won't kill herself," Hati said. "Didn't Luz say she wouldn't? She's grown too hard for that. She listens to all we do and say, even if the voices are quiet."

Norit went out of the tent and stood in the burning heat. Eventually he went, swept her up in his arms, and carried her inside. When he set her on her feet she abruptly sat down and stared out unblinkingly at the daylight.

"Luz," he said, kneeling and shaking Norit. "Luz, you're killing her. We love her and you're killing her."

There was no seeming awareness. Norit simply stared.

He gave up, took his hand away, then on a second thought laid hands on Norit and made her lie down. She stayed as he disposed her, and he went back to his mat, next to Hati.

The au'it slept. Tofi and the freed slaves slept. A rising wind stirred the broad canvas of their shelter, and everyone but Norit roused to see the sight. They had seen nothing else living for days, not even the flight of a bird. The land seemed dead around them.

Then the canvas stirred slightly and lifted like a breath of hope.

Then the southwest wind began to blow, but it was the breath of a furnace, as unkind as the silence. They packed up and moved on, the beasts complaining, and by evening the wind was a west wind, in their faces, picking up sand as it came. In the pans, uneasy dust flowed in small streams along the harder surface of the sand.

They crested a broad, gradual ridge as evening fell, and before them, as far as they could see, the otherwise flat, stone-littered plain of the Lakht beyond showed strange new wounds, pale sand circles in the old, weathered sand, two nearest that overlapped each other.

Had some desperate band of travelers, as lost as they, attempted wells all over the plain?

"What creature made that?" Hati asked Tofi. "Have you ever seen the like?"

"No," Tofi said, sounding for a moment like the boy he was. "Never in my life."

Their downward path took them alongside one such pale spot, a shallow new depression in the sand, with dark red, unweathered sand thrown out around it. The beasts lowered their heads and nosed the area, odd behavior in itself, and pawed at it, but they found nothing buried there.

They pushed on across the plain, not liking the vicinity. They put it far behind them by next noon, when they pitched a belated camp.

The earth shook itself, like a beast shaking his skin; and they who had been stretching rope, and the two freedmen, who had been pounding a tent peg, stopped their work.

They all stood still, except Norit, who had sat down at the start of their work, and who sat like a stone. The peg, half-driven, pulled loose.

"What was *that*?" Tofi asked.

"The earth will shake," Norit said, breaking days of silence. "The earth will crack like a pot and spill out fire."

Marak looked at Hati, and lastly at Tofi, who stood with a tent stake in his hand. Stark fear was on his face.

"Should we sink the deep-irons?" Tofi asked.

"Do that," Marak said. He himself had no idea what next would follow. The stars fell. The earth itself had turned unreliable. Whether deep-irons could pin them to the earth and keep a shelter over their heads he had no idea.

The earth shook again while they were setting the stakes, and the now-freedmen dropped their hammers and looked as if they would run for their lives, if they had any idea at all where to run.

"What will this bring?" Marak asked Norit, who had never stirred from where she sat. "What does this mean?"

"The end of the world." Tears overwhelmed Norit, who

began to sob quietly, covering her face with her hands. "Luz doesn't think so. But I do."

It was a whisper of Norit's old self, free, for the moment. That in itself lent him encouragement.

"The end of the world it may be, but we'll die well fed and well watered. Get under the tent, Norit. Go."

Norit obeyed him quietly. It was her task, when she would do it, to unpack their noon meal, such as it was: dried fruit and grain-cake, and tea, if they chose to heat water.

He wielded a hammer, and Hati helped him. "Get to work!" Tofi chided his helpers. "You're free men. Act like it!"

The earth gave a shudder, and the beasts bawled alarm as the poles swayed and strained the ropes of the tent. They pulled to steady them, and sat down hard on the sand. It was that violent a motion.

The shaking was brief, and left no apparent damage. If the earth would crack, there was no sign of it.

Marak, having fallen hard on his backside, gave a laugh. "Well, the earth tries, but it can't shake us off."

"If the earth cracks, what will we do?" Hati asked, with real fear in her voice. "Perhaps we *will* die."

"Maybe we won't," he said, sitting there, toe to toe with her. "*I* don't intend to. You're on your own if you do."

Hati gave a shaken laugh of her own, threw her head, and got up, dusting herself off. "I'm not that easy to kill."

They went under the shade of the tent, Tofi and the slaves as well. They broke grain-cakes and ate well, and drank. Twice more while they slept the earth shivered, and both times they waked.

"Perhaps at least the shaking is done," Marak ventured to say, as dark fell with them still camped. They had been reluctant to pull up the deep-irons and venture out.

Just then another shudder ran through the earth, so that neither earth nor heavens seemed stable tonight.

"Speak of misfortune," Marak muttered.

Tofi went outside the open sides of the tent to see to the beasts, and came running under the tent again, a shadow in the dark.

"The stars are all gone!" Tofi cried.

Marak gathered himself up in alarm, with Hati and Norit close by, and indeed, as he walked out beyond the edge of the tent, the whole heaven was black. All the land was dark.

"All the stars have fallen," Hati said in dismay.

"They are there," Norit said calmly. "The star-falls have kicked up the dust to the sky. That's all."

"That much dust?" Hati asked, but had no answer.

Marak could see nothing in the pitch-black, except shadows against shadow.

Then in the far west white fire chained through the murk in the west, and thunder cracked, as sometimes it would in the great western storms.

A storm was indeed coming, and weather-sense had failed him. Now he was very glad that they had driven down the deep-stakes.

"We should put on the side flaps," he said, and, difficult as it was in the dark, they began to do that.

Before they were done, a sudden wind came and battered at the canvas, making it boom and rattle while they worked. "Make sure of the ropes!" Tofi shouted at the ex-slaves. "Do it right this time, or you go out alone to tie it down!"

The beasts got up and settled down in the lee of the tent. The food and water all had to be moved inside, for fear of it all being buried in blowing sand; they made a wall of the rest of the baggage, and the side flaps had to be battened down tight. As an added measure, feeling their way in the dark, they made the tent sides and the roof fast a second time to the baggage, and to a second line of stakes, which they drove down inside the tent.

Then, sitting against that wall of their possessions, they were ready for the earth to shake and the heavens to be carried away.

The wind roared and the thunder boomed above them. The canvas bucked and thumped away, anchored by the deep-irons and the heavy buffering on the windward wall, inside their tent. Having worked so hard and so quickly, and having nothing left to do, they ate an extra ration of sweet dried fruit and grain-cakes in the pitch-blackness and settled down to rest through the wind and the storm.

The air grew far cooler, even cold, strangely smelling of dust and water.

"It smells like the inside of a well," Hati said in wonder.

It did. But rain never came to the Lakht, and only twice in his life in the western lowlands.

Thunder crashed over them, the wind roared, and in the overthrow of the heavens and the battering of the wind, Marak held Hati to him for warmth. They tried to gather Norit into their embrace, but like the au'it, Norit stayed apart, somewhere near the big tent pole, waiting, waiting. She began to sing to herself in the dark, a tuneless song like the wind, drowned intermittently by the thunder and the crack of the canvas.

Lightning flashes showed through the seams of the tent. A terrible crash of thunder hit their ears.

A pattering followed, as if pebbles were falling on the tent.

But in the rain of pebbles battering against the canvas over their heads, Marak realized the singing beside had stopped a moment ago.

He gathered himself up and felt toward the tent pole where Norit had sat.

"Norit?" he asked the dark, and the roaring and the thunder gave him no answer.

Were it Hati, he would have thought she had simply gone off to the corner of the tent on intimate business. But a moment ago Norit had been singing, and now she was not where she had been. That warned him something might be amiss.

Then he felt a sudden gust, and he knew for certain. The tent flap blew and moved in the dark, its cords loosed, admitting a dark less absolute than the dark inside, and a fitful flicker that picked out a horizon.

He went out it, flinching as pebbles struck him . . . not woundingly hard, but hard enough, and when he put a hand to his bare skin he felt his skin slick and gritted with sand that immediately stuck to it. In the lightning flashes he saw small shining objects lying about him, like jewels in the lightning. He saw others bounce as they hit, and felt the sting of others, an impact on his skull.

"Norit!" he shouted into the wind and the falling stones, angry, willing finally to leave her to Luz.

But he heard her voice on the wind, sobbing or laughing, or perhaps both.

"It comes," Norit cried. Lightning showed her dancing along the ridge.

On that dim, lightning-lit sight he ran out through the pelting from the heavens, knowing that only fools and suicides wandered away from tents in storms. He reached her, he seized her in his arms and precisely reversed that trail, aiming straight for the tent door, in a sudden, blind dearth of lightning.

"This way!" Hati shouted from ahead of him.

He went toward that voice and as he made the doorway, fierce, familiar hands seized on him and on Norit. Lightning showed him Hati's face, a series of three flashes.

"Fool!" Hati shouted at him over the roar of the wind. "Get in! Get in!"

Even in that time pebbles had bruised his back and his head, and with Norit in his arms, they burst through the windblown door and into the numbing stillness and blackness inside.

Tofi asked in the dark, "What's falling on us?"

"Pebbles," Marak said. They all were struck and bleeding as best he could tell, and he set Norit down on the mats, trying to tell whether there was any injury to Norit's head: he found grit and wet in her hair, her aifad carried away in the wind. He felt wet on his own skin, and on his clothes, and a profound chill followed. The three of them, he, and Norit, and Hati, all huddled together shivering while the thunder raged.

In time he warmed, and rested. And uncommon storm that it was, the air grew still before the dawn. Tofi got up and put his head out to find out what might be going on.

"The stars are back," Tofi exclaimed, "and more are falling down."

After this, Marak said to himself, nothing could astonish him. He got up to see, found it true, then went back to rest, in the knowledge that at least there were stars in the sky. The convulsion in the heavens had settled again, if only to a steady ruin.

Marak, Marak, the voices said, back again, after such long silence, and rocks and spheres collided, and the heavens fell. He could have wept. They were not lost. The voices knew how to find them. The visions were back. He never thought he could be glad. *West,* the voices told him. *West by northwest.*

"Do you hear?" he asked Hati. "Do you hear them?"

She moved her head against his arm. He thought it was a yes.

The sun, relentless, came up as sane as ever. They unfastened the lee-side tent flaps and let in light, welcoming the sun, and where Marak had expected half-healed wounds, he found no fever and no swelling. Where he expected blood from the stones, he saw no blood, rather a patchwork of dirt on his arms and his clothing, and on Norit's, and on Hati's, as if they had been pelted with mud.

He walked outside, seeing the ground all likewise splotched and spattered, and the canvas the same. The beasts were all but laughable, having a coating of dried mud all over their backs, and the pale, spread canvas was a patchwork of red and rust like him and like Hati.

"Raindrops!" he exclaimed in astonishment. He laughed aloud, having expected blood and bruises, and finding them marked like fools. "Water drops. No wonder we were wet!"

"In the far north," Hati said, "sweet water fell hard as stones, and became water again in the sun. So the grandfathers tell it."

Norit had come out, and so now did Tofi and his men. Norit, too, was splotched with huge dollops of rust, and at some point tears had run down from her eyes, trails through the red smears. Now her eyes, red as fire, were fierce as Hati's.

"So it has rained on the Lakht," Norit said in a low, hoarse voice, "and it will rain. The floodgates of the heavens will pour it out. A man can *die* of too much water."

That was almost the last of his patience. Of all Luz's utterances, this one seemed sinister, intended to frighten them, he still had bruises on his skull, and for a moment he vowed he had made his last effort for Norit, as a vessel for Luz. But a second thought showed him Norit beneath the dirt and behind the burning eyes, and he said to himself that her skull likely had more bruises than his, and her head rang with worse than voices and a useful sense of where to go.

"Go sit and wait," he said gently, to the wife from Tarsa, not to Luz. "Rest. Dust yourself off. We'll be moving on."

The animals had to be brushed clean of grit so sand would not gall their hides under the packs. The mud had to be swept off the tent canvas, or it became a heavy weight of dirt for the beast that carried it. Before all was done they all had bleeding hands and sore arms, but they dug out the deep-irons, packed the tent, reorganized their baggage, and moved, over a rise and down across a landscape dotted with thousands of small pits.

This morning, however, they saw wild creatures, furtive shadows that dived beneath rocks at their passing: the waterfall had brought them to this plain. A handful of plants bloomed and withered with the day's heat, leaving a gold spatter of their life-bearing dust on the rocks. Water spilling on stones. Spheres falling into spheres. Gold dust scattering on the wind.

West by northwest. Hurry. Hurry. Hurry, Marak.

Marak tucked his foot up and rested his arms on his knee as he rode, rested his forehead so, trying not to think, to hear, wanting not to imagine what would be their fate if they had been on this plain when the stars fell.

Luz bore no grudge. And could he fault Norit, after all? Had harm come? It was only water. It was only pride. They had laughed, and the laughter, half-crazed and weak as it was, had healed them.

Had Luz, in driving Norit to the edge of collapse, managed their escape from the falling stars? Had she preserved their lives as mindfully as she preserved Norit from harm, and had she directed them around the region of worst damage? He wondered what had become of Pori, and the plain beyond.

A trail of fire went across the heavens. A star fell by daylight, smoking as it went. It went to the south: it was one whose direction was clear, and it fell beyond the hills, like a guide.

Two days later they rode again within view of the Qarain by sunrise, and the day after that found one of those caravan traces that led toward the holy city.

The au'it had learned to accommodate the beast's rocking gait and now used her journeys as well as her rests to record her observations.

And this, too, she wrote.

All the things they had seen and done the au'it had recorded. All these things she would present to the Ila, the unprecedented fall of rain and mud, the fall of stars alike.

And what would her book say?

That the stars fell? That their hope of safety lay in the tower, in the white tents?

The one even the Ila could surely see for herself, and of the other, Marak thought, they had no proof, even for themselves.

13

We have seen the stars fall in their thousands. The book contains no event like this.
—The Book of Oburan

The ragged upthrust of the Qarain, that division from the Anlakht, was a wall on their right hand as they went. They were on the edge of desolation.

And by the next day they joined a recently used caravan trace and followed it in an abrupt turn toward the north, toward the Qarain.

Marak thought he had crossed this place before. He thought he recognized the vast, stone-littered pan and the rocks beside it.

Tofi recognized it, too. "Besh Karat," he said excitedly, pointing a thin arm to the left of the trail, where a ridge of rounded rocks stood, looking like its name, a burdened, sulking beast. "We're at Besh Karat, at the bitter spring. And these last tracks are only a day ahead of us. Another caravan."

A little after that Norit suddenly reined back her beast, which squalled a protest and fought the rein. "Stop," she said. "Stop here."

Marak shifted his foot back and took in the rein. Osan

stopped, putting his ears up and laying them down. They were just passing among the rocks, an easy hiding place for vermin, and they were short of the bitter spring. It was not ordinarily a point to rest, and the beasts knew it, and complained.

"A little farther," Marak said, which was only common sense. "Not in the rocks."

"No. Here. Now." Norit tried to get her reluctant beast to kneel: it would not, and came close to veering off the trail in besha obstinacy, but stopped as she began to dismount all the same.

"Damn," Marak said, and slid down and went to rescue Norit. Tofi and Hati dismounted, and Hati assisted the au'it to dismount. They were at a stop. The freedmen got down.

"For what do we wait now?" he asked Norit, apprehensive and impatient both.

She answered him with one of those cold, clear stares that said Luz, more than Norit, was hearing him.

The vision of rocks and spheres followed, one crashing into the other, the sphere with fire at the point of damage, and a spreading ring of disturbance, like a stone cast into a fountain.

"Make the beasts sit down," Norit said.

"Why?" he asked.

Norit said nothing. She only sat down, herself, her legs tucked up at a slant to avoid the heat of the sand.

Marak looked at Hati, both his temper and his dread reaching a near boil. They were so close to reaching Oburan: they were on the very trail to the holy city, and was there another calamity?

"Can she not *explain,* damn her?" he muttered under his breath, meaning Luz, and complaining to no one but the wind and the desert heat. "Do we need the tents? Is a star about to fall on top of us?" They were sitting next to Besh Karat, which indubitably housed vermin . . . he hoped they were small and timid vermin, nothing larger.

The vision came to him, the ring of fire, so vividly it blotted out the sun. He ground his hands against his eyes, fighting for a sight of Osan's rein as he tried to grasp it, and shook his head to clear it.

He settled Osan, and if Osan sat, Hati's beast and the au'it's settled, complaining. The pack beasts were always willing to settle, in hopes of shedding their packs for a rest, but here they were uneasy, and circled and made trouble, two of them wanting to stray off from their accustomed order. But they settled.

Tofi and the freedmen did not then unpack the baggage, and the beasts complained about that, squalling and rumbling in the heat.

So they sat, all of them, like fools, and waited for this danger, and they waited, and the unwilling beasts shifted their limbs under them and complained noisily, with no relief from the packs or the saddles in the sweltering heat. Tails whipped, beat the sand, thump.

Suddenly the beshti set to bawling again.

The earth shook itself like a beast twitching its skin, a hard shaking. Tofi's riding beast, which had started to rise in panic, plumped back down again, unhurt, but rolling its eyes and bellowing to the heavens.

Norit sat with her hands in her lap, combing out a tassel on her headcloth.

The tremor passed. Tofi swore and hid his face in his hand, looked up again as if to be sure it was over.

Norit showed no inclination to move.

"Shall we go?" he asked Norit.

"Not yet," Norit said. She stared into nothing, the tassel forgotten.

The sphere fell against the greater sphere. The ring of disturbance went out. Marak saw it. He knew Hati did. Hati's hands were clenched on her quirt until the knuckles stood white.

The au'it, having endured one shaking, grimly gripped her book and her ink-cake, and wrote, braced for more disturbance.

Time passed.

"Shall we pitch the tents?" Tofi asked at last. The sun was

high. It seemed now that they would not go beyond this place before noon.

"No," Norit said shortly, in a tone not inviting question. "Stay still."

Marak shrugged and found occupation sharpening his boot-knife, as Hati and two of the helpers had tucked up and attempted to sleep.

Norit combed out the one tassel and three or four others.

Then a haze in the west caught Marak's eye, a fuzzy seam on the far horizon that grew wider and wider and wider every instant.

"Hati," he said as it grew. And to all of them, "*Storm.*"

Damn Luz, there was no time to pitch the tent. The storm came like sand flowing downhill: it went from that seam to a band across the horizon to a towering wall faster than he had ever seen a storm move, less like a wind than a landslide. In hardly longer than a panicked mind could think about it, that wall filled the sky, and rushed over them with a stench of earth and heat like nothing Marak had ever smelled.

The beasts did not attempt to rise: with successive shoves of their knees and hind feet, they shifted about to present their backsides to that oncoming wind, burdens and all.

Sand began to blast over them, stinging exposed skin.

"Get together!" Tofi shouted, flinging his arms about Marak and Hati. The au'it folded her book and put away her writing kit. Norit moved closer to them, the au'it joined them; and Tofi's two men, and they all pressed themselves against the sun-heated earth, together, making a single lump, robes tucked up for shelter.

The moving sand deafened them and dimmed the light. Marak protected his eyes with the headcloth and tried to see through that veil, and found only greater dark and lesser. It grew hard to breathe through the folds of cloth. The smell was that of a sandstorm, and of hot sand and of deep sand and of burning.

There was no substance left in the air; they struggled for the least whisper of breath, losing strength, until at last the air came, tasting like the wind off a forge.

Lying together, faces buried in each other's robes, they gasped and breathed such as they could, fighting for the dusty air they drew, and dared not move, while the wind roared over them, and kept on, and kept on.

But air there began to be, if only a trickle through cloth; and the sand that blasted over them began to settle long enough to become a weight in the folds of their robes. It found ways in among them, in the crooks of arms and legs, building supports under them, finding crevices to fill, threatening to bury them alive.

Breathing was the greatest concern. They fought to stay behind the wall of sand that built against them and atop what built under them. It seemed forever before the gust front passed and they could stir out of their sand-choked huddle, still wind-battered and blinded by the blowing sand, but able to stand.

The beasts had suffered. One was down under his pack, alive, but unable to free himself until they removed the baggage that trapped him at disadvantage, and by then he had been lying so long he was paralyzed. They had to rock and pull and haul him to rights and up to his feet. Three had painful windburns on their rumps, where the hide was blasted bare and red, and the canvas that wrapped the packs, part of the tents, was worn through several layers on one edge.

They were all alive, that was the miraculous thing. They were alive, though the sky was still a sandy murk, and the air still stank like hot iron.

"If we pitch a tent," Tofi said, muffled in his veils against sand and dust, "it will not stand with this constant shaking. Best we do as we have done, build a wall of the baggage and stretch our canvas from it. I've never seen a storm come on like that."

"Will there be another?" Marak asked Norit, hard-edged. Norit said nothing. "What should we do? Luz? What comes next?"

The vision of the spreading rings repeated itself in his mind, over and over and over, making no sense.

Came another shock, a great one, a long one, and the one beast that had gotten up staggered and bellowed its distress.

"Norit!" Hati shouted.

"Camp here," Norit said.

Pressed to invention, they and the slaves unburdened all the beasts and contrived to stretch canvas from a stack of baggage to a few anchoring stakes, lashed down so it would shed sand that accumulated from hour to hour.

That gave them a measure of comfort. They slept, but slept by turns to go out and keep the two entries clear. The sand-fall, no longer blasting, but a general murk in the air, went on and on into true dusk, then a night so deep and so cold they huddled together, men and women, freemen and freedmen together.

When morning came creeping through the murk, there was no talk of moving on. Those habituated to the desert were used to waiting out storms, and were schooled to patience even this near a goal. So they waited, deciding finally that the ground had stopped shaking enough to try the pegs. They pitched their tent for comfort, and salved the animals' seeping windburns, which were crusted over with sand.

At that, they and the beasts alike had proper shelter, and they rested wrapped in double robes against a cold unlike any they had ever felt.

"I've never seen the like," Hati swore, shivering. "In the deepest desert I've never seen such a storm."

"Tomorrow the sand-fall will be less," Norit said.

There was no question in Marak's mind that Norit knew exactly what would happen. Norit crept close to him and then Luz shoved away. Alone, Norit bowed her head and wiped her eyes in silent tears. There was no solution he could give. He offered his hand, and she jerked away. It tore his heart to watch her.

Hati shook her head as if she could read his thoughts, and rubbed his shoulders, making him realize his muscles were set like stone. She had clever fingers and knew where to press. He stretched out finally and slept, and for a few hours the dreams left him in peace.

On the next day the storm abated somewhat; but the taste in the air was that of sulfur. The wind stank, and it burned the eyes. They ate beneath the canvas, and carefully shielded their food from the foul stuff that blew in from the sky, under a yellow murk in which the noon sun was a spot in the haze.

"The grass and the grain will wither," Norit said. "All the west is ruins. But that's not the worst."

Kais Tain was in the west. All his father's household was in the west. Marak wanted to strike her senseless. He had done all he had done, he had survived all he had survived, and Norit told them calmly that nothing lived in the west.

Marak, the voices said in the midst of it all, clamoring for his action. *Marak.*

Norit said, aloud, "We should go now."

"When did she become god?" Tofi cried. Their voices had become raw and unpleasant from the dust, and Tofi's voice broke on the shout.

"Obey her," Marak said wearily. "Where else will you go?"

"To hell," Tofi said bleakly. "We're all going to hell."

But Tofi roused up the freedmen, who moved about loading their baggage and getting the beasts up.

As they were packing up, a small thing that lived in buried rocks came out and hissed and dived back again. One of the men threw a rock at the burrow in the Besh Karat.

"It will die on its own," Norit said.

The bitter spring was covered by deep sand. It would not flow again until the vermin dug it up. The beshti themselves, water-short, still showed no disposition to seek it out.

What Norit prophesied haunted Marak as they rode away from that place.

Should even the ill-tempered creature in its house of stone perish? Should winds like that cover the wells? From that small comprehension he truly began to grasp the height and depth of the devastation, east to west, from the highest to the lowest.

He wished he had stayed at the white tents. He wished he had told Hati to stay. He wished he had never undertaken this fool's errand with Norit. There was no way out of this. There *was* no safety. He was a fool, and he had led them all to their destruction.

But he had lived before by imposing strict conditions on his death.

He would not die and leave Hati and Norit alone to face what came. That was his underlying resolve. He would not die without speaking to the Ila and relaying what she had asked to hear. That was his mission; and it was not that far. They would at least attempt the return, whatever the Ila did, and if, in the Ila's wrath, he could not, *they* would go back to the tower. He would put the fear in Tofi and have him promise that.

Both these things he promised himself, while he roused Osan to his feet and turned Osan's head toward the holy city.

Marak, Marak, Marak, the voices said to him. By noon, they passed bones that jutted up from the sand, a besha's carcass already stripped by vermin. They came to others, four and five, and the bones of two men on the other side of the caravan track, but those bones were gnawed for the marrow and scattered, dug up by some creature after the sand had covered them. A scrap of canvas lay against a distant rock, looking as the wind had carried it and bunched it around the base of the boulder. It might have sheltered a man, but if it did, that man was dead by now, beyond their help. And the visions were now of fire, fire flowing like water from a broken spigot, fire coursing through land and eroding it.

They found other remnants of passage, as if bit by bit the whole caravan before them had come to grief, overwhelmed by the wind and the sand. Other debris was blown up against the rocks, far from their path, which now was as smooth as if no caravan had ever gone before them. When the desert destroyed, it both preserved and obliterated, even this close to the holy city.

But the day-early mirage that usually heralded the holy city failed. The sky was dirty yellow, and the air was cold. They doled out a little water to the beshti, and wondered what was ahead of them.

He contrived to speak to Tofi alone, riding side by side with him for a space, while Hati lagged back with the au'it. "I have a proposition for you," he said. "We both have a promise to the Ila. But she may reward *you*. If things go badly for me, as they may, take Hati and Norit and go back as fast as you can."

"To the tower?" Tofi asked.

"There," Marak said. "There's no safety here. You know that."

"I already know," Tofi said unhappily. The young man who had thought at the beginning of this trek that the world would survive now had different ideas. "There *is* none here. We're lucky it's not our bones lying back there in the sand."

"We had warning. They didn't. *We* have Norit. Listen to her."

"The question is, what's *there*? Is it any better there than here?"

"Norit will know," he said. "I think she knows as well as anyone what the state of the tower is. If anyone can get you back there alive, she can." He thought of the Ila's promise to save his mother and his sister, and now he knew that calling the Ila into the tangled affairs of his family might have put Hati and Norit in danger, and if things went wrong in the Ila's eyes, and she decided to blame him, he knew that she would never release those related to him: that was not the pattern of the Ila's justice. He could not ask Tofi to save his mother and sister in that case: there was no likelihood at all that Tofi could pry them from the Ila's hands and far less that Tofi could rescue him. But Hati— Hati was not a name the Ila even knew about.

"Don't let Hati come with me once we reach the city," he said. "If you have to carry her off by force, do it. Claim her as if she were *your* family."

"Can you argue with her?"

"I'll give her that instruction. I'll tell her to take care of *you*. Go along with it."

"I'll do my best," Tofi said, and joined the scheme to get the most of them back. "If the Ila's men ask, I'll lie and say she's my wife."

That was the measure of Tofi's courage, his loyalty to a stranger . . . that he would lie to the Ila's men and rescue Hati. It was what happened to men on campaign together; and Tofi was no longer a boy, no longer a youngest son, struggling with a man's burden. The ex-slaves obeyed him . . . respected him, that had happened day by day.

Now Marak discovered the courage that was in Tofi, as great as any man's he had ever ridden with; and he went to Norit, too, riding alongside her.

"Tell Luz," he said, "if anything goes wrong, go to Tofi and tell him to get you to the tower. You'll need Hati, too. I can promise you, you'll get nowhere without her. Hati's of the tribes. You don't know enough about the desert on your own to live the day out. Your advice is dangerous to the inexperienced."

Norit looked at him, frightened, as all her waking hours were a chaos of fear and Luz's presence. For a moment it was Norit, wholly Norit who gazed at him. Then the fear dimmed, and it was Luz. "Do what you came to do," Luz said sharply, and that was all she would say, leaving him angry and worried both.

He delayed talking to Hati. He knew it would be an argument.

Haste, the voices said. *Don't stop. Don't rest.*

The sky remained the same dirty yellow toward the night, until the sun went down in a red sky the like of which none of them had seen; and that night the stars were hidden by cloud. Now and again in the far distance a trail of fire came through, and once a great boom resounded across the pans.

Day came with a different shade, gray murk above their heads, streaked with dirty yellow high, high aloft.

They had ceased to point at wonders. Tofi looked up gape-mouthed at this one, and so did Hati. The au'it began to write, and seemed to lose heart, and folded her book under this leaden sky.

Norit had nothing to say.

"We should keep moving," Tofi said. "The mirage has failed us. But I know we're not that far."

The yellow dust of the western pans was on the move. Sometimes, being newly fallen, dust ran along the ground, a light film of it, streaks across the red sand of the Lakht.

But by midmorning a dark haze was on the northern horizon, and by noon a low black pall obscured the face of the Qarain's red rock.

"Fire," Hati said. "*Smoke.*"

It was the city itself they were seeing. They saw nothing like the tall graceful towers. The city lacked its towers and was surrounded by a field of dull gray and red-brown their eyes had taken for sand.

Tents stood on the outskirts of the holy city . . . many, many tents spread all about it.

But there was no city. All the fine dwellings, all the wealth, all the power of Oburan had come to this. The holy city was a hill of ruins.

14

The extent of the calamity of the heavens has yet to be known, but Oburan has opened its gates to the desperate: everyone who comes to the Ila's Mercy may come in.
—The Book of Oburan

They did not rest. The beasts remembered water or smelled it in the air, and even after so long a trek they stretched out in that smooth halfrun the self-saving creatures rarely sustained, flagging occasionally but still moving at a walk, until they caught their breaths. Then one of the riding beasts would take it in his head to run, and off they would go again toward that distant ruin, maintaining the pace so long as their wind lasted, pack beasts jogging along behind.

The leaden sky had turned red with sunset before they reached the outskirts. The color dyed all the canvas in sight as they reached the first of the tents that ringed the city— dyed their party, too, with its ill-omened stain.

In a certain area were Ogar tents, round and center-poled; and others were tents from the west, longer than wide. There were tents from the deep Lakht, square, with rope webbing; and tents from northwest, a simple cone-shape, made of hides.

"This is not all Oburan," Marak said. Hope rose in him, seeing that motley gathering. "Those are from the lowlands."

"Those are Keran," Hati said, rising on one knee in the saddle, pointing to a group aside, on the outskirts. *Her* people were here, and they rarely came in from the deep desert.

"Kopa," Tofi said excitedly, naming a tribe from the south. "Drus. Patha. And Lett!"

When the stars had started falling, then from all about the inhabited lands, people in terror of what was happening must have come here, using the summer tents, the shelters they used in festival, in harvest, in birthing. They must all have crowded to the holy city for answers, thousands of them, an army of the desperate, the shattered, with possessions, with domestic herds, with beshti, whatever they could pick up and bring.

The outermost tents were entirely catch-as-catch-could, tents of varying size and style, and they had suffered from the recent storm: sand was piled up, in many cases well up on the tent walls.

But, proof of authority somewhere at the heart of this confusion, some rule had laid out a broad road on which those tents did not encroach, and work, not nature, kept it clear of sand. Some power had said, camp here, and not there. Some of the encamped tribes had feuds, and none were completely at peace with Oburan, but here they camped together.

Might Kais Tain have come? His father had signed the Ila's paper, her armistice. Might he have gathered up the district and come here, seeking escape from the star-fall and the storms? Dared he hope that, though the west had suffered, his father had come in?

Might his mother's tribe? Haga tents, though the Haga visited the Lakht, were like the rest of the west, long, light canvas, the common fiber, neutral brown, green-striped with dyes. He scanned everything in view and could not find them; but tents ringed the city on all sides, thousands of them, more than he could see at a glance: they spilled out past the walls, past the Mercy of the Ila. Of the reed-rimmed pool itself, the tents were so many and so close that he could see no trace but a small interruption in the sunset-dyed canvas.

They entered and rode past disheveled groups who paid them little attention, children who stared, adults who failed to look at all. They were only a handful more arrivals. Of what interest could they be?

And the beasts were bent on water. They resisted the rein; they had nothing else in their heads but their thirst and the relief from their packs.

Marak, the voices said. Fire ran like water across his vision. *Marak!* the voices cried, while his eyes searched desperately in the fading light, through the distraction of the visions. *Marak, Marak, Marak!*

One thing the visions wanted. One thing he was supposed to do. If anyone could find his mother and his sister in this mass of people, the Ila could find them; if anyone could save a life or damn one, it was the Ila. He had to go there first and take the risk.

And if shot through the heart now, the beshti would continue to seek water, where, at the end of this single street, up past all this chaos of tents, it poured out at the Ila's Mercy, under the glass-crowned walls of the city.

Those walls came into view, cracked and ruined, above the tents. The gates stood lastingly ajar on a heap of rubble, and the Ila's Mercy spilled out a flood that wet the cracked pavings and seeped into the thirsty sand. People came and went here with jars, with waterskins, and crowded close not only about the drinking basin but about those troughs below it that were meant for beasts.

No one stood against the beshti when they arrived, squalling and threatening. Men and women scattered from hazard as Osan forced his way to the trough, as Hati's mount did, and Tofi's. Men scrambled for safety, scooping up a precious last jarful of water, taking a half-full water bag, as the ex-slaves' beshti, and Norit's, and the au'it's, shoved and pushed their way in, heads down, gulping up water as if it would never exist again. Then the whole string of pack animals arrived and pushed their way in, nipping and yanking at the rope that prevented their maneuvering: two tangled, and bit, and squalled, a fight that itself made the two room at the trough, the two ex-slaves risking life and limb to get the pack line free.

Marak slid down. Osan sucked up water in a steady stream and never lifted his head or noticed as Marak squeezed between the tall bodies and helped Norit down, bringing her back of the line of rumps.

Hati had helped their au'it . . . their au'it, their au'it: that was how they had come to think of her. She joined him. Tofi came close to him, looking about him in the overthrow of everything they knew of the city.

Sunset had gone to twilight as they rode. Now a few tents nearest the water, at heart of the camp, shone with inner light—white tents, glowing from inside.

There *was* wealth and power still in Oburan. Authority still existed, even if chaos ruled the outskirts.

Above those tents rose the cracked and broken wall, and beyond that, beyond the gates that sat ajar, was the ruin of all the hill, wall thrown on wall, bricks and stone blocks broken and cast down like a midden heap.

People climbed on that ruin even at this hour, carrying lamps, frail, small lights, that bobbed and moved all the way to the crest of the hill.

The inhabitants of the holy city, perhaps, searched the rubble for their dead, or perhaps the destitute of all the villages in the world sought what they could salvage.

"The Ila must be here," Tofi said anxiously. "Omi, we need to find the Ila's captains. I daren't leave our tents here."

Tofi had the right of it. Tents and beasts were life itself now. Water flowed free, but food and shelter might be another matter. "They're our escape," Marak said. "Claim the Ila's hire. Say that to whoever asks. We're leaving as soon as we can. And watch out for Hati." Her people might be here, but they had given her up, and she had as yet made no move to go to them. "Keep an eye on Norit, too."

Tofi looked about him, pointed, where armed men stood in the dusk by the largest of the tents. "The Ila's men."

"Stay close," Marak said, and took the au'it by the arm. "Hati, help Tofi."

He moved quickly, walked as far as the guards, who immediately came to attention. The au'it, their au'it, in her red robes, holding the book clasped against her chest, simply walked on into the tent, then beckoned.

The guards made no further move. Marak walked into the lamplit interior, where a second set of guards admitted the au'it, but barred his way.

Then he knew to his dismay that Hati had followed him, and that Norit had. There was nothing he could do. The presence of the Ila's guards was no place to dispute who had followed orders and who should be kept out of the Ila's grasp.

"I'm Marak Trin," he said in a voice unreliable with dryness and exhaustion. "I'm on the Ila's commission, with her au'it." He almost asked the man to report their presence, but before he could, their au'it held the curtain aside with one hand, holding her book with the other, and nodded, a gesture for them to follow, the guards doing nothing at all to prevent her.

So they walked through, into a small space between curtains. An officer stood there by a camp table and a chair under a lantern, and that worried, wearied officer was one of the Ila's captains.

"Marak Trin," Captain Memnanan said, as if he had met the dead. "Marak Trin Tain."

"I have a message from the far side of the Lakht," Marak said. "Obidhen's dead. His son had a chance to stay safe, the other side of the Lakht, but he came back . . . his father's duty, he said. He needs help: two freedmen and too many beshti to keep contained out there at the well. These two," Marak added, meaning Hati and Norit, his last attempt at cleverness, "these two can help with that. The Ila will *need* those animals. And the master."

Memnanan heard all that with a weary, dazed look, and then went to the curtain and passed curt, coherent orders to the soldiers to get slaves and assist at the well.

He let the curtain fall then, and looked at the several of them, dusty and dirty as they were, in this immaculate place, Hati and Norit making no attempt to leave.

"I am the Ila's au'it," the au'it said in a soft, little-used voice, "with *her* book."

She might have said *I am the god's right hand*. It was that kind of utterance.

"Go through," Memnanan said, and lifted his arm to forbid Marak. "Have you any answer worth delivering," Memnanan asked him, all other things aside, "considering what you see outside?"

"I have the *only* answer worth delivering," Marak said, and succeeded at least in surprising the man.

Came a rumble in the earth, then, a shudder, and the walls even of this tent billowed and moved. Cries of panic resounded outside the canvas walls, far and away across the camp.

He saw pools of fire burning in the dark, walls of fire racing across the land.

Be patient, he told his voices, and threatened them in desperation. *Be still—or fail.*

Memnanan moved as soon as the earth was still, and swept that curtain back. Servants moved it farther, sent it traveling on gold rings that sang as they went. A desk was beyond, and servants, with a black curtain at their backs. They parted it.

Behind that curtain a red one.

Slaves hastened the third curtain back, gathering its folds in their arms, carrying aside several small chairs and a lamp from what had been a small room.

The Ila maintained her state beyond, on her gold chair, on a wide dais of far fewer steps. She was robed and gloved and capped in red. An au'it—not their au'it—sat cross-legged at her feet.

They stood at the edge of a priceless carpet, the three of them, with boots scuffed and coated with dust, in the dusty gauze robes of Luz's tower.

Here was what remained of power. Above them was white canvas, extravagantly lighted with bronze lamps. About them were all the trappings of wealth and control of the lives of men, even in the desolation of the city.

But above that canopy was thunder in the heavens, and under their feet was the shiver of a newly restless earth.

The Ila lifted her hand, motioned, and from a shadowed curtain an au'it came, holding her book, and scurried to sit at the Ila's feet—their au'it, dusty and soiled as she was.

"Marak Trin," the Ila said.

He walked forward, three paces, four, until the guards at the Ila's far left and right reacted, until the Ila herself, in the same moment, turned to him the back of her uplifted hand. *Stop.* So he stopped. Hati and Norit stopped somewhere farther back.

The Ila looked at him, assessing what she saw, or realizing what she saw: Marak had no idea, in the quarrel between Luz and the Ila, how much either knew of the other. For everyone else's sake, he waited, asking himself where to find the right words, the few words that might catch her attention, and her belief.

"What have you found?" the Ila asked.

Where to begin? Most desperately—where to begin?

"There's a tower off the edge of the Lakht," he said, "ruled by a woman named Luz. She says she's your cousin." He saw the Ila's breath come in, deeply, and go out. That was the only sign of emotion she gave. "More," he said, risking everything, "she speaks through us. I think she sees through us. She guided us a new way through the storms. The mad stayed there at the tower . . . with Luz . . . but they're no longer mad. There's water. There's sweet water, and tents, and all the madmen that ever wandered away from the villages are camped around the place, as sane as . . ." As the rest of us? he almost said to that white, implacable face, and stopped himself in time. "She chose us three, and took us into the tower. Its doors open with no one touching them. Lights burn without fire. She talked to us. She gave us a message for you. She sent us because it's not too late."

Rocks hitting spheres, and pools of fire. Luz was aware at this very moment, aware of all three of them, he was sure of it. Luz was looking out through Norit's eyes, and dared he make the Ila aware of that fact? What would she do to Norit if she knew?

"Nanoceles," Norit said from the back of the chamber, taking every guard by surprise, and she strode forward. Men started to move, but the Ila lifted her hand and stopped the drawing of weapons, stopped their rush to prevent Norit, who took her place at his side.

"You understand that word," Norit said in that cold, clear, terrible voice. "You know what you've done, you know what your predecessors did to the world of the *ondat*. In revenge they've begun to reshape this world, but with us, your cousins, they have peace. And I came here to offer you a choice that they allow me to offer you."

"Luz takes her," Marak said, with a distracted glance at Norit. Her face was white and still, terrified. "She can't stop it. She's a woman from Tarsa; she's never been outside her village. She isn't doing this."

"This is a dangerous woman," the Ila said considerately, the hand half-lifted. "This is an extremely dangerous woman."

"I'm your hope of salvation," Norit said sharply. "You've *lost*. Your enemies have found you. We bargained with them for your lives. We've worked here thirty years to save *something* of what you built, first, because we couldn't come closer to you inside your guards and your protection, and second, because we didn't think you *would* hear us, and third, because we wouldn't lose the rest, trying to save *you*. When we knew we had Marak Trin among the mad, we *tried* to take the Lakht and gain your attention, but he couldn't reach his father, and his father couldn't reach *you*."

"With Tain's army?" The Ila laughed as a man might laugh at a very grim joke, on his father, on his entire house and all their effort, and it stung. "From the beginning, that wasn't likely."

"But you reached *him*," Norit said, while Marak remained paralyzed by this step-by-step disclosure of the facts of his life, a simple process of logic and history. "Knowing what we had made him, but not *that* we had made him, you chose him for your messenger. Entirely reasonable. There was no one better, no one more likely. And having sent a messenger, I assume you intended something more than to wish us well."

Luz *dared* to challenge the Ila, to question her. The guards, the whole chamber poised and braced for retaliation.

"Because," the Ila said, as if it were no consequence, and with a turn of her wrist, as if she deflected a blow. *"Because we wished to send him, cousin. Because through him you challenged us.* Because he is less mad than the rest, and because I saw if any of that herd would come back across the Lakht, he was the likeliest. And if there were madmen appearing across the land, it was as clear a sign of something arrived as was likely to come. Yes, I sent him. I sent him to find an answer to the madness, and to explain it, and he has, beyond any doubt."

"But they're no longer mad, those I keep. They are safe. They *will be* safe in what will come. You know the nature of their voices. You know the source of their visions. I don't need to explain. More than that, you feared, Ila Jao, you *feared* we were the *ondat*. We are *not*."

"But in their service."

"Not in their service, only having made peace with them. You know what they fear and why they fear it and why they will reshape the world."

The Ila stared, stone-faced. "I can guess."

"Omatbarat. Do you know that name?"

"I know it. I was not there."

"As we know. You were not there."

"Yet they come here to destroy the world."

"To reshape it. To stir the pot and be sure that what arises here out of the soil of this world is shaped by this world, *not* by you, Ila Jao. When *we* say to them that the makers *we* loose have had their way with the world, then, *then* the armistice will hold and the *ondat* will admit their war is over. But until that day a handful of us of your own kind have set ourselves down here, damned ourselves along with you, for *your* fathers' sins, Ila Jao. We bear you personally no ill will. More than that. We can save you, if you aren't a fool."

There was a heartbeat of terrible silence.

The Ila's white hand lifted abruptly, made a gesture for silence as a hushed murmur began among the officers. Pens made rapid strokes—ceased, as the aui'it stopped, both of them.

"And the other madmen?" the Ila asked.

"Remained at the tower," Norit said.

"Who is this woman?" the Ila asked aside, of Memnanan, and, looking straight at Hati: "Are you a prophet, too?"

"No," Hati said. "No, Ila. But I saw the tower. I saw tents all around it, white tents, that cool the air. I saw a river with green banks."

"White tents," Marak said, drawing the Ila's dangerous attention to himself, "and as much water as anyone wants. Craftsmen. Farmers. All that survived to reach the tower are in that camp. Luz wants you to come there before it's too late. She wants everyone to come."

The Ila looked straight at her, eyes burning in her white and angry face.

"Listen to him," Norit said—-*Luz* said. "You know. *You know, Ila Jao.* There's nothing to gain. Your war is *lost.* You knew it was lost when you came here, five hundred years ago, and you knew it was hopeless when your makers couldn't defeat what we loosed. You couldn't cure the mad. You tried, but you couldn't, so you sent to know what we are. But it's not hopeless. I'm offering you a refuge from what you've brought on yourself."

"Take that woman out!" the Ila said, and the guards moved at once.

Norit held up her hand abruptly, as yet untouched, and turned, and walked of her own accord toward the curtain.

There she stopped, faltered, *fell* like the dead.

Marak started to move without thinking. But guards had reached Norit, and felt of her pulse.

"Fainted," a guard said.

"It's Luz in her," Marak, appealing to the Ila, for fear what consequences Norit might suffer. "The body is only Norit. She's an honest woman, a shy, gentle woman . . . she'd never say what Luz said. She wouldn't know how to answer you."

"And are you Marak, and only Marak?"

He had never wondered. It was a terrifying question. "As far as I know."

"And this?" The Ila gave a wave of her gloved hand toward Hati.

"Hati. An'i Keran. She knows the desert. She knows the way to the tower as well as I do. She helped me reach Oburan." He had no idea of the Ila's motives in asking, or her intentions afterward, and had no idea whether it was better for Hati to be important or invisible, but now he had no choice. "Out on the pans we've seen two storms on the way. Stars fall in their thousands. We passed places where they make pits in the sand. We saw rain, on the Lakht. Luz said the world would change. And it's changing all around us. The earth is shaking. The storms are like nothing anyone's ever seen." He had trouble thinking of the wreckage the other side of these canvas walls, but it was all around her: how could she be ignorant of it? "She says we're almost out of time. That something worse is coming."

"I trust all the things you saw on your journey are in the au'it's book," the Ila said with a glance at their au'it, and the au'it nodded slightly. "So. I will read them at my leisure."

"Everything we saw in our visions," Marak said, desperate for time to make his point, such as it was, "everything we saw came true. All the mad had the same visions. And now we three, Hati and I, and Norit, as far as I know, we're the only ones who see visions beyond those. We see rings of fire, spreading over villages. But if we come to the tower, Luz claims she can keep everyone safe there. I don't know what the truth is. I don't know who's right. I told you I'd come back, and I came back, and I've made my report, such as I can. I don't *know* what's right."

"Come here," the Ila said, beckoning, and beckoning twice called him forward, and forward again, and a third time, until he stood face-to-face with her.

The earth shivered under them, a little tremor, the like of which happened hourly.

"Lay your hand here," the Ila said, and indicated the arm of her chair.

He by no means trusted he would be safe to do that. Yet he did. Within her place of power, the Ila's directions were the only safety at all.

"Captain," she said, holding out her hand to the side. "Your knife."

Marak did not move. He looked at her eye to eye as she held out her hand and Memnanan gave her his belt-knife.

She clenched her fist and stabbed the blade down into his forearm. She was not adept with weapons. The point hung on the gauze and turned, though it scored his arm deeply enough. Blood ran down and divided at his wrist, thin streams that dripped down past the arm of the chair.

It was a demonstration of her power to harm, perhaps. He demonstrated his own, not to flinch from her threats.

"You may move back," the Ila said then calmly, and handed the knife to the captain.

Marak stepped back, blood dripping off his fingers. He disdained to stop it. Knowing it was a test or a chastisement, he knew he had had worse, and stared still straight into the Ila's face, as she stared at him, a long, long while.

Then the Ila dismissed them all with an abrupt gesture. "Care for them! Give them my hospitality. —Don't bandage the wound."

That was a strange exclusion, Marak thought, relieved and stunned. He bowed and, with Hati, went where Memnanan directed, the rings singing on the rods, and singing again as the servants drew the curtains together again. Guards carried Norit and brought her with them, unconscious, unaware, unresponsive . . . but safe.

The servants directed them into a narrow chamber still within the huge tent, a curtained area warmly lit with lamps.

There Memnanan drew the curtain aside, and the Ila's women-servants attended Norit, and wished them to separate, the guards urging Marak alone to a second chamber, but not far. It was apparently for modesty, and he did not resist.

Memnanan stayed with him there a moment, as menservants stripped off the gauze robes. "Did you lie?" Memnanan asked him when he stood naked.

"No," he said. The servants turned back the carpets, laying bare the sand beneath, and moved him onto that spot beginning to wash him with sodden, herb-smelling towels. One overwhelming question had fallen unasked in Norit's assault on the court; and to ask it might bring down consequences as yet unconnected—but not to ask might lose him all chance to ask. The Ila's honesty was in question; so was Luz's.

And he cast back his one measure of truth, and promises kept. "I didn't lie, in there.—The Ila promised my mother's safety, and my sister's, if I came back. Is that true? Is my mother here? Is my sister?"

The slaves had stopped their work. Memnanan studied him and bit his lip. "What if I said she was here?" Memnanan was no fool, to give away the Ila's points in advance; but he was a decent man, Marak had sensed it once, and he believed it now, in the silent war in Memnanan's eyes.

"I'd believe you if you said so," Marak said.

Memnanan changed the subject. "Your arm has stopped bleeding."

It was an inconsequence. Marak bent it, glanced at it, expecting what he would see, that the wound was dry before the blood was. The area had grown warm with fever, and would swell.

He had denied all his life that he more than healed quickly, foolish notion. Now he knew that what lived in his blood would keep him alive through far worse than this. It might be a disadvantage.

"The Ila will hear you again," Memnanan said in leaving, "I'm relatively sure of it. Ask *her* about your relatives."

"The people out there . . ." Marak began, and Memnanan stayed from letting the curtain drop between them. "Did she call them in, or did they come?"

"They came. When the misfortunes began, where else would they go, but Oburan? One village passed another on the road, from farthest west inward, from south to north. So the trickle became a flood. They've left most of their harvest in the fields. They've eaten most of their provisions. Now they deplete Oburan's." Memnanan divulged his own worries, the coming, undeniable privations. "We can hold out a while. This tower you saw . . . this green-sided river . . . can it supply all the people in the world?"

"I don't know how many. It supplies a good many already. If she hears me," he said. "If she listens, then we have that much chance. If she asks you, tell her that. I could have stayed there in safety. I chose to come here, for my mother's sake, to rescue her, and anyone else I could."

"And the Ila?"

"I made her a promise. I'm here. I came back."

"So you did."

"Is she disposed to listen?"

"The earth shook. Everything came down. I don't know what her disposition is. But you were right in what you guessed. And the woman said far too much." Memnanan had already told him far too much, himself. Memnanan let the curtain drop and left him to the servants.

"Omi," they said, and came with their basin, and poured clear water over him, and washed his hair.

"I can wash myself!" came from beyond a curtain, and his spirits lifted. Hati was not threatened, or bullied. Hati was Hati.

It was Norit he could not account for. He knew that Memnanan was right, that Norit was deeply at risk. He saw no way to help her, more than he had already done, and had a slashed arm to show for it. He could argue with the Ila for Norit's life. He might have his way, if the Ila wanted the things he had to offer.

But what stopped Luz? What prevented Luz making things worse?

The servants dried his hair, dried him, gave him a sleeping robe of fine blue cloth, and drew back the curtain. Hati was there, damp and not yet robed, water a fine sheen on her dark skin. She cast a burning glance at the female servants, snatched the robe from their hands, and slipped it on, disdaining to fasten it.

The servants ebbed out of the chamber, through the curtains as she came to him. Hati wished to see his arm, which had already grown fevered and swollen.

"It will heal," he said. But Hati knew that, no less than he. "Where's Norit?" He failed to see her anywhere about the chamber.

"They took her away," Hati said. "I don't know where."

Hati's bath chamber provided a gilt-framed bed, and he led her to it, and they lay down, under the bronze lamps, weary, and able at least to rest. Thunder rumbled in the skies, and more than once they felt the earth give a slight shudder. That brought the crack and crash of stone as the nearby ruin settled.

"She's too proud to listen," Hati said, as they lay there wrapped in each other's arms. "She's lost everything she had, and I think she's too proud to take this offer."

"You were supposed to leave and go with the beshti," he said. "You were supposed to be with Tofi, safe, so I didn't have to worry."

"Not as I see it."

"You saw your tents. The Keran are here. Could you go to them?"

Hati shook her head, a tumble of moist braids on his arm, a scent of oils and herbs. "No. And if the Ila agrees to be sensible and go, we'll all go. And if she doesn't, I'll go and tell the Keran the truth, and then see what they do."

"Don't threaten her." He moved his left hand over her braids, smoothed her brow as she leaned her head against him. "Escape this place. You can walk out there, change your robe, and be one of ten thousand."

Hati heaved a long, deep sigh, and in that sigh was the chance of violence and dire actions considered, and denied.

"Only with you. If you wish me to leave, man of my choice, we both go to my tribe."

"Memnanan hinted that my mother and my sister might be here."

"Fine. We'll rescue them. We'll go east. We know where the stars fall. We'll go fast through that part."

It was dreaming out loud.

And it was dangerous, counting the thin curtains that surrounded them. The whole of his life had turned fragile, and all of life he trusted, all of life he held as his was in his hands, in Hati's slim, hard arms, in the confident look in her eyes. There might only be this. They might die at any moment. And life had never been worth more to him.

"The Ila knows about the healing, doesn't she?" Hati asked.

"I think she does know," he said. Above the tent he heard the thunder, and heard the distant shift of uneasy stone in the ruins. He was too weary to make love. He thought that Hati was, too. They simply looked at one another until Hati's eyes began to drift shut, and then did close.

He lay very, very still, for Hati's sake, despite the muttering of heaven and earth, and had one lengthy sleep toward what he thought must be dawn.

Then men-servants came in and provided them clothes, and brought them dried fruit and fresh bread, with butter . . . butter, which was a rare treat.

Memnanan came next. "Marak Trin," he said. "Come. The Ila wishes to speak to you."

Hati was immediately concerned, and was a move away from getting up to go with him, but Memnanan had a word for her, too. "Stay here. He will be safer if you do."

Hati sank back down and cast him a look as if to ask if he thought that was the truth.

"Do as the captain asks," Marak said.

15

It is the Ila's will that the abjori should exist, and at her pleasure and on a day to come, they will cease to exist: for this hour they are the trial of her people, gathering all her enemies together so that everyone may know them.
—The Book of the Ila's Au'it

Memnanan brought him alone through the maze of veils, stopped him in a narrow space, and nudged his arm to gain his attention.

"The Ila spent the entire night with the au'it," Memnanan said. "Watch yourself. Rein back that temper of yours. This time it won't serve you, or the women."

"Why do you warn me?" Marak asked, trying to catch the man eye to eye. "You being the Ila's man, why should you warn me?"

"Would you come this far, through so much, to tell her a lie?"

It was the plain truth, he discovered of himself. He was not set on the Ila's destruction.

Then what don't you believe? he wanted to ask Memnanan, seeing Memnanan believed him that far. What don't you believe, and what doesn't *she*?

But Memnanan *was* the Ila's man.

"Come with me," Memnanan said, and led him through

the last three curtains, where the Ila sat as she had sat last night, with the au'it by her. Another au'it—who might be theirs—sat nearby, on a carpet at the side of the chamber. Lamps still burned here, hung on golden chains, but with the leaden light seeping through the canvas the lamps seemed less bright than last night.

"Well," the Ila said. "Well." She held out her red-gloved hand and beckoned him. "Come," she said. "Show me your arm this morning."

Marak came close enough and pushed up his sleeve, no more surprised than she to find it only pink flesh.

"So," the Ila said.

"I heal well," he said, letting fall his loose sleeve. "I always have."

"So again," the Ila said. "And do you understand the makers, as this Luz calls them? The nanoceles?"

"No. I don't, at all."

"Falling stars," the Ila scoffed. He was accustomed to shame, regarding the visions. But these were no visions. He had seen the pits where they fell, and he would not be dissuaded.

"There are," he said.

"So this *Luz* has appointed herself our savior. Our god. And wants me to go to her."

"She wants everyone."

"Oh, doubtless she does! You're *still* mad," the Ila said. "Have you looked about this tent? Do you see the size of this encampment? And you'll lead us all to the edge of the Lakht?"

It was a question, a very terrible question. And the aui'it wrote it in their books.

"If we have to do it, we have to do it," Marak said quietly. "These encamped are the villages. They have their harvest tents, and beshti enough to get here. There are the tribes, who know how to get anywhere they choose to go. All I have to do is tell them 'beyond Pori,' and they'll know."

"And will this *Luz* stop the fall of stars?"

"I don't know. I don't think she can." That sort of honesty

was his besetting fault. It had gotten him his father's chastisement a hundred times before he could learn prudence. But he plunged ahead. "I don't know what she can and can't do. Or what you can. She's a stranger. I came to ask you, can *you* stop this?"

Perhaps no one had ever asked the Ila to do something impossible for her. She frowned at him, frowned long and hard.

"Such faith."

"I don't have faith," he said. "I don't trust strangers."

"Or me."

"At least you're not a stranger."

"So she wants me to come there. For what?"

It was the foremost question, and he could not answer that.

"If we stay here," the Ila said, and in that little time the earth shivered and shook, so that the aui'it gripped their books tightly as they wrote. "If we stay here, we will die. Do you believe that?"

"I know that for a truth," he said, trying to gather his wits, beset by her and the restless earth. "I know the *way* to the tower beyond Pori." It struck him that the Ila had *sent* him to Pori, not to the west, not to the north, not to the south, but specifically to Pori. She knew where the tower was. She had known before she sent him.

How much else had she known before she sent him?

"And you can guide us," the Ila said.

"If I can't, I have Norit."

"*You* have Norit," the Ila scoffed. "*Luz* has Norit."

"When Luz is done with her," he said, "she's my wife."

"Your wife!"

"Norit has no part in what Luz does."

"Have *you*?" the Ila asked him sharply. "Have you any part in what Luz does?"

He asked himself. And shook his head. "No." He added, because it was the absolute truth, "I don't *trust* Luz."

The Ila lifted her chin, looked down at him with hard and suspicious eyes. "Do you trust me more?"

"*You* never offered me anything."

The Ila made a bridge of her gloved hands. "Oh, but I did."

He shook his head, denying it. "I asked a favor of you, and you agreed. You never offered me anything."

"So I sent you out," the Ila said, "a man who eluded my patrols for three years, and this *Luz* took you up as quick as seeing you. Or quicker. She knew who you were. I doubt she had to listen to rumor to know you for the great Marak Trin Tain. You are her prize among the mad. What did she offer you?"

"What she offers everyone. Paradise. Paradise in white tents beside a green river." That image came back to him, but the more urgent visions were of disaster. "That was before the stars fell. I have no idea what's become of that place now. I think it's still safe. I think Norit would act differently if anything happened to her. Luz hasn't left her but moments at a time, all through our journey."

The Ila's lips rested against those bridged fingers. Her eyes burned, dark and deep.

"I have your mother, Marak Trin, and your sister. And your father."

So. He had steeled himself against caring. Against anything that could be a weapon in her hands.

"So you promised," he answered quietly. And suspected everything she said, every motive in her heart. "So I kept my promise to you."

"Virtuous of us."

She prodded at him, wanting an answer. He could think of none. He simply kept still.

"Suppose I said to lead all these people to the tower, Marak Trin. What would you do? How would you manage it?"

He drew a deep breath, a fleeting chance to think of first things, and second. "Do you want me to answer in specific?"

"Do."

"First, put in charge of each unit those who led them here. If a unit has beasts, they keep them. If they have tents, they keep them. If they have waterskins, they keep them. It's only fair. They have foresight. It makes them the likelier to live. Have the order of march and camp understood. Set the tribes to the fore: they would move quickest. Whoever moves slowest, falls behind, and who falls behind . . . there's nothing anyone can do. They'll die."

"It's that simple."

"Nothing can be simpler. The Lakht is the Lakht. It's never different, no matter who asks."

The Ila lowered her joined hands to her lap. "Captain."

"Ila," Memnanan said from back near the curtains.

"Assist him in this undertaking."

Marak blinked, thinking, Surely not, not that easily, not that quickly.

Not me, not over all this.

But silence followed. He understood dismissal, with that, and began to back away.

"Marak!"

He stopped. "Ila," he said, as Memnanan did.

"When will this people set out?"

When did not rest in his hands. *When* rested in the starfall and the calamity in the earth.

Marak, Marak, the voices clamored, suddenly riotous with urgency. Norit knew what was agreed. He was sure she knew. And then he was sure that Hati did.

"Tonight," he said, and took his life in his hands, for what had to be said. "I would advise, Ila, that you yourself use a common tent, one that two men can raise and pack, for your own safety. That you carry more food and water than weapons."

An implacable face met that judgment. "You would leave each segment of the caravan to its own decisions."

He had not asked himself why he chose as he did. It had seemed evident. Now he did ask. "The line of march will stretch too long. The leaders can't be everywhere along the line. The fastest have to go first. I will, however, give them advice, such as I have. Shelter, water, food, and then weapons. Beshti won't take the Ila's orders: they limit their loads."

The aui'it stopped writing. Everything stopped.

The Ila lifted a hand and made a gesture toward the second au'it, a command to rise, a second command less apparent.

The au'it went to the curtain behind the Ila's seat, and drew it back, and there sat, pile after pile, books, books of the aui'it's recording, hundreds, thousands of books, leather covers, canvas covers, stained books, ornate ones tattered with age and use.

"This is the knowledge," the Ila said. "And what will this *Luz* give to have it? And how will you move these, Marak Trin? Tell me how you will do it."

He was stunned. A village house could scarcely contain that pile. His voices clamored at him, *Marak, Marak, Marak,* and he had no idea what their desire was, or if Luz understood what he saw, or what it meant. They were the books of the aui'it, all the knowledge, all the recorded history there was.

"This is my condition," the Ila said as the earth shuddered, a small thump, like a heartbeat. "Not the tent, not this piece of furniture. They can go to hell. Where I go, *this* goes. Can you find beasts enough?"

"I'll find a way," he said on a deep breath.

The Ila regarded him thoughtfully. "Do that," she said, and moved her fingers in dismissal. "Do it by tonight."

That was all.

Marak, the voices said. He tried to manage his retreat. Memnanan guided him, held the curtain aside for him, took him by the arm. He saw fire, and ruin.

By tonight.

"I need the two women," he said to Memnanan.

"Not your father?" Memnanan asked. "Not your mother?"

"I have no time," he said. He remembered his father's parting with him and had no desire to see him. And for his mother and his sister there was no time.

Marak, Marak, Marak, the voices said, let loose, given sudden free rein. In his vision the rings of fire spread again and again: pools glowed red as iron in a forge, and he could all but smell the smoke.

He struggled to think and make lists. "I need Tofi. I need Hati and Norit. I need every leader of every tribe and village to meet me on the edge of the camp, on the caravan road to the south, inside an hour."

Memnanan looked at him, then passed the order to a subordinate who waited nearby. "See to the meeting," Memnanan said, with a wave of his hand, and that man gathered two others.

So the matter would spread, without their help. But Memnanan stood fast. "The two women. Luz's eyes and voice."

"One is Luz's voice," Marak said. "The other is an'i Keran. That tribe of all tribes will survive to reach the tower. If my mother and sister are here, let them go to the Haga. If they're there, that's all I need to know. They'll be safer than I can make them."

"And Tofi for his skills? He's a boy."

"Not since his father died. I want him, and his two men. He of all the masters understands exactly what's out there. I want him to manage the Ila's tents. Our tents."

"Beasts to carry the books?"

The captain might have his own estimate how many that was, a massive caravan unto itself, able to carry neither food nor tents.

"In the deep desert," Marak said, "we lost a besha on a slide and it started a mobbing. The mob left not a bone, not a scrap of leather. The besha was taller than either of us. The largest of the vermin in it didn't top a man's knee. We didn't wait to watch, but I'll imagine a man could watch it vanish."

"A remarkable sight," Memnanan said. "The god's wonder you lived. What do you mean?"

"That you don't need beasts to carry the books. You need the strongest, the likeliest men to live, of every village, every tribe."

Memnanan said nothing for a moment, frowning, but with thoughts sparking within his eyes. "Allow the books into the hands of the tribes?"

"Do you want these books to come through?" Marak asked, and saw that Memnanan listened to him intently. "Will these books pitch tents and manage a half a hundred beshti? Men do that far better. The books will have thousands of feet, and if one is lost, they won't all be lost." He drew a breath, space to think. "This caravan can't camp in a ring. They'll be strung out like beads on a necklace. We can't help that. If fools drink all their water, we can't help that. Water the beasts to the full. Feed them. Fill every waterskin in camp. Even the bitter wells are uncertain."

"That saves the villages. Oburan itself has few tents at all . . . few beasts, except the breeding herd. They're city folk. They don't know the desert."

"Apportion the important ones like the books, a few to every band. If there are too many walkers, they go last, enough strong hands to drive stakes, a besha to carry the canvas and keep them headed right if they drop behind." The beasts would smell the way to those in front, given any breath of an east wind or a lingering scent above the trail. A caravan this large would assuredly leave scent. It would leave a trail of waste, breakage, vermin, and all too many lives.

Memnanan, like him, was a man in authority, one who saw bitter necessities when they were laid in front of him, who knew how to make a rule for the good of the many. Individual compassion, for the two of them, was a vice secretly practiced.

"It's a chance," Memnanan said. That Memnanan knew the desert, Marak suspected, as the Ila's men generally knew enough of it to live . . . knew it as a place where they were strangers, being on their way to a place, on their way from a place, never at home in it. The villages existed within the desert: they had never quite lost their skills. When the big winds blew and ten men could die going out to secure an orchard netting, when sand could choke an unprotected well, when hunters caught in the open could easily die, if they failed to take the right steps . . . the knowledge of the desert was not that far removed.

"If you have a household," Marak said to the Ila's captain,

"put them with the tribes. Or in my tent, with Tofi and his men. I trust you'll be busy with the Ila's company, and I'll have room."

Memnanan gave him a look. "Too many old, who can't walk. A wife six months pregnant. The city has far too many."

"Put them with me," Marak said. "Get beshti for them. We'll get them up and down. Save your worry for the Ila. Be selfish, man. Give yourself this one gift. You're due it. I've asked several. We'll need to get the books down to the gathering. Give them to the leaders. Leaders survive. They have a duty to do that."

Memnanan said not a thing to that. He walked, and led him back through the veils, where he found another subordinate, in the chamber with his desk. "Bring the an'i Keran," Memnanan said, "and the village woman, the prophet."

But Hati came on her own, through the other curtain, expecting him and Memnanan, trailing an embarrassed guard. Madness had its advantage, in that regard, that no one had struck her; Hati reached him unhindered, seized his arm, wound his fingers into hers as Memnanan dismissed the confounded guard. In a moment more, Norit followed her, guard-led, with that calm, still face that told him Luz was entirely in the ascendant. Memnanan dismissed that man, too.

"We're going outside the camp," Marak said to Hati and Norit, "to talk with the leaders. We'll be moving this evening, with the Ila, with the tribes."

They did not question what he said. The three of them walked out of the tent with Memnanan, under a sky slate-colored and menacing. The water-gatherers at the Mercy of the Ila moved about their business. A handful of wretched people carried bundles out of the gates of the city, bent beneath their load. It was all useless, that gathering of resources.

Memnanan sent men for beshti and for wheeled carts to carry the precious books to the edge of the camp. "The priests moved them here," he said. "They can bring the books down. We'll rest here until they're ready. The god knows there'll be no rest tonight."

There was a little shaking as they waited. They sat on mats, under an awning, as wealthy folk passed time, while filling of the Ila's household waterskins and the watering of the Ila's herds took precedence at the Mercy of the Ila.

Servants brought them food and drink during a second tremor. The poles of all the tents shook, and the canvas shook. Behind his eyes, Marak saw a lake of fire spreading outward and flowing over desert rock. He saw the falling stars. But he ate and drank, and took his ease, the last that any of them might see in their lives. Memnanan went aside now and again to pass particular orders to his men, then came back to join them.

A rider came up, perched like a boy, bareback. Welcome sight, Tofi came riding up, clearly not expecting to see them disposed as they were, like a handful of wealthy enjoying the afternoon breezes, with the Ila's Mercy pouring out its abundance of water nearby and the searchers still busy in the rubble of the city beyond the ruined wall.

A flash of recognition preceded an immediate solemnity and formality in Memnanan's presence, and Tofi dropped from his saddle to stand the ground, light and quick as he was, wide-eyed and anxious.

"Men said to come, omi."

"That they did," Memnanan said.

"This camp will move tonight." Marak rose from his seat under the awning and came out into the wan, clouded sun. "You're to go among the first in a caravan of all these camps. You're to go in among the tribes. You can spread the word to the other caravan masters in the camp: if it gets out to the tribes, no harm done. There'll be no hire given but the lives of all of us, and you know the truth as well as I do: tell it to them. Rumors can fly, for all I care. Gather up all your tents, every beast, every man."

"Where shall we go, omi? Back?"

"Back, as fast as we can. You'll carry those persons the Ila bids you carry: the aui'it, the Ila herself, her servants and her men. Have you kept the freedmen?"

"I paid them wages," Tofi said, "and I don't know how

they found it. There's not a tavern working, but they're drunk."

"Hire them or not, but get skilled help, first, before the rest of the masters get wind of it. Where are you camped?"

"To the southwest edge," Tofi said. "On the flat. There's no other out there. Some have let their beasts go forage. I haven't. I waited."

"Good. We'll use our tent, the same we have used. It was a good size. Give the best one to the Ila and the aui'it. Her men will camp with us, with their households, I take it, in tents they will provide." Memnanan, standing close by, failed to contradict him, so he supposed the instruction stood. The Ila would move from this white grandeur into ordinary brown tents two men could have up and down again in haste, and her men would have the tents the Ila's men used in the desert. "Go see to it."

Tofi bowed, and bowed again. "Omi," he said. "Captain," he said to Memnanan, and ran to scramble up to the saddle of the waiting besha, making him extend a leg.

In an instant more Tofi was off down the street, vigorously plying the quirt.

16

The book of an au'it may not be opened except by an au'it and it may not be read to the people except an au'it read it. If a village wishes to know what is in an au'it's book, let them ask the au'it.
—The Book of Priests

The priests came to the Ila's tent with their besha-drawn carts, and the chief priest, a haughty old man, strode angrily past Memnanan, went into the Ila's tent and came out again with his hauteur aimed solely at the junior priests and with a very chastened demeanor toward Memnanan.

"We are," the chief priest said, every word labored, "to take the library in our charge. Where shall we dispose it?"

"Men of mine will guide you down," Memnanan told him, and with a nod of his head toward Marak: "He has the Ila's authority in this matter."

The priest looked at Marak in dismay, and turned to the junior priests to give orders. Aui'it came out, bearing books; and so priests went in, and servants, so that it became a hand-to-hand stream, loading the leather-bound books into their arms, one to the next past the veils and curtains of the interior, and servants passed books on to priests and soldiers outside, and they laid them carefully onto carts which would have fared very well on the pavings of the city. Now, with the increasing loads, they bogged in the wet sand around the Ila's Mercy, and required the beshti to labor to move them. "Not so many in a load," Memnanan said, and added under his breath, "fools."

"To the outside," officers shouted as they filled each cart. Memnanan sent an officer down with precise instructions, while Marak and his companions sat on mats in the shade of the awning and rested, truly rested in the bawling confusion. Norit slept longest, curled up in a knot. Hati waked and sat sharpening a knife. Neither of them had use in what proceeded. Marak himself let his head down and catnapped in what should have been the heat of the day, but was in fact cool and pleasant.

Important men and women arrived at the tent, and Marak lifted his head, overhearing that rumors were suddenly rife in the camp, regarding caravans leaving. "Caravans may indeed leave," Memnanan told them. "And if I were you I'd see to my herds, and have the beasts watered before the Mercy grows crowded."

Priests' white robes were now brown-edged with soil from the spring, dusty and stained by the moldering dye of the books; but on they worked, better men than they looked, in Marak's estimation.

The aui'it labored with them so far as loading the last carts, and two of them in their red robes went with the carts, down the sole straight road that led from the Mercy through the camp, and if rumor was not now running the circuit of the camps, nothing less than a star-fall in their midst would rouse curiosity.

Servants hung about in the doorway of the Ila's tent with worried looks on their faces. They had sent all their treasure out, at the Ila's order, under a sky leaden and disheartening. The guards themselves looked desperate, expecting further calamity, and looked about them as the ground shook, as if they now realized that cataclysm had reached the heart of their lives.

Traffic around the fountain increased to a point of panic, slaves of the caravans restoring their supplies, servants of households taking up water in jars, jostling with common folk and villagers: if one house was watering, then all would. Beshti moved in and out, with their handlers, snarling and grumbling.

The beshti Memnanan had ordered arrived to water, too. Marak was glad to see Osan among them: and the rest that appeared were fine animals, decked out in gear that shone with brass and fine dyes.

Memnanan's men came to report the carts outside the city and disposed under guard of the priests. It was time to move.

Norit slept like the dead, for all the rest she had not had, and they had not disturbed her. But now Marak shook gently at her shoulder, and met for a moment the gentle face, the sensible one. She had a frightened look, in her interludes of sanity, as Marak could only imagine. Norit's plunges into madness were deep and dark, and left her haunted by things she half remembered, half understood.

He tipped up her face and kissed her, and Norit kissed him back, her fingers woven with his, reluctant to let go.

"Priests have already gone down," he said gently. "With the last of the books. We'll ride, with the captain and his men. Can you get up, or shall I help you?"

"I *want* to go," was her answer: Norit's answer, as if she had half heard everything until now, or as if she wished to say that going back to the tower was her choice, apart from Luz's wish.

"Come," he said, and helped her gently to her feet. He and Hati together picked out a fine gentle beast and helped her up to the saddle before they themselves mounted up.

Then Memnanan rode his besha to its feet, and the rest of the company got up, a good twenty men besides, good, agile riders, armed beneath their robes, and carrying heavy quirts, Marak noted, not solely for the beshti.

"I've ordered the books to a ridge beside the road," Memnanan said, swinging in close to Marak as they walked their beasts past the fountain and through the confusion there. "And I've sent messages calling the lords of the villages and the tribes there to hear us. If I were doing it, I'd have the Ila down the hill to speak to them, but she says rely on the priests to persuade the people. She sends her messages through the priests. I have less confidence."

"In the priests?" Marak said. "I have none at all." The visions momentarily haunted him with sights of fire and destruction to come . . . then failed entirely, and even the imagination of the next handful of moments eluded him, leaving him bereft of any resource. From instant to instant he believed what he saw . . . and then saw only disaster in attempting to get all this mass of people on the road in any orderly fashion, without fatalities even in the process itself. He imagined no one would take the books. No one would care. He and Memnanan had deliberately let rumor loose, foretelling the movement of a caravan, and fear became a bitter dose at the fountain, where rumor spread.

Now a tide of worried people shouted questions at them: "Where are the caravans going?" and: "What will the Ila do?"

Marak had no idea on the latter and wanted no pause for questions, not yet, not here, disorderly as the road through the camp proved to be. "Wait," he shouted at the importunate. "Your leaders are going down to hear. Stay here! Pack your belongings!"

There must be a fervor to carry them, a wild, a mad, an unstoppable urge: he stirred it, and knew what he did . . . he reminded them of their belongings. He hinted of movement. If the leaders denied him, the people themselves would be behind, pushing, demanding answers of their leaders, who had only one place to get answers. But it was a dangerous action. It could end in looting, in murder, in people trampled, or robbed, or stabbed and shot. Any leader knew it. Any leader who had not gone out to the summons would know he had to go, he had to find out the truth of their situation.

And it could not wait another day.

"You're running a risk," Memnanan said.

"They have to move," he said. "They have no choice." More people crowded in on them. Three times more he told them the same, before the rumor was running the camp on so many legs that their appearance was only confirmation, the outflow of authority, the imminence of movement.

The road poured them out of the camp and onto the vermin-hazard of the open sands, a fast-moving company of riders. A relatively few curious had come, the anxious, the frightened, representatives of households joining their leaders on the flat. They came in their hundreds out to the ridge, a mobbing not for blood but for news, and pressed outward in greater and greater numbers, hysteria in their faces. In some areas of the camp behind them, tents were already collapsing.

A ridge of sand along a face of rock: that was where Memnanan had ordered the priests and the aui'it to take their cargo of precious books, and that was where Memnanan had told the lords and the leaders to meet. The Ila's men had gone out to protect the priests and the aui'it, and spread out across the ascent to prevent others.

The priests tried to make themselves heard, trying to take authority to themselves, crying out that the judgment was on the city.

"The god has sent this!" they shouted out to believers within hearing. "The god has decreed a judgment! Repent of your rebellion and your greed, and the Ila will intercede for you!"

"We have to silence that," Marak said as they came within earshot. "They don't know a damned thing, and they have no authority over anything but the books. Quiet them."

Memnanan had a worried look, but he gave orders to his men as they reached the ridge: the guards went to the priests and ordered their leaders off the ridge, down at the base, where the carts were. There the junior priests had spread out and made a useful defense of themselves, a line of bedraggled white between them and the press of the crowd.

A greater and greater crowd gathered, both from the edge of the camp and from the far side of the city perimeter. There were thousands afoot, and tribesmen mounted on beshti, all pressing toward one point, one source.

"This is dangerous," Hati shouted at him above the noise

of the crowd. "They all want to know what's happening. What will happen when they know?"

"They will know," Norit said in a loud voice: *Luz* shouted. "*This is the day of judgment! Hear Marak! Hear the messenger! Listen to him!*" But even Luz could not make herself heard, and the soldiers plied their quirts, driving back those the crowd behind shoved forward.

In that moment Marak feared for their lives, knowing he had set too much in motion too fast. The beshti they rode snuffed the scent of the crowd, the palpable scent of fear, and swung their heads this way and that, ready to fight, sensing a mobbing and knowing only one answer to that. Madness was not the sole property of the mad, not now. The crowd stretched now almost as far as the tents, under the clouded sky. The leaders who came forced their way to the base of the ridge, the tribesmen and some few village lords riding, most afoot, pushing, shouting, arguing with the priests and pushing at the soldiers, whose whips only frustrated the press, and did nothing to hold it back.

Then Memnanan drew a rifle from his saddle gear, and fired several rounds into the leaden sky. The reports echoed off the cliffs, startling beshti, bringing a moment of relative silence.

"Marak Trin Tain!" Memnanan shouted out. "The Ila's answer to your questions. Be quiet! The god speaks through the Ila, and the god has appointed an escape for his people! Be still. Stand still!"

"That's Aigyan," Hati said, edging her beast close to Marak's, pointing. "The man with the red sash. Lord of the an'i Keran. He sees me. He may suspect revenge. *There* is trouble."

They could not be heard in the mutter around the ridge. Marak saw the veiled tribal lord, one of a handful of the deep Lakht tribes he most wanted well-disposed to them—and one that he least wanted against him. He knew the challenge he would face; but Memnanan had given him his moment, his only moment, and he rode Osan to the center of the ridge, looking out on thousands of misgiving, mistrustful faces. Men below looked up, a moment, a single moment in which the crowd expected an outcome, a miracle.

"*Safety!*" Marak shouted out in the inspiration of his heart. "Safety! That's become more scarce than water on the Lakht! The refuge you came here to find, all of you, water, food, and shelter enough for every household! I, Marak Trin, I've come in from across the Lakht with a caravan and we're going out again, to bring you all to a place where one refuge for you exists, off the edge of the plateau, beyond the village of Pori! I've seen it! I've seen a river green-sided with palms. I've seen beshti wandering free of harness. I've seen craftsmen in their tents, working for the pride of their craft! I've seen the heart of the tower that provides this place and keeps the star-fall away from its land! I've been inside it, and I know it exists!"

Cries rose up to him, one and another just out of earshot trying to position himself to hear and the attempt crushing those nearest.

"I say *safety,*" Marak repeated for those who were in earshot of a shout. "I say a caravan leaving the holy city, going to an oasis where you and your children will *live!*"

That created its own babble, repeated mouth to ear among the crowd, and now, caught in the press of bodies forward, riders controlled irritated, snappish beasts.

"The tribes will move first," Marak shouted, while the fire boiled and bubbled within his vision, while the stink of heated rock assaulted his imagination. "The Keran and the Haga, of the deep Lakht, will go first. Then the Ila's caravan. Then tribes beyond that. And the villages! Let every tribe, let every village, let every man forgive their feuds! What is the law of the Lakht? What is the god's law? That when the wind rises, any man may come into a tent, regardless of feuds, to the number the tent will bear! No just man can deny shelter!"

Grim veiled men nodded. It was the law. And now for the first time there was a hush over the crowd. Those who could possibly hear leaned close.

"The Keran are the kinsmen of my wife, the Haga are the

kinsmen of my mother," Marak shouted, as loudly as he had in him, "and to them I entrust the guidance of the caravan. The Ila will go with me, in my band. Then the rest of the tribes, in their honor, as they determine precedence, then the villages, as they determine precedence. Those of the city, you with no tents, no knowledge of the desert, each tent of the villages will take one or two of you, and those who have to walk, will walk following the beshti, with riders to guard you and to set the pace. Each lord of a tribe will govern his tribe, each lord of a village will govern his village." *Fire,* the visions said to him, overwhelming all sense of what he had to say. Random words welled up in him, not his own, warning of this disaster and that, and he smothered them, fighting for his sanity and his own sense. "More, —*more!* each strong and reputable and god-fearing man will carry, besides his day's water, the wisdom of the aui'it, on his person, one book! These strong men will bring the wisdom of the aui'it to the new land and they will have their names and the names of their houses written down forever! One book, *one book* with a man or a band or a tribe will assure the carriers of it a welcome in the paradise the Ila will rule! If a man of the tribes and of the villages wishes to carry that burden for himself, let him come forward now to the priests and present himself to the aui'it, who will entrust him with that honor! Spread that word! *Paradise* for the bearers of the books!"

The priests had by no means realized what sacrilege he intended. Perhaps they imagined they alone would carry those books, pulling their carts through the deep desert. Perhaps at very least they expected more order about it, a making of orderly lists: but the mood and tenor of the crowd was not in favor of long lines and meticulous recording of names.

"No!" the chief priest shouted at him, and a murmur went out from the ridge, all the way back, over the grumbling complaint of beshti and a lone, frightened voice shouting above the rest, "What did he say, what did he say?"

"Paradise!" he shouted. "Water enough and food enough for you and your children!" He lifted his arms and shouted with all the strength that was in him, half-kneeling on Osan's saddle as he did. "When men think they will all die, they gather together, not to die alone. You all came here to *die,* and not to die alone, but we have better news! We know the path to paradise! We move at sunset. We're not going to die. We refuse to die! Those who survive this journey are all going to *live,* in a paradise *on this earth!*"

A young caravanner of the tribes leapt up onto his feet, standing barefoot on his saddle, waving his arms and shouting in excitement.

He was not the only one. Men waved their arms and cried aloud. Those at the back of the gathering were still trying to find out what was said; but those near the front saw the books and rushed at them, overwhelming the priests as men took books for themselves, snatched two and three in their passion for rescue. Pages were imperiled in squabbles. A cart axle cracked in the press of bodies, and spilled its load of books onto the sand, priests scrambling to save them as the crowd utterly mobbed the carts.

Norit screamed above the cries of the crowd, wild-eyed, a madwoman beyond any doubt. "The hammer of heaven is coming down!" Norit cried. "Listen to Marak Trin! Prepare to move!"

The priests shouted to their own wild-eyed hearers, "Respect the god, in the Ila's name!" Believers cried out, "The god and the Ila, the god and the Ila his regent!" while fire rained down in Marak's vision.

Now he knew the city folk would follow, and follow with the passion of belief, never mind what they believed, only *that* they believed, and drove their bodies with the strength of that belief. It *was* the god that would save them, because they would go, and go, and go, believing in paradise.

Marak, Marak, Marak, his voices dinned at him, ill timed, goading him, urging precipitate action, urging him to lead this mob, when he most wanted to use his wits.

"A judgment on the earth!" Norit cried over all the tumult: "The hammer of heaven is coming! Do you see it, Marak, do you see it? *It's coming! We're losing time!*"

Luz was afraid. *Luz* herself was gripped by fear. He saw in his vision a falling rock, saw it strike, saw a ring of fire spreading out from it; and a taste like copper came into his mouth. *Haste, haste, haste* dinned in his head until he could scarcely think, as if a message had held off as long as it could and now that the essential thing was done, Luz told them, unveiled what unnerved even her.

He saw Hati similarly afflicted by the vision, her hands clamped over her ears, and he fought to still his own shrieking voices, trying to use his wits for what still had to be done.

"Captain!" he shouted at Memnanan. "As soon as you can get there, bring the Ila to us where Tofi's camped, at the southwest corner, on the flat. He's waiting for us. He'll need help there: he has the beshti, and he has to keep them!"

"Do you want a detachment with you?" Memnanan asked him.

"You'll need them for your own safety!" Marak yelled back. "Go!" He turned Osan's head, tried to speak coherently to the tribal lords, less bothered by the shouting below, at the carts than at the noise in his head, the flaming rings that obscured his sight.

Memnanan led his men off to the north, off the edge of the ridge. But to the face of the ridge, coming up toward them, was the lord of the Keran, still among the foremost, and he looked no happier.

"Norit, stay with us!" Marak said, and turned Osan's head, suddenly within close-range shouting distance of the veiled man, in the surrounding tumult, both of them mounted, over the heads of the pandemonium below. "I'm Marak Trin Tain," he shouted out across the racket. "I've married this woman. She's never complained of your fairness. And I've heard nothing but good of the Keran, and I want you to the lead, omi! Forgive me for putting it forward without begging your goodwill, but the sky gives us no time for such courtesies."

The veiled man glared back, looking at him, not at Hati. "What is your request, villager?"

"Lead a caravan east, past Pori, past the rim of the Lakht,

where there's safety from the star-fall. No one knows the eastern desert better than the Keran. *She* proves that."

The eyes above the veil were hard as black stone, and no more revealing.

"Marak Trin Tain, is it?"

"All the world's come here expecting to die. If someone doesn't lead all the world *away* from here, they'll starve, if the stars don't destroy them first. The crops will fail. The star-fall will only get worse. Soon there'll be no food to sustain this mass of people."

"I bleed from grief. We'll ride away safe."

You came here, it occurred to him to say. You came here because everyone else was coming. . . .

But that was not the way to win this man. Not this man.

"I'm amazed your *pride* isn't sufficient," Marak said, leaning an elbow on his knee. "Hati had said you'd want to lead, not follow."

"Lead this *refuse*?"

"To lasting glory. A caravan. A caravan of everyone in the world, toward safety. No one will forget your name. Aigyan, they'll say. *Aigyan-omi, the great tribesman, the most famous man in all the tribes.* You can't be famous if there's no one to tell the tale."

"I hear you're mad as she is." It was Aigyan's first acknowledgment Hati existed.

"At least as mad as she is," Marak said, "but both of us have the Ila's forces under our command. That's Memnanan himself that's just left here. Do you know the name?"

"Marak Trin Tain commands the Ila's army, and Captain Memnanan takes his orders. The *Ila's* mad, too."

"No. The Ila's gone sane. She wants to live. I ask you: lead. You'll go first, the other tribes, then the Ila with my company."

"That white whore! In her billowing white canvas!"

"None of the big tents: small ones, fit for the desert. It's our only chance."

"And what's at the other end? There's no oasis beyond Pori!"

"Have you been beyond Pori? I have."

"My father was there. And there's nothing there."

Pieces came together. Made sense. "Thirty years ago. This began thirty years ago. There was another Descent. And I've seen the tower. I've seen the river. A green oasis, past Pori and off the Lakht a few days." He had only the eyes to reason with, above the veil, dark and fierce as Hati's, but they were attentive, and he took a chance. "I tell you this well knowing you could find your own way there and leave the villages to die. You came here because you hoped the Ila had an answer for the star-fall. You came because you know how bad it is out there. Well, so do we. We just crossed the Lakht. And we know that a skill like yours is the best help we could get."

The eyes narrowed above the veil. For the first time they swept across Hati, acknowledging her existence. "This *is* Marak Trin Tain." That was a question, flatly stated.

"Marak Trin, no longer Trin Tain," Hati said, "because *Tain* is a fool. Be patient. He'll make you an honest grandfather yet."

What had he just heard?

The an'i Keran swept aside his veil and spat to the side. It was a superstition, ridding the place of devils, and Aigyan stared across at them, unveiled, a man the sun had weathered about the eyes, a man whose face showed deep scars and an unforgiving mouth.

"Daughter of a devil. So now I'm to follow *you,* is it?"

"Join me," Marak said urgently, before things flew out of hand. "Lead the caravan. Take the place of honor across the edge of the Lakht. Can a man ask more?"

"Your mother is *Haga.*"

Aigyan might as well have spat as said that word. There was an old feud, old as water boundaries.

"Damned right his mother is Haga!" rang up from below, where other tribesmen had forced a way toward them, brown and green, Haga riders, six or seven of them.

One rider suddenly drove his besha up toward them.

"My enemy," Aigyan said, unveiled, and Menditak, lord of the Haga, likewise unveiled himself as he arrived.

"Water thief!" Menditak hissed.

"Hold off," Marak said, and drove Osan between the two. "To you, omi, the lead." This he said to Aigyan. "And Hati goes with me.—And you, omi, mother's cousin . . ." The last was for Menditak of the Haga, heartfelt. "I've reserved a place of honor for you. I hope you have my mother and my sister. I knew if there was any safety for them, it was with you, and I know if anyone will bring all his tribe through, you will. That's why I want you on the one side and the Keran on the other, because you're the wisest, the canniest, and the quickest leaders alive, and I *need* you both, not one, not the other, but both of you in your right minds and your good judgment! Your peoples' lives, all our lives depend on it!"

"New land, you say! Paradise!" The last was mockery from Menditak of the Haga. Few of the tribes believed in the god behind the Ila. They had their own ways, their own paradise, their own devils, and one of the latter *was* the Ila.

"To each his own!" They could all but hear one another normally, with the sudden ebb of the crowd from around the ridge. Tribesmen had drawn swords and villagers and priests alike scrambled out of the vicinity, not that they were targets, but that a tribesman had as soon ride over them as around them. "Water and safety is what I offer! I came back to save as many as I could! It was beyond my hope to get word out to the tribes, but here you are, and now I see a chance for the rest of the lives out here under this unfortunate sky! It's gotten worse, and it will get worse than that, rapidly, trust me that I know. Paradise of water, of shade, of everything material, and honor! Not forgetting honor, and the respect of all the villages as well as the tribes." They were both there, they were both listening, and neither had ridden at the other. "Will you ride away from honor? Will you ride away from renown greater than any man has ever had? Or will you ride at the front of the greatest caravan the world has ever seen?"

"We go first," Aigyan declared.

"And you next the Ila's men," Marak said before Menditak

could take umbrage at that, "and not less in honor. It takes *two* of you, setting aside water feud, to demonstrate to all the tribes how great-souled men can behave! One isn't without the other! It takes you both, and both of you will have that reputation. Ever after this, whenever men talk about wise agreements, they'll say, Like Aigyan and Menditak, after their example. You'll become a proverb for wise men. You'll put all the rest to shame, never yourselves."

They hesitated. If the wind blew contrary, if a besha sneezed, if anything tipped the balance the other way, it was calamity. But the wind stayed still.

"My fathers," Marak said, in the way of the tribes with other men, paying his respect. "We need you."

"To Pori," Aigyan reminded him. "And how do we move these city-bred fools?"

"As the tribes move. If men fall behind, they fall behind. Take the south road tonight and wait for me by the Besh Karat, do you know it?"

"As I know my own backside," Menditak said.

"I trust you to know," Marak said—whatever and any flattery to keep the peace. "I have to gather the Ila's beshti. If anything should happen to me, leave, lead as many as you can keep alive and go to the village of Pori. Do you know a northern route? It's safer."

"It's reputed there's a northern track," Aigyan said. "Our oldest may remember. If not, I can still find my way."

"Ha!" Menditak said.

"Go for Pori, then east, down off the Lakht, east still, and ten marks off east to the south. There's the refuge!"

"There's nothing out there!" Menditak protested.

He resisted the voices' cry for haste. Resistance was all that gave him sanity.

"There is now. A second Descent."

"And another Ila?" This was no good thing to the tribes. "Hell with that, sister's weanling!"

"A rich land. Water. Palms thick as you please. It's Oburan, before the city rose. It's the heart of a new land, uncle, the heart of the people the tribes will supply with goods and trade. What have you left here? What will you have left, if the Lakht becomes a smoking waste—as it will! As it will, uncle! More than the mad have seen it now. All of you have seen what we warned you would come down, and now we tell you there's a way to live, and live well, rich as the Ila, every one of you, if only you get there with the people's gratitude. The people's gratitude is better than gold, far more powerful. Live! Don't despise what I tell you. The people need you now. Who else can we look to save us?"

"Flatterer!"

"I've become a prophet, uncle. And I tell you both the truth. Keep the peace, and be there, by the Besh Karat!"

He kept nothing from them. If he had resources, he poured them out to those that knew how to use them.

But he believed his own urging, and delayed no longer. "Hati!" he shouted. "Norit!" He gave Osan a whack of the quirt, trusting him to find its way down from the ridge, trusting the two feuding lords to find their way to their own tribes, Memnanan to find the Ila, and the two women with him to stay behind him.

But another rider barred his path. He saw his sister among the Haga riders, and his sister saw him, there at the very foot of the ridge.

"Patya!" In utter astonishment he reined Osan to a halt and dropped to the ground by the mounting loops. His sister slid down, her feet within knee height of the ground, but Patya, silly girl, failed to know it, and held on.

He simply swept her up in both his arms like a child, flung her rightwise about to look at her, and hugged her breathless.

"Marak!" His mother, Kaptai, dismounted beside them, a plummeting of brown veils and a clash of bracelets. He caught her, too, and swung them both around, veils flying. He pressed their faces against his, and he smelled the smells of home and hearth about them, everything that had kept him alive on the trek to Oburan.

"You're safe," he said. "The Ila kept her promise!"

"They said you were back," Patya said, still hugging him. "No one believed you'd come back, but we believed."

"I love you," he said to her. "I love you," to his mother. As far as he remembered he had never said that word to either of them, and least of all to his father, but now it had become a word he owned; and when he said it he knew he had forgotten Hati in a moment in which he was home again, before Hati, before everything had changed.

"You came back," his mother said. "You said you would come back, and you did."

What had he said? He had made a hundred promises when he left them, all lies; but unlikely as they were, he had kept them all, every one.

Hati had gotten down. He felt her familiar arm slip around him. He took her hand, and put it in his mother's. "This is Hati," he said in utter, untrammeled joy—then saw the dismay, the look from head to foot.

An'i Keran, tribal enemy under this foreign sky.

But his mother, of the Haga, hesitated only for a heartbeat, and gave her an embrace, his mother rattling with the wealth of a lord's daughter, a lord's wife: she had come away with everything, and Hati with only the bracelets he had given her.

Patya embraced Hati, too. "For Marak," Patya said. "For him."

There was another rider near them. Norit was there, and her, too, he showed to his mother. "This is Norit, from Tarsa. I have *two* wives."

"Two?" said Patya, a child of the west. But his mother never blinked. "Daughter," Kaptai said, while the earth shivered. She reached up a hand, the token of an embrace, but Norit for whatever reason did not get down, and Menditak had come down, urgent to be away.

"Damn this shaking!" Menditak said. "Bargains with the omi Keran! Come on, there! Will you delay for a damned festival?"

"Up." Marak heaved his sister up to her saddle. His mother, like Hati, needed no help. He made Osan extend a foreleg, and caught the strap and got up, recklessly, pridefully mounting like a tribesman in front of this arrogant old man, and Hati did the same.

"Away!" Menditak shouted, above the rumble from the skies and the earth, and the earth shuddered as Menditak took his company toward the north and east and Marak rode ahead of Hati and Norit toward the north and west.

"The god's vengeance on the Ila's enemies!" some lingering priest cried from the side of the ridge. "Salvation for the righteous! Pray for the Ila! Pray for our salvation!"

Tents were already beginning to collapse on the edge of the camp, adding to the confusion an unintended consequence. Essential landmarks were disappearing. Confusion multiplied. He rode through the diminishing crowd, past a camp edge that itself was blurred by so many, many people milling about trying to find the lost, the strayed, the ones who had to know what they had just heard. People shouted at one another, waved arms, cursed or pleaded. The noise of their confusion went up to the heavens.

Someone recognized them as they rode. People ran at them. Hands caught at their legs, at their beasts' harness. People shouted questions, what they were to do, what the Ila might do. The lifesaving frenzy he had helped create threatened to overwhelm them.

"Pack and get to the south road!" Marak shouted, and brought his quirt down sharply on his beast's hindquarters.

Osan leapt forward, scattering men who were closing in ahead of them, and Marak took that gift, rode after, trusting Hati to keep Norit with her and both of them behind him. A man went down, knocked aside: it was not his concern. He had held the visions at bay, he had spilled out everything he knew to two tribes of twenty, and now that the need to speak was past, he could no longer think, or see anything but the ring of fire.

Marak, the voices cried, wanting, demanding something more of him, urgent with this new, this ill-timed vision. *Marak!*

He and Memnanan had created this panic. They had primed the people with fear and uncertainty and the sense of one essential escape from their plight, one door by which they might exit, and it to the south. He had used every tactic, every wile he had, he had said he knew not what in the urgency of saying something, promising something to get the people to move. He had abandoned his own mother and his sister to the safety they could find, and now his only companions were companions in the madness: he was through with dealing with sane people, ignorant people, desperate people.

Tofi, who had seen the tower, Tofi, who had the tents, was the missing piece, of all the structure he still had to assemble, and he knew where Tofi had said he would be, one young man and a handful of beasts and two slaves, on whom he depended, out across the flat, to the southwest of the city and imperiled by men desperate for tents and transport.

Leave me alone! he raged at the voices and the visions, and rubbed his eyes until they were shot full of dark and red stars. *Let me alone! Let us alone! Let me see and hear!*

"There's Tofi!" Hati cried, riding up even with him and pointing ahead, on the flat where Tofi had said they would be.

There, through a haze of dust and the running figures of men bound for the tents, Marak saw beasts, all seated, all ready for their packs, and Tofi, who was waiting for them, waving them in while confused and desperate men ran past his goods and his beasts.

"Omi!" Tofi cried, as they rode in. "Omi, we're here. We have everything. What are we to do?"

"Stay where we are," Marak said, though Tofi was clearly ready to load on the instant. The ex-slaves, Mogar and Bosginde, were with him; so were older, hard-faced men, caravanners who might know their trade, and more slaves, young and strong ones as anxious in this confusion and the threat of the heavens as any free man. All this Marak saw with a glance. "The captain's on his way back to the Ila. He'll manage that part. She'll arrive with her tents." He reined Osan about before leaving the vantage of Osan's high back, with Hati by him, but Norit was nowhere in sight, and Hati was looking anxiously behind them, scanning all the way they had come, through a milling crowd.

He did not immediately see Norit, but he knew her coming, knew her presence as a magnet knew iron. He saw her riding through a gust-borne cloud of dust and waved to her, signaling her.

She rode toward them, and priests labored in her wake, white-clad men afoot, crying out after her, but a surge of running people poured between and cut them off.

Norit reached them, her besha wild-eyed and still trembling from fright. But they were made whole, the three of them together again, and safe for the moment. Their madness had become linked, one to the other, and where one was, the others would come, and where Luz was, they would know Luz's intentions, all three of them: there had been no chance they would lose her while she was free to ride, Marak was sure of that now.

"Everyone's gone mad," Tofi lamented, standing on the ground beside him. "We can be robbed if we stand still!"

"Far worse than that can happen," Marak said, conscious of the lead-colored heavens over their heads and the crowd seething back into the camp on the edge of outright panic, a narrow margin between the urge it took to move this number of people and the fear it might set off an utter panic. "Stay mounted," he said to Hati and Norit. "All the rest of you, mount up. Let no one cross here. Use the quirts. Make stragglers go around us and the baggage!"

Luz was satisfied, exhausted. The voices and the visions dimmed in his head and ceased to drive him.

In the gray sky above them a shooting star streaked beneath the clouds, sputtering fire as it fell. Tofi's men cried out and pointed, and priests, in the chaos of the crowd, pointed aloft and raised their hands in prayer.

"The priests may come into our camp," Marak said. "They're useful. But for the rest, don't pity anyone. We know the way. Our resources are for us and the Ila to stay alive. Without us all the rest will die." He felt a chill as he made that pronouncement, facing the scene in front of him, the ruin of a city ringed with tents as far as the eye could see. He made an exception for the priests. With all his heart he hoped his mother and his sister were safe, but he knew his mother could ride, and knew they were safer with the Haga, come what might: the Ila's close company had dangers of a kind he had to be free to deal with.

Most of all they would be happier not seeing him as he was, prey to madness and harried at times beyond love for anyone.

For the rest, there was one, only one alive who could hold this mass of people together, and she, red-robed, their life-long enemy, amid that tangle of canvas and ropes and panicked crowds.

If no one else in the city escaped, *she* must come down, soon, very soon, because if this mass became a mob, it was no more rational than any other mobbing in the desert, no mind, no wit, only desperation and self-seeking, devouring its own to satisfy the panic hunger, and they would have to take to the road and get ahead of it or die.

The ex-slaves had gotten up on their beasts. Tofi's common sense for convenience, never knowing this would happen, had set them out of the convenient track for traffic going back and forth along the edge of the camp, and well toward their road. So when men took a notion to go far out of their way to encroach on their stacks of baggage, or to cast desperate, covetous eyes on their beasts, they could be sure it was no innocent encounter: they took their quirts and beat them off time and again. The would-be thieves were not brave, and went to plunder more helpless prey.

But quirts would not be enough when dark fell, as the camp ripped up the stakes and folded its canvas and began to quarrel about the life-and-death question of who rode, and who walked, and what they had to leave behind.

There would be a brief period of looting, Marak was well sure: when this huge camp utterly broke up, the wise would leave what fools would think they desperately needed; and there would be that sorting out of goods. Some, too, would elect to stay with the ruins, seeking shelter there, in the ruin of the Beykaskh, ignoring prophecies as they ignored the evidence of their eyes. Those few might even be right. The wealth there, and the burrows they might make in the shattered stones, might suffice to save them.

He would never wager his own life on it.

The sun sank in the clouds. He kept his eyes sweeping the south, where the caravan had to form, trying to discern whether the tribes had yet moved, sure that the first hint that one tribe was on the road would set off the others determined to secure their place in the march. He had said sundown: sundown was what he aimed for, and he feared delay for its own reasons: tonight the ones in utter lack would run riot in the ruins, predators and prey alike.

He waited, and he waited, and sure enough, as the sunset widened across the clouds. A handful of the more organized rough element made a determined sortie against their belongings. Marak saw it developing, and joined Tofi and his men, not just quirts now, but knives as well. None of the knives in fact drew blood: the skilled snap of a loaded quirt across a man's arm or head was no small deterrent, and the ex-slaves enjoyed giving back what they had gotten. The ruffians drew back to regroup, nursing bruises.

"*Marak.*" Norit caught his attention, pointing.

A line of riders descended the hill among the collapsed tents, tall beasts gliding through the smoky chaos of the camp with the beshti's classic arrogance. The foremost of those riders were armed men and the center of that column were riders all in red.

At that presence people all across the camp were distracted, and the straggling priests found a focus for their prayers to heaven.

A great number of the dissolving camp surged toward the Ila, those who worshiped her posing a more serious threat than bandits. Silver flashed in the dim sunlight as the Ila's guards cleared a path for her safety.

So the Ila and her court came down from the hill.

"Get the packs on," Marak shouted over at Tofi, who sat his saddle sweating and pale from the latest fight. "Pack up! We're through with this! We have an armed escort now. And we're going to move!"

17

Give shelter to an enemy and you hold a knife by the blade.
—Miga proverb

The Ila might never have ridden in her life, Marak thought, but ride she did, at Memnanan's side, and behind her rode the aui'it, a broad gout of jewel red in a landscape otherwise brown and rust and yellow, under a murky sky. Behind them came the Ila's guard and the Ila's household, down to the servants.

Then came the pack beasts, to the number of about a hundred, all under Tofi's direction, and under the management of his freedmen and his slaves: the Ila's staff had no idea how to pitch a tent.

For so large a group, including tents for the guard, it was a modest number of beasts: Memnanan above all that staff understood the necessities of the Lakht, and might have enforced his choices on the Ila's will. Tofi had had the foresight to gather help, at a time when skilled help had become as precious as water.

None of Tofi's doings needed question. Marak only waited while that line of riders clove its way through the confusion and turned toward them.

At the last, calmly despite the recent armed confrontation, he simply lifted his hand to confirm his location, if Memnanan had doubted it. Memnanan lifted his hand. They saw one another. It was accomplished, all they had set out to do.

Now it was a matter of getting this mass of people directed south in some kind of order.

Hati moved off to consult with Tofi, but Norit stayed by his side, silent, watching as Tofi's men hurried to attach the packs to the saddles. "Hup-hup-hup!" Marak heard, that call that had afflicted the mad on their march, but this time it came as a welcome sound, a promise of freedom. Beasts snarled and grumbled and got up to work.

Tofi himself brought a waterskin for him, and the two freedmen brought Norit's. They had secured none for themselves: it was the way the day had progressed. "I have your gear packed aboard," Tofi said, "all of it."

"I'm in your debt," Marak said. He had regarded Tofi as a quick-witted young man; he was not surprised, or disappointed, either. "If debts will ever be paid in this life."

"Save us from the Ila, is all," Tofi said under his breath. "Don't let her cut my head off, and I'll be grateful."

Tofi went to his business. Hati rode up beside him, and slowly the Ila's column wedged a straight course through the confusion toward them.

"Form up," Marak called out when he judged it time.

Tofi moved, shouting to his men, who already knew their places in the line of march.

The Ila approached, at Memnanan's side, and Marak waved a signal, sweeping to the south and never even stopping for courtesies. Marak fell in smoothly with the head of that column, he and Hati and Norit.

The Ila was behind them, in the heart of their protection, not leading. An au'it, their own au'it, fell in with them and rode with them, her book on her knee, writing as she rode.

"Ride with me," Marak said to Memnanan. "Is your household with you?"

"Within the column. They'll come to your tent when we

camp," Memnanan said. "I've told them. You have my lasting gratitude. And your relatives?"

"With the Haga," he said. "I hope they're there." For the first time he thought of that second question. "My father?"

"Released," Memnanan said, and Marak suffered curiously mixed feelings about that.

"It was that or kill him," Memnanan said. "I'll not have him near the Ila."

"I well understand," Marak said. A certain part of his heart wished he had seen Tain. A certain part of him longed to linger back and wait for Kais Tain to pass: See, Father, he could say. I've done something useful with my life. I've saved all of you.

And another part wanted to say, I've survived. I'm still alive. So has my mother, so has my sister, damn you for a devil.

He did neither. They filed out along the road, past that trampled ground near the ridge, past the wreckage of the carts, where not a book remained, only a vermin-covered body. The junior priests might not have lingered to bury their chief priest, or, do them credit, perhaps they had, and misjudged the tenacity of the vermin. In either case, even if they had carried him back to the city for burial, the vermin would get the body, with more or less work.

On that thought, Marak rode aside from the column and looked back at the city.

A pall of smoky haze hovered above the hill that had been Oburan, and over the Beykaskh that had been the heart of it. It was the last of sunset. The glass dome and the glass-rimmed walls caught no light now. Their fire and their life was extinguished. The vast camp had gone down, collapsed, beshti rounded up, pressed back to the work of carrying riders and baggage.

And some had none. People had come in from the villages using them; and only if they were strong enough and forceful enough, they rode out with them. He knew with all his experience of desperate men that the desperate and the hard would have beasts to ride and the forgiving and the gentle would have no one to defend their rights.

Oburan's people in the city's fall had passed through a sieve, through which only one kind survived, and it was not for the better, and it was not for the kindest, except as they had protectors more ruthless as the worst . . . and the Ila had moved to the fore of the line, being that ruthless. So had he. But the Lakht as it had become was a far finer sieve, a trial from which fools and those led by fools did not emerge at all, and a leader who had too much pity for the few would kill everyone who trusted him. Witness the caravan they had passed, bones, naked bones in the sand, and a leader who should have known his business had miscalled the storm and the proximity of safety. Norit had warned them . . . and they had used that advantage.

He saw the tribes drawn up along the road, different in proportion of beasts and goods than those caravans of the villages, for the tribes had less, used less, were much the same as each other in weight carried, in every aspect. There were subtle differences in colors and patterns, but all tribal patterns, even the brightest, blended generally with the beasts, with the rocks, with each other, as if the same haze of desert dust lay over them all. The Ila and the aui'it were a splash of scarlet in his company, the priests that had attached themselves a glare of white, and then the rest of the tribes poured in, following their line, more dusty hues half-obscured in dust as the sun sank to leaden death.

As for the villagers, beyond his view, people of every color and every pattern, inexpert with the beshti and a hazard to themselves and others in the high desert, he could only wish they hurried onto the road and kept the pace behind them as best they could. He would not turn back in this deep dusk to see how they fared, what they chose, what they did. So far as they would survive, behind the tribes' example and advice in front of them, they were on their own.

Hati paced him, riding by him. Norit scarcely bothered. They both knew where she was, back among the rest, and nowhere, drifting in her mind in a dark place, cold, peaceful, remote from them.

Marak, Marak, Marak, the voices said, as if he could be several days' marches farther on, and they would never be satisfied.

They rode past familiar formations, and on and on. There was no fall of stars tonight. The cloud obscured it.

Throughout the night the villages camped around the ruin would still be setting themselves on the road. Perhaps into morning, the halt would ripple down the column to those just setting out. They had thought they would make better time than they had on the way back, with lightly laden beasts, but with the incidents on the road, it turned out they had not. Now by no means would they set any greater pace on this trip, with the beasts as laden as they were, burdened most of all with shelter and with water. The slow pace was unintended mercy for those afoot. It was danger to the rest of them, and still the hindmost might not survive . . . but they would have a trail to follow, the more they straggled. They would have it until the wind blew and erased the slate and buried the bitter wells too deeply to dig out.

Marak slept, rocked by Osan's motion, safe in Hati's company. At times she slept, and he stayed awake, both of them exhausted.

Past the mid of the night, Memnanan came forward.

"The Ila asks when we will take a major rest," Memnanan said. "I think I know your answer. But these people are unaccustomed to riding."

"At noon," he said. "Granted no delays. Tell her I regret the discomfort, but this is to save her life. Twenty and thirty tomorrows will have no more pleasant answer."

Memnanan rode back to tell her so.

How the Ila had received it he was not sure, but Norit came forward then, and rode with them a while, and slept in the saddle: Norit had finally learned to do that in their travels . . . had learned her balance, and how to brace herself, and rested as secure as a woman of the tribes.

The falling object hit the sphere, again and again and again. The lake of fire flowed down over the rocks like a spring let loose.

Norit waked, and said nothing to either of them.

When the sun came up, a gathering light along the line of the Qarain, Marak rode up the line a little. Hati paced him as he rode past their column, not pressing the beshti for any speed, but gaining, slowly, slowly, comfortably, as riders moved within the column. They entered the Haga column.

Patya saw them. She rode over just out of range, looking for a signal, but she was no great rider, and she could hardly guide her mount with any subtlety. Hati waved to her. Marak would not bend to acknowledge a close relationship, not now, not since the caravan was under way, but she could come to him, and it was his hope that Patya and his mother would move toward him if he came up in the line. He had no need to ask whether their mother was safe: she drifted close, a far better rider, and stayed just within sight of him, presence enough to assure him she was safe and well, but she, too, had her dignity before her new neighbors, her relatives. She would hold off as long as there was Patya to run the errands between them.

"Are we really going to the end of the world?" Patya asked, as if she of all these leaders and all these people could have the precise truth from him. "And is that woman with you a real prophet?"

"You mean Norit," he said; he was aware of Norit having followed him, also at a distance. "Her name is Norit. She's my wife. Is that what the priests say?"

"For what the priests are worth." There was never any great reverence for priests in Kais Tain. "But if you say she is, I believe it. And your wife, too. You've joined the tribes like us."

Tribesmen might have more than one wife.

"I suppose I have," he said.

"She's very pretty," Patya said, meaning, he thought, Hati, but Hati said nothing.

"Where did you meet her?"

"On the road," he said. "After the Ila sent us east." He found there was a great deal he dared not tell his sister, not about Luz, not about the tower, not the least detail from his own mouth. Now he regretted he had come up here, or that the questioning had taken this direction. Let Tofi gossip, let Hati, if she chose: but what he said, men would repeat as coming from authority, and that was substance: men would debate it, dispute it, argue over it, dice it fine and begin to reject parts of it or to substitute their own notions. He could not.

"Did Father send you away," he asked Patya, "or did you just go?"

"Oh, we were going to, but Father—" Patya hesitated, trouble shadowing her brow. "But the Ila's men came and arrested us. And we rode to Oburan."

"Did they treat you well?" He had not *ridden* to Oburan: that, at least, indicated that Patya had fared better.

"Oh, they gave us everything. You never saw such food. And fine clothes, and everything. But Mother wanted to leave."

"I'm not surprised."

"Then the sky started doing what it does." Patya was brimming with things she likely had no words to say. "And everybody was scared. Why does it do that?"

"I don't know," he said, which was only the truth.

"The tribes started coming in. And the villages and all. Father packed up Kais Tain and left. That's what we learned, anyway. We were living in the Beykaskh until it shook down, and then we lived in tents, and then the servants told us we were free and we could go to the Haga, outside the camp."

"That was what I asked Memnanan to do."

"What's going to happen to us? *Is* there a tower?" His sister knew he could lie. His sister wanted the truth the Ila and the tribes and all the villages might not get from him. And would repeat it.

"There is a tower. I promise you there's a tower."

Patya looked relieved at that. "I'll tell Mother."

"Good."

"You can ride here a while," Patya suggested, falling a little behind as he quickened Osan's pace. "You could ride over and see Mother."

"She knows you'll tell her. I have a job to do." He put the quirt to innocent Osan, who hardly needed that vigorous an encouragement, but he wanted away, quickly. Hati was with him as they rode forward in the line.

"She seems a fine girl," Hati said. Around them the sun had brought color to the land. The desert had acquired detail while he talked with Patya, so rapid the sunrise was on the Lakht.

"So she is. But full of questions."

"The same with Aigyan," Hati said. "I won't answer him, either. I'd rather not go that far."

He saw that clearly enough.

"Have you a mother? A father?"

"Both gone," Hati said. "Gone in the war, with my uncles. We fought the Migi for the southern wells. The Migi are dead. But so are most of Aigyan's house. Don't go there yet. Don't talk to him. He'll only argue. Don't talk to Menditak this morning, either. You'll only make Aigyan suspicious. Let them settle out, on the trail. Let Aigyan declare his camp with no one advising him. That will be soon enough."

Marak, the voices dinned at him, a rising echo, a warning.

The vision was back, the star-fall, the ring of fire.

He took the warning. He reined back, to the side of the column. They need only wait there as the column proceeded, until they could simply set the beshti in motion to rejoin Tofi and Norit.

"Is everything all right?" Tofi asked.

"Well enough," he said, and the au'it, closely attending them, wrote.

They rode through the morning. There was a minor shaking, and toward noon a star fell on the horizon, a bright stuttered trail beneath the scattered clouds, then a loud boom. It frightened Tofi's slaves. The two freedmen and Tofi had grown accustomed to such sights.

Noon came with the sun a white spot in gray cloud, and the sand was hotter than the air as the column stopped, the decision of Aigyan, far ahead of them.

The Haga stopped, and they stopped. All down the column, camps would set themselves where they could, in whatever circumstances they might manage, all the way back to the city, it might be: the line might still stretch to there.

The air was cool. It was a question whether they even needed use the tents, and the tribes might choose not; but it was better to work out the hesitations of a new party in quiet air rather than in a rising gale, which tomorrow's camp might bring: better, too, to let new tentmates find their places and settle in. He gave Tofi the order, and they unpacked the tents and pitched them as the soldiers did.

Memnanan came to their tent and brought his pregnant wife and four old women: the wife's name was Elagan, and the old women were Memnanan's mother and three widowed sisters.

Those were the additions to their tent, suffering as new riders did, and Elagan six months pregnant. The women wanted to do little but sleep, the old women were already miserable and would wake unable to walk, Marak was sure. He urged them to use liniments and use them abundantly before they slept.

He lay down on his own mat. The warm sand and the cool air and freedom from the city combined made a strange sort of luxury; and having Hati and Norit close by him was better still. For the first time in days he slept like the dead—waked once as the earth gave a little shiver, then wondered whether it was that illusion of movement that exhaustion brought.

It was their first sleep on the road, and so many unaccustomed riders and so many that had worked feverishly to get them under way were equally abandoned in rest. In all the camp there was no sound but the restless grumble of a besha, and one answering far away.

In late afternoon Marak waked, roused up off his mat, and went out. The Haga had stirred forth. Hati and Tofi joined him outside, and the two slaves and a couple of the hired men.

"Pack up," Marak said. "We'll move. In this, we order the Ila."

Tofi gave him an uncertain look, but ordered his men to

work, and the beshti began their usual complaint. Soldiers stirred forth from their open-sided shelter, and so did a handful of priests. The Ila had not stirred yet, but before the first tent, their own, billowed down, the Ila had sent an au'it to complain.

"Tell the Ila we are behind, and running late," Marak said, when the au'it posed the objection. "There's no leisure to sleep. This is for her own safety."

The au'it went into the Ila's tent. In a few moments, back came the au'it. Now their own au'it was on her feet, and the two of them put their heads together and talked in voices so soft as to be inaudible in the flap and shake of the nearby canvas as the slaves rolled it.

The Ila's au'it went back inside.

In a matter of moments Memnanan came out to report the Ila was not pleased.

"But I have advised her that this move is necessary," Memnanan reported. "I trust that it is."

"Necessary now," Marak said, prepared to be utterly obdurate, "and it will be necessary, every day for the next thirty to fifty days, regular as can be, and after that if we haven't come to the tower, we may die out here, so there will be no further requests. Tell her she has to learn to sleep in the saddle. We all do. She may rule in Oburan, but she doesn't rule the Lakht, or the heavens."

"I certainly don't want to bring her that advisement," Memnanan said.

Marak was amused. "Then save it for a better moment. But we have to pack the tent. Good luck to you."

"Long life to you," Memnanan said dourly, and went back to bear unwelcome news.

The villages behind would doubtless learn, too, at what hour to be up and moving, or lose their priority in line.

Certain individuals, however, had been moving during the rest: a number of priests had found their way up the line, without tents or guides. They simply lay on their mats, and rested outside the Ila's tent, exhausted, men afoot, traversing the line at need, mostly the Ila's needs.

Marak regarded them uneasily. Since their chief priest had fallen dead beside the distribution of the aui'it's books, they had no leader, so far as Marak was aware. The priests had waked, too, and were rolling up their mats, with no water, no food, no provision for the desert. And whether they followed the Ila, now, or had some way of consulting their own god for more obscure and divine messages, and immaterial sustenance, he was unwilling to have them underfoot.

More to the point, he was unwilling to have them taking up rations in the Ila's camp.

Memnanan had come out again. "She will move," Memnanan said.

"And the priests," Marak said. "They should fall back and find some village who wants them. What do they intend to drink? Prayers?"

"Prayers," Memnanan said. "And the Ila's charity. Like the aui'it, they have their uses."

"And their water needs." Marak was far less convinced. "They'll drink up half their weight in water and endanger the Ila. They have to be under someone's authority."

"I'll speak to them," Memnanan said.

Before they were under way, and before all was said and done, the priests went under the Ila's remaining awning for an audience: Marak saw them kneeling and bowing and speaking at some length. He wished them to the vermin of the desert: bad enough the several they already had, now there were twice that number, and he wondered how many more of this white-robed lot were loose among the tents of the caravan.

They were parasites, every one of them, in his estimation.

But the Ila called him, next, having dismissed the priests. Her tent remained uncollapsed. Its veils were down. But while the Haga were well toward finishing their packing, the Ila sat on her chair, the only chair in the desert, unless some villagers were equally fool enough to pack furniture instead of food . . . and sipped tea under the only tent still standing.

Marak went under it and sat down. His au'it went with

him and sat, and her au'it sat cross-legged at her feet, with her open book and her pen in hand.

"The captain has told you we should be moving," Marak said before the Ila said a thing. He made up his mind then and there not to pay abject courtesies or to play the courtier to the Ila's whims. It would not serve her, him, or the people in their threatened thousands. He measured his retreat, if he had to, and he knew that not all the Ila's men could or would prevent him and Hati and Norit riding up among the tribes at the lead, ignoring the Ila, and ruling from there. Their lives, and hers, were too precarious.

He did not intend it should come to that. But he did not intend to have the Ila delaying them in daily argument, either. Or to have other appurtenances taking up their supplies.

"The priests," he said, "are a waste of water. They can pack canvas."

"The priests will go back to the villages with my word," the Ila said, likewise in the serenity of absolute power, and joined her gloved hands primly before her lips. "And keep me apprised of matters behind us.—How is your mother?"

"Well enough."

"I hear you've sheltered Memnanan's wife."

"A matter of gratitude." He was cautious. Lives ended, on the Ila's whim. He might be secure, but others were not.

"And a matter of personal favor," the Ila said, behind joined fingertips. "Are you corrupting him?"

"He pays *you* the favor," Marak said. "The captain is devoted to you. For me, it's a personal debt, and I'm paying what I owe him."

"For what?"

"For not being jealous of me. He might have been, seeing you gave me command of this caravan. But he's an honest man."

"I know he is. A hundred have fallen, and Memnanan stands.—Do you still hear your voices?"

"Sometimes."

"And the fever?"

He was not sure he had ever told her about the fever. Instinct waked instantly and warned him. He was on his guard, in a heartbeat retracing everything he had said, and asked himself again whether the Ila would be fool enough to threaten his life or that of someone near him.

"The fever from the wound?" he asked. "Gone. I'm quite well."

The Ila regarded him curiously and in silence for a moment. She had protected her white, white skin, even beneath the clouded sky. It was as white as ever. If anyone in the camp washed with water instead of sand, it would be the Ila. The smell of the Beykaskh went about her still, perfume, or incense. Even in the oily, sun-warmed musk of the air under the tent, he smelled it, like a taint of holiness.

"And the wound itself?"

He pushed up his sleeve. The wound was entirely gone, leaving no scar. He had no idea what she thought, having seen that, but she seemed not entirely pleased with the sight. She lifted her hand.

"You may go," she said, having asked nothing about their destination, their schedule, or their pace.

He gathered himself up and left, with his au'it, who never said a word.

And having escaped the tent and the interview, and saying no word to Memnanan, he gathered up Hati and Norit.

Tofi came over. Beyond them, the Haga were starting their beasts to their feet, ready to move, in the breakup of that last conference.

"I think you can pack the tent now," Marak said. "Speak to the captain."

"What did she ask?" Norit asked him, when Tofi went off to do that.

"I asked her about the priests, and she asked me about Memnanan's wife."

"Nothing else?"

"The voices, the wound, the fever."

Norit said nothing, but frowned at the last.

"Why?" he asked her, as they three stood in the dissolution of their camp, the au'it at some distance, writing.

Norit was a moment answering. He had all but given up on her answering at all, no infrequent thing that Norit remained completely absorbed in her musings. But she said, faintly, "The makers."

"What about the makers?"

"That was her question to you," Norit said. "About the wound."

He and Hati looked at her in dismay, silent. It was clearly not Norit speaking to them. It was not Norit who had asked that question, as he had the strong suspicion it had not been Norit for days. "She wished to know about the makers, that was the intent of her question. Whether the strange makers still work in your blood. That's why she asked you about the fever."

"She asked whether I'm cured of the madness."

"Exactly that?"

"Whether I still hear the voices," he amended it.

"Yes."

"Did she think not?" he asked. "As if, when we reached Oburan, the madness would just let us go?"

"Perhaps she poisoned you," Norit said, "with her knife."

He was appalled, and asked himself had Norit been there to see the attack. She had not. "To test whether Luz's makers cure poison, too?"

"They can," Norit's lips said, while Norit gazed blindly at the horizon. "She knows that."

"Would she take such a stupid risk?" Hati demanded angrily. "Would she poison the only ones who know the way?"

"It depends on the poison," Norit said in that same distracted tone.

"What do you mean it depends on the poison?"

"She set her makers into you. But you still hear the tower's voice. You still hear me. You still see your visions. She asked about the fever, and you reported it fallen. So she knows her makers were defeated and ceased fighting the makers from the tower. She knows she's failed."

"What, to have her makers give me voices in my head?"

"I frankly doubt she has that ability. The First Descended

had the skill, but not the resources here. We, on the other hand, do. Yes, she tried a small contest against you, and now she knows she's beaten. Now we can prove to the *ondat* that we can defeat her, and we can show them how. It also proves there's no need for the star-fall, but they won't stop: they wouldn't even hear our protestations that we could prevent the need for it. They're reshaping the world because they have the power, and frankly, too, it's simply politics. Their people have to see their enemy utterly defeated, ever to feel safe. But she's beaten, face-to-face and at her best."

"Because your makers fought a war in me. And they won."

"With the fever, they won, yes. It's a very good thing she tried. She's proven our surmise, that we *can* overcome her. We've also proven it to her, and she's not happy about it."

"You mean——" It was probably useless to look at Norit, but he did it instinctively, in outrage. "You mean you invite her into your refuge knowing she has these *makers* in her, and she's going to try some other way to get them into all of us."

"She may try several times. But she'll lose—again. Oh, make no mistake. This will be a series of battles. She sent you out to us in the first place with makers that didn't survive . . . as everyone in the world has her makers in them. She just now tried it again, with a direct effort, with the best she can create, and she's lost again and her makers lost."

He found there was a limit to what he wanted to know about this war in which his soul and his body were the battleground.

"You mean she'll go on doing this, and you'll try, and she will."

"I've no doubt that she has something yet to try, and will. We're equally determined it won't work."

"An attack on us. In us. Again."

"I fear so."

Anger welled up in him, a distracting, overwhelming anger. "You listen to me. Your voices can damned well let me alone when I have something to do. There's no need to be chattering at me the way you do. You're sitting in the tower. You can tell your damned voices that while you're at it. And you can let Norit go! Let her be! She's not yours!"

"She's an excellent viewpoint. You're far too inclined to turn and twist things into what you want to say. And you grow distracted and don't listen. I need to know where you are."

"You know damned well where we are! Let her alone! Give her her nights free of you, at least!"

"It's too important," Luz said. "I won't lose all of you just for her comfort."

"Then talk to *me* a while!" Hati said.

"You won't do, any more than he will."

"Give her some rest!" All this talk of makers fighting makers had disturbed him. He saw nothing to do about that, but Norit's plight, at least, seemed within their reach, a point on which they could reason with Luz. "You'll make her sick if you go on at her like this."

"I'll let her rest," Luz said quietly.

Immediately Norit blinked several times and seemed herself again, a little distressed, a little lost, a little confused. Marak put his arms about her, and Hati did, and Norit shivered, and shed tears, then simply sat down on the sand and sobbed.

"Everybody," Norit kept saying. "Everybody," but they made no sense of it.

"What can we do?" Hati asked him in dismay.

"I don't know," he said. He had no idea now whether it was worse for Norit to be awake and to know what she might know, or whether during those times of Luz's possession Norit simply took refuge somewhere Luz failed to bother her, and Norit only realized the nature of what had flowed through her once she waked . . . but whatever Norit saw that they failed to, it seemed terrible. He squatted down and wiped Norit's tears, and all the while Norit's tears kept flowing, tears for what she saw in Luz's visions, tears for what had happened to her, tears simply of exhaustion: he had no idea what caused them.

"Find Lelie," she said once.

He remembered Norit had shouted that name once, in her greatest distress.

"Please find Lelie for me."

"Where shall I look?" he asked, but of course it was Tarsa he should search. In those days before their march to the tower, Tarsa was all Norit had ever known.

"Who is Lelie?" he asked, but Norit failed to answer him.

In a moment he got up and exchanged a glance with Hati. "I'm going to try," he said.

"If this goes on," Hati said, "she *will* go crazy, crazier than we ever were. I think it's a sister she's lost. Maybe someone she knows from her village can reason with her."

When Tofi and his men had packed down the Ila's tent and when Memnanan and his men had seen the Ila and the aui'it mounted and ready, they got up on their own beasts. Norit seemed calmer by then, though whether it was the calm Luz imposed in her reign he had no idea. The Keran had already begun to move, and opened an interval on them.

There must be gaps all along the line of march now, similar disparities in readiness. Some afoot might even turn back after their first or second camp on the road, losing courage for the hardship. He decided he had no wish to know the personal stories of those behind him in the line. He wanted no faces for those that were bound to die, no situations to haunt his sleep and his waking.

But he went to Memnanan and asked the service of one of his men.

"I need someone to ride back and find Tarsa in the line," he said, "and find someone named Lelie."

"Why?" Memnanan asked.

"One of Norit's kin, I think. I don't know. But I want this Lelie found. It's a favor."

He left that statement to lie unadorned between them. There were favors passed, indeed there had been favors passed between them. Without comment, Memnanan called a man over and put him under that instruction.

"Find out who Lelie is, and if there is a Lelie with Tarsa's

company, bring her with you and protect her from all un-
pleasantness. A member of this lord's party wants her."

The man reined aside from the column and rode back
alongside it. There was no telling where in the line of march
Tarsa might fall: it might be a journey of one or two days.

By morning the man Memnanan had sent had still not
come back. By then Marak began to know it was no small
favor he had asked, and by afternoon, after their rest, that
most likely time for the man to catch up to them, he began
to worry about the man, and about the favor he had asked of
Memnanan.

He found nothing comfortable to say about the situation,
only to shrug apologetically when he met Memnanan and to
wish the man safety and a safe return.

"The line is very long," Memnanan said. "It may take a
while."

But none of them, not even those experienced at reckoning the number of a group by looking at them, knew how
long the marching line would be. All methods of measuring
failed against the scale of the undertaking, to move everyone
in the world to shelter. Marak found himself in Memnanan's
debt, and in debt to the messenger, who had surely had no
idea, either, the size of the task when he left.

Morning, too, brought a stiff head wind that kicked up
the dust in their faces and made the pitching of tents at noon
a far more difficult operation.

Rumor filtered up the line during the rest, one group talking to another next in sequence. An old man had fallen off
and broken his leg. A woman of the villages had given birth,
and men had carried her on a litter while she did so.

Life in the column went on, no matter its difficulty.

But the messenger had not come back by then, either, and
no rumor reported the messenger on his way.

18

If a good well turns to bitter water, the village dies: there is no remedy.
—The Priest, in his Book.

The wind that had made pitching the tents so difficult at least blew the clouds away. Tofi laughed when they waked after noon rest and saw a bright blue sky. "I thought we might never see the sun again," he said. His voice attempted levity, but it was relief everyone must feel.

Norit seemed calmer, and had done with crying. She seemed to have forgotten having named Lelie, and they failed to mention the messenger. Norit rode with them, and measured the fringed edge of her aifad, over and over and over, lost in her own thoughts, or in Luz's: there was no telling. The voices were quiet.

But that night as they rode, the stars fell again in all their terrible glory. No few were the fiery sort, that stitched their way in silver and gold across the night before they plunged below the horizon.

Memnanan rode with them a time. The messenger had not yet returned.

"I regret asking the favor," Marak said. "Something may have happened."

"It may," Memnanan said. "But it may not. I'm not yet worried. It may simply take that long."

"I hope for his safety," Marak said. Norit was near them, but he had never yet told her about the search.

"Has the fall been this thick before?" Memnanan asked, with a look aloft. This was a man who had spent days before this in the heart of the city, where lights blotted out the sky.

"It's become ordinary these days," Hati said. "I suppose it will be ordinary for a long time."

"No," Norit said suddenly. "It's not ordinary. That's why we have to hurry. The hammer of heaven will fall."

"The hammer of heaven," Memnanan said.

"A very large star," Marak said; that was the way he interpreted it. "Where will it fall, Norit? On the Lakht?"

Sometimes Norit seemed to intervene in Luz's answers, or failed to understand them. She turned and pointed, back, behind them. "Not on the Lakht. Out in the bitter water."

"Then not on us," Memnanan said with relief.

"But wherever we are, still, the wind will reach us, and when that wind blows, the sun will stop shining and the stars will vanish. The earth will ring like an anvil. When it comes, we have to be off the Lakht. If nothing else, we have to be off the Lakht, and down below it. The wind up here will be terrible."

"Is this the truth?" Memnanan asked.

"That we have to be off the Lakht before this great star comes down?" Marak said. "I don't know about the sun and the stars. But she's saved our lives before." Under the streaks of the star-fall, the desert showed cold, and the wind bit as it came. The sand blew along the surface, a light film of fine dust, and in Norit's doom-saying, it struck him with peculiar force just then that in all this riding since starting out from Oburan, he had seen no birds, no vermin, and no trace of them. It was more than strange, and what was strange lately became ominous.

"Can we reach the edge by then?" Memnanan asked.

"If the weather holds," Norit said. "If it turns against us, we don't know. I can't prevent the storms."

Memnanan laughed at the strangeness of that *I can't prevent,* as if he thought it a grim and impertinent sort of joke, but Marak was less sure. Luz would want to prevent the storms. If anyone could, Luz might be able; but she told them it was beyond her power.

Their own contingent, third in line, moved at the pace of a very large caravan, which was to say, very slowly, still, despite Norit's warning. It was his intention to anchor the line, not to let the Keran and the Haga and the tribes with their travel-hardened beasts run a race to the detriment of all those village contingents behind. The villages, unaccustomed and containing many weak, could surely go no faster, and those afoot above all else could not match the tribes' pace.

But now he wondered if that kindness to the hindmost was not risking all of them. "We could go some bit faster," he said to Norit, when Memnanan had gone his way, "but that would mean those afoot will likely die. What should we do?"

Norit looked for a moment apt to burst into tears and shook her head distractedly as they rode.

And for the first time he added up the fact that all the mad had heard the same voices, their own, and seen the same visions, at the same time, and so had Norit, on the way. But now he became keenly aware of what they had begun to believe beneath the surface and never saying it: that Norit had special warnings, and special visions, and that Luz's constant possession of her was different than what afflicted them.

In a way he had known it for days; he had known it when Norit had warned them of a storm he had had no idea was coming. He had known it when Norit ran mad, alone, under the sky.

It was not that he was hardheaded and failed to listen; it was not that he and Hati were too resistant to the voices— but that Norit's voice was a special one, and that it had begun to be a special voice in the tower, where he and Hati and Norit had spent an amount of time they had never added up. Now he believed Luz had done something special to

Norit. She had done something special, and cruel, and Norit was not the same as she had been. Norit heard things constantly, and that flow of images that had once united the mad did not reach them . . . only Norit, who suffered.

There was nothing they could do for her but find this lost person named Lelie. Norit had asked for that. But whether Norit would even continue to care for this Lelie, there was no promise. Every time he made an effort to get her back from Luz, Luz's possession of her was fiercer and harder when it set in.

He looked at Hati, riding near them, and found no better answer. He no longer knew what to do: but he knew that he had no wish to end that possession entirely—their lives depended on it. Even Norit's life depended on Luz's voice continuing.

And all night long the star-fall continued, obscured at times by threads of cloud, dark strips in the heavens. By morning those strips glowed pink, then faint purple, then white.

Even by this morning, there was no word from the young man they had sent down the line. Marak tried to imagine how far that was, and whether in fact it did extend all the way back to the holy city.

But now he had to reckon that perhaps the young man had come to grief . . . nothing to do with vermin or bandits. The Ila's men were not loved in the villages.

By midmorning two of the younger priests worked their way up the line, afoot, breathless, to ask the Ila questions, it seemed. They were from among a small set of priests taken in by Kasha village, among the first behind the tribes, so they said, they had not paid attention to the small traffic along the line, and after a brief sojourn near the Ila, but never directly with her.

"Have you seen a young man of the Ila's guard?" Marak asked them afterward.

"Yes, omi," they said. "But only going. Not coming."

What had they asked the Ila, or what had they to report? Marak wondered, but dared not ask.

They offered Norit their courtesies, wished the God's

blessing on her, and by implication, he supposed, they asked for enlightenment. "Have you seen other visions?" the seniormost asked.

"The hammer will fall," she said. "We have to hurry." After that she waved them away, disinterested in their prayers, having no more cheerful prophecy to give them, and no counsel.

"Omi," the priests said to Marak, and the same to Hati, seeing that they were a group. They paid their parting respects to him and Hati as much for being associated with Norit, as for leading this company, so he suspected; but he felt better for their gesture. They rejoined their companions by the simple expedient of going outside the line and sitting still for as long as they had walked double the pace, and were gone.

The au'it recorded their visit, afterward, but that was all the information they had from it: Norit had posed them no questions, the Ila offered no answers, and being distrustful of priests, he had made no detailed inquiry, either.

The sun grew fever-warm. The air seemed to give less sustenance than usual. At noon he lay beneath the tent, numbed his mind, and sweated: he rested with his arm pillowed on his head, secure in Hati's presence beside him, and the au'it and Norit sleeping at his back.

For two more days it was like this, with the stars falling at night and the sun burning by day. Once more the priests came. He asked them the questions he had reserved, what they had seen, whether the people were keeping the line together: they were, the priests said. But the Ila's messenger did not come back, and the priests had no news.

"I fear I've brought that man to grief," Marak said to Memnanan when they discussed the matter. "I don't know where or how an experienced man fell into difficulty, but I'm very sorry for it."

"The desert has its dangers," Memnanan said with a shrug, and that was the end of it: Memnanan showed no enthusiasm to send another man, and he would not ask it. So there was no answer about Lelie. There was no way to trace the man without risking another, and of the rumors that found their way up and down the line—of births, of deaths and calamities: vermin invading a village's food store during rest, but they had not lost it all—for two more days there was no word, and they gave up hope. Luz was quiet, the au'it recorded little but the arduous routine of camp and cooking, and one tremor in the earth that lasted longer than any before. It did no damage, beyond the collapse of the soldiers' tent and the disturbance of the beshti, who complained from camp to camp.

Escorted by two villagers, at the next morning, on a day of high wind and dusty haze, priests came into camp to seek the Ila, and failing her civil reception of them at this hour—wind had put out the small stove that heated the Ila's tea, and she was indisposed—they came to Norit.

"Pesha village has lost two tents," they said, speaking for two dour and mistrustful village men. "What shall we do?"

"Has Pesha lost its water and its food?" Norit asked, consulting no one, though Marak stood by and listened to this audience.

No, the man from Pesha insisted, and tried to present more of a case for being given tents from some other village. "We have elderly," he said. "Our lord is an old man. We need the tents."

Norit lifted a hand, as autocratic as the Ila herself. "If they lost two, give them no more to lose. Let them all go to other tents, and settle in the village behind them in line."

Marak was astonished, and the Pesha villagers wildly outraged. It was a desert judgment from a softhearted village woman. And on that thought, Marak knew Norit had not made that choice.

"This isn't just!" the men cried.

"The desert isn't just. Those who lost two tents should have better leaders."

"They have a book," the priest said, over the protests of the villagers. "Shall they keep it? Or shall it also go to their hosts?"

"It should go to their hosts," Luz said through Norit, but Marak thought it was Norit who added: "and the village lord should beg the pardon of Pesha village for losing the tents. He may be a wise man in his own village affairs, and he can command again after we reach the tower, where we're safe, but he should leave pitching camp to those that kept all their tents, and thank them for keeping his safe."

The priests and the chagrined villagers bowed and went away with their message.

Well judged, and well said, Marak thought to himself in their departure. Even Luz could learn the exigencies of the desert; and even Norit could moderate Luz's harsh judgments.

But that disaster was not the worst. Tofi reported grimmer news relayed to him up from the tribes, a concern that small vermin had moved in near the caravan track back among the villages, and showed increasingly disturbing courage over the last two days. The tribes nearest the villages had warned them to be more careful with their waste, and the priests, in evidence of very bad judgment, had not reported it when they reported the lost tents.

Tofi, however, knew the dire seriousness of what the tribes observed, and stood waiting for a solution from him.

The vermin came to the moisture and waste of a caravan. They always followed caravans, but they never, almost never, attacked one on its march: the noise was too much, the activity too threatening. Vermin were interested in everything a caravan left or shed . . . starting with the latrines, and the small insect vermin that burrowed there, and the larger vermin that came to feed on them, and the largest that fed on the larger. They were habitual pests, no more than that, on the average route, at worst startling some caravanner bent on private business in his tent's latrine, in some three-day camp.

But no one had ever seen a caravan that took a day or more to march past a given point. No one knew what happened when the rule that vermin never mobbed a large caravan ran up against the rule that vermin always gathered and moved in on an abandoned campsite.

In their all-inclusive caravan, only the Ila's party and the tribes and the villages in front marched over clean sand. Past the first half hundred or so camps, the entire route of march of those behind was through one continuous campsite, and Marak was appalled that they had not once thought of that ominous situation. They were fools.

He looked at Tofi, took a hitch of the aifad to obscure his dismay. The dust stung his eyes. It made the air itself smell like hot sand. "They're marching over old ground," Marak said. "There's never been a caravan so large its back end marches over its own trail after breaking camp, not that I know."

"We must stretch out at least a day's march, maybe two," Tofi said, over the thumping of the nearby tent, which slaves were working to take down. "It's going to happen, isn't it?"

"The city people, those afoot . . ." Marak shuddered to think of the situation of the hindmost: beshti were some defense. But for a man afoot . . .

"I'll tell Memnanan," he said to Tofi, and went and immediately called the Ila's captain apart from his men, the two of them curtained in the blowing dust, partly sheltered by the Ila's tent.

Memnanan listened grimly, as appalled as he. He had fought in the desert. He knew the hazards of vermin, and the rules of a clean camp, no matter what city people understood. "Wait," Memnanan said, and went to talk to the Ila, reckless of her bad mood, and talked for several moments, urgently, before he came back.

"The Ila understands," Memnanan said. "She gives us leave to do whatever is necessary."

"If we increase the pace more than this," Marak said, "we'll lose lives. But if we don't, we'll lose villages. Send a letter back through the line. Tell the villages to dig their latrines as deep as they can. Cover everything they leave behind as deeply as they have the strength to dig. Let the strong dig for the weak, and let them make only as many pits as they can make doubly deep. Digging will delay the vermin and give us time . . . if only they don't go for the stragglers: there may *be* a mobbing, but we won't be there to see it."

The earth shuddered. They had all but learned to ignore such moments.

"Kinder, perhaps," Memnanan said, "to leave the weak behind all at once, and not to drag the inevitable out in days of misery."

"Kinder to poison the lot of them this evening," Marak said above the thumping of the wind-stirred canvas, "and not leave them for the vermin to eat alive. But we're men, and we don't give up. Sometimes we win. Sometimes even villagers win."

"You were already safe at the tower," Memnanan said, chasing that old question. "If it was safe. You knew you were risking everything. Why did you come back?"

"For my mother. For my sister. Wouldn't you?"

"So you have them. Why don't you ride off ahead of the rest?"

He had no idea why he stayed. But he shook his head again, thinking of thousands of the helpless, all the mothers and fathers and sisters and brothers and children in the world. "We do what we can," he said with a shrug, "or nothing at all gets done, does it? Nothing ever gets done, and no one gets saved, if we aren't fools at least some of the time. Why don't you run for the tower with a few men and the best beasts? You know the route. Why does even the Ila march at this pace? We're fools, is all."

"I'll instruct messengers to go back," Memnanan said. "I don't trust your written message."

Marak had a vision of the line stringing out as they marched, farther and farther separated, the strong leaving the weak, and the villages beginning to know it.

"There'll be panic," he said, thinking of the last messenger they had dispatched, and took a small, personal chance. "You might inquire of Tarsa, if someone gets as far as that village. Tell them ride through the column, not down the sides."

"We do what we can," Memnanan said, and they parted, and went each of them to see to their own necessities.

His were simple, to see everyone in his own tent mounted up and ready. Tofi had packed the tents. The beshti and the waiting riders stood like ghosts in the blowing sand.

He had no desire to imagine their collective situation if

all the vermin in the world began to turn toward the only caravan in the world as their only source of food. He declined to mention the notion to Hati and Norit and the rest as he joined them: if Luz had not bothered to tell them in relentless detail, he kept the secret. Tofi looked at him questioningly, and he said: "The captain's sending instructions back."

By the time they began to move, behind the Haga and the Keran, the dust was blowing steadily at their backs, and the Keran, foremost, had surely gotten the message from Memnanan's first messengers. The Keran moved out, and they did, and they set a faster-than-usual pace as the wind helped them along. The strong west wind was an assisting hand behind the weak in these first hours; but the dryland gusts carried moisture away from them, too, and made them drink more often. The wind stressed the weak, some of whom would die today. Marak could not but think of it.

Three times that morning the earth shook, but the line never faltered, not, at least, that the foremost could see when they looked back. At noon they made the ordinary measured rest, and pressed on.

The Ila through the day spoke rarely and was cross with everyone. The aui'it went in healthy fear, and theirs was likely glad to be serving them, writing down their daily progress and little else, ignorant, perhaps, of what Memnanan had told the Ila. In the late afternoon Marak rode up a time to see his mother and his sister, and they had heard the news: the Keran had told everyone in their camp.

"Are we in danger?" Patya asked, being half a villager, and doubtless she had asked their mother the same question.

"Not us," he said plainly. "The last ranks are dead men."

The knowledge of the situation cast a pall on their meeting. Kais Tain might be among the last. He had never yet seen his own village in the lines. But they never mentioned Tain, and they never mentioned their village. He dropped back to ride with Hati and with Norit, and Luz was quiet, apprised of the hazard around them: so by then, might they be, but he told them.

"Vermin are moving in. The end of the caravan is in danger."

He saw only Norit's eyes above the aifad, but he imagined the worry. He raised no hopes, said no word of Norit's lost Lelie, and neither did Norit.

By evening, the wind had sunk notably. The Keran had found a bitter spring in the rocks, and dug it out. The beshti drank, and the Keran marked the place for the other tribes and the villages as they moved. The spring scarcely kept up with the demand of the beshti, and no man could drink it, but the beshti, whose urine was at times poisonous even to vermin, were content with what they drank.

By morning, there was cloud above the blowing sand, and by the hour they camped, the cloud was such that they could not use the sun for the heating-mirrors, and could not cook their rations or boil water. Only the Ila had tea, using precious lamp oil for fuel as well as light.

Her tent, of all the rest, surely, in all the long line of all the tents left in the world, glowed in the gathering murk, stained with the light of lamps inside. It must be all of them lit, Marak judged, profligate waste.

"The Ila shouldn't burn the fuel for tea," he ventured to say to Memnanan. "Or light. We may need it in the storms. We've been lucky so far. Can anyone reason with her?"

"She's angry," Memnanan confided in Marak. "It's become the tea, the clouds, the wind, the dust, but mostly it's the situation. Men are dying behind us. She lights the lamps. *She* will have tea. I don't know why. Sometimes I think this is how she grieves."

The Ila's messengers through the day had come in with news of lost tents, straggling walkers, and persistent vermin, and said four young villagers had died or would die as fools, drinking the bitter water—but as yet they had had no disasters beyond the loss of a few sacks of grain riddled with hardshells. They were not doing that badly. It was strange to hear Memnanan's observation . . . that the living goddess grieved, and sipped tea.

He marked, too, that Memnanan had not visited his wife

or his mother. Memnanan had only spoken to them outside the tent, obsessed strictly with duty, or perhaps commanded to that obsession. And still the Ila grieved.

"More useful if she saved the fuel," Marak said. "We haven't seen any excess of vermin this far forward, and that's good news. But we can't say about the weather." The west had made him increasingly uneasy, in the steady wind. For two days he had been free of visions, but when he said that, he saw the ring of fire.

More, he saw the ring become a sheet and a wall of fire and rush across the land as high as a dust storm, towering up to the heavens. He took in his breath, lost to ordinary use of his eyes, lost to his sense of balance.

"What's the matter?" Memnanan asked.

Out across the flat pan, with his eyes, he saw the streak of a falling star pierce the cloud, and fall and hit the earth. It shook him. He was not sure it was real. "Shall I talk to the Ila?" he asked. "I know how to give her bad news . . . and how to call her a fool. If she kills me, she loses her guide."

"Not now," Memnanan said soberly. "Not today. Not even you."

"What, besides the haste?" he asked.

"The haste, the wind, all these things." Memnanan heaved a sigh, looked at the sand under their feet and, looking up, gave a fourth reason. "The priests came. They call your wife a prophet. The Ila isn't pleased."

He had been aware of messengers coming and going. He remembered a visitation by priests, afoot. He had not reckoned that for the cause of the Ila's mood, but it made sense. "I'll speak to Norit," he said, and knew that, far more than that, if the Ila was growing chancy and destructive, he had to speak to Luz about the danger.

"Say nothing of it," Memnanan advised him. "The matter is settled now, and quiet. If she sends for you, you never witnessed such audiences as I did. She *won't* send for your wife."

It was a statement begging for a question. "Why not?" he asked.

"Your wife speaks for the tower. The Ila is increasingly distraught. She finds the connection intolerable."

"So does my wife," he confessed, in this moment of truths somewhat excessively given. "She doesn't like what's happened to her. But she does tolerate it, being mad, like the rest of us. She can't help it. And she's our guide."

"Oh, the Ila knows that," Memnanan said. "She knows it very well. I would even say she forgives your wife, if I had any belief in her forgiveness."

"You don't."

"I don't."

"Yet you serve her."

"So did my father's father. And we've done very well, until now."

They parted. They went their ways. Memnanan stopped for a word with his wife and his aunts and his mother. Marak settled down with Hati and Norit, and they slept a peaceful, abandoned sleep.

Marak, his voices said, for the first time in hours, and waked him and them all at the same moment. *Marak.* He saw the ring of fire.

Norit lowered her face into her hands and wiped her hair back, distracted and unhappy.

"In the bitter water," Norit said. "A great fall. A shake is coming. It's coming soon."

"Not a danger to us," he said, hoping it was the case.

"No," Norit said. But in only a matter of moments the earth shook itself like a beshti clearing dust. The tents swayed and the beshti bawled their distress. It did so twice more.

The wind had fallen off markedly by then. And as Marak came out of their tent to inspect for damage, a few drops of cold water fell from the leaden clouds. Sheet lightning showed in the distance, to the east, and as Hati came out under the sky, a spit of rain came down and pocked the sand all about them.

Marak gave a desperate laugh.

"What's funny?" Hati asked him. Worry had settled on Hati like a heavy weight these last days. She looked at him now as if he had become the madman again.

But before he could explain himself, more rain fell, and she took on a strange look and began to laugh and laugh, and laugh. "You're right," she said, and laughed again, until Tofi and the freedmen came out to see what was funny. She wiped her eyes with a dusty knuckle. "We'll *drown*, next." She kept laughing.

"What's funny?" Norit asked next, completely seriously, and he and Hati both set to laughing, which brought a tentative laughter from Tofi and the freedmen, as if they dimly understood the joke.

"We'll drown or we'll be eaten," Hati said, and laughed. Norit simply looked puzzled and troubled.

"There's a storm coming," Norit said. "But a small one."

That was from Luz, Marak thought, and he had Tofi move to strike the tent, determined to get the canvas down before it gathered water weight. The Keran were taking those down, and meanwhile one of Memnanan's messengers had come in, and he went to know what the news was.

"We've lost contact with the farthest contingents," Memnanan said to him, after talking to that man. It was sifting rain, now, a mist as fine as dust. "We've heard nothing yet. I hoped this man had ridden back that far, but he didn't. The weather changed, and he grew uneasy and came to report."

"It's possible they're that far off," Marak said.

"Or vermin ate them. But vermin aren't our only worry," Memnanan said. "There are bandits unaccounted for in all of this. They've doubtless picked over Oburan's bones. If they're starting now to pick at the column, there's nothing we can do about it. They'll scavenge the weak."

"Like the rest of the vermin," Marak said, all trace of humor gone from his heart. It was a reasonable suspicion, and one their plans could not deal with. "If that's started, our line will grow shorter until they have too much to carry. Or they'll tail us, picking off what they want, when they want it. We can't divert our march to deal with them." He knew this kind of war, this bandit harassment. He had practiced it himself, against the Ila's caravans. He had equipped bands of raiders that way.

"It's not in our hands," Memnanan agreed. "But we'll send no more men back there."

"I'd say that's wise," Marak answered him, "if it was for me to say anything."

"Oh, you're the desert master, Marak Trin. I listen."

Desert master because the abjori had fought from the desert, and Memnanan from the city, always from the city. And Memnanan remembered, too, what the marks were on his fingers.

"I've no better advice," Marak said. "I haven't, and Luz hasn't, nothing that I know."

The Ila remained secluded, and peevish. They parted, and Memnanan returned to his duty with a grim face. A short spate of rain soaked them, and then the clouds broke and shredded, and went flying along with amazing rapidity.

At sunset of that day a brilliant seam of color showed on the horizon and persisted after dark.

Clouds, some said. They had seen plenty of those.

Fire, others said. But the glow went out after dark, so they decided it had been cloud, and that foretold weather.

Sphere hit sphere in Marak's vision. Hati was as downcast as Norit, and kept looking behind them as they rode. Stars fell, not many, but large ones, one of which left a stuttered trail for a long distance.

By dawn both those clouds and the wind had reached them, and it blew stiffly at their backs, raising the dust—if not for the dust, the wind at their backs would have been a benefit.

"How will it be?" Hati asked Norit, for she, more than they, had become a weather-prophet. "How long will it last?"

"It should last," Norit said quietly as they rode. "But it won't blow hard. Not enough to fear."

Not enough for the labor of deep-stakes, that was, and still, as the dust rose, Marak thought of using them, because they dared not take risks with their lives and their sustenance, for the sake of all the rest. But Norit seemed right: by every scrap of weather-sense he possessed, he felt it would be a windy day, and the dust would get up, that curse of the pans, where a silken fine dust mixed with alkali and tasted bitter.

By noon of that day, the fine dust was thick in the air. The Keran, ahead of them, were shadows in the curtain of dust, but it was not enough to worry them: the day was still bright, not that all-darkening gloom of the great storms, and the beshti made light of it, blowing the dust from their nostrils in occasional noisy gusts. They camped without the deep-stakes, and since the Ila's men attached the flaps on the windward side of that tent for her comfort, Marak ordered the same for their tent.

It gave them a few hours of relief from the wind. Dust seeped around the single wall, but far less of it. He and Hati even made love in the noon quiet, discreetly, hanging their robes on lines strung from the nearest center pole to the edge. Norit and the au'it were there to witness, but the wiry little au'it kindly went to sleep, and Norit lay with her back turned.

Marak slept afterward with his arm around Hati, next to Norit, who snored gently, troubling no one. The gusting of the wind, the thumping of the canvas, had assumed a quiet sameness.

Then someone came running. That was the impression that waked him from half sleep, that someone was running, and that someone coming into the tent had disturbed Memnanan's family from their rest.

He sat up, and moved the curtain. Tofi and his men, free and slave, were awake and upright on their mats, startled from sleep. It was a young woman . . . his sister Patya, her aifad trailing loose, her hair flowing wildly in the breeze from around the windbreak. Her expression told him something terrible was amiss.

He scrambled to his feet. He snatched his robe off the line, flung it on, beltless.

"Marak," she said, then: "Mother," and burst into terror and tears.

"What is it?" he asked.

"Father. Father came. She told me—"

That was enough. In leaden fear he ran out from under the tent, and Patya and then Hati ran with him. The au'it, too, snatched up her kit, but what she did, Marak did not stop to know.

He ran through the blowing dust, back through their camp, in among the Haga tents, among a gathering of men and women roughly waked from their own noon sleep. Patya had his sleeve, and guided him straight to the heart of the camp, in among the tents. "She told me to run," Patya managed to say on the way. "She said run, and I ran."

There was a crowd, shadows in the blowing dust, foretelling the worst. He pushed their way through, and saw, on the ground among them, a woman, their mother.

He fell to his knees and gathered Kaptai up into his arms. He felt the life weak in her as he lifted her, immediately felt the moisture of blood on his hands, under her back. "Marak," she said, just that, her eyes half-open. Then she went limp in his hands.

Just that. Only that. He had held the dead before. He knew that absolute shift in weight. She was gone.

Patya gave a great sob and tried to chafe life back into their mother's hand. His, damp with blood, tested for pulse and breath, and he knew that Patya's tears would bring nothing of their mother back, ever.

He let their mother slide to the ground and got up, conscious of all the witnesses around them, the Haga, and Menditak himself . . . conscious of rage, and grief, and a mind slipping toward unreason.

"It was Father," Patya said. "He did it. He came into the tent while everyone was sleeping. He wanted Mother to come outside with him, and she did, and I did, I knew it wasn't good, and she said run."

Kaptai had known enough to leave her husband. But, prideful to the last, she had not known enough to cry out and wake her tribe to deal with Tain. No, she had gone out to deal with him herself, sending her daughter to safety, to get his help. As a consequence, she was dead, and Patya might have been.

Why? screamed inside his head. Why would she not turn the Haga on Tain? He had deserved it. He had entirely deserved the shame, and being driven out like intruding vermin.

For love? For love, even yet, had she gone out to meet with him, even knowing to send Patya to safety?

"We missed catching him," Menditak said grimly. "We've sent men out, looking."

"See to Patya!" Marak said to Hati, and turned and ran back to Tofi's tents as fast as he had run getting to the Haga, blinded by dust that stuck to his face and collected about his eyes.

Inside his tent, he snatched up his aifad from where he had been sleeping and put that on. He put on his belt, and snatched up the *machai* and his waterskin, all the gear an abjori needed in the desert.

Tofi was awake and on his feet, staring at him in dismay. "Wake the captain," Marak said, measuring his breaths and ordering his information as if he were back in the war, hiding and fighting among the dunes. "Tain's killed my mother. Tell him!"

Tofi ran to do that.

The au'it had come back with him, and sat down on the sand, writing, writing all of it, in that heavy book. Hati and Norit came back, bringing Patya, who was convulsed in tears, but his began to dry, and his mind ordered matters in small, precise packets.

"He's gone to the south side of the column," he said to Hati. "He'll likely cross it again when he reaches some village band, and cross it several times after to confuse the track. He'll hang off our flank and wait his chance at me, at Patya, at the Ila. I should have dealt with him before we set out."

"What are you going to do?" Hati asked.

"Find him. And kill him."

"No," Norit said sharply, and not Norit, but Luz. "No! You have a responsibility."

"The hell with my responsibility!" He strode out the door,

with Hati hurrying after him, and Patya seizing his arm. He shook them both off, and rounded on Norit, who had followed as far as the doorway of the tent. "The hell with my responsibility to the whole damned world! This is mine. This is my *responsibility*! You can do what I do. You hear Luz. She talks to you nowadays. So do it! And, Hati, don't you follow me! Don't do that to me. I know his tricks. He'll be after me, and you, and the Ila, next. I count on you to take precautions, and keep this camp safe!" It was on Hati he relied most, Hati's interference he most had to stop cold, Hati's life that mattered most to him, even above Patya's. "Guard my sister. Hear me? Don't make me lose her, too! Patya, behave yourself. I'll be back."

"Don't go out there alone!" Hati said to him. "Get Memnanan."

"I *know* what my father will do, and the Ila's men don't. I know he's not alone. And I don't want Memnanan's men out there: it stirs up the old abjori, and that gives my father what he wants." He reached Osan among the beshti and got him up. The saddle was near. He flung it on, adjusted its padding. "He'll go to supporters in other villages. He'll persuade some here and there along the line to come out beside the column." He tightened the girth. "He'll take tents, and gear, and beshti, and he'll *create* his army to harass the line. This is war he's declared. And the Ila's soldiers aren't well loved in the villages he'd try to convert, but *I* have friends there. Trust me that I know." He made Osan put a leg out, and seized the mounting loop and swung up. He saw Memnanan coming through the dust, with Tofi, in haste. "You explain it to him," he said to Hati. "You're in charge."

"Marak, be careful!" Patya cried. "Don't die out there! Please don't die."

"Do everything Hati tells you. Stay with her and don't be stupid."

He took up the quirt and gave Osan a hard hit, leaving before he had to explain anything. The Ila might not forgive him. Memnanan might not.

He might not forgive himself if he let his father do to all these people what he knew his father intended.

The dust came between them. It had veiled his father. Now it veiled him as he rode.

19

A bitter tree must be cut down. Its shade has become tainted. Its soil shall be dug out and cast away. None of its leaves and none of its fruit shall be eaten or pressed for water. All its substance and progeny shall be burned.
—The Book of the Law

A small band of Haga had already ridden out on Tain's track. Even in the blowing dust and the rapid fill of the surface, the traces of their passage were plain in the sand, where no other track had been, out between the dunes and then back alongside the caravan track.

But it was more than footprints that Marak used. A besha tracked others: set a besha on the trail, persuade him not to go back to the main caravan, which was his initial and overriding instinct, and by sight or by scent he tended to follow any other track where other beshti had gone, the strongest and most persistent trail as his first choice. It was a useful instinct in a native of the deep Lakht. It was useful to the riders as well as to the beasts, and Marak rode quickly, confident of Osan's senses.

But it was not Tain Trin Tain he found. Haga lay at the end of that trail, four of them, in among the dunes, dead on the ground, half-sand-covered. Vermin were already worrying at their bodies. Those scattered as he rode onto the scene, but he delayed for no rescue of the dead and no moment of sympathy or respect, either. He knew Tain's tricks, and the skin between his shoulders felt the threat of ambush. He turned Osan away quickly, seeking the side of the wind that his father would use.

But in the dunes he only found the tracks of beshti going away from there, as beshti would, back to the caravan, reporting their own dead. There was the track of one, only one, going to the west, back along the caravan trace. That was his father, doing what he thought his father would do.

So now the toll was five.

It might be the politic and prudent course for him to go back to the Haga, to rouse all of them in indignation at this killing and lead them out on the track, but that kind of massive excursion had never availed anything against Tain's subtle kind of work. He had a single hot trail back toward the tents of the encamped line, and he knew Tain would move quickly to lose himself where it would cost lives to get him out.

He chose not to go back. He followed Tain's tracks, as he thought, and that trail took him back beside the tents, not crossing the line of march yet, but proceeding straight back alongside the encamped tribes.

Among the foremost there had as yet been no detectable movement to resume the march, and none came for a long time. Whatever was proceeding, whether the Haga had recovered the four riderless beshti and had left his mother's burial to go out hunting on their own, it was early in their noon routine. Tribes behind the Haga in line were still asleep, still unaware what had happened up in the Haga camp.

He knew, too, that if he lost Tain's track, he might lose more than he had lost. Tain might immediately double forward again to attack Tofi's camp, and he might be wandering back here; or if he followed too fast, Tain might realize who was on his trail and lie in wait for him.

He expected ambush minute by minute, as he was sure Tain expected him. The dust made shadows of the encamped tents and the resting beshti . . . themselves a temptation for a man who might want a relief mount; but Tain had not struck here, not yet: beshti disturbed at their rest would not settle so complacently, would alarm their owners and rouse out a camp, and nothing of the like had happened.

Marak, Marak, his voices whispered to him. It came to him they had spoken before and he had not been attentive . . . nothing had been in his head at all but the necessities and the dangers of the chase. *Go back,* his voices said to him.

"Go to hell," he said to Luz. "It's my mother. Do you understand that? Did you *have* a mother?"

Marak, the voices whispered.

"Go to hell!" he said, and, on clear trail for a moment between dunes, he diverted Osan into a tribal camp. They were the Rhonandin, allies of the Haga. "Rhonan!" he shouted out, waking the camp, and roused men out from under their sheltering canvas. They came in alarm, clutching swords and pistols.

"My name is Marak Trin," he said to the Rhonandin. "Marak Trin *Tain,* to the point. My mother is Kaptai of the Haga, Menditak's cousin, Tain Trin Tain's wife, and she's dead."

"What do you want of the Rhonandin?" a man in authority asked him.

"Tain's murdered my mother up in the Haga camp and killed four of them in ambush when they rode after him. I ask you send a messenger to lord Menditak and tell him his men are dead. Tell him I'm on Tain's trail, to kill him, and I can't lose it."

"Montend," the man named one of his own. "Go to the Haga. Antag, you and your brothers, go with this man."

"I'm in your debt," Marak said fervently, "for water and peace. I honor you as my grandfather, omi. But they'll have to follow me. The wind's taking the trail, and I can't stop that long."

Beasts were unsaddled for their noontime rest. Men ran while he rode out to recover the trail. He recovered it, and in a very short time Antag and his four brothers appeared out of the dust behind him, armed with hunting spears and swords and one long rifle wrapped against the dust. Under the circumstances it was a weapon worth ten men, and one which Tain would kill to get into his hands.

"Omi," the foremost said. "My name is Antag. These are my brothers."

"In your debt, all." He never delayed, scarcely took his eyes off that quarter of the horizon where he guessed the trail to lie. "My father intends to raise a war within the caravan. He'll ride across the camps somewhere. There are those that might join him."

"The Ila is no friend of ours," Antag said. "But the Haga are."

"I'm outside the Ila's orders. This is a blood matter. And life and death for us. If Tain starts a war between the villages and the Haga, and these villagers get to acting like fools, they'll shed blood, and we'll feed the vermin, all of us. He doesn't care. He's angry, and now he's attacked the tribe that were his friends."

"You're sure of his track, omi."

It was tacit acceptance, respect for him. And an essential question. "He has no second beast, unless he got it from the Haga, and I didn't detect it." It was a tribesman's trick, to confuse the trail, steal a second besha and let his own go, to confuse pursuit as the freed beast wandered confused between the known company that abandoned him and the larger lure of the caravan.

"The Haga are friends," Antag said, and the four Rhonandin stayed with him, following the tracks in among the dunes, over the edges.

The blowing dust made it harder and harder to keep the track, but it remained a single track. They passed one and the other of the tribes, and sometimes the trail came close, and then veered off. Tain had found the beshti too restive, set within the circle of tents as the tribes tended to keep such valuable possessions.

"We'd best tell the tribes as we go," Marak said. "Their livestock is at risk, if not their lives, tonight. Are these near us within your kinship?"

"These are cousin-tribes." Antag sent the two younger brothers off to the side, into the camps, where a kindred tribe would meet fewer questions and gain quicker compliance. Meanwhile Antag and the one brother stayed with him, in and out among the dunes, trusting the other two brothers to find them again by their pace and their direction.

"He's running hard," Antag judged at a moment they found a clear set of tracks, and Marak agreed: there was the movement of a man bent more on distance than on cleverness.

"He taught me every trick," Marak said grimly. "And he's not panicked. He has a lot of them left."

He tried not to plan what he would do, or what he would say when he found Tain. He planned only to kill him before there were any words to haunt his sleep. His mother's blood was on his hands and before he was done, his father's would be. He promised himself that, and grew as crazed as he had been when it was the voices. Luz wanted him back. Luz tried, but he refused, continually refused, and bent the sanity he did have in one direction, into the sandy haze and toward his father.

They passed the last of the tribes and along beside the village camps. There Tain's track moved inward, ran beside the tents, past one camp and a second.

Then as they might have guessed, that trail went into the midst of a village camp, and straight through its center and into the next.

Here was where Tain might change beshti, and steal one or two, but as yet they found no trace of that: besides that, the trail grew confused, Osan taking the scents of dozens of his kind, growing distracted: they would have to pick up the trail outside again, and that would cost time.

Sleeping men stirred beneath the tents, lifted heads from their arms. Or they were not quite sleeping, since the last intrusion.

"A man rode through," Marak said to the villagers. "Where did he go?"

Several pointed the same way, back through the length of the camp, not to the side.

"Which villages will shelter him?" Antag asked, as they followed that track.

"The western," Marak said. It made him think of home, of the walls of Kais Tain, irretrievable. Of neighboring villages, red walls and known wells, and boyhood friends, and pranks, and the shade of village gardens.

Marak, Luz said, trying to recover him. He had shown weakness and she found it. *Marak, Marak, Marak, listen to me.*

He refused.

He tried not to think about the villages, those times, those lessons, the years he had loved and respected this man as the god of his life. In his boyhood the sun had come up every morning over Tain's shoulder, and all the world had been right . . . or would be if he could be quick enough, hard enough, strong enough, to win Tain's approval.

In those years the western lords had all been Tain's allies, and there had been no hint of the quarrels that would break the abjori apart. They had all fought against the Ila's rule, which was eternal, remote from care of them and their needs. They had fought, and their cause was right.

The western villages clear to the edge of the Lakht had gone to war. They had engaged the sympathy of no few of the tribes, who themselves had disdained the Ila's law. Tain had had close and friendly relations with the Haga, and won a Haga wife.

Now they would chase him to the ends of the earth.

Now Tain had lost all virtue in tribal law. He had struck at the woman who had run his household and shared his bed for thirty years, at the woman who had borne his children and bandaged his wounds . . . struck at her because the war failed, because even then there were cracks in the structure of alliances Tain had built.

Struck at her because *Tain* could not be the source of the madness and *Tain* could not be at fault for losing a war.

So Tain stole up on a peaceful, allied camp and called a woman out, not to reconcile and beg her pardon as he ought by rights to do, as Kaptai had every right to hope he might intend—but to murder her and then run like the felon he had become, challenging every tribe to kill him.

There was no forgiveness. There was no one left to ask it for Tain.

Antag's two brothers overtook them, calling out as they took shape out of the haze, to be sure of identities. The warning was given. The tribes knew, and sent out messengers and hunters of their own.

They asked at every camp they passed: "Has a man ridden through?" and at five camps the answer was the same, but at the sixth there was confusion and an instant's hesitation.

"I'm Marak Trin Tain," Marak said. "*Where is my father?*"

The people of that village, a village from the rim of the west, stayed unmoving, so many statues staring up at him with frightened eyes. Tain was known to take bloody vengeance on betrayers. Did he not know that?

But one old woman pointed to the side of the camp.

"You said nothing," Marak said to her. And to the rest: "It's your mistake if you pity him. The tribes are against him. The Ila is guiding you to water, out from under the star-fall. His own son guides this caravan. Do you want to die?"

For an answer, they only stared, so many wind-rocked images, and he and the four Rhonandin turned off where the old woman had pointed.

There were faint tracks. Tain had crossed back to the same side he had ridden before, and now they followed tracks rapidly growing dim in the blowing dust, then merging with others along the side of the camp, where the feet of men and beasts had made a complex record.

No track went out from it: Trin's course lay within that trampled ground, on to the next camp, but all the camp was ringed and crossed by that kind of track.

"Keep with it as best you can," Marak said, and rode into the village camp alone to ask whether any man had gone through.

"No," they said, and this was the village of Kais Mar. "Someone rode by," a child said, and pointed.

Marak turned Osan's head and rode back to join Antag and his brothers along the outer edge.

"There's still the gaps between camps he might use," Antag said. Particularly in this stretch, the camps did not abut up against one another: the villages pitched their tents often in confusion, not in orderly fashion, and one would end up closer and another farther, and such trampled gaps existed. At every such gap there was the chance of losing the track.

And now there came a stir within the camps, as somewhere far forward the Keran must have started moving, and gotten on their way, and now that movement had spread backward through the line.

They came to a western encampment, the village of Dal Ternand, and there Marak called out a name: "Mora!" It was the lord of Dal Ternand he wanted, and when the old man came out from the shade of the tent, the last left as the young men packed up: "Mora, you know me. I'm looking for my father."

"With no good intent," Mora judged. "You're the Ila's man now."

"I'm the guide for this caravan, the *master* of this caravan, and it's my job to get it to safety, with all that's in it. Tain killed my mother just now, and ran like a coward. I want him, Mora!"

"Killed Kaptai?"

"Killed her with a knife in the back, with no stomach to face me and not a damned care whether this caravan lives or dies ... whether all the people in the world live or die. *Where* is he?"

"He went the length of the camp. That's what I know."

"Pass the word. Tain's shed Haga blood, and from behind. They're after him. And I am."

"The Rhonan are after him," Antag said, "for the Haga's sake. And so are the Dashingar. Spread that word. This is a dead man."

Marak sent Osan on, along the route Mora of Dal Ternand had pointed out, and so into the next and the next village camp.

In the next after that, he knew the lord lied, and there was a suspicious dearth of able men packing up the tents: it was Kais Vanduran, where his father had veterans, and where he had his own, men who ought to be here.

"Where's Duran?" he asked old Munas, the lord of the village. "*Where's Kura?*" That was a man who had ridden with him, no older than he.

There was no answer, only a troubled look from Munas.

"He's killed Kaptai," Marak said in a hard, disciplined voice. "And four Haga. The tribes are after him, and I am, to the death, Munas. This isn't a war against the Ila. This is a war between us. If you hear from Kura, pull him back. Duran, too. I don't want his blood. Only Tain's."

"They aren't here," Munas said stubbornly. "I haven't seen them."

"You've let most of your men go with him," Marak said. "The wind's up. What are you going to do when the sand moves? What when a tent needs help? Did my father ask you that?"

That scored. But Munas had his jaw set and his mind made up.

"You're in danger," Marak said, and rode out with the Rhonandin, knowing that what he feared had happened: Tain had called up his veterans and declared his war against the Ila, against the caravan, and against his son.

They kept riding down the side of the lines, in a wind that got no worse, and no better, either. Larger vermin scampered from under the beshti's feet: the smaller, less aware, died there, and vanished in the blowing dust. When they came into the line again they saw some villagers had their baggage loaded and were ready to move, waiting for the village group in front of them.

"Have you seen men riding through?" Marak asked of them, and when they said no, lingered to wave them past. "If you're ready and your neighbors in front are not, move past! The whole line can't wait on the slowest! Camp as far forward as you can, and spread out from the line of march if you need to, to get to clean sand and keep clear of vermin."

That might provoke arguments when it came to camping at night, and he knew it; but let the word spread: no waiting, once the line began to move. No villager would pass the tribes, but he saw how delay in these unskilled folk became a contagion, spreading from one to the next.

They moved on, circled out among the dunes and back again, in heavy, blasting wind that made them keep the aifad up close about their eyes: they found no tracks out there, only the numerous scuttling vermin, so they went back to the villages, and on back, on tracks steadily growing obscure in the blowing dust.

After two more villages they were moving beside a moving line, going counter to the flow, so movement had spread back along the caravan. To each of the villages Marak posed the same question: have you seen men pass you? He gained an admission from one that they had seen riders coming back, but the village took them for the Ila's men.

Armed men, and more than one. That was no surprise.

They passed the villages more rapidly now, the caravan's motion carrying them past as they rode toward the rear: Kais Goros, Kais Tagin, and Undar went by: the westernmost villages were not the hindmost in the line.

They passed Kais Karas and Kais Madisar, and the wind was, if anything, fiercer, coming in gusts that reddened the air with sand. They had come into a place where a deep wash rolled down to a dry alkali bed and where there was little room on the column's right hand. By then, shadows had begun to gather, the sun dying in murk.

But on that rock Marak saw the bright scratches in the slope where a rider had gone down, and another where he had climbed up again and onto the far side, and so toward the low stony ridges.

"No knowing whether it's Tain himself," Antag said, and Marak said to himself that it was true. He would wager if he looked to the other side of the camp he would see other tracks, and that Tain had sent a man out to divert pursuit and himself taken another route.

"He's gone straight through the camp," he guessed suddenly, and rode through the traveling column, dodging between riding beasts and pack train.

It was the same story there, tracks on the far side of the line, perhaps another diversion. More, it was the village of Mortan, and two men he asked for by name in this village of the western Lakht were both missing.

They rode on. Another and another village they searched, and heard nothing, and found nothing. The next village had seen men riding through, and had no idea who they were, except they thought they were bandits.

Tain might have abandoned diversions, ridden straight back to Kais Tain, wherever it fell in the order of march.

But in his doubt the voices, hitherto silent in this business, began to echo in his head, Luz's summons, Luz's urging: *Marak, Marak, come back. This is too far.*

They passed new graves, walking staffs marking the place where someone of the villages, likely the old, had simply given out during the last rest. Vermin had already dug up the dead, and fought and snarled over the pits, not a good sight. But there was no longer any hint along the trampled side of the tents that a band had gone this way or that. There might by now be ten or so men weaving in and out of the camps to confuse pursuit, men going off across the sand to lay false trails and coming back again.

Marak! the voices insisted, out of patience with his desertion, and he knew, as surely by now Antag and his men knew, that they had lost Tain's track.

"He may double back on us," Marak said when they reined to a pause, and as the caravan had begun to move. "I can't ask more than you've done. He may double back tonight, he or some of the men with him. He's gotten away."

"He deserves his reputation," Antag conceded, leaning on the knee of the leg tucked against his besha's neck, while the wind battered them. "Now our tribe is against him, and he may strike at us."

"Go back. Spread the word among your allies. Spread it among all the tribes, and into the villages. He'll try to kill the caravan guides—the only ones that know where we're going.

He'll try to stir up the old abjori, as many as he can find, to take the leadership for himself. Then he'll lead everyone away from the only safety there is. He doesn't know what's coming down on us, and what he does know, he doesn't believe." In his vision the ring of fire went out again and again, and he shivered in what had become a chill wind. "Nothing we've seen yet equals what's coming."

"You'll go back with us, omi."

"I want to go on. I need to find Kais Tain. It's my village, as well as his."

"It's foolish to go on. You'll be traveling in the dark."

"I'm a villager. I know these people. I can talk to their lords."

Marak, Marak, Marak, the voices said, but he ignored them.

Antag asked his brothers what they thought, and they shrugged. Antag said: "We'll stay with you a while. You're taking too much risk, for one of our guides."

"I know I am. But my wives are up front. They know."

"We'll still stay with you," Antag said. "We'll be sure you get back. Easy to go back in the column. Hard to catch up with it while it's moving."

It was the truth Antag told him. The beshti had their limits, too, and almost, he surrendered to the voices, almost, he was willing to go back.

But not with his father loose, not with harm apt to come on the whole caravan, and him with a chance to prevent it.

They rode in on village after village, he and Antag and Antag's brothers, asking their question, naming their names and spreading their news. They rode beside the village leaders in each village only long enough to do that, and then reined back moved farther back in the line, quickly lost in dust and dusk.

Two more of these village lords Marak knew: Kefan of Kais Kefan, and Taga of Kais Men.

"Killed Kaptai?" Taga asked, in a tone of great indignation. "That was a good woman."

Taga had always loved Kaptai, had always been a friend of the house, and Kaptai had always welcomed the old man.

"He's gone madder than I was," Marak said. "Now I'm the sane one, and he's trying to kill the lot of us. Stop him if you see him. At best, persuade the rest not to follow him."

But in all their wandering back in line they had not yet come to Kais Tain, and they had come a long way back. They rested the beshti beside the column, letting them sit a while as the dark gathered about them. Some village bands, passing them, sent to know who they were, and they told them, and advised them about Tain and the danger to all of them.

Meanwhile the dust stayed up and the wind kept blowing, a stiff wind at the caravan's back . . . far better than a facing wind. The sand piled up against the beshti's feet as they stood by the wayside, and vermin prowled about, prompting an occasional stamp and threat.

In that rest they shared a little of their provisions, that water and that food which every tribesman carried against emergency, and to increase the food and water store of their group.

It was soon dark, a sand-choked night in which Marak saw it was folly for the villages to keep going: the weak lagged, and if not for the beshti's following, other beshti might well stray off the track and lose themselves in the dunes. If he were at the fore of it, secure in the heart of the tribes, he might not himself realize the struggle back here, the fragile contact between straggling village groups, with village-bred beshti, many of them not the swiftest, not conditioned for long treks, rather beasts of local burden, soft as their local handlers.

As the Keran and the Haga had not realized it. As Hati had not. He tried to make Norit hear him, through Luz, but that never succeeded. Luz seemed to look through his eyes only seldom, and with difficulty, and if she spoke, it was less loud and less real than the wind rushing past him. The villages dared not stop, and the vermin got in among the beshti, quarreling over the latrine sites and the cook sites, which became a seething mass of small, unwholesome bodies.

How long they traveled then they had no idea. There were no stars to measure time, no light at all in the heavens. The earth shuddered briefly, and people on the march cried out soft, weary alarm.

Something mid-sized and furtive slipped up on them, encountered them, and shied away, vermin that feared the beshti. After that several others likewise shied back from the beshti, and lost themselves in the dusty dark.

Antag and his brothers were brave men, and not stupid ones. They must long since have known what had taken him longer to admit.

"There's no hope in this," Marak said, tugging Osan to a halt. "He's gotten away from us. The best thing we can do now is go into the line and move up gradually, and tell every camp we meet that he's outlawed. It may take us more than a day to reach our own tents, the way the weather's going."

"As you will, omi," Antag said, and no more than that. But Antag and his brothers were relieved, Marak was sure. They rode in among the line, and passed the word to the village of Faran as they did, a Lakhtani village out of the south, where Tain would find little sympathy—it was their goods, their caravans that Tain had raided in the war, and Tain's son was little welcome: Antag did the talking. Marak was glad to ride out of their midst, bound forward, but it was only to another Lakhtani village, one he had no more knowledge of.

Then in their moving forward they came to a village contingent they had not addressed, one that had passed during their rest.

"What village?" Marak asked, and hearing it was Tarsa, asked after the lord, having no idea who it was.

The lord of Tarsa turned out to be an old, old man, Agi, wrapped in the wind and the dust and the night, and drowsing as he rode.

"Omi," Marak said to him, drawing near, and told him the matter of Tain and a rebellion within the caravan, not knowing where Agi might fall on the matter of Tain's war, and the abjori. He was a voice in the dark. So was Agi.

"We'll keep an eye to it," Agi said as they rode.

"Have you heard where Kais Tain might be?" Antag asked. They had asked that of every village.

"I've no idea. Forward or back of us, it's all the same to me. This is a fool's errand, this moving to another tower. Stupidity. You're Marak, are you? Tain's son? Tain Trin Tain?"

"The same."

"Fool. Fool to bring us away from Oburan."

"Oburan's dead," Marak said doggedly. "There's no other place, no other destination for caravans after this. I've been to the tower. I know it's there. I know what's there."

"You're the prophet."

"I'm the Ila's man. With Hati an'i Keran." He added, fully cognizant that there might be feuds: "With a woman named Norit."

He could make out only that the elder turned his head to stare at him. The veils, the sand, the night, made their emotions invisible to each other. It was impossible to placate this man with a gesture. There was only this one chance to talk to him; and he knew Norit had not been a widow: she was a married woman, and by the law, yes, they were adulterers.

"Norit din Karda is dead. Her mother is dead. Her father is dead. Her aunts are all dead. And she's dead."

"To the life she had in Tarsa, yes. She is."

The old man made no reply.

"Is Lelie dead?"

Still there was no reply.

"She named that name to us," Marak said. "Is it a sister? A mother? A daughter?"

The old man was still a while answering. But Marak waited.

"The girl's with her father," the old man said. "As she should be."

"A daughter, then."

"Yes."

"Does the father treat her well?" He as much as any man knew the situation of an unwanted child, and the fate of one dragged into the affairs of state and the angers of leaders.

"She's alive," Agi said flatly. That was all.

Not a good situation, then. And Marak made a quick decision, a desperate and dangerous decision, since if there was one person on whom thousands of lives relied, it was Norit, through whom Luz spoke most easily; and if there was one person whose sanity was in greatest danger, it was Norit. "If the father isn't happy, then give her to me, omi. I'll relieve the father of an obligation and take good care of her."

The old man considered the proposition.

"This is a great lord," Antag said across the wind-battered gap. "What he says he'll do, he'll do, omi."

The old lord reined aside to one of his own men and spoke.

Then that man, no skilled rider, managed to turn aside in the storm and the dark and the stubborn persistence of the beshti in evading the wind, and to go back into the caravan of Tarsa.

No one spoke. The effort to converse was too great, and Agi had no great desire to speak to them, that was clear. Marak waited, thinking how he had come out into the caravan to take a life close to him and now bid to save one he had never met.

Memnanan's messenger had never gotten here. Why that was he still had no idea, and saw no profit in asking: it was the desert at fault, the abjori, his father, or Agi himself, but it was nothing he could mend now, under present circumstances. In some measure he was a fool even to trouble what was settled, a fool to think of taking a young child back the route he had come. It was a dangerous enough ride for him and the Rhonandin, and he had no idea of Norit's frame of mind. One might: *Marak, Marak,* his voices raged at him. But he paid no attention. He shut his eyes. He rode without attention to anyone. He waited.

Men moved forward in the line, one that might be the old man's messenger, the other that might have some answer about the child, both faceless shadows in the violent, sand-edged dark.

"Where is this Marak Trin?" one asked. "Who wants this child?"

Marak saw no child in the man's possession. "I'm Marak

Trin Tain," he said, to have that clear. "I want this child for a woman who asked for her."

"My wife is dead," the man said, and Marak had no idea of his name, though sharing what they shared it seemed he ought to know that small fact.

"Do you want the child for yourself?" Marak asked him. "I haven't come to take it, if you want it. But I'm telling you there's one who does, desperately."

"Is it my Norit?" the man shouted across the wind. "Is she the prophet we heard? Is it really Norit?"

"She is the prophet," Marak said. "And she speaks well of you. And she misses Lelie."

"I have a new wife," the man said. "My Norit is dead."

"She loves you," Marak said to him, deciding he might feel sorry for this man, deciding that his rights here were limited and circumscribed by older ones. "She's well. But she suffers."

"Is she sane?" Shouting across the wind robbed the voice of inflection. It might have been an accusation. Or a heart-felt longing.

"Sane enough she guides us all," he shouted back. "Sane enough to this hour, but her duty won't bring her back, not likely, not if you've married again. Give her the child if she's a trouble to you. If she isn't, then be a father to her. And if you want Norit back—" He had no power to give Norit to anyone. "Come forward in the line and ask her for yourself."

"I have my new wife," the man answered him. He unfolded his robe and unskillfully managed his besha closer to Osan, to pass across a small bundle, a half-limp child who waked on being exposed to the blasting wind, and struggled fretfully.

Marak reached across and took it under the arms, a light weight, a girl, he thought, maybe about a year of age, maybe two. She seemed light for her size.

"Do you want to give her up?" Marak shouted at the father, at Norit's husband. "Don't do it if you don't! I'm here to offer and ask, not to order! The Ila's man came asking. Did you ever hear him?"

"I heard nothing," the husband said back to him. "But Norit is mad. So Lelie may be. And my new wife doesn't want her."

"Then I'll take her to her mother," Marak said, and opened his robe and snugged the infant into that warm shelter. The baby fought him. He hugged her tightly, preventing her struggles. He feared even so that he had robbed the father, but if what the father said was so, maybe he had saved the child a warfare with a new wife, one that wanted no reminders of a marriage the father had not willingly left, a villager that would never reach such an accommodation as he and Hati had with Norit. "I'll take care of her," he said. "Shall I say anything to Norit?"

"She's dead," was all the husband would say, as Agi said, as everyone in the village might say.

"Antag!" Marak called out, gathering his companions, and rode forward with the storm at his back, on across the gap at which Tarsa lagged behind the next village. He felt obliged to explain himself; but he had no explanation that would make sense to strangers.

"We were looking for this baby," he said, feeling that life squirm against him. The wind drowned its outcries and its fear. He was holding it too tightly, and eased his grip, and patted it inside his coat, trying to still its crying. *Her* crying. Lelie had ceased to be an abstract question, and became a living distraction, a personal folly.

If he had been alone, he might have said to himself Tarsa was not all he wanted to find. Tarsa was not what he had looked for. But he had found Tarsa, all the same, and he had pursued a question which was not his question, and met a man he had never wanted to meet, and acquired an answer that had already cost a life.

And now if he did anything but go back to the Ila he risked more than himself, and he risked these men, and more. The squirming bundle against his side, trying to kick him, told him how much he had risked already, and reminded him there were other concerns besides his blood debt, and his mother, and his grief. He wanted no part of these concerns . . . if he had his own way he would hand the baby to Antag and keep going; and he could do that.

But thinking once meant thinking twice, and thinking twice told him that if it had been rash to come out here, it was increasingly his father's territory, back here among the villages, among men whose loyalties were in question. His loss might lose all the rest, and he had something to live for . . . he had two women, and a young man, and even the Ila's captain, who had trusted him with all he personally cared about.

He could not go back to Kais Tain. Having seen a father part with his daughter and a village agree with that act, he could no longer delude himself that Kais Tain would ever confess their own guilt for turning him out. They would never change their minds, or give up their allegiance to Tain. He had rescued Lelie, but no one would rescue him, if he went on into territory where Tain's word had more credit than his, and where a man who spoke for the Ila was the enemy.

He hugged the child more gently, a living prize, when the ride had begun with a death. He knew Kaptai would have hugged Lelie. Kaptai had had a large soul. Kaptai had loved his father, which took particular persistence and patience—and too much patience, and too much belief. He knew now what she had never confessed: that she never should have left her tribe, and now Kaptai lay somewhere ahead of him in the dark, that, for all her love and her loyalty . . . not prey to vermin, not now, not like those shallow-buried others . . . not when the sand got up like this, and not when, knowing it, the Haga raised a mound over their dead. The sand would cover her, make her the heart of a dune, turn her to one of those strange dead the sand gave up rarely. She had loved the high desert, and now it took her in, and he could do nothing to mend her death and nothing to get her back.

"This is my wife's baby," he said to Antag, shouting over a gust. "She's divorced from her husband. He'd kept the child and didn't want it. At least there's this."

"A good thing," Antag said, as they moved along beside the next village in the line. The baby's wail for a moment was louder than the wind. "She's likely scared. The wind's no lull-aby."

"She'll sleep," Marak said. Her struggles were wearying, but they were nothing to him. "She'll grow tired."

"So do the beshti," Antag shouted back. "We can gain a lit-tle distance, still, tonight, but we ought to camp with one of the villages next noon, and maybe get that baby some milk or something. Not to mention changing her."

There was a young man who knew infants with complete common sense. Camping with one of the villages was also better sense than he had been thinking of.

And he was willing to do that.

"We should pick a group now and keep their pace," he shouted at Antag and the brothers. "No sense wearing the beshti down. We'll sleep, gain back a little tomorrow, ride back if we can."

"That's good!" Antag yelled back at him.

So they fell in with the pace of the third contingent up from where they were. The village was Kais Kurta, a western village, and Andisak was its lord: one of his father's veterans, a man of his father's generation, but one who had broken with Tain before this. Marak was dismayed, meeting An-disak, to know where he had arrived.

"It's possible I shouldn't be here," Marak said. "Tain has killed my mother in the Haga camp. I've hunted him for my mother's life as far as the tracks lasted and found nothing that tells me we'll come on him tonight. So I'm going back to my camp, but we can't make it all the way tonight. And I wouldn't have come here if I'd known this was Kais Kurta. What do you want? Will you take us into your camp until the next rest? Or shall we move on? I'll take no offense if you de-cide that's best."

"Stay with us," Andisak said, and he was western, so that was that: if Andisak himself invited them, there would be no treachery within the camp, on the offender's life. Andisak's reputation was at stake. "Give me the news," Andisak said, "what the state of affairs is between you and my old ally."

Marak began to, in the sinking of the wind for a space,

and they rode at that pace the night long, resting sometimes, talking with Andisak in the intervals when the wind allowed easier speech, and they kept very close to the contingent in front, even commingling ranks with that village in the confusion of the wind and the blowing sand. Andisak was wise, and allowed no gap between his village and the next, but that spoke only of Kais Kurta. If any village let themselves lag behind, they could stray off the track in the storm and consequently lose all the rest of the caravan, never to find their way again.

It was a terrifying realization. For the first time Marak understood how fragile the chain of life was, far back in the line. The tribes would never break and lose their way . . . but the villages had no experience at this business of caravans. For most the only journey they had ever made in their lives was the matter of getting to Oburan on a well-traveled trade path. Now the weakest village lord, and his bad decisions, could kill all the rest of the people in the world, and vermin had begun to be a threat, much bolder than ordinary, much bolder than they had been since the war, when they had gathered thick about the battles and preyed on the wounded . . . the vermin could change their habits, and had begun to encroach, even within the line, where beshti feet cracked shells and where seething masses in the night and the blowing sand denoted some latrine left by a prior tribe.

That was not ordinary. Nothing of the sort was ordinary.

And where was Kais Tain? Somewhere at the rear of the line of march, at least far enough back that a day of riding against the flow of villagers had not located them. Kais Tain was in danger, and those who walked were doomed.

"Have you seen anything of messengers?" Marak asked Andisak, and Andisak said he had.

"They went on down the line, but never came back," Andisak said. "And the priests come and go, the Ila's priests."

The priests were never well loved in the west.

"We have one of the Ila's books," Andisak remarked at one point. "At your urging we took it. If you ask me, as the priests did, but I didn't say, it's damned dull. Court proceedings. Are they all like that?"

"To my knowledge, probably," Marak said.

"I'm not sure I want to be written in the Ila's book," Andisak said. "What if I keep this book?"

"I'm sure it won't be that much use. It's what's in it that matters; it's all the books together. The Ila wants that." So did Luz. So, very much, did Luz, who suffered through this dialogue and nagged him, saying his name over and over: *Marak, Marak,* until he grew distracted. *East, east, east,* Luz chided him, impatient of the delay.

20

Every child must be written down by the au'it and its shape accounted. When a child is born the priest must see it.
—The Book of the Ila's Au'it

They talked at times, Marak and the Lord of Kais Kurta. They rode at that easy pace the night long, into a sandy, murky dawn, and on into the day, letting the beshti rest from their long trek back in the line.

At dawn, when Lelie became fretful, Andisak found a woman to take Norit's baby and tend it, and Marak let it go. He had not known how heavy that load had been, in all senses. He slept in the saddle after he had turned the hungry, fretting child over to a strange woman. He slept the sleep of the exhausted, and at the same time Antag and his brothers slept, trusting Andisak's honor.

All that morning, at Marak's intermittent waking, the wind blew and the sand still moved. They went over a desert continually being rewritten, discouraging the vermin, making the vermin's constant hunt for leavings more difficult. The pickings were constantly richer toward the end of the caravan.

That was where trouble gathered. Those were the people

with most to fear. Was it possible, if a mobbing started, that all the vermin in the world could sate themselves with a handful of villages and spare the rest? *Marak, Marak*, his voices chided him, but mildly now. He was sure Luz now had some idea where he was, and that he had turned back toward his duty: she seemed content with that. Whether Luz had also told Norit what gift he had with him he very much doubted; and whether Luz approved of his collecting Lelie along the way, he had no idea.

But he was glad of the voices as a guide, as an indication that Hati was well and Norit was well. He had no idea about his sister, but he had trusted Hati and Norit to take care of her, and if they were well, then that was cared for.

"I'm coming back," he muttered aloud, to Luz, if she heard him. "I'm all right."

They dismounted, unsaddled, and rested a while, at noon, as Kais Kurta pitched its tents. And in that rest he took the child from the woman and tucked her up next to him.

"Is it a child you know?" the lord of Kais Kurta asked him, sitting near him. "Or one you found?"

"My wife's," he said, and touched a small hand . . . incredible to him that a hand could be so small, and his sun-dark and marked with the killing-marks, one for every finger. She played with his fingers like Patya when she was a year old. She made him remember.

"We had enough war," Andisak said with a sigh. There came a broad shadow in the wind, as the industrious young men put up a side flap of their tent, to give them shelter a while from the constant buffeting. Before them, the next village was camped, and the sun sat at a sullen yellow noon.

But now the wind grew chill as it did at times when a larger storm was coming. Haste, the weather said. Make all possible speed. The ground shook, shivered like a besha with an itch.

"So had I," Marak confessed, "had enough war. Enough of a lot of things."

"Is this the whole truth?" Andisak asked. "Is there a safe place?"

"I've been there," he said. "I've seen the river, the water. Everyone is fed. Everyone has shelter. The ones who went with me stayed there, all but Tofi and his freedmen."

"I saw you," Andisak said, "on the ridge. It was a relief to hear someone we know say so."

"It's all true, omi. I wouldn't bring this many innocents into the desert on a lie."

"I know you wouldn't," Andisak said, and nodded slowly. "And the tribes aren't fools. They're up there at the front of all this. To the umi of the Rhonan: welcome."

Antag nodded, and took down his veil, as a man did with a friend. So his brothers did, and they all did, while Norit's Lelie slept, collapsed across Marak's knee.

They shared the prepared meal, but not to their fill. They had riding yet to do. In no more than an hour, they tightened girths and prepared to set out, with Andisak and his household bidding them a courteous farewell.

The weary beshti launched only token complaint. They did not belong with these beshti, and were restless, outside their own camp.

So were they all. The voices dinned a constant noise as Marak got up into the saddle.

From Antag's hands he then took Lelie up, and she waked and struggled and cried in fretful, constant misery, tears running through dust on her face, but Marak took her inside his coat, and took up an offered aifad for her, and sheltered her and wrapped the cloth about her small face, veiling it, and keeping her close.

"We owe you," Marak said to Andisak. The woman who had cared for Lelie was the one who had given the aifad. She had turned up among the foremost to see them off, not without regrets, Marak thought, perhaps very much wanting the baby; but Lelie was Norit's, and once she resumed her place across the saddlebow, wrapped within his coat, she quieted.

They rode out. He had done nothing that he had set out to do, and acquired something he had never planned on.

When, as they rode through the dust and fought the

wind, Lelie opened her small arms and took a strong grip on his shirt, he found unaccountable satisfaction in that, and hugged her with his free arm, like a close-held secret.

Marak, Marak, Marak, the voices said, a guidance as the earth shook, once strongly enough to stagger the beshti.

They had learned to duck low when that happened. No one fell. The beshti had no liking for the sensation, and a few younger ones in the column bolted and had to be reined in.

Lelie, too, waked and cried, and Marak opened his coat and talked to her: "Be still. I won't let you fall."

"Mama," Lelie said. "Mama, mama, mama."

Not papa. Marak heard that clearly enough, justifying what he had done in taking her. "Hush," he said, drying tears and leaving mud on her face instead. "It's just the wind. It's just the earth twitching its skin, like a besha. Such things happen these days."

He flinched, himself, when something boomed, and the earth shook like a table jolted by a fist—all of it in murk that only gave them shadows to see, hulking tents with the flaps down in some instances, and others which had only pitched canvas halfway, as windbreaks, not a safe proposition, if the storm should worsen. It was better to have enough stakes down and more canvas spread.

He said as much to villages where they passed in their long, long ride, and they might have listened to those who looked like tribesmen, as villagers were always wise to listen to those who knew. They were not pressing the beshti now, not asking more of them than they could reasonably give. They rode generally to the outside of the column, to left or to right, on untracked ground, and the beshti startled vermin that were otherwise scuttling about at the edges of the pitched tents . . . flattened a few, which became snarling balls of other vermin. If he had known nothing from the priests, it would have been troubling, that the vermin were so quick, that they came out of nowhere. They were growing hungry. They had found a food source.

In their ride, they passed priests walking along the spread tents, and exchanged greetings with them . . . these men he had despised proved hardy and resourceful, and carried messages. He gave them one in the Ila's name, that the villagers should never pitch lean-tos in a gale, and they nodded solemnly and promised to repeat it.

They moved on past the resting tents. In the lulls he talked with Antag and his brothers, idle talk, for the most part, those things that strangers could say to each other . . . he clarified rumor, and answered questions on the tower, questions about the land there, about the camp and the nature of the strangers . . . all these things. Lelie grew fretful and wanted down, and went and squatted in the sand with five men to guard her moment of vulnerability. So they all took the chance, and even while they were occupied at that, Marak saw five and six of the beetles that haunted such sites, and one of the creepers that preyed on the beetles, though the sand was blowing and quickly covering any damp spot.

It was not good.

They moved on, and the wind grew fiercer, and they struggled to keep going as the beshti leaned into the blasts and wanted to turn tail to them. Lelie cried, and exhausted herself, and slept again. But they kept going. The time passed that the camps might begin to stir and pack up, Marak thought, but no one moved in front, and so the villages down the line stayed put later, and later.

The dim glow in the murk that was the sun had inclined halfway down the sky and no one had stirred. *Marak, Marak, Marak,* his voices said, and he began to fear that Luz was holding the whole caravan for him. On the one hand they might be wiser to rest this storm out, and on the other it was loss of time, precious time, time that was worth lives, if there was any chance of moving at all. He had no foreknowledge of better coming, only of worse, and when he shut his eyes, now, which were crusted with dust and sand and running tears, he saw the ring of fire, over and over and over, worse and worse as he grew more tired.

Once he had been terrified of the visions for themselves. Now he had a warm weight against his side, and village lords telling him, if he asked, that they understood everything, oh, yes, and all their precautions were enough.

He began to understand a diffuse sort of fear, not acute, but widespread, a sense of disaster shaping about them. He began to understand he cared in more than the abstract, that he cared for the weight in his arms, and that it was all too large. He had not been able to ride all the way to the back of this mass of people, and that there was more to be done to save the people than one man could do, more to be done than any ten men could suffice to do.

His father had one answer. The Ila might have one. Luz had, and moved to execute it. There were all these competitors, when the vermin were gathering to feed on their corpses.

The best thing he could ask was for his father to gather all the discontent, the core of the abjori, and trail the column, so that perhaps the fact that the column reached refuge and the fact that the things Luz warned of came about would make Tain understand, and change his tactics, because after the caravan entered sanctuary, there would be no caravans to prey on. Ever.

And no one out here yet understood that. No one understood that where the producers of affluence went, those that ate the scraps would follow after, more and more desperate. The land would not be the same, and such as Lelie would not inherit anything her elders would recognize.

That was what he held in his arms. That was what breathed and wriggled and fretted against his heart. It was time-to-come. It was After. It was what-next, insistent with its sole question and tearful in its protests about its situation.

It made him aware that his own vision stopped at Norit's hammerfall, again, and again, and again repeated in his sight: it reached that point and stopped, just stopped, with the scouring of everything he knew from off the face of the earth. Antag and his brothers asked him questions, What will we do? Where will we trade, when we're there? and he could not answer any of them, except to laugh hollowly and say that he supposed they would lie under palm trees in paradise and eat until they had an idea.

Antag laughed at the joke, somewhat desperately, gallantly. Marak reached inside his coat and held his hand on Lelie's back, and felt her breathe, quiet as she was. Now he was afraid of what-next. What about Lelie? What about the children? What about the books, safe in the hands of every elder?

Antag had asked him, "What do we do when we get there?" and he had said, "Lie under the palm trees," but what resounded in his brain over and over again, with the visions of damnation, was the building of a city, a city like Oburan, around the Tower.

We make a city. We grow strong. *We build,* woman, and we *make,* and we *do,* no matter this enemy we never asked to have. We *fight* against our ruin, woman. And we get children to inherit what we build, and we live, woman. I give *you* a vision. This is what we have to have.

Marak, Marak, Marak, hurry, the voices said now. *We're waiting. Keep coming. Weather's moving in. Hurry, hurry, hurry.*

He picked up the pace as they came across the first camp of the tribes. The caravan still waited, lashed down tight against the storm that was coming. And if that stayed true, Osan would have his rest at the end of the ride, and if it was not, if he had to stop to rest, then he would camp beside the moving caravan and wait until Osan was fit. Antag and his brothers asked no questions of his intentions. But they kept with him; and "Mama," Lelie wailed against his heart.

Had she never ceased to call that, in all the time since the Ila's men had taken her mother away?

And had the man in Norit's songs waited so little time before taking another wife?

"Hush," he said to her, just beneath the wind, just beneath what his companions could hear. "Hush."

Your mother's waiting, he said to Lelie in his mind. *Luz won't have all her attention now. It's not fair, what she does to your mother.*

"Be still," he said, "be patient. It's only the wind, and the beshti can see the way, if we can't. They always know the way."

They passed camp after camp, and now the beshti had some recognition in their heads, or some sense in them that said their own bands were close. They began to move faster and faster, and they passed alongside the tribal camps, one and the next.

They reached the Rhonan, and there Antag and his brothers reined back their beshti from the goal they wanted, only for a word or two.

"Good luck to the mother of the child," Antag said. "And good luck to you, Marak Trin, wherever we go."

"My thanks to you and your lord," Marak said. "My tent will always shelter you and your tribe."

It was what friendly tribes said. They were pleased: despite the veils, he could see that.

"And ours, yours," they answered with the ritual courtesy. "At any time."

The storm battered them. They had said all that had to be said. He was within easy reach of his own camp, and he gave Osan the signal to move.

"He may be out there," Antag said to his back. "Tain is a clever man. Be careful."

"I will be." He gave Osan his head, and they rode beside the column, he with Lelie, at a traveling clip. People in the Haga camp had put up the tent sides. Warnings about the weather had passed from Norit, or the tribes sensed it themselves, and not empty fear, either. From moment to moment the dust cut off all view: the sun was on the horizon now, at his back, and cast no shadow at all in the thick air.

He rode finally alongside his own tents, and Osan made a jogging, eager approach to the beshti he knew, the comfort of his own herd. The side flaps of these tents, too, were down: the wind was cold, and he hoped for help as he rode Osan in among the beshti of his own tent and began to get down.

A gun went off. He stopped in mid-dismount, with Lelie in his arm, and was thinking of having to unsaddle Osan on his own when that strange thing happened: he was still thinking of it as a bullet tore through him where he held

Lelie. Osan shied, finishing the motion, and went out from under him.

He fell toward his back because Osan's motion had flung him that way, and the shot had, and he was conscious of holding Lelie, but not being sure he had her as he went down. He was astonished at the turn of fortunes.

Then he hit the sand full on his back, and hit his head, and heard Hati shout and swear . . . he thought it was Hati. He lay there winded, dimly trying to find out whether he held the child, and aware that she was wet and hot, and trying to cry, not fretfully, but in earnest—but she was as winded as he was, and could not somehow get her breath.

"Get them!" Hati shouted at someone, and immediately a hand came under his head and an arm tried to lift him.

"It's a baby," someone said. "It's shot, too, right through the leg."

He was shocked, and angry, and tried to see the damage the bullet had done, but he could not get his head up. He would not let go of Lelie. He had held her, he had protected her, and he went on doing it until Hati pried his hand off the baby. Her, he trusted. Norit, he would trust.

If he was shot, it was his father's doing. There was no one else. They were all in danger.

"Get him," he tried to tell Hati. "Get under cover. *Someone get him.*"

"The captain's men are going after him," Hati said. She understood him. Someone was trying to press a cloth against his side, where Lelie was lying, and wanted to pick her up. "Let go," Hati said. "Marak. Let go. Let them take her."

"It's Norit's baby," he said. "It's that Lelie she asked for. Her baby." But he was not at all sure Hati heard. He had no idea where anyone was, and that was unusual, as regarded his wives. His voices failed him. His whole sense of the world was fading. Their sense of presence had faded. He was sinking, and they tried to turn him over, which further confused his sense of the world.

"It went out his back," Tofi's voice said. "That's good."

"It could have carried threads into him. Heat some oil."

Lelie had been shot, an innocent, if the world had one. The bullet had gone through her before it reached him. He had meant to save her, Lelie's father had failed her, and his father had meant to kill him, and this was the way it all came together. It was his own father who had done all this mischief, his father who had won the throw. He had no doubt of it. His father had been more clever, still more clever, after all these years. His father had won, at least the contest between them, and he might die. Not dying was the only way to spite Tain. He told himself that.

Men were still shouting and running around him. The beshti complained, that noise which had underlain half his life. He heard a cry, a thin, desperate kind of baby cry, absolute indignation, it seemed to him, and justified, if ever a cry was justified in the world. "How bad is the baby?" he asked Hati, when she leaned close.

"She's shot, too," Hati said. "Norit. Norit, *take* her, damn it. Don't stand and stare like a fool!"

The baby still cried, more distantly. Pieces of his recollection scattered, like coins across a floor.

"Someone had better unsaddle Osan," he said. "He's been under saddle since yesterday. Maybe longer." He could not remember. "Rub his legs."

"We'll see to him," Hati promised him.

"Is he going to die?" That wail was his sister's voice. He could not remember why she was there. "Is he going to die?" He tried to answer her for himself, though he could not see her. "No," he said.

But after that men picked him up by the edges of his robe and carried him into the walled tent, where they had an oil light.

They let him down. He was content simply to breathe. The wind failed to reach here. The noise and the dust was less. He could have sunk into sleep, quite gladly.

But they brought hot oil, and poured it into the wound, repeated doses. He felt other faculties dimming as a fierce throbbing attended the hurt.

"It's swelling," someone said. "It won't take the oil."

The makers were at work. His makers. His protectors. About the baby he had no idea. He simply lay still, shut his eyes, tried to ride through the pain while they probed and cleaned: he fainted, and came back, and fainted again, but by the second waking there were wet compresses on the wound, and they had given up on the hot oil.

Hati was by him. He found no need to talk. The pain was all, for a while, and he could not organize his thoughts to want or wish anything beyond that. He simply lay still, wondering whether they had delayed for the storm, or for him. He vaguely knew Hati could answer that one question, but he had no wish to open a conversation he could not carry further. He was growing delirious with the fever, and his head hurt worse than any headache in his life. He decided he was willing to die, so long as no one disturbed him or hurt his head. The veins in his temples and in his ears seemed apt to rupture, the pressure was so great, and tears leaked from his burning eyes simply because there was nowhere else for the pressure to go.

The makers might not win this one, he thought, and if that was so, then he urgently had to muster the wherewithal to talk to Hati. There were instructions he had to give.

"We can't stay camped," he said, and what he tried to say was: "The moment the weather allows, we have to move out of here. Something's coming."

"I know," Hati said. "Be still. Sleep."

"Did you hear me?" he tried to ask. He still heard Lelie crying, and he lost the thread of communication with Hati for a while, but he thought about it while he rested.

Marak, the voices said, and he tried to listen and learn this time. He hoped Luz could reach him, explain to him, understand their situation and get them to safety. He saw dots before his eyes, but it was one of those kind of visions he thought came from fever, not from Luz.

Then the dots, red and blue, mostly, acquired significance, individuality. They moved, and followed patterns. Life depended on them, and they made chains, spiraling like the flight of vermin.

It was surely fever. In a remote part of his mind he knew he was delirious.

Marak, the voices said again. *Marak.*

And in his dream, "I'm listening," he said aloud. "Tell me what to do."

You've been foolish, Luz said.

"*I know that,*" he said in this dream, but he was mesmerized by the dots, wholly absorbed by them, as if they were the secret to all the world, just revealed to him.

You're looking at the nanisms, Luz said to him. *These are the makers. Are you listening this time?*

"Yes," he said. "*Help us get out of here.*"

They heal you when you're injured. They're my creatures, at work now, patching the damage you've done.

"*I've done. I didn't do it. My father did.*"

Small difference.

"*That's fine. I'll get well. Go away. I'm in too much pain to talk.*"

The swelling can't be helped. Your body does that when the nanisms rush to an injury: there are so many they congest the area. They diverge, you know: the makers aren't the only sort. The makers make other makers, some of them the body's own nanisms, if you like.

"*If I live I'm sure I'll appreciate it.*"

I'm sure you will, Luz said. *Are you hearing me now? It's rare that I can get your whole attention.*

"*I'm trying.*"

I'm sure you are. But know this: you carry these nanisms wherever you go, and shed them into the soil and the water. Or into blood. They work very efficiently in the bloodstream.

"*Nice.*"

You took it on yourself to bring Norit's baby. You risked every life in the world for one child.

"*As you did, to get the Ila.*" Now he roused almost to consciousness, and for a moment the dots and their movements were not the whole world. "*The baby is Norit's child. She misses her child. Is that such an offense to you?*"

It's certainly an inconvenience to her. But we have the child

*now: your blood shed new makers into her, not the old sort, not
the sort she had from being in Norit's body, rather the new ones
we gave you at the tower. An unintended gift, and we get very
little of sense from her, but she does try.*

"Damn you, let the child alone."

*She'll heal, thanks to your makers. As you will. And you'll
shed your makers wherever you pass. You constantly shed them
into the sand, and beetles take them up . . . small use, those. But
we can direct their structure. You shed them everywhere. You've
begun what the ondat decreed. You are that change. You war
with the Ila simply by breathing.*

Dots built intricate structures, moved, shifted, built towers and strings and divided. Some beat like imprisoned
birds, only fast, far, far faster. Some turned and shed pieces of
themselves. It became incredibly sinister, the activity of those
moving forms.

*Big eaters eat little eaters and on they go, our makers, the Ila's
makers. They carry on warfare, and that war spreads wherever
you go, and they change what they touch. If the Ila offers a man
a cup of water, these nanoceles, these makers, go with that touch.*

*If a man goes back to his village and sleeps with his wife, so
the makers will spread, and spread when she prepares a meal,
or goes to the well, or kisses her child. All through the world,
these makers renew themselves and become newer kinds.*

*And all these things the Ila does, because she contains her
master makers. As you contain mine. And mine are essential.
You have to live.*

"That's comforting to know."

You have to live. Tain has become my enemy and her friend.

"Tain wouldn't like being the Ila's friend."

Do you hear me? Repeat what I say.

"Repeat it, repeat it, repeat it. God, I have your makers in
me! The Ila has her own. And you're against my father and
he's *for* her for some reason. But I don't understand. And I
don't give a damn." He wanted the rapid dots to stop, slow
down, cease their actions. But he would not betray a weakness. His father had taught him that among his first lessons,
never betray a weakness, never admit to one.

Had reticence and deceit helped Tain? Was it a reasonable way for a man to live, who hoped to be loved?

"Hush," Hati said, and wiped his brow. "He's dreaming."

The world became a treasure set way up on a shelf, something he could almost reach, and was not tall enough. His mother had used to put things above him, and frustrated his reach. He would sit below the counter, discontent with whatever was in his grasp. He remembered the tiles near the kitchen table. One was cracked. It sat not quite level. Out of such incredible fine detail a man built his life, his remembrances, his loves and his hostilities.

Once loosed into the world, Luz said as he sat there, *the makers spread out to any creature, high or low. Your Ila came here with resources we now count primitive. She shaped the beshti to be what they are. She shaped men to survive the harshness of this world. Now we in turn shape you.*

"I tell you I don't understand. You're saying the Ila has these things in her, that she put in everyone alive. But you put different ones in me, and where I go, I shed them and other creatures take them up and they have them. So how am I different than the Ila? How are you different?"

You aren't. And I'm not. That's the point, isn't it?

"Damned nonsense," he said to her in the dream.

But this is the tricky part. Her makers have fitted men and beasts not only to live in this world . . . but to destroy the ondat. That's what the ondat fear: a buried instruction. That's why they insist on raining destruction down. Nanoceles can simply lie hidden, a small handful of makers that won't not breed without a signal to do so, and that signal may come from outside, or inside themselves, and it may come today, or tomorrow, or in a hundred years. Do you see why they should worry?

He lay feeling the tides of pain, the waves of burning fever, deep in listening, in the deafening wind, in the thump of the canvas. He listened so hard he became remote from the chill, and the wind, and the pain.

But if the world changes, Luz said, *the makers change. Life changes life. Life changes the makers. It must. It's what they do.*

Change the world and you change all its parts. Change the world and you change all that the makers do. To so alter this world that the rules of survival are utterly changed—that's the way the ondat intend to destroy the Ila's creation and scour it clean of all life. But we persuaded them we need to be here. They know nothing of guilt. Nothing of repentance. Nothing of redemption. They aren't like us. But they do know need, and they know we're more dangerous to them than the Ila, if we wished them harm. They need our knowledge to repair what the Ila's kind have done to them, and to win that knowledge, and not to have us do again what the Ila did, they've come to an agreement with us. That's the fine point of the matter. On that your life rests. Hers rests. All this world rests. Do you understand that?

"No, I don't. Not at all."

In his dream he tried to look away from the breeding dots, the red and the blue and the yellow dots, endlessly fluttering and spiraling, and in them he could not find the sky.

Everyone alive has the makers, Luz said. *Over enough time, the heavens will grow calm, and the earth will grow green, and clouded. Some of these stars that fall are water, only water. When the world is new, oases will go from horizon to horizon.*

"Paradise," Marak said. He had no idea why so beautiful a thought should batter at his heart and make him long for things less safe. But then the word came to him. "Freedom. What about freedom?"

Freedom is relative, Luz said. *Can you leave your world? Can you see the things I've seen?—I gave my freedom up for you, you damned ingrate! So did Ian! Appreciate the gift!*

He laughed. He saw no humor in Luz's situation, or in his, but still, he found a soul in the woman, and that was more than he had looked to find. The last that she said was true, and he believed it.

"You don't like paradise, either," he said.

For a moment the visions and the voices were utterly silent. The earth quaked, one of those small, frequent shudders, and was still again.

Your paradise is my hell, Luz said. *And Ian and I have come into this hell to satisfy our consciences, because of what your Ila did, the fool.*

There was another small pause, in which the wind was louder than thought, or than the slight whisper of Luz's voice, and the earth remained unsettled. He was nearly awake, and sank back again.

In the vermin, you see the result of makers run wild. They breed too well. They die too seldom. They eat up the world, and every generation of makers grows more adept, and more clever at what it does. Her makers are very, very good at living.

But so are mine. Her makers would destroy her, given another five hundred years. Destroy her, and all she's made. But mine will heal this world.

The wind battered at the tent. Something hit it, startled him, a piece of cloth, perhaps, or a loose mat. His heart sped. For the first time in many moments, he thought of Tain.

We do value you, Luz said. *I tell you, we would deeply regret it, Marak Trin, if the hammer comes down before you get to safety. Get well. Sleep now, and get well.*

"The hell," he said.

He tried to move. Hati was there, washing his face with precious water, while somewhere in the distance, in the skies, something boomed and crashed.

"Hush," she said. "You're talking to Luz, but I don't hear her."

"She's dividing us one from the other." That they had all heard one thing had been a curiosity, and then a comfort to them in their madness, and they were losing that. The makers changed things. The makers themselves changed. Was that not what Luz said?

"Hush, you're not making sense."

"Where's the baby? What happened to her? Where's Norit?" He reached after Hati's hand and held it, held it fast. "I passed by Tarsa. I was there! The captain's men never got that far. I asked. Her husband has another wife. He let the baby go." He wanted to see Norit with the baby. He wanted that desperately, but he could not lift his head. He remembered. "My father shot her, with me."

"She's fevered. The bullet went through her leg. But she may have makers of her own. She should have died, and she's mending."

"I bled into her," he said. "Our makers overwhelm everything the Ila put into us. That's what Luz says.—Damn!" The pain overwhelmed him. "Is Patya all right?"

Hati gave a nod over her shoulder. "She's there. She's not left you. Norit's with the baby. So's Patya."

"Good for Patya." He tried to glance that far, but it hurt his side and his back.

He was due for a night and a day of misery, at least, healing at his ordinary pace. He expected a long, long misery.

But after that the pain began going away, and Hati grew quite dim, and he could not move his hand from hers.

"Has he fainted?" Patya asked, leaning over him. "Is he all right?"

"I think so," Hati said. "I think he'll be well now. The makers are working. Go take the baby. Norit's left her."

There was so much sharpness in that tone. So much he wished he could mend. He had rather have the pain back than to have his mind racing, and his body numb.

His eyes were still open. He saw Hati take Lelie from Patya's hands, and saw Hati hold her, and rock her, and talk to her, because Norit had walked away. The baby was as still as he was, and perhaps heard everything.

Luz! he tried to shout, but could manage not a word. *Luz, let the woman alone! You call the Ila cruel . . . damn you, let Norit alone! This isn't a time to talk to her . . .*

But Luz gave no evidence she heard him, and Norit stood in the edge of his vision, staring at the wall of the tent, alone with Luz, the two of them talking, numb to Lelie's pain and Lelie's distress.

"Lie still," Patya told him. "Hati, he's sweating so much. Is he all right?"

"He will. It's what we crazy people do when we heal. Don't be afraid for him."

Not be afraid for him. Not be afraid for Norit, or Lelie, or Hati? There was a great deal to fear.

The star fell from the heavens, again and again and again, and hit the sphere, and the ring of fire went out from it.

Again and again and again.

21

Every good beast and every grass that produces grain and every tree that produces fruit is the gift of the Ila. The grasses and the trees she gave to the villages and told them to build gardens, instructing them to make covered conduits and to make basins of fired brick.
—The Book of Pori

Marak mended, in pain and fever. Patya stayed close by him while the storm wind blew and racketed about the canvas. Tofi came and laid a hand on his and reported to him in meticulous, quiet detail on the state of the camp and the Ila's temper.

The au'it sat nearby and wrote all these things.

Memnanan, too, came and stood over him, asking in the Ila's name how he was. Marak heard. He could not see Hati's answer to the captain, but he could hear it, and imagined Hati's shrug, which was Hati's characteristic answer to mysteries.

"Healing," she said to Memnanan, and through him, to the Ila.

That visit meant the storm was not bad enough to prevent Memnanan reaching them from the Ila's tent. That meant they remained in camp and he knew they had to move: something was coming. *East, east, east,* the pitch came to him now, urgent and frequent. His inability to move was the decreed torment for his sin of desertion.

Priests came and looked at him. That, he could not account for, and thought he might have dreamed the visit in his fever. He saw three of them in their white robes sitting on a mat and contemplating his condition. He grew increasingly perturbed about the situation, and still could not wake far enough to tell them to go to hell.

He fretted and he sweated, and eventually Memnanan and the priests left him to Hati's care, saying that it was clear there was something remarkable about his healing, and about the child.

The au'it wrote. Norit remained as she was. In the distance he heard Lelie crying, and crying.

"Someone," he tried to say, "someone take the baby."

"Norit! See to that child!" Hati said sharply, but Norit sat still, lost in her visions. Hati herself got up and fetched Lelie and put the wounded child into Norit's grasp. "Take care of her!" Hati said.

Norit never waked from her visions, but held Lelie against her, her hands absently doing things a mother might do. Her eyes were still set on the distance, full of fire and fear, experiencing that place and time Norit saw more clearly than she saw the sights around her.

"We have to move," Norit said, and said it more than once. He willed her to say so, when he could not. "Hati, we have to move."

"I know we have to move," Hati said. "Everyone knows we have to move. We can't see our own feet out there in the dark. We'll move when there's light."

That was good. At least Hati knew. Marak wit-wandered, then, watched Norit with Lelie, with nothing else to watch. He was glad Norit had said it for him. He was glad Hati had agreed he should not slow the caravan.

He could only move his head. Hati came and wasted water, washing his face. Extravagance, he said to himself. She gave him water to drink. He had a burning thirst. He always did when he healed.

Lelie abruptly began to sleep, that hard, heavy-limbed sleep of a child. She hung like a doll in Norit's arms, and now

Norit waked from her visions, spoke to the child, talked to her.

Now at last he saw the mother he had brought Lelie here to find, and now Norit perhaps realized what gift he had brought her at such effort.

"My baby," Norit exclaimed, with tears pouring down her face. "Lelie, Lelie, Lelie."

He was content. The world seemed very much kinder then, its natural laws restored. He trusted it enough to shut his eyes on it a time, though the tilting still bothered him, though he desperately wanted to tell Hati and Norit and Tofi to put him on Osan and move the caravan this hour, this moment.

But there was a weight on his senses, a wall between him and speech, and the will to speak grew faint and less frequent. Norit spoke for him, and even she found distraction in the dark, in the howling of the wind.

He waked as they moved him, and as they shifted him over something hard on the ground. This proved to be the pole of a litter, and the two freedmen carried him out into the wind under a sand-hazed sun, whether morning or evening he could not tell, but he thought it was dawn.

He was still fevered, and this waking brought him acute pain, so he knew this healing was longer and this wound was probably worse than any other in his life. He thought he should get up and ride, but he failed, and lay there thinking that someone would move him sooner or later.

Strange sights passed his eyes meanwhile. A good number of Haga were in the camp—surely they were still in the Ila's camp. Then he thought no, he was mistaken, there were tribesmen, but they were Keran. It was curious. It seemed one, and then the other, when neither belonged there.

The camp meanwhile packed down the tents and loaded them on the beshti. A second time he tried to get up and walk so that he could get to the saddle on his own, to save everyone the trouble of getting him up there as a dead weight.

But having lifted his shoulders perhaps a handbreadth off

the mat, he simply fell back, weak, with his head throbbing and the desert alternately showing twilight and sunlight around him, and the tribes still coming and going.

It was not the star-fall, he decided: it was his own head, feeling as if it expanded, and with it all the sky expanded and then contracted.

He might have fainted. But in what seemed only a moment he heard Hati giving orders, and Memnanan and Tofi shouting, a comfortable and ordinary sound. The camp was moving. At any moment he had to get up and ride.

Then someone else overshadowed him and picked up the poles of the litter.

This was a priest, a presence which he found almost as strange as tribesmen coming and going. He could not see who had the poles at his head, but he thought it likely another priest.

It was the Ila who ordered all priests, and if there were priests doing useful work, that was probably not a bad thing.

But why priests?

They brought Lelie, too, and laid her on him. She was a heavy weight, and it hurt, but she was not overall a burden. Lelie was fast asleep and he could see the wound in her leg, too, ugly and swollen . . . but healing, as he healed.

He was bemused by that fact. They had bled into one another. Maker fought maker. Or Norit's were in the child, potent from conception. Could the makers pass like that . . . through a mother's blood, if not through a father?

Marak, Marak! East, east, east! The world swung, and his head did, and he fell flat. He saw the rock hit the sphere, again and again and again. He heard the rhythmic sound of water, and saw a shore where endless water washed against the sand.

It might be the bitter sea. Stars fell into that sea and extinguished themselves. Plumes of water and smoke went up and joined the clouds. The sun went down in sullen red, and more stars fell.

He remembered where they had to be. They had to reach Pori. He tried to tell Hati so, to be sure he remembered the truth, and had not come adrift in visions. There was water at Pori, water necessary to all these people, whose ranks marched on and on, stretching across a star-battered plain, whose dead lay in rows beside their road.

The priests changed off with other priests from time to time. He waked at such moments, and blinked at the priests, and wondered at the vision. Intermittently, too, the caravan suffered from the wind, which gusted, and blew red ropes of sand across his vision. The priests staggered, and sometimes jolted the litter. Lelie waked at one such jolt, frightened by the wind, hungry and out of sorts.

"Hush," he said to her tear-stained face, and she knew his voice, and broke into a loud wail, in pain and crying for her mother. But Luz had her mother, and he could bring her to Norit, but he could not get Norit back . . . he failed in that, continually, and tried to comfort her.

But Lelie cried and snuffled against him, weak and miserable.

"Call Norit," he said to the priest at his feet, wincing as Lelie hit his wound. But before the priest could decide to obey him, Lelie fell abruptly asleep, perhaps Luz's work. Then he slid down into sleep, too, and that was the end of that.

When he next waked it was at the shift between bearers, and Lelie was still asleep, her spritelike face shaded by the aifad. The sun warming them in a clear sky.

It was afternoon, he decided. He tried to reckon where they were, and tried to fit an east direction into the angle of the distant ridge and the flat expanse of pitted sand. He could lift his head, he discovered. He moved a leg and a shoulder grown unbearably stiff with lying compressed between the litter poles, and found the pain of his side and his back was less, the swelling diminished.

The war of the makers for his life and health seemed won. And where were they? And how many days had it been? He began to know fear, and to care where he was. If it was not toward Pori, he thought, then he had to do something. He had to know.

"Where are we going?" he asked the man at his head, but, tilting his head, he saw only a back, and had no answer. Riders on beshti moved at the limits of his vision. That was as it should be.

He looked down past his feet at the priest carrying the litter, a strong man, a patient man. "I may be able to get up," he said, under Lelie's peacefully sleeping weight. "To ride, if not to walk. Stop."

The priest stopped, and the pair carrying him drew aside from those riders immediately to the rear. They set the litter down. They were at the heart of the column, and beshti had to move around them, a tall shadow of legs and undersides as Marak shifted Lelie aside and tried to lift himself.

He could not quite sit up straightway. He gathered his breath and rolled onto a knee and both knees and his hands on the dusty sand, encumbered by the litter poles. Slowly then, in blood-stiffened clothing, he attempted to disengage his shirttail from under Lelie on the litter and get up. The priests' belated help impeded as much as assisted him, and he shook off the offered arm, rested hands on his knee, shoved himself to his feet.

As he succeeded and dragged his shirttail free, Lelie waked, and sat up, too, rubbing her eyes with a bloody, grimy fist. He stood swaying on his feet in the passage of beshti on either hand—looked down at his little prize in numb curiosity, wondering what he was to do with her, and where Hati was.

Marak, his voices said, beginning their normal litany. And the pitching feeling came, reliable as sunrise and destructive of balance. *East, east, east.*

He saw Lelie catch her balance, too, and sit afterward wide-eyed, her small mouth open in dazed startlement.

"It's all right," he told her: madness seemed to have grown in the child like a seed. "Your mama's here. You're all right."

She cried. It was beyond him to pick her up. She reached up hands to be taken. It was the other priest who picked up the baby.

"She's Norit's," Marak said. "My wife's. Norit. Let the baby ride with her." He had no idea where anyone was, but he wanted not to be left afoot. "Where's my wife?"

They both, the one holding Lelie, and the other, looked at him as if they had seen the dead rise.

And perhaps, he thought, staggering into a first step, that was very nearly the case. He knew where east was. He knew that.

Then, arriving from behind, a rider shadowed them, and that was Hati, who slid down in a welter of windblown veils.

"What are you doing?" she cried.

"These men have blisters," he said, meaning the priests: he had seen their hands. But he saw her face all exhausted and worried, too, and added, "I'm all right, wife. Trust my judgment. I'm all right."

Hati did not embrace him, not in front of strangers and priests, but she came and put an arm about him, guiding him along with the walkers, leading her besha with the other hand. Bosginde, one of the freedmen, had ridden near, too. "Get Osan," Hati ordered him, looking up. "My husband will ride now."

Bosginde left in haste, applying the quirt, and still the riders streamed past.

"Someone may have to put me up," he admitted to Hati, for her alone, and again, having become sane again, saw something was clearly different about the company in which they rode. Around them were more riders, dark-clothed riders. Tribesmen. He had not been dreaming that.

And he stumbled, trying to walk.

"I don't think I can hold on," he said.

"Someone will help you," she said. Her voice was tense. Her hand on his arm was gentle and anxious. She had changed her clothes for the dark-striped robes of her own tribe, and her arms flashed with gold and honor. "I thought you might die in spite of the makers."

"Or to spite them." It was a bad joke. He saw that in Hati's worried face. And among the accumulated confusion in the world he was unsure how much time had passed. "The makers won't let me die. Last night, it seemed a disadvantage. But I'm improving fast. I'll ride. Where are we?"

"Two days from where you found us."

"Toward Pori."

"Toward Pori," she confirmed, and relieved his anxiety on that score, at least.

"The tribes are here." It was assuredly the Ila's caravan. Bosginde was here. He saw beasts he knew. His memory could not account for her gold and her change of robes. He himself stood in changed clothing, a loose shirt, trousers not tucked into the boots . . . they tagged loose about his ankles, and blew in the wind. "The Keran have joined the camp?"

"When you were shot. The Haga came in. They were angry because the Ila's men couldn't protect the camp. Then Aigyan heard the Haga were here, so he came, in the storm and all, and he and Menditak talked. Then they got to arguing with the Ila's captain, and they got hot, but I said they were all fools."

He could imagine the scene. Hati would say that. And Memnanan, who was not a fool, and Aigyan and Menditak, had all been in one council, while Hati had her say.

"Menditak gave you a gift," Hati said, and let him go to pull rolled cloth down from her saddle ties. She shook it out, a coat of Haga colors, and held it out for him, while beshti passed them and passersby, the Ila's servants, gazed at this private proceedings. He put it on, a heavy, warm coat, and was troubled about what it said, a declaration of tribal colors; but before he could half think the thought, Hati flung an aifad about his neck, a fine one, of Keran colors. "Aigyan's gift," she said.

They marked him with both sets of colors. It was without precedent that the tribes should mix camp with each other, let alone with the Ila's men, the enemy, the lifelong enemy. But so was this journey without precedent. So was the Ila's presence among the tribes unprecedented.

He fell to Tain's bullet, and there was power, to be had, and both the Haga and the Keran moved in on it, possessed it, guarded it from mishap, supplied him with what he needed. Could he fault them for seeing to their own? Memnanan could only be grateful to have added their force around him, with Tain threatening the caravan, but he saw abundant reason Memnanan might not be easy with the situation, too, and had an idea now why Memnanan might have come to stand over his healing carcass . . . to estimate the chances of his recovery, and whether he might take that power back again, and whether he could.

He had to talk to Memnanan at the earliest opportunity—once his head stopped reeling.

"So how long will this truce among the tribes last?" he asked.

"They're staying," Hati told him. "Aigyan and Menditak have sworn water peace forever. They've merged the camps." Hati waved a gesture forward. "Aigyan's up there, leading. He insists on that." And back. "Menditak is just behind the Ila's company, next behind her men, running the camp. The servants are behind him. So are the priests, and they don't get past the tribes unless Menditak says they do."

A lasting peace. Access to each other's wells, fiercely defended for generations. The Ila all but imprisoned in the camp and effectively deprived of her priests. He was gone one day and two, and the rules of march all changed.

"What did the Ila say about it? What did Memnanan say?"

"The captain took the offer for the Ila's sake. What was he going to do? I told him the Ila shouldn't give the tribes any orders, that they're too valuable to offend, if you were down, and I warned the captain they won't talk to her, so not to expect it. But they have talked to the captain, all the same, and he's talked to his men, and we're guarded on every side. They don't intend to see any more shots fired into this camp. They want you and me and Norit in tribal colors. Less of a target."

"A damned good idea," he said. The tribal presence more than thickened the head of the column and made sniping into it more difficult. The union of Haga and Keran carried an unprecedented force of tribal will, as well. If the tribes were upset about what Tain had done, and if the Haga and the Keran now ruled the Ila's camp, then the Ila's camp became a tribal camp—if Tain violated that, there was a price on his head, on the part of every tribesman.

Tribal unity—and around the Ila.

And around him, and Hati, and Norit . . . Norit, who added in the villages, and, he saw, also in dark-striped cloth.

"It's not been easy," he said to Hati, grateful for her level-headedness.

"No," Hati said. "It's been hell. Don't leave me like that. Don't ever leave me like that."

"I won't," he said. "I was crazy. I was crazy for a few days, and you weren't. I wouldn't even listen to Luz. But I'm sane now. And won't ever be crazy again. I promise you that."

"I hold you to it." They were within the witness of all Tofi's workers, packing the baggage. Her hand stayed steady, holding his arm, while she had the rein of her besha with the other, but her voice was a soft touch, a gentle forgiveness. "Let Tain ride up and down out there where the vermin are. Let him take his chances being eaten alive. We all need you. I need you. And the Ila won't get you either."

"No," he agreed. He saw one of Tofi's slaves ride up with Osan in tow, saddled and ready for him. Bosginde and Mogar rode next behind that man, and got down to help him up to the mounting loops and into Osan's saddle, holding Osan from his usual step forward.

That meant Osan swayed, taking his weight, and his head did, and he forgot all about tribesmen and dark riders and vermin mobs.

He hit the saddle, and the feeling passed. He took the rein when they passed it to him, and being on Osan's back was good, despite the giddiness of the perch. It was far better than lying under Lelie's weight and better than the occasional jolts of the priests' handling. He saw that the priests had taken up the litter, and walked near them, still carrying Lelie.

"Hand the baby up," he said.

"You'll drop her," Hati said, and it was true: his side was sore, and that arm was not dependable. In the end Hati mounted up and took the baby up to her own saddle. Then she excused herself and rode up the line to Norit, where she gave Lelie to her own mother.

Marak let Osan travel up through the moving line and

met Hati halfway on her way back. There were tribesmen on either hand, as they had drifted back. The colors were Haga.

He rode forward with Hati, and also overtook Norit, who failed to notice his presence. She rode with Lelie half in her arms, half-sitting on the padded saddlebow, and talked to her daughter.

It was, for that moment, and rare that he was sure of it, only Norit in that Haga-robed body. Luz was silent, in his mind, in his ears and, he hoped, in Norit's.

"Luz," he said under his breath, reeling with the strangeness of the day, but rewarded by what he saw, Norit happy, and for a moment sane. "Luz, do you see what's going on? I'm up and riding. We're on the road. The tribes have come around us to protect this camp. There's no danger at the moment. You can let Norit alone. Give her a day. A day to herself."

He heard nothing by way of answer. But that silence was what he wanted.

Then Tofi overtook them.

"You're alive," Tofi crowed. "And riding! It's a miracle of the god!"

"It's the damned tower's doing," Marak said. "If I thought it was the god, I'd complain to the priests and the Ila. It hurt like hell."

Tofi thought that was funny at first, and having laughed, looked as if he had swallowed something questionable, and it was too late to stop swallowing.

"I'm glad you're all right, omi. All of us are glad."

"So am I," Marak said. He heard that *omi*. He saw the decent respect give way to outright fear, which he had no wish to have in those close to him.

His *father* had wanted fear like that among his subordinates . . . fear, and worship. Tain had trusted no one who failed to be awed by him, but Tain's son trusted no one who did fear him . . . that was his rule. He had never wanted to be worshiped, or to become the focus of dim-visioned men who wanted to be governed by fear. He had been an outright fool to go after his father alone, knowing the quality of the men who surrounded Tain and fed him with their worship, men in whose eyes Kaptai's murder had to be justified, because everything Tain did had to be justified. He had been a fool to go by his father's rules, in his father's territory. He knew that now. He was lucky to have fallen in with the Rhonandin instead of his father's men, because it never would have been a fair fight. "I shouldn't have gone after him," he said to Tofi. "But I lived through it. Tain got away, and good riddance. It was a damned waste. His whole life is a damned waste. So are the men with him."

"It's not *good* for you to kill your father," Tofi ventured to say to him. "It's not good for *you,* omi, no matter what your father's done. You can't. Don't go back there again."

He could have taken offense at Tofi's meddling in his private business. But Tofi's was the courage and truth and constancy to a course that he saw Tain's teaching had never given him: Kaptai had, if anyone. "I don't plan to try again," he said to Tofi. "Be glad we're not farther back in the line. It's hell back there. Good luck if we don't lose half the caravan, if they don't just walk off the trail on a cloudy night. And there's nothing we can do about it if it happens. That's the hell of it." He looked out to the edges of the column, past the shield the Haga tribesmen posed, riding on the edges of the column. Their way lay among low dunes, over hard ground, rises too shallow at their highest to hide a rider.

That was good. So was the Haga's added protection for the Ila's camp. He raked his memory, trying to remember how long this area lasted, or where they were on their journey. He had no idea how long he had lain on the litter.

"It's only been two days I've been out," he said.

"It's been two days you were gone, before that, omi," Tofi said.

His brain had been rattled. Time had slipped away from him. Location-reckoning mingled with the trip back and forward in the line, and with the fever. For a moment of panic, he had trouble recalling even which trip this was, and which trail of the two possible routes they were following. That eye-blink lapse scared him.

But he remembered: he was clearheaded on the facts. It was the northern route. They were approaching an area of alkali pans, where concealment was much more difficult. The open land was a protection . . . for a time, and if the weather held. If the water did. The pans might hold some water. He hoped so. They had not tried here, on their way to Oburan.

Marak, the voices said, if only to let him know they were there. And dizziness assailed him with, *East, east, east,* so that he gripped the saddlebow.

"Would you truly have killed your father?" Tofi asked him, out of nothing. They were all in a group, he and Hati, Norit, and Tofi, with Patya not far distant. His family. His people. Would you have killed your father? Tofi asked him, and he gazed at the horizon, trying to steady himself in that answer and Tofi's assault on his purpose.

"Yes," he said, trying to mean it, trying to insist everything he had done had been a good idea.

But he suddenly discovered the limit of his detestation of his father, and perhaps the limit of his love of his mother, now that he had wives, now that he had others leaning on him. Now he found he agreed with Tofi . . . and hoped that somehow even with blood between him and his father, that the matter of his mother's death would dwindle to a lifelong feud, with never any further action.

Shoot Tain if he had to . . . yes, that he still thought he would, and after all his father had done. He thought he would do it without regret. But he knew what Tofi was saying to him, a son who lately had buried his father. He had no wish to be a parricide, at any price, mother *or* father, and his parents' quarrel with each other had never been his. He had no idea the roots of it, only the bitter fruit.

"I feared you *wouldn't* kill him," Hati said under her breath, an'i Keran, and far harder than Tofi, from birth. "That was my greatest worry, all the time you were gone."

"It was a question I asked myself," he said. His time among the abjori, the killing-marks on his fingers, those had changed him in one direction—but Kaptai had changed him in another, reshaped all his father's work in him year by year. And that, he decided, was his father's ultimate and personal defeat. It was Kaptai who held all debts, now, forever; his father had nothing from him or in him, not even the desire to shoot him dead. "I know I would, now, if I had to, but I won't look for him, not even for this. I don't give a damn whether he lives or dies; that's all it's come down to. I don't give a damn for him, not before the duty I have up here. I won't take that chance again."

That satisfied Hati, he thought. He wanted to set himself back where he had been, in the post he had deserted—not with a right to have it back, but understanding the way his obligations balanced, now, better than he ever had done. He was *fit* to lead, he said to himself, now. He was fit to lead: he understood things better than he ever had.

But the thought of riding forward, of reporting to the Ila, daunted him. He saw the red robes in the distance ahead of him, but he still felt a certain dizziness and unsteadiness, effects of the fever, and doubted whether he could deal with her subtleties and her threats. He felt a queasiness, too, in the voices that dinned in his ears, distracting him, as if to say he had deserted that duty, too, and earned trouble for himself and everyone under him. *Fool,* he imagined Luz saying, and he was put to asking Hati and young Tofi how the supplies stood, and how far they thought Pori might be . . . he knew they were on the track, but he had come loose from all his reckonings, and lost the threads of information that were life itself.

A ridge lay due east of them, uncrossable. *East,* the inner voices cried, but *east* was impossible, and Pori, south, was essential . . . they could not cut cross-country as they had on the journey from the tower: they had to reach Pori, had to, had to, no matter what the voices clamored. The sweet well there was life. He had seen the fragility of the camps behind them. He had a grasp now how very far that line stretched, how endangered, how little the skill of the village lords in the deep Lakht.

Pori was two, three days from this plain of stones, at the

pace they had traveled on their way to Oburan. He knew that ridge. He began to know where the rim of the Lakht was, just beyond that horizon line, that implacable, uncrossable ridge.

Memnanan, meanwhile, dropped back in the line, reining in his besha until he fell in beside him and Hati and the rest . . . the Ila's voice, it might be, the Ila's curiosity personified.

Or Memnanan's own.

"Faring better," Memnanan observed. "No end of miracles, it seems."

"Better than I expected," Marak said.

"The Ila was not pleased," Memnanan said.

"My apologies," Marak said, not contritely enough; but his own stubborn will would not admit to her what he had learned about himself. "Well enough that the tribes stepped in where I wasn't.—How does the Ila view our escort?"

"She knows," Memnanan said. "Where they ride is nothing to her."

It was the Ila's sort of answer. That meant the Ila knew she had no practical way to stop them, and would not try.

"She wishes to speak to you," Memnanan said.

"I've no doubt," Marak said. He was sore and entirely unwilling to deal with the Ila today. His head spun. But he valued Memnanan's goodwill, and he knew he had tested it to its limits in the last several days.

"He's not recovered," Hati said. "He needs his rest."

Useless excuses with the Ila. "No, I'll go," Marak said.

"Then I'll go with you," Hati said.

"Best not." Hati and the Ila alike had hot tempers, and Hati's, like the Ila's, had been sorely tried. "Do me the favor: stay here."

Hati frowned. He fixed that dusky stare in his heart and rode off with Memnanan, alone, and straight up through the column, among the red robes.

The head of that group was the Ila herself, veiled in red, gloved against the sun.

"Ila," Memnanan said. "I've brought him, at your order."

Marak drew alongside. "I'm here."

"I sent last night!" the Ila said peevishly. "And where were you?"

"Dying."

"Deservedly! You left against my order!"

"I'm here now." It was the old give-and-take with her, not unreasoning anger. He was reassured in her purposes, her demeanor, her control of her anger. "You wanted something?"

"What is this baby?"

"My wife's baby," he said. "Mine. I take it for mine."

The Ila did not look at him, rather sniffed and stared straight ahead, thinking what, he could not guess, until she asked: "And Tain? Tain shot you. *Tain* got the best of you, Marak Trin."

"He did." There was no denying it. "The Haga lost four men on the trail, shot from ambush, and I don't think he was alone. The Rhonandin helped me search back along the track as far as I was willing to go, but he wove back and forth through the column. We lost them in the storm."

"Those helping him."

"I know he gathered certain followers. Not an army, I think. If I thought that . . . I'd be concerned."

"Water is running short among the villages," the Ila said, still in a prickly mood, and waved a red-gloved hand, an elegant spiral of evanescence toward the heavens. "Even for drinking. So I am told. But in your travels you may have discovered it."

"We'll come to water at Pori. As we planned. There's the well, the only good well we'll meet."

"You need not inform *me* where the springs are," the Ila said in all hauteur. "I'm aware of Pori."

"We're on schedule," he said. "More or less. Some villages may have drunk more than they ought. They're not experienced in the Lakht. But what can we do, but shorten our own supply?" He spoke to the woman who had her baths, daily, whose daily tea delayed the column. "Luxury for one may be life and death for a village, Ila."

"Luxury, you say."

"I say go unwashed, Ila! It's not that long to water. A little dust is bearable."

A flutter of red fingers. "Is it bearable for you?"

"And for all of us, Ila. Give up your noon tea. Make *some* sacrifice!"

"To what end? Will it bring water to the hindmost? Will you ride back and carry it there? Leave it for the vermin? Oh, I know your villages. Some may take to robbing their neighbors, and Tain Trin Tain is back there fomenting trouble. Certain villages have decided to squabble, when even the unlettered *tribes* band together to defend us."

"And the tribes will not respect a leader who washes her body in water people might drink," he retorted. "There's the truth for you, Ila."

"And do they respect a man who leaves off guiding the caravan on a whim and a fit of anger?"

"My wives know the way," he said. "They know it. We were never lost. Trust Norit, if no one."

"Trust *Luz*," the Ila scoffed. "Trust the all-seeing Luz, who prepares a shelter for us, who mediates for the *ondat* and *lies* to them. Tell me why you should live."

It came to him like one of his visions, a dizzying perspective that came so clearly, so absolutely: he ought to fear the threat and failed to, utterly.

"Because, Ila, no one else serves you and Luz at the same time and very few tell you the truth. You know and I know that I could have led the people away from you days ago and left you to travel at odds with the tribes; you know I could have left that very first day with my own tent and a handful of friends—but I didn't do that. I didn't do it because *you* have importance to the world, and what do I know else? Only what Luz tells me, and I don't think that's enough to go through the rest of our lives with—so I want you to get there alive. I want you and Luz both to settle the *ondat* and save what's left of us. So I stay and I tell you the truth. Stop taking baths with our water and pay attention to what the tribes tell you and, most of all, win their loyalty, Ila!—which you damned well won't do by bathing in the drinking water.

Win *their* loyalty, since you created us, and *be* the god on earth. *You* know us as our mother *and* our god. *You* made the makers that made this world, and apart from you we can't hope to know who we are and what's right and wrong for us to do. Call in the au'it if you want to know the secrets I tell my wives, and have Memnanan shoot me dead if you think I threaten your life or your authority. But I think I support it. I think you *want* someone to say what I say, and tell you the unpleasant truth, or you wouldn't call me in to talk to me. You're not mad, and I'm not mad. We're both terribly, unhealthily sane, and we're going to go on living, because we *have* no illusions and shooting us doesn't kill us, does it?"

There was a lengthy silence, and the red gauze veil obscured the nuances of her expression. He saw her in profile, considering all he had said.

"Oh, we have a great many illusions," she said. "We shape them and make them, and now one of them has risen up to call himself my equal."

"Equal to you and to Luz," he said. He was utterly reckless at the moment, whether Luz possessed him or whether it was his dive toward death and back, but he saw all life hanging by a thread, and tired of this woman threatening it. "Because without me, and without Hati, you and she would sit still, and most of the world would die. You don't know how to be loved. I can tell you: save these people's lives. Do something with your makers, if you can do it: make them strong enough to get to the tower, and then what you and Luz do with each other is your affair. Until we get there, it's mine."

"Marak," Memnanan said quietly, a late, a desperate warning. "Be still."

"Dare you order him be still?" the Ila asked. "Dare you?"

"He's our guide, Ila. We need to keep him safe."

"Then see to it he doesn't leave," the Ila said sharply. "See to it he's not twice a fool."

"I will," Memnanan said.

"Tain knows which tent is mine," Marak said, seeing dismissal coming. "He was lying in wait. That means he's watching. He knows the layout of this camp, and that means he knows which is your tent." He saw he had the Ila's attention a second time. He knew he would have Memnanan's. "Tain may be near there to this hour, likely stalking us and wondering what he can do about the Haga and the Keran moving in to guard you. If the men with him are sensible, they've seen the tribes in this camp and they know—"

"I'm not a fool!"

"Then you'll listen to advice."

"How many men do *you* think he has?"

"Twenty, perhaps, perhaps more. He rarely likes to move with more. How many may be loyal to him . . . reliably so . . . perhaps a hundred. I doubt he'll gain more who have the strength to ride with him."

"Do you know their names?"

Suddenly, knowing the Ila's ruthlessness, he knew what direction this was going. And refused it. "Folly to go back there and deal with them. Make one mistake, *one* innocent man, and there *is* a war, where right now there isn't."

"Captain!"

"Ila," Memnanan said, as aui'it all around them wrote zealously.

"Hear me instruct him! Don't ride out again, Marak Trin Tain. You will not leave this camp without my direct permission. *Write it!*"

"I don't intend to," Marak said. "Unless I see an immediate way to end the threat to the Ila."

"Did I say not? I think I said not!"

"He would have shot you instead of me, if he could get so far into the camp and be sure of getting out again! He's not a fool. He wants to rule, not die. I'm not sure *you* care which."

"Marak," Memnanan said again.

"No, let him say what he wishes. And let him hear! I saved the lives of everyone alive in the world. I've preserved the lives of their children's children, and for my comfort and long life, it was a sensible transaction. Now after all this time, it seems I offend enemies I never met, that *I* never fought. Luz blames *me* that these enemies rain destruction down on the world. Tain Trin Tain blames me that I take tax. Yet a farmer comes to me if a windstorm flattens his fields and say, 'Ila, we have no food.' And what should I say? We have no warehouses? Will Luz have warehouses? And wherein is *she* virtuous, above me? Wherein is *Tain,* and what will he do for the world, in my place?"

"I can't talk about Tain," he said in a faint voice. "I don't understand Luz. I only know where water is, and where safety is. That's *all* I know, but it makes me your match, out here. Once I've gotten you to Luz, my job is ended, and I lose all importance. It's my greatest ambition, to lose all importance."

"No, it isn't."

"What is, then?"

"To escape alive," the Ila said. "How dear will you hold that ambition, in a hundred, in two hundred, in three hundred years? How dear will you hold it, when you've watched the whole world die, twice and three times? And how tempted will you be, to eliminate the fumbling and the foolishness and the damnable *waste* of stupid creatures that repeat the same mistakes and die and feed the next generation of makers, and the next and the next and the next after that . . . I provoke you and you do nothing! I tread on you and you bleat that you need me! I save your world for you and you never learn! Do you want my power? Take it, and *you'll* bathe in the drinking water in half my life span."

The Ila rode beside him, veiled, a riddle of intentions, in command of armed men, on her way to an enemy's refuge, an enemy whose deeper motives he also did not know.

And all his experience told him that nothing was as fatal as lying to the Ila, that her sanity, like his, was precarious, and that he, and Memnanan, and all he loved were in danger at every moment he failed to keep her wondering.

"Are you mine?" the Ila asked him.

"I am not hers," he answered.

"What if I said to you that *she* is the enemy of the *ondat*?"

"Why would they save her tower and ruin yours, if that were true?"

The Ila cast back her veil, precisely, with red-gloved hands: exposed her face to the wind and her eyes to his curiosity.

"Indeed?" she said. "Do you know they do things as reasonable men would do them? And are these *ondat* your friends?"

"No," he said. "They're not likely to be. We agree on that."

"Ah," the Ila said. "Indeed. Is *she* the enemy of the *ondat*, who destroy us to carry out their law . . . and the rest of our kind—and there are others, Marak Trin!—allow it, in their laxhanded way? But only so you think on it, Marak Trin, I tell you something I believe Memnanan understands, too. If he doesn't, explain it to him. I trust nothing but a man's own best interests. And I believe you've discovered yours, and mine. You've made yourself safe in my company. You've made yourself essential, personally essential. Go on amusing me, Marak Trin. On that thread your life hangs, and will continue to hang. I've not had a husband in a hundred years. Do you feel lucky?"

Marak, his voices said, outraged. *Marak, Marak, Marak,* as if they would not let him think deeper, ask deeper, act on those thoughts and those questions, or countenance sanely the Ila's outrageous proposition. The world swung east, *east!* with a vengeance. He swayed in the saddle, all but fainted in the dizziness, and caught at the saddlebow to save himself.

Memnanan also caught at him, riding close on his left.

"I've annoyed Luz," the Ila said to Marak. "Poor Luz. Go console her. And don't leave the column again."

"Ila," he said, and had no idea what Luz thought, or what the Ila thought, or what either of them meant. He talked about the safety of every living soul in the world, and the Ila reduced it to a personal argument.

It was like bathing in the drinking water. It took the question of survival to an individual one.

But did they refuse to drink the water? None of them refused.

He reined back. He understood her conditions, and the points of her argument. She did what they allowed her to do, and they allowed her, because she was the god on earth . . . because without her they had no god, no devil, either, except the *ondat,* and no man in the caravan wanted to contemplate dealing with them: most failed even to understand the *ondat* existed. For them it was all the Ila, and not even Luz was real.

"Memnanan," the Ila said as he retreated. "Watch him. On your life, watch him. Don't let him disobey."

Nothing protected Memnanan. And she threatened her own captain. Where there was leverage, she found it.

And she was right: those who destroyed so many lives were no friends. Those who *would* destroy this many lives were no fit rulers. That was all his battered wits came up with for an answer: that their fit ruler was madder than the mad, and had been saner in her long life, but she was still—for reasons most of them never understood—their god, their precious ruler, the definition of what they were. Was it virtue in her, some last remnant of sanity, that she bent every effort to make them hate her, and spared them when they failed to kill her?

He, on the other hand, held Luz's makers. And what had he just tried to do? He had ridden after Tain, and now he defied the Ila.

Now he committed himself to one more mad act, and rode toward the head of the column, increasing Osan's pace to a run that jolted his side. It hurt: it jarred to the roots of his teeth, but he was not done being mad: he rode up among Hati's tribe, up where Aigyan rode among his household, all on lofty, richly ornamented beasts. Bells attended their going. Swords and the occasional long barrel glinted in the sun. This was armed might the likes of which Tain and the Ila herself had to reckon with, and it did not obey Hati, or him.

But it had arrived in his camp, and pitched tents around him, and he meant it should justify its presence with him and with the Ila.

"Omi," he said, bowing in the saddle, respectfully enough, and the au'it, his au'it, who had chased after him into the Ila's presence, now arrived after him in some disorder, and unfolded her book to write when he had said no more than that word.

Marak, his voices said, however, and could the au'it write that Luz was agitated, perhaps outraged? She had asked for his attention. The Ila had stirred her up, and now she was back, a ceaseless din. He set Luz and her complaints to the back of his attention, and meant to have command of his own camp back.

"Awake and alive," Aigyan said, looking him over as he rode. "Bullets, then, have as little power over you as the Ila's orders."

"The mad heal well." The voices rose nearly to a point of distraction, irate, and he fought stubbornly for his purpose. "I came up here to pay my proper respects, omi. I've had your help, the help of the Haga, the Rhonandin, when I rode back to settle with my father. They sent out four men, too, and lost them to Tain; and I owe them for those lives as well as for my mother. That's four lives besides hers." With the tribes, the tally of favors and grievances mattered: he was aware of that priority from days long before his dealings with Hati. "The Rhonandin were with me when I recovered my wife Norit's daughter. Tarsa village had the child. The Rhonan helped me get her back, but I failed to find Tain. For my obligations here, I had every confidence in the an'i Keran, my wife. Nothing disappointed me, not her and not my in-laws. We're growing short of water, but we're not that far from Pori."

Aigyan shrugged, a mirror of Hati's gesture, an answer for a good many things: *I accept what you say,* whether happy or unhappy. "Give greetings to Menditak when you see him . . . if you haven't."

"I will." That was a question, as much as a request to know which he had answered first, whether kinship or official precedence; and his answer, indicating that he had not yet seen Menditak, seemed to please Aigyan. The reasons Aigyan and Menditak had for making water peace might be broader and deeper than either admitted. They used their kinships. They moved in on them, and neither let the other have all the advantage. And they sat in power, now, both tribes. "Get us to Pori, omi. Beyond that, there's a trail over the rim. There's no mistaking our way. But water, first. The villages back there are stringing far back, and it'll only get worse. No matter what the Ila does, no matter what you hear from the priests or anyone else . . ." The din in his head already debated him. "We've got to get to water."

And Aigyan studied him, the madman, his relation-by-marriage. "Off the edge of the Lakht," Aigyan said. No ruling tribe had ever left the Lakht, the center of their range. "To this tower in the middle of the lowlands. So we find this paradise, do we? Wish that water thief your uncle the peace of the day."

"I will." He understood the uneasy agreement, one in which Aigyan had only moderate faith. Aigyan challenged him, since he had made the gesture to come up here and assert direction of the caravan. He had made himself Aigyan's equal, if he was not the Ila's, and he had not gotten full courtesy out of Aigyan . . . being an upstart, in Aigyan's eyes. The tribes were here for kinship's sake to the dead, and for rivalry to each other, but not to rescue him. *Marak, Marak, Marak*, his voices said, urging him to the east. And he defied those, too. "Pori," he said. "If we get there, those can stay that want to and those can part that want to." Those that stayed or parted from them would die, he was convinced of that. His responsibility was to the caravan, and *east*, the voices urged him, no matter that east of here was a long, uncrossable ridge and a drop down a cliff. *Pori*, he insisted, and reined back, dropping back through the ranks. "I'll see you, father-by-marriage. I'll see you there."

He fell back, dizzied, beset by contrary voices, having lost all capacity to argue with Aigyan: but no matter the Ila's whims, no matter the priests, no matter Luz's will, he had delivered their chief guide his direction, and meant it. The au'it who had followed him up in the ranks followed his retreat, struggling to rein back her besha, which wanted to follow the others. But he simply rode slower and slower, let beshti pass him, one after another, until finally he found Norit and Hati.

By now Patya was riding beside them, doubtless wondering whether he had gone mad again.

"What did the Ila want?" Hati asked him. "And what did Aigyan just have to do with it?"

"A courtesy, in both cases. They wanted to know how great a fool I mean to be after this. But I can't offend Menditak, either. I'll be back." He threw a look at his sister Patya. "Stay with them. Keep where Hati and Norit can see you, at all times, hear me? If our father lays hands on you . . ."

"You're the crazy one!" Patya shot back. "Be careful!"

"You're right," he said, while the au'it wrote, mercilessly recording, making casual utterance into lasting record. "I won't do it again. And don't you be as crazy. Hear?" He remembered what Patya could not: his mother's worry when Patya was born a daughter; Tain sulking and drinking all night and breaking crockery because he had a daughter and not a second son.

He remembered things Patya might remember, too, Patya very early lamenting to him she was not born a boy. She was the one in the family without illusions. She was the sane one, and knew their father failed to love her. These things the au'it could not write. Not even Hati knew the pain that Tain had inflicted, long before he murdered Kaptai.

"There's four of us of the household, now," Marak said, lingering by Patya, deafening himself to the voices. "Tain's not our father anymore. Hati and Norit are your sisters. That baby's Lelie, and her father didn't want her. I'm not sure Norit does, when she's crazy. Help her."

Patya's eyes still carried shadows of Kaptai's death and Tain's hate. But there was courage in her. There always had been, a finer, steadier courage than his. "I'm fine," Patya said, pressing her lips to a thin line. "I'll get myself a husband. If a rock from the sky doesn't fall on us. I'll marry you some help."

"I *have* help enough," he said. "Marry for love. Bring some peace to the house. That's what I want.—And stay to the center of the camp. Don't go on the outside edge, and I promise you won't." They both had to fear every night and every day from now on that their own father might be aiming at her life or his, or at anyone Tain thought they cared for. He put it in words, and knew that somewhere the feud had to have a bloody ending.

But not today. Not this moment. *Marak, Marak,* his voices nagged him, and *east, east, east,* when life and water lay south. Luz would make him crazier and crazier. She would drive Norit, and Hati, who must hear the same urge, and find it harder and harder to resist—off a cliff, no less. He would *not* have Luz dictating Patya's life. Patya was always and forever the sane one.

"Stay with Hati," he said. "I'll be back before we camp. I'm not going anywhere near the edge. Hati?"

Hati paid sharp attention.

"Water," he said. "Water, at Pori, before everything."

"Something's going to happen," Hati said, and Norit, with no sanity at all in her eyes: "There's no time, Marak."

"The hell." He reined Osan back a second time, with the au'it lagging back after him. He let them slip farther and farther back, past the Ila's pack train, and all the Ila's servants, city-bred men and women wrapped in white, under the fierce, bright sun. *Marak,* the voices said, and the rock hit the sphere, vividly, persistently. Luz was increasingly upset with him.

"I understand you," he said to Luz under his breath. "And you want the damned books, don't you? Every village that dies, you're losing a book."

The vision came again, repeatedly, blinding him. He rubbed his eyes, coming among the Haga, among the most familiar of tribes.

He found Menditak, and Menditak went veiled in the aifad, withdrawn, in mourning or in anger: it was impossible to read. Dust was on Menditak's shoulders. That, too, was mourning, for Kaptai, for four good men—he had no clear idea who those men might be, whether uncles of his, or close to Menditak. There was a debt here, and he had come riding in unveiled, mad, distracted by visions.

"Omi," he said to Menditak, raking his sanity into one coherent heap. "I had to come back. I risked the caravan to keep chasing him. But I haven't given up, either. I've carried my report to the Ila and to the Keran, forward: but you, *omi, you* are my father. I haven't any other."

"Tain Trin Tain will die," Menditak said, from behind the veil. "Word is out, against him."

"The Rhonan joined us," Marak said, that *us* that meant the tribe. "Certain of the villages have helped me, against him. He's lost. He won't be welcome where we're going. We'll come to water at Pori, and we'll go on over the rim, and if he stays on the Lakht, he'll die. If he comes in reach of us, he'll die. He has no choice, *omi*. He won't get anything from me."

"He'll die," Menditak said again, and asked carefully what Aigyan had said, and about the Rhonan, and their lord, and all the while Menditak's son was nearby, listening to everything, as the au'it wrote, and for the same purpose.

"I don't know about your paradise," Menditak said. "That water thief Aigyan moved in when we did, and insists he's leading. It's no time for a fight. The whore in camp bathes in water while honest mothers run short of drink. But we wait, Marak an Haga. We wait. Tell that to the Ila. There will be this paradise of yours."

"Before that, there's Pori," Marak said, and the voices in his head put up an argument that made his temples ache. "You'll live, and Tain won't." He could not muster courtesies, could not track the convolutions of tribal custom. He simply rode ahead, suddenly, his hands doing one thing, his mind distracted in visions and a whispering in his head that would not be still.

He rode through the ranks. Norit met him, on her way back.

"*It's coming,*" Norit said to him. "It's coming. There's no stopping it."

It was the sort of thing Norit raved about. "Where's the baby?" he asked harshly, trying to call her and him alike back to common sense. "Where's Lelie?"

He only confused her. Norit rode back through the line,

shouting that the hammer of heaven was coming, terrifying the Ila's servants.

He rode forward, up to where Hati was, where Patya rode, carrying Lelie on her saddle. "Did Norit find you?" Hati asked, and looked back behind him, but Norit was not in sight.

The au'it wrote that, too, it might be.

"Shall I go after her?"

"I know where she is," he said. It was impossible for them to lose track of one another. The moment he wondered, he knew, and Hati seemed to, the same.

"So do I," Hati said. "She doesn't care about her daughter. Norit wants to, but Luz doesn't. Patya said she'd take care of her. Or Lensa will." That was Memnanan's mother, who rode with Memnanan's wife, Elagan: Laga, they called Elagan, a stronger woman than seemed likely, all belly, now, and very small limbs . . . endured the ride, simply endured, day after day, smiling sometimes, bravely—while Memnanan's allegiance had to be elsewhere given, and while she grew closer and closer to her time. *Lensa will.* Lensa and the aunts, frail and one sickly, had enough on their hands, and he had brought Lelie back to be an inconvenience to everyone . . . to fight Luz for Norit's sanity, and now Norit went raving back along the line, wearing her besha's strength down, frightening anyone who would listen to her, among the Ila's servants and among the tribes, that being all she could reach.

Them and the priests, he thought.

That was where Norit had gone, to tell the priests, and the priests told everyone, simply, clearly, without distortion or reinterpretation. That was their value to the Ila, and that was their value to Luz.

As rapidly as word could pass, at their noon camp, as rapidly as single priests could walk to the first of the villages, and village priests, and that man to the next, and that next to the village following, word would spread.

"Tell them there's water at Pori," he muttered to Luz. "Have her do something useful. It's not damned useful to scare everyone."

East, the word came to him. *East, east, east,* and an overwhelming sense of urgency, but he denied it. The needs of a whole caravan short of water denied it. Pori was the destination.

They camped. They had to, and he had reached the limit of his recovered strength. He sat down until the slaves had the tent ready, and he let Hati unsaddle Osan.

And curiously, without any threat in the heavens, every tent deployed side flaps on every side but that facing their line of march, an arrangement which both gave them deep shade and prevented the air moving as efficiently.

It cut off the view of anyone trying to find a target within the tents.

Norit came back to them, saner than she had left. She sat down under the tent, and Patya gave her Lelie, who was fretful and confused, as what child might not be?

But before their noon meal Norit had Lelie sleeping in her lap, and smoothed Lelie's fine hair . . . unthought, repeated gesture.

"Come," he said to Norit, to Hati. "Lie down. The baby, too."

They did, their mats set together. Lelie squirmed and fretted, still fevered with her wound, and found a new soft place between Norit and him. Memnanan's mother and that household sat at one end of the tent, and Tofi and he and his at the other, but when they went out to get their bowls filled at the common pot, with the rest, and came back to sit and eat, they made one circle.

There Lelie, still fretful, injured, discovered willing sympathy in Memnanan's mother, and left off scratching her healing wound to sit and be coddled on the old lady's knees. The mother of the Ila's own exalted captain fed a village waif, and Memnanan's wife, uncomfortable at every angle, carrying a child of her own, smiled, a transformation of a plain, thin face into a remarkable woman.

Patya and Tofi sat and talked together. Marak lay down with Hati, alone with Hati, at peace for a little time. He wondered at himself at times, that he could go through such a day and suddenly think of making love to his wife. But thinking was as far as it got.

Come to bed, he wished Norit without saying so.

Babies grew and changed so quickly. Perhaps Norit could not figure where the missing weeks had gone. Two months, and three, and the child was not the infant she remembered. None of them had recovered what they had lost. Everything fell through their grasp so quickly.

Fire blazed through his vision. Rings of fire spread outward.

Marak, his voices said, and something else. Lovemaking became impossible.

Damn the Ila, damn Luz, damn the *ondat.* He saw the structures start to build in his eyes. He shut Luz out, remembering music, remembering voices, remembering the courtyard and the garden, and the old slaves gathering fruit. Go to hell, he said to Luz. Lines became the base of the garden wall. Voices became the sound of water.

The earth trembled, reminding him it was the Lakht, after all, and that hours of sleep were hours of life irrevocably lost.

22

The Anlakht is the land of death, but it is also the mother of wells and waters. Fortunate for the world that mountains rise beyond the Qarain and trap the water that rises in the wind. That gift, passing through the hard rock of the Qarain, feeds the wells of the Lakht.

In the same way the Lakht sends water down to the lowlands, turning bitter water into sweet. The unkindest land feeds all the rest. On that one circumstance the whole world lives.

I am the Anlakht of my own creation.
—The Book of the Ila

Stars fell, and multiplied streaks of light across the night sky as they rode through the dunes that night. Some stars vanished beyond the distant wall of the ridge, off the edge of the Lakht. Some sank themselves in cold waves of sand in front of them.

One exploded overhead and left a trail that twisted slowly in the sky.

Marak, Marak, Marak, the voices said constantly, allowing him no rest from warning. Norit rode with Lelie asleep across the saddlebow, and had her eyes shut, listening or seeing visions, but Hati seemed doggedly trying to sleep, head down and arms clenched as she rode.

Over hours, the ridge to the east played out. The sand stretched level as they traveled south. There was the way to the rim, that track they had taken before, avoiding Pori. The night went insane above them, one streak and the next.

East!

The voices suddenly redoubled their efforts, as if the tower had just wakened from sleep and found out where they were.

Marak! East! Now!

Marak bit his lip, and kept going as he had set their course, as he had told the lord of the Keran, who was deaf to voices and blind to visions.

Lelie began to cry, wordless, plagued, perhaps, by prophecy even in her young age.

Norit suddenly reined in her besha and diverted it from the line, obstructing the course of beshti behind them. Tofi and Patya scarcely avoided colliding with her.

Marak rode close and leaned from the saddle, evading the irate snap of the besha's jaws. He seized the rein and led Norit back, and Norit jerked at the rein and tried to seize control of the beast.

"East," Norit insisted. "The hammer of heaven. We have to go east."

"We know it," Hati said, entirely awake now, and in bad humor. "All of us know it's coming. But we're not going east. We haven't any water. Make Luz understand that. We can't kill all the villages."

Lelie kicked and squalled. Patya rode close, far more skilled a rider than Norit, and held out her arms. So also Memnanan's relatives rode near to offer help, asking what was the matter, while the caravan moved around them, never pausing. Children grew fretful. Families held discussions. It was no one else's business.

"Give Patya the baby," Hati said harshly. "Give her to Patya! You'll drop her if you go on."

Norit would not. Norit held Lelie and hugged her close, hushing the cries, and the look in her eyes, in the light of a star-streaked heaven, was a hell of fear and desolation.

"It's not safe."

"Nothing's safe," Marak said. "We're not safe if half the villages die of thirst."

Rock hit sphere, over and over. He was blind for the moment, but he jerked the rein from Norit's hand and the besha, misused, squalled and backed and jerked its head, dragging painfully at his grip, compressing his fingers.

But he held. He kicked Osan and started forward, and the besha, glad, perhaps, to have a direction compatible with the herd, walked, Norit willing it or not, and Lelie still in her possession.

"We'll die!" Norit cried. "We have to go east, we have to go over the rim!"

"Shut up!" Hati said. "If you let that baby fall, I'll hit you!"

Marak paid no attention to the argument, or to Norit. He led, blind with visions that argued Norit's opinion, and knew when they passed the track that had turned north of Pori the last time they had made this trek. They passed it by.

"We'll die," Norit muttered. "No safety there. No safety. No safety."

"There'll be water," Marak said, weary of listening to her, distracted by the vision of the star-fall. "There'll be water, and we'll be there by morning. We'll be straight on to the rim with no more than a camp. It's the best we can do."

"No safety," Norit said.

He was not talking to a sane woman. He feared if he let go of the rein, Norit would be off through the column, creating a panic, and as it was, the Ila's servants looked at them askance, and the slaves looked fearful.

In time Memnanan came to ask what the disturbance was, and went to report Norit's vision. The au'it stored up things to write at sunrise.

"It will be the worst," Norit muttered under her breath, and hugged Lelie to her while dying stars streaked the heavens in their hundreds. "The earth will crack and pour out blood. Smoke will go up and blot out the sun. It's coming, and nothing can stop it. Fool, Marak. Go east."

"No," he said.

"What does she expect from us?" Hati asked. "Why won't she just give up and let us go at our own pace?"

"Who knows if the *ondat* even exist?" Marak said in despair and exhaustion, and regretted saying it, knowing that Luz was listening. He amended it. "Probably they do exist."

"Someone's throwing stars at us," Hati said, a bitter try at a joke. "If it isn't these *ondat,* it must be their cousins. Maybe their uncles."

"That's clearer than we've gotten from Luz."

Norit held her daughter close now, and sang to her, not a madwoman's song, but the clear, quiet tones of a lullaby.

"Child, sleep soundly in my arms.
Nothing can harm you here.
Dream of springs rich in water,
Dream of palms of shade and fruit.
Dream of fields gold with grain.
Dream of cool breezes.
Our house is shut against the night.
Our door is strong, our shutters tight.
Stars are brightly shining."

A star exploded on the horizon while she sang. The explosion lit the sky like a northern sunrise, so bright the column cast shadows.

A wind came after that and ran up the beshti's backs, a wind from off the Anlakht, where the blow had struck, but it did no harm.

At dawn, the au'it began to write, and wrote and wrote, furiously, fighting the pages flat in a light breeze.

At midmorning Norit suffered another fit, and Marak was quick to seize her rein again and bring her under tight control.

The rocks that broke the horizon were those of Pori, that height which poured out the water.

East, east, east, the voices said, maddening, frantic, and he could no longer believe that Luz was blind and deaf to their situation.

"I'm going ahead," he said to Hati. "I'm going to have a look." He no longer took responsibility for Norit: she was in Luz's hands. But they were close enough to see the landmarks, and he had his strength, Hati her keen eye for situations on the Lakht, and for the lives of all of them, he could no longer ignore the two-way pull on his instincts. It was another day to the descent, another waterless day, with no water at the bottom of a climb that was itself bound to cost lives, and the villages' strength was surely running out. They needed to camp. Pori would let them recover their strength for the descent, gather into a large mass and pass instructions before the descent: and if Pori village was already gone, there was still the water. There was a stone cistern. There was surely that.

He rode forward, Hati riding beside him, and they paused only to let Aigyan know his intention.

"What of Tain?" Aigyan asked. "What of ambushes?"

It was possible Tain had gotten ahead of them. That was always possible. It was possible for the rest of their lives.

"We have a premonition," Hati said, "and we need to know where we're leading, *omi*. We need to be sure about Pori. We'll go and be back before noon camp."

"Not without escort," Aigyan said, and named two men and two women to go with them, men and women of Hati's kind, dusky-skinned and wrapped in the dark-striped robes of their tribe, two of them with rifles.

Marak made no objection. They quickened their beshti's pace and rode out to the fore, and far separate of the others. Another rider joined them. Norit, with Lelie held close, had come for a look of her own, and he said not a word to note her presence. He bent all his attention to the land, keeping his eyes tracking every roll of the sand, every stone that might mask ambush: sand-colored robes and a well-laid ambush was the abjori style of attack, and he was alert for it.

It was the way they had plundered the Ila's caravans and killed her soldiers. It was the way they had enforced Tain's will on the villages and made the west for the better part of a decade a difficult place for Memnanan's men to travel. But he saw nothing of ambush, only a furtive movement of vermin that vanished ghostlike into tumbled rock, persuading the eye it had been mistaken.

"Paish," Hati said. That was one of the larger sort, knee high to the beshti, strong and tracking mostly by scent. He saw it go over a ridge just ahead of them, a red-brown flash of a flank and a tail, then gone.

One rarely saw them.

The beshti, on their own or subtly cued by the Keran riders, picked up the pace. For half an hour or more they proceeded, up and over ridges, down again into the general pitch of the land toward the edge of the Lakht.

Two stars fell by daylight, paired bright streaks across the sky that vanished beyond the hills. The boom that went out shook the air and made Lelie cry.

One more ridge, and the roll of the land gave up a strange sight, the ruined sticks of trees, the jagged edges of walls.

A star had fallen here. The well had broken open and continued to flow, soaking the sand.

Marak drew Osan in atop the ridge. So all the rest reined in. They stood atop the ridge and looked out on what had been an oasis, and now was a sky-reflecting pool of water, around which the red sand writhed. Small clumps of bodies detached at various places around that edge and floated out . . . hundreds, thousands of vermin gathered and pressing in on the sweet water, a living carpet of predators and scavengers that fought and preyed on each other, and waited only for the smell of death or waste to draw them all outward in a ravening swarm.

"Dead." Norit said faintly. "Pori is dead."

"Marak," Hati said, pleading with him, turn, move, and quickly.

He drew Osan's head about—his hands moved before his vision had finished taking in the danger. He was wrong. He had been wrong all along.

"Ride softly," a Keran tribeswoman said. "Quietly, please, *omi.*"

He knew. The sound, the scent, any whisper of presence might send the outermost of the mob toward them. They had the whole caravan advancing toward this place, and he could only be glad Norit had raised the doubt in him, and could only wish he had listened to Norit, to Luz, to the warnings Luz had tried to give them before now.

They rode away behind the ridge at a restrained pace.
Lelie began to fret and to cry. Norit hushed her with a hand
over her mouth, and hugged her close. It was more than their
own escape they had to manage. They dared not draw the
mob after them, and the beshti, uneasy, wanted to travel
faster, to break into a run that would take them back to the
herd . . . that was the beshti's view of things, get to the herd
and bolt for the horizon, faster than the mob could follow.

Osan fought to get free. Norit's besha, beyond her
strength or skill, suddenly jerked the rein and pulled Norit
half from the saddle, and a tribeswoman seized her before
she could fall free . . . seized her robe in one hand as she
swung to the side, but the besha went out from under her.
Lelie fell from her grasp, and Norit herself fell to the sand,
her besha running free, rein trailing.

Hati reined in beside the accident as Marak did, and before he could get from the saddle, Hati jumped down and
swept Lelie up in her arms. Lelie had had the wind knocked
out of her, and got her breath back, and screamed, Hati trying in vain to prevent her crying. Meanwhile one of the two
tribesmen, retaining a tight grip on his rein, had leapt down
to haul Norit to her feet.

Marak rode past Hati, grasped the baby by one arm as he
did so, and yanked her into his grasp, smothering her against
him to silence her cries as he reined around. It seemed forever then. Hati fought to steady her panicked besha long
enough to get back into the saddle, a lifelong-practiced set of
moves, and made it—got her hands on the harness and was
up into the saddle, leaving Norit still down, still dazed by a
thump of her head against the sand. But one of the men of
their escort immediately gathered Norit up, supported her,
staggering as she was while the other man pressed close to
control the rescuer's besha.

It was all a matter of heartbeats, scant moments—but
there had been too much noise, far too much for their safety,
and as the one tribesman held Norit on her feet against the
side of his besha, Marak's anxious glance found an ominous
furtive movement among the rocks on either hand.

"Up!" Marak said. *"Luz! Get her up!"*

Norit managed, winded as she was, to take hold of the saddle loops, but the tribesman shoved her from below so that she landed like baggage, and never delayed to mount as with a frightened snort the besha moved out. Vermin poured out of the rocks: one besha moved and they all moved, for their lives. The man's grip on the mounting loops held, keeping him with his besha in a maneuver that carried him along faster than a tired man could run, clinging on the side of the saddle, hitting the ground with occasional strides. "Go, go, go!" the Keran all insisted, and that man no less than the others. The tribesman had a death grip on the mounting loop, and before Marak, burdened with Lelie, could ride Osan in to his assistance, his brother tribesman came by on the man's left side to seize his hand, leaning down, boosting him higher off the sand in two strides, until the man was able to get an arm past Norit and haul himself half-over the saddle behind her.

His grip after that embraced Norit, and kept her across the saddle like a water sack while he reached forward for the rein. It was a feat of skill no villager would match, and it freed them all to run all-out.

No one had bled, no one had died, no blood had encouraged the vermin: distance widened between them and the mob, and when Marak looked back he saw clear sand between them.

He slowed. Far enough in the lead to know they had room, they all slackened to a staying pace, but kept moving. He held Lelie. He had Hati and Norit as safe as any of them.

Norit's besha meanwhile was long over the horizon, headed breakneck toward the caravan to join the herd it knew. Unrewarded, behind them, the vermin had straggled out, and most would go back to the water. A few might follow the track they inevitably left—less dominant outrunners, more desperately seeking moisture or carrion, or living prey.

They were not out of danger, but they had gotten away from the heart of the mob.

Marak finally became aware of Lelie's struggles in his

arm. He had kept her still, carefully managed his grip to let her breathe, and now he soothed her frightened, wounded sobs and sheltered her in his coat as he had on the ride that brought her.

He thanked the god he doubted that he had had the instinct to doubt his judgment and investigate before bringing the slow caravan with all its weak and helpless all the way to Pori.

But there was no water.

"Hati," Marak said. "Go. Take the women with you. Warn lord Aigyan. We've no choice but to turn toward the rim. Have them turn, don't camp, and we'll catch up on your new track."

"I'll see you there," Hati agreed, and called out to the two women and laid on the quirt. She was gone over the roll of the next hill, vanishing in the dust they left.

"I warned you," Norit said in a brittle voice. The tribesman had gotten her upright.

"That you did," Marak allowed. He had no wish to take up a quarrel with Luz. He doubted even Luz had known the danger there was at Pori, or Norit could have warned them in far clearer words. The truth was that Luz had not known, had had no idea until now about the mob there. But: *East, east, east!* the voices urged, as if they had always been right.

He said, he hoped sanely so, and calmly: "Well, we can't water at Pori; that's clear. Norit *was* right: we can't camp and rest. We need to get all this mass of people as far east as we can. If we're out of water, we're out. We'll do what we can."

East. Surrender to Luz settled him into a familiar track. He knew the way down the cliffs to the east of Pori, and he knew that the gathering of vermin had just doomed a good number of the caravan to a struggle they might not have the strength to make without rest and water.

But if the continual footfall on the earth of the last caravan in the world drew attention from Pori, if the smell of them wafted on the chance wind, if the vermin still following the column met those feeding on Pori's ruin . . . if any one of those three things happened, the unthinkable became a certainty.

He led. They veered just slightly off the track they had taken getting to Pori, and for the better part of an hour they moved over trackless sand.

Then as they crossed a shallow pan they saw, as Marak had hoped, a distant haze of dust below the line of a far ridge. That hazy disturbance in the sameness of the Lakht marked the caravan's passage, and it had, indeed, turned eastward.

Hati had reached them safely. Aigyan had heard the warning.

The sun stood at noon, and the caravan pressed eastward, not camping, not resting.

Marak kept his pace, not pushing his own party. The beshti under them were tired, worn down by days of travel and now coming within sight of water and hazard at distant Pori—only to turn away.

But the beshti had not called out after the water at Pori: they had seen for themselves a hazard and smelled a smell that ruffled the ridge of hairs down their backs—Marak recalled that fine line of fear on the nape of Osan's neck, just before he had known there was trouble. Tails had gone half-up, and stayed bristled, even now. The beshti left the promise of water and traveled back to their own caravan without a sound, thirst and self-preservation at war in their keen instincts. Only once in the next hour the beshti stopped, braced their feet, snuffed the air. The earth trembled slightly. But as it proved no worse, they resumed their progress toward the distant caravan.

Lelie, drained of tears, had seized hold of Marak's coat at that instability and held on after that for dear life, not releasing her hold. She was bruised and scraped from the fall, but the makers were surely attending to that. It was the wound to her soul, her mother's casual forgetfulness, that the makers could not cure: Norit had never asked to have her back, and as he rode, Marak stroked her hair gently, told her in a low voice that all was well, that they would go down to a safe place . . . half lies, all, making it sound easy, making it sound like tomorrow, when the next instant was Lelie's tomorrow, in her young perception, and her mother rode dazed, lost in Luz's visions.

Soon, tomorrow, very soon now.

How many fathers must be making that desperate promise today, short of water, themselves short of strength . . . and how many fathers must be giving up their ration to their children today, not knowing themselves where the end of this was, not knowing whether it was wiser to consume the water themselves, to keep their strength, or how much privation a child could bear?

"Luz," he said aloud, to the presence behind Norit's glazed steadiness. "Can you bring water to us at the bottom of the climb? We need your help. Too many of these people will die. Can you send Ian? Can you lead us to water closer to the cliffs?"

He begged for help. He bargained with their fate. Pride was nowhere in his reckoning. He prayed to a second goddess-on-earth for a miracle their Ila could not provide, and all the while the skin between his shoulders was uneasy, as if they had not shaken all the vermin off their track. He felt calamity organizing around them, and the people for whom he held all responsibility were in greater and greater disarray.

Marak, Marak, Marak, was all his own voices said in reply. He saw the sphere and the rock and the rings, twice repeated. That was the help Luz gave. She *had* done better. She *had* reached him before, and now found nothing to say to him but that: *go, go blindly,* giving him no reasons.

He suspected the fault lay in himself, that he was mosttimes deaf, and unreceptive . . .

Like his father. Like Tain, deaf to things he needed most in the world to hear.

But unlike Tain, he broke his silence. "Norit," he said, pleaded. "Does Luz say anything about water? Does she offer us any help?"

"There's nothing," Norit said, sitting in the embrace of the tribesman who had saved her. "Nothing I can do."

Norit never yet asked how her daughter fared after that fall. *Luz* had never asked. Luz involved herself not at all in the welfare of individuals, cared nothing for the workings of Norit's heart. Later Norit would shed tears, but Luz did not let her shed them now.

"It's coming," Norit said further. "It's on its way. We have two days. Just two days. You won't reach the tower in two days."

That was the plain truth, and it offered them no water, no help. It occurred to him to ask Luz if there was any point in trying, but it occurred to him, too, that he had no interest in hearing the answer one way or the other: it would not change what he would do. He could not sit down in paradise. He could not sit down in hell, either. He was going to try to reach the tower . . . he was going to try to get all his people down off the Lakht and into the lowlands before the hammer fell. He was going to get them as far toward safety as he could get them. They had him for a leader: that was what they bargained for.

"Why didn't you tell me this *before* we went to Pori?" He did ask that question.

"You weren't listening. Now you are. Get below the cliffs. Get behind rock. Get the stakes down. I don't know what may happen. I'm trying to know where the hammer will come down. It's not good for where it falls. It's not good for the other side of the world either, and that's what we have to worry about. The earth will crack at both places and melt the rocks in its forge."

Luz made the visions. Norit said them as best she knew how, out of things she had seen: what more could she do? Sometimes they were things no one alive had ever seen, and Norit tried to describe them, out of a village wife's meager experience.

"The prophet," the tribesmen said to each other in muted tones, and meant Norit. The tribes regarded no priests, but the Keran had learned that this one spoke for the power that led them, and they were in awe at this strange conversation, this matter-of-fact consultation of their oracle.

And there was no comfort in anything Norit could say.

They traveled toward that haze of dust that marked the passage of the caravan across the land at the same steady pace.

And uneasy as he was about the land behind them, Marak became aware, in that sight, that he knew where Hati was. He knew it as well as he knew Norit's location beside him, as steady, as reliable as the pole stars in the general fall of the heavens. She was there in the heart of the column. The constellations might be shaken, but he could not *get* lost in the world that contained the other parts of himself.

The caravan had no need of another dreamer, another guide as mad as Norit.

It needed a plain, headblind madman to say only: *I've been there before. I can lead you. I know a way down. Don't hesitate, don't camp.*

It needed Tain's son, too: it needed him to say: *Don't have pity on the dying. Don't hesitate. When the line goes, go.*

He rode toward the column, and on the edge of joining it, on the very moment of crossing toward safety in among the plodding beshti, he realized their party had been one member short on the retreat. He was so used to the au'it following him and Hati and Norit that he had failed to notice that this time she had not followed them out from the caravan.

Surely she had not come out with them.

"No au'it followed us," he said to the Keran, half a question. "You saw no au'it tracking us at any time."

"No, *omi*."

At least they had not lost her. He thought they had not.

He rode in among the Ila's servants, and near the Ila, and up to Hati's side.

"I advised Aigyan," Hati said first. "He knows all the situation. He's going to keep the line moving. We're going over the rim."

Hati looked aside. The Keran had let Norit down off his besha, and Tofi had gotten down. Norit's besha was, not surprisingly, walking with the rest, riderless, and Tofi called out to Bosginde to catch the beast and bring it. The caravan, meanwhile, never stopped. Such small exchanges dropped behind temporarily, and caught up again, beshti tending to seek their own herd.

But if anyone was as likely as the Ila's priests and servants to be alive with the Ila's own makers, if there was anyone in the Ila's service who could be as aware of the Ila's whims as he was aware of Luz's moods and desires, it was the aui'it.

Her priests, her servants knew the Ila's wishes and obeyed her.

The au'it had reported, that was what.

Looking back, he saw Norit had gained the saddle again, in the weary, moving throng. There was no eagerness in the crowd around them. A kind of glazed desperation had replaced fervor and mirth and anger and all the rest of motives that kept men moving toward the unknown, away from calamity.

"Let me take the baby," Patya said, riding close to him. "I'll hold her."

Marak passed her over, glad to surrender the responsibility. "Norit can carry her on the descent," he said, and added, because with his own experience, he pitied Norit: "Her mother doesn't know. She's gone where she goes."

"Will she come back to be—?" Patya asked, and to her mad brother, tried to find words.

"Sane again? Will she be sane? I hope so." But he saw no sign of it, not now, not for time to come. "If she doesn't, we'll take care of her, Hati and I. And you." He saw how Patya took to the waif. "We'll take care of you, too. We're family."

He had to promise that to Patya. But he foreknew her relation to him might soon become a hazard to Patya's well-being, to her very life. He suspected their au'it had been making an extensive, perhaps not favorable, report, that her whole account had gone to the Ila now, and he had to know, before he set out on this risky descent, before people began coming to the Ila, mad for water and in terror of the star-fall, what the Ila meant to do about that report.

He rode beside Hati, not reporting to Memnanan, or to the Ila.

He waited for the Ila, riding within sight of him, to send for him.

He waited for Memnanan to ask him what he had seen out there, or why they had ridden back in disarray. Even if Memnanan had gotten a full report from Aigyan of what Hati had told him—it was good sense to ask the firsthand witness, at least, what he had seen, and why he had changed his mind about Pori.

No query came from either. The au'it—an au'it—rode near them, rode veiled, as she often had, appearing out of the dust.

Why she had left them remained a mystery, one with, he was sure, the Ila at the heart of it, and Memnanan's ignoring him as the wrapping on the affair.

"The Ila asked you no questions?" he asked Hati.

"Not a one. I only talked to Aigyan."

"Don't look back," he said in a low voice. "The au'it's back there. Did you see the au'it immediately when you got back?"

"No." Hati sounded startled. "I don't think she went with us. Or did we lose her?"

"One is with us now," he said. "Something's happened. I don't know what, I don't know why, but something's happened."

"About the Ila, you mean?"

"She didn't want to know about Pori. She only took the easy chance to call the au'it back, maybe to read the book. We have an au'it back there now. I don't know that it's the same one. Memnanan's not talking to us. I can see him. He's not even looking our way. He's under orders."

"We can't completely trust him, then."

"We never could completely *trust* him," Marak said. He tried to think what reason the Ila might have for not needing to know about Pori, and all he could think of was that the Ila had foreknown there was no use in their mission there. Failing that—her need to have the au'it's report on them had become more important than her need to know what they did out there at Pori.

Perhaps it was a consultation before their descent of the

plateau, her wish to know everything they had said in secret before she went into Luz's territory. Perhaps the Ila herself perceived the approach of the hammer and pondered leaving his venture south, and going east, instead. She was well watered. There were makers in her blood. She might be, herself, mad.

But if the Ila had found out something of Luz's intentions, it was not the au'it who told her, because *they* had no idea and could not have informed her.

The Ila had ceased her daily baths. The Ila's servants no longer cooked for the camp or made tea for the Ila. Presumably the last few days the Ila ate the same dry ration as they ate.

Perhaps the Ila held some intention of dealing with Luz and everyone that served her.

"Do you think she means us harm?" Hati asked him.

"I don't know what she thinks. I wonder if she's begun to hear the voices herself."

"Luz's voice?" Hati asked.

"The makers could do that. Her makers haven't cured us of Luz. Our makers keep us what we are. Maybe they've gotten into *her,* now." He paused on a thought. "Maybe she fears they're going to get into her—maybe she didn't *want* to drink water that didn't come from the Ila's Mercy."

"All our water did," Hati said. Her dark eyes went wide and troubled. "And our food came from Oburan. Everything. *Pori's* wouldn't. Pori belonged to Luz. Didn't it?"

"I think we shed makers," he said. "What if we breed them continually and shed them like old skin? What if we shed them into the sand and into the water? And the Ila's servants cook for the camp, or they did before we ran short. And the priests, the Ila's priests, they come and go up and down the line. Maybe it's a kind of war going on. What if the Ila would lose altogether if we took water from Pori, and everybody watered there?"

Hati simply stared at him, the two of them riding side by side. "She hasn't given up, then."

"I don't think she's given up," he said.

"Do you think she's planning some sort of attack on Luz?"

"I don't know. But Luz hears us." It was hard to remember that they were spied on, constantly. But it was true. "Luz knows, now, everything we just said. We can't help that. I hope Luz figures how to protect us." The last he said like a petitioner in a village court, hoping Luz was listening carefully. "She's asked all these people to come to her tower. If she meant all of us to die, we could have done that in Oburan. *Surely* she has something she can do. She won't just turn on us, because of the Ila. She wanted her. I think she still wants her. But the Ila doesn't want to be taken." He was afraid, as he said it. He had met two small anomalies in the way things had worked: the au'it's desertion, and now her return, and neither might mean more than that the au'it had decided not to take an arduous journey, an ordinary simple decision.

But the Ila was going into danger at the very heart of their safety: he understood more and more that peace between the Ila and Luz was not likely, and he grew as worried about what the Ila might do as they came closer to Luz, as their journey became harder and the decisions more dangerous.

He worried about the Ila's unanticipated action now as he worried about the failing water supply, as worried as he was about the beshti's strength, about the *people's* strength to make the climb down from the Lakht—as worried about all those things near him, perhaps, as he was about the remote calamity coming to the world. The hammerfall was still distant: the Ila's independent action might come before they reached the cliffs, before they entered Luz's domain, and it might be anything, even a decision deliberately to kill all of them.

And she might be mad. She might be as mad as the rest of them. She might do things that only made sense to the mad, just before they attempted the climb down with many, many people that, already, would not survive.

But *east* and *down* was increasingly the only choice that would serve. If calamity was coming as a star-fall, then surely, he said to himself, it would be something the like of which they had accompanying the lesser star-fall. They had their forewarning in that: it would be quake and wind and blowing sand, ten times, a hundred times worse than before. And *that,* unlike the Ila, could not change.

He gathered up his wits and his courage for confrontation and went to Memnanan instead, who rode behind the Ila's servants.

"Pori's lost to us," he said.

"So I gather," Memnanan said.

"The Ila knows?"

"She knows."

"Quake and storm are coming," he said plainly, "worse than we've ever seen. And it's coming soon. This next camp of ours will be only a short rest, with no stakes driven. After that . . ." He felt his way onto quaking ground, with a man he had generally trusted, who had trusted *him,* more to the point, and who had the Ila's ear. "After that, and it's not far from here, we go down the climb off the Lakht, and we try to get as many as we can alive to the bottom."

"Is there any spring at the bottom? Is there anything near the cliffs?"

"Not that I know. But we do what we can. We get down off the edge, and we immediately get the deep stakes driven, and we trust the cliffs to shelter us." He wanted to ask, and saw no course but to ask. "Pori was completely infested. Did the Ila already know that?"

Hati, to his dismay, had followed him. Now both of them rode beside the captain, one on a side, and the au'it trailed them at a distance, as she always had.

Memnanan had a grave, a worried expression, and did not look quite at him or at Hati. And failed to answer.

"You don't need a report," Marak challenged him. "Why don't you need one? Why don't you ask? Isn't she taking advice?"

"The Ila said let you try what you could, and if you couldn't, or if you didn't come back, then we would go down to the lowlands without you." Memnanan did look at him then. "She believes in your calamity. She expects a storm. She doubted Pori would be enough shelter." Memnanan seemed to weigh saying something further, then did. "She thinks most will die, and if anyone will live, we have to assume most will die."

"More likely we'll die if we sit on our rumps. We're going to try not to. Tell her that. Tell her she needs to listen to advice." Tell her she was not in charge of decisions? Tell her she would not give orders to the tribes? That was too much to expect of Memnanan. If he tried to make that point, he would lose this man, and everything. "Tell her we can't rest long. Not a moment more than we have to."

"I will."

"What did the au'it tell her, in her report? Good, or bad?"

"I don't know," Memnanan said.

"Is that the same au'it with us now?"

Memnanan's eyes traveled in that direction, and back. "I have no idea."

"If the Ila orders anything that prevents us getting down off the rim," Marak said, "for her life, don't let her. Don't do anything to prevent us. It's coming. That's all I know now. It's coming."

"I said: she's in favor of the descent," Memnanan said. "As soon as possible." He added, in a low voice, with as much desperation as a man might feel: "I trust you for my household, Marak Trin."

Memnanan's wife, his mother. His unborn child.

"I'll have a good man walk beside your wife when we make the climb down," Marak said, reassured that Memnanan had asked the favor, not quite admitting it. "To steady the besha."

The au'it had moved up beside them. She wrote as she had written all the conversations before, all of which the Ila now knew—at least those the au'it might think most important.

It was their au'it, he decided, in one glance, and then in the next, had his doubts return.

He knew their own au'it's face, her mannerisms. And how often in the past had it been some different woman, when the aui'it frequently wore the veil, against the unkind sun and the drying wind? Their own au'it might still be reporting. The Ila, riding with the aui'it, ahead of them, might be making her own plans, outside Memnanan's knowledge.

The Ila had no need to ask him questions, if that was the case. In the au'it's report she proved to herself whether he would lie to her, or to his companions, and when he posed himself that question he grew calmer: he never had lied, so far as he recalled. If she was sane, she would know he had never worked against her.

Perhaps the Ila even *trusted* him, as far as she trusted anyone, even Memnanan. That was an unlooked-for conclusion.

But whatever the Ila thought, whatever she schemed, whatever she intended toward him, if her intentions agreed with his, getting this mass of people down off the Lakht before the hammer came down, he decided not to confuse the issue any further with questions.

Or reports.

Or speculations.

For the next number of hours, her motives and his motives might both demand they get off the Lakht and stay alive.

For the next number of hours, if that was her thought, it was good enough.

23

In the abyss above the sky, I saw death. Below the heavens, I have made all choices I could make not for lives, but for life itself.
—The Book of the Ila

They rested for two measured hours on the tribal clock, simply looking at the sun and trusting the sun, no matter the fate of the world, to stay on its course. They pitched no tents, only unrolled their mats. The Keran and the Haga drank very, very little, allowing the water to stay in their mouths for as long as possible. They gave sweet water to their beshti, as much as they could give, to sustain the legs that carried them. They sorted even the sparse goods that a tribe owned, paring down the weight the beshti carried to the least possible, while the sky above them was blue.

At that stop, the horizon of the world was closer than it ever had been. The drop into the rolling flat of the east was clear and distinct to see, seeming so close that Marak would have driven himself and his own to keep moving and to reach it, and to go down, but the distance in that vision was deceptive because of the scale. It was another long walk away, and desperate as they were, they had no choice but to rest—and to ask the Ila, through Memnanan, to be wise: to do as the tribes did, and to cast away anything that could be cast away. The tribes made a small heap of what they abandoned. Yet nothing from the Ila's baggage joined it, and for the Ila, her servants spread a side flap as a canopy and a curtain for a wind-break: the Ila would not lie down in the witness of others, and what she owned, she would not cast away.

Hati had lain down with her veil pulled over her face, like the dead. Norit rocked Lelie . . . rocked sometimes, simply because she was mad, but it chanced to calm Lelie, all the same, while it calmed Norit.

"Soon, soon, soon," Norit said to no one in particular, and exhausted herself, refusing rest. Marak saw how worn she had come to look, how the bones stood out in the hand that rested on Lelie's back.

It was no wonder. He had watched it happen. He blamed Luz, and hoped Norit had strength enough to carry her down the cliffs. The child—Lelie—was a hazard on the descent, when a suddenly ill-placed weight, like too much weight, could cause a besha to miss its footing, and where one besha falling could wreak havoc on those below. But Norit had taken Lelie back. And he summoned up faith that Norit would make it—hope that she would make it. She was a better rider than Patya: she had become so, on their ride. He appointed the man to go beside Elagan, and keep her steady, and he appointed another to go beside Memnanan's mother and his two frail aunts.

He trusted them. He trusted their own party to get down intact: the tribes knew what they were doing, if the Ila's men did not.

But what disasters would happen after, what would happen if the hammerfall overtook them on the descent, what would happen if the weather turned, what would happen when inexperienced villagers attempted to ride down the cliffs under adverse conditions—during earthquake, or in storm . . . those were questions with one plain answer, and he blotted it out, as far as he could, while anger at the Ila's obstinacy churned in him—about her decisions, he could do nothing.

He thought he should station someone to check the villagers' loads before they started down. He should have someone to advise certain villagers, inexpert riders, to walk, and certain others to adjust their packs and lower the height of them before attempting the descent.

He might find some tribesman that brave, to linger back behind the tribes, to stand among the damned and save those he could. It galled him to have to ask that of the tribesmen who knew better and had managed better all their lives, and one part of him said he should not; but he imagined the calamity among the helpless and the weak, the unjust, undeserved calamity of villagers who had never learned the Lakht and had no reason to know, and the *ondat*, serene in the heavens, hurling stars at men and women as innocent as the old slaves in the garden. There were gods-on-earth, and gods in the skies, so far as men of his ability could ever deal with them, and *reason* gave way to blind luck and *justice* had no place in the reckoning: like the wind, death just *was*, and he knew he was going to fail to save some—and more than some.

His orders from Luz were running out. He had gotten them this far. He considered the Ila's arrogant canvas, and began to ask himself what he himself was worth, more than the rest, and why should *he* tell another man to stand back at the beginning of the descent and advise villagers on the way to get down?

His job was to save lives and get them on their way. But he had done that. Norit would see the rest to safety. She was their guide. Anything he could do, Hati could do.

Was he holier and more righteous than the Ila in her shelter?

And then he looked at Hati, asleep beside him, and knew in his heart that Hati would stay with him, no matter what. It was never just one life that he would risk, taking that hazardous post for himself: he would kill Hati by that decision.

And if Norit was not enough, if they lost Hati, too, what application of common sense were all these people going to get in their leadership?

None from the Ila, nothing that did not favor her own comfort, her own survival above all. The people deserved some leader who cared about them? And did that attribute make him holy? Or better?

He ceased to have answers. He thought that he should go down. He thought that he should stay alive as long as he could, and do the most that he could, because he had no way of knowing what might happen after they reached the bottom, or where he might find a use.

But if he went down, what man *could* he ask to stay? Or should he ask any man who might live to risk his life?

He was looking at the ex-slaves, at Mogar and Bosginde, men who least of all had relatives depending on them, but they had each other, and could he ask those two men to risk their lives, even when no village would value those two lives? *He* knew what good men they had come to be, and how, in any other time, if there *were* time left in the world, those two would turn up masters of their own caravans . . . but there was no time left for good men to do anything but scramble with the rest and stay alive.

If all the good perished, it left only the rest to have their way. And was *that* good?

He was still thinking that when Tofi came to him and squatted down to talk, and he realized Tofi and Patya had been sitting off to themselves, and that now Patya was hovering suspiciously in the background. Marak shaded his eyes to look up at the young man.

"*Omi*," Tofi began. "We may all die."

"I don't certainly intend to."

"I don't either," Tofi said sensibly, while Patya hovered behind him in unaccustomed silence. "Your sister, *omi*, she doesn't intend to, either. But—we don't know about tomorrow. A star could fall on us."

He suddenly realized where this was going. He understood Patya's desperate, anxious silence. They were young, and there was no time for decent understandings—that was the very point. The desperation in the air drove more than one older, more sober couple to their mats, trying to beget their way to immortality. The desperation gave no time for joy, or hope—or patience with custom, or modesty.

"Out with it," he said. "Time's short. You're using it all up."

"Patya and I . . ." Tofi tripped over his own need to breathe, or the need to remember what he had meant to say, exactly those desperate, calculated words.

"Patya and you," he said. He looked at Patya. "Is this your idea, as well as his?"

"I want—" she said.

"You want. Everybody wants. Go to it. Good luck to you." He got up from his mat and took Patya's face between his hands, kissed her on the forehead. "The *best* of luck," he said, and knew, for himself, in the back of his moiling thoughts, that he could not risk himself for more than the immediate needs, either . . . he had more than a wife to constrain him.

He had the Ila on his hands, and her dealings with Luz. And not Memnanan nor Norit nor any of the tribal lords could deal with her as he did.

Patya blushed. Tofi did. Patya hugged him. He clapped Tofi on the shoulder and sent them away. There was no privacy in the whole camp.

But lovers managed. They went off among the beshti. Inventive. He expected that of them.

"That was sweet," Hati murmured, beside him. "I like him. I like your sister, too."

"He's a good young man," he said. He fought off despair for their situation and exhaustion deeper than any since he had come on this trek. He touched Hati's shoulder, just touched her, wanting comfort for himself. He had not even spared half a thought for the appropriateness of his sister's choice. Kaptai would have married her daughter to a young man of more prospects than Tofi had. But who, in this hour, had more than Tofi?

He was thinking of the deaths of hundreds and thousands. He had begun to plan for that carnage as inevitable. What share had Patya in his obligations?

Obligations all came crashing down on him with a smothering weight, all the first ride to Pori, the trip back,

Kaptai's death, and his failure to do anything for the ones who most relied on him, like Norit, like Patya. And Hati.

Marak, the voices said, always there in these hours, along with the urgency to move, move, move, go east, and he would, he had to, but ultimately he had no power to save the weak, the feckless, the ignorant. He tried to call what he felt in his soul *responsibility;* but it was beyond any sense of responsibility: it was simply doing what he could do, as long as he could do it, like a man walking on his last strength.

They settled. Norit, meanwhile, rocked, rocked, singing, quietly, mad as they came. Her head dropped several times, and a final time, and she slept, Lelie sprawled in her lap. There was nothing he could do for them, either. Hati slept, and he knew it was his own duty to rest and to become sane again, but *Marak, Marak, Marak* was all through his brain, and it would not let him go. Thoughts raced and circled through his head, what to do, whether he could find the exact spot where they had descended off the Lakht the last time.

Most of all—the chance that storm might come while they were exposed to that edge, that the earth might shake while they were on that climb—all these things.

And the sand-fall below the cliffs—he had forgotten that. Sand came off the Lakht, wind-carried. They could get down and find that their tame slope, their trail, was under a wind-borne waterfall of sand, the trail changing under them and a weight of sand simply crushing them down—but if they were too far away from the cliffs, the sand-charged wind would kill them. He struggled to imagine what the balance was, how close they dared be, whether the fiercest wind that ever blew might simply carry all the sand-fall up into the storm. Might it be the best gamble to pitch tents closer to the cliffs and risk being buried?

What was right? What could Luz know about conditions no one had *ever* seen?

"Marak," Hati said, and sat up and tugged at him, wanting him to lie down and be reasonable. He would not. Could not rest. Not with that realization. They had to do more than just reach the bottom. They had to get a camp pitched that would save their lives.

And he had to guess right.

She leaned against him, and put her arm about him, her head against his shoulder. "Luz is noisy today. She should shut up."

"It's coming," he said. "It's coming for sure. Luz wants us to move now. She's never walked this desert. She doesn't know what she's asking of us. But we don't know what we're facing."

"She should shut up," Hati said, laying her head against his heart. "She should let us alone. We're doing all we possibly can."

"If there's no water down below, before we reach the tower—" The worries obstructed clear reason, his thoughts going back and back again to the cardinal points. "She's got to do something, is all. I can't. I *can't* get the villages to move faster than they will. And if we don't camp close enough to the rocks at the bottom, the wind will kill us, and if all the sand falls off the cliffs, it may bury us. What's the answer for us? How far is safe?"

"We've done all we can," Hati said. "We'll go down, is all. We'll do what we can, by what we see."

Norit, who might know, who might hear Luz's answer, only rocked and sang to herself.

There was nowhere any peace. He could look to the edges of the camp and see the furtive action of a few creepers, harmless things, but their disturbance could trigger others— all that mass at Pori, which stayed near the water, preying on itself, the stronger on the weaker. They had not walked into it. The chance that they might have walked in with the villages behind them still haunted him. But he tried to do what Hati said: he tried not to think.

A wind blew, sulfurous and unpleasant. It might have stormed for days during their passage, and instead the weather had favored them, their one piece of blind luck. Not even Luz could have arranged that. He thought that calamities were piling up on him, but if he looked, he saw a few

signs of luck still with him, a few signs that the odds could
be shoved into better advantage. If a man paid attention. If
he did think of all the possibilities.

He kissed his wife, rested his head against her, shut his
eyes a moment.

"Up," Hati said after a dark space, giving him a little
shake, and he realized she had held him, bracing his weight
for however long he had slept, steady and sure. "We're moving," she said, and they were: the Keran were rolling up their
mats. The Ila's servants had struck her shelter.

A little sleep seemed for a moment worse than none. It
was hard to move. He gathered his scattered wits, helped
Hati up, waked Norit, but not Lelie—her he picked up, and
heaved her, still sleeping, to his shoulder, to hand her up to
Norit once Norit was mounted.

Hati rolled up their mats and went and tied them on, and
led the beshti back.

Marak saw Tofi help Patya up. The aifad cheated him of
the sight of Patya's face, but Tofi looked happy, and the lan-
guage of their hands, not quick to part, was a reassurance.
They looked only at each other.

"Do your jobs," Marak said to Bosginde, who stood staring. "*He* won't give you orders." Meaning Tofi. "*You're* in
charge. Prove what you've got."

Bosginde went and with Mogar did his ordinary duty, and
saw the girths were tight, then helped Memnanan's wife and
mother up. Tofi became cognizant enough to join them, with
looks back at Patya the while, the look of a young man with
only one thing on his mind.

Bosginde elbowed Mogar, with a grin and a knowing look
on his face, before they helped Norit up and both got to the
saddle . . . as if it were any day, as if nothing in the world was
unusual. The Keran, meanwhile, were setting themselves into
motion, the Ila's servants were attempting to get her
mounted, and Memnanan and his men were up. The Haga
began to flow out around the edges of the lump that was the
city-dwellers in their midst. Marak saw it all, the amusement
of the slaves, Tofi and Patya with eyes for one another, and

Hati's amusement, and all of a sudden there was a commotion in the Ila's camp, the Ila's white besha having escaped out through the camp, and two more followed it.

Everyone began to laugh, he laughed, and then the earth shook them all to sobriety: that was what had startled the beshti, and the Keran quickly caught the fugitives. The Ila, veiled and angry, allowed herself to be helped up.

They could still laugh, the ex-slaves at the ex-master, the tribesmen at the city folk—all of them had laughed except Norit, who sat expressionless and staring blankly at the commotion. She would go where the besha went. Whether she herself got her baby down the descent safely—she had no particular care—but Luz would see Norit survived, if anyone did.

"Here." Marak made his decision and handed Lelie up to her mother, live or die, the best he could do: then he went and mounted up, the same. He turned Osan to follow the Keran, and Hati went with him, and Norit did, and Tofi and Patya, and the whole camp and the whole caravan began to set out.

The wind fell. The afternoon grew hot, and the air utterly still as they traveled. The edge of the world was in front of them, a horizon unnaturally clear now that the wind had let the air clear.

"Talk to me," he said to Hati. "Distract me."

Marak, Marak, his voices said to him, and he saw a vision, the fall of a great star, as it seemed, and the earth splitting, and fire running in the cracks.

"I think it's coming," Hati said, offering no comfort. "Something much bigger than the rest."

"It's coming," Norit confirmed, catching a breath. She hugged Lelie close. "In the bitter water. Not yet, but soon."

Conversation was no comfort, except to know the tormenting vision was the same for all of them. They saw the vision over and over and over, with the sun shining at their backs as clearly and as brightly in a clear sky as if there were never a threat.

And by late afternoon the edge of the world developed a

crack, and by evening that crack became a cliff edge, bright red with sunset where they were, and shadowed beyond, until the distant sand caught the light again.

It was the edge of the Lakht. It was the way they had to go down, and they were not yet where Marak hoped to reach, not near their former descent: that was southward, toward all the hazards of Pori.

"The climb down is at a notch," he said, riding up to Aigyan before Memnanan or any of the rest could question him. Only Hati came with him, and now he quickened the pace ahead of the Keran, and took the lead himself, with Hati, and then with Norit and Tofi and Patya, and last of all the au'it, all of them that had come this road before.

The light was leaving. The smallest stones cast strange, long shadows on sand turned red as fire. They were running out of daylight and farther from a downward path than he had hoped they would be.

But they rode up on a depression along the cliff edge, and there was their path, just as the sun was shining its last, there where the sand had slipped away down the edge of the plateau, and rocks thrust up like giant sentinels.

"There it is!" Hati exclaimed: trust the an'i Keran to recognize a landmark she had once passed. This was the place. *East,* the voices still urged them, and now *east* was possible. Marak turned Osan about and looked back to the long line of tribesmen that followed them, and to the red among white that was the Ila's household, and Memnanan, and the dark of the Haga.

All the tribes would follow without question. All the villages had to, for good or for ill. The descent showed treacherously steep, a winding stair of sand and rock where they had lost a besha on the last descent: bad enough the last time, and now they had the old and the sick to get down.

Marak, his voices called out, demanding, urging him down that trail. His heart hammered in the disturbance the makers created. But he and his house all waited until Aigyan had reached them.

"Will you go first?" Aigyan asked, offering him the honor

of the leader of all of them, and he shook his head, knowing *that* was not his place.

"I'll wait, *omi*. Go down and set the edge of the camp closer to the cliffs than a sane man would dare, and drive down the deep-stakes and take every precaution: I don't think the sand will fall down. I think the wind will carry it to the ends of the earth. There's a storm coming. It's all I know—a wind stronger than any wind. Better be closer to the cliffs than not."

Aigyan heard him, and thought about it, and nodded, frowning in that consideration. He thought Aigyan understood him.

But he had second thoughts of Tofi and Patya, and when Aigyan and the Keran had started down that slope, he wanted to see his own charges go down early and be safe. "Take care. You'll have our tent. See to it. Don't make any mistakes."

"Yes, *omi*," Tofi said, and asked no questions. But Patya did. "When will you come?" she asked.

"When I've seen the most of our own camp come down. And the Haga. Don't worry about us. If anyone knows the time to go down, we do." He knew, when he had just said it, what compelled him to stay above, the simple drive to see what was coming, whether he was right about the choices he had made all along, and about what he had just asked Aigyan to do—to violate a basic rule of safety in all storms before.

But he could not overstay the margin of time they had. "Just take precautions," he said to Tofi. "I know there'll be a storm. The earth may shake. I don't know if the cliffs will stand, but they're all the windbreak we have. Be very sure of those stakes!"

Patya went with her husband. He was not easy until he saw the both of them pass that place where the besha had died, and until he knew they were down on the easier part of the trail.

Vision flashed across his senses, blinding him. Rock hit sphere.

Norit's besha started forward, compelled by so many

beshti it saw moving. But Marak still reined back. "Go down with her," he said to Hati. "See she doesn't break her neck, or the baby's."

"She doesn't need me," Hati said, defying him. The au'it, also, was having trouble holding her besha, but she held it, and Hati did: two stubborn, purposed women, each with their own intentions. But Norit—and Luz—left them.

Orders could not send Hati away. He knew that Norit had obeyed her voices. He had second thoughts about his own judgment, and wished now he had intervened to keep Lelie and give her to Hati, but Hati was in as much danger, staying with him . . . all of them up here were in danger, on the rim, when the wind came.

Memnanan rode over to them, right at the edge of the descent, as the Ila's servants began to pass onto the downward trail.

"It's bad news from behind us," Memnanan said. "We're hearing that vermin have moved in, right on the line. The priests absolve the living of the duty to bury the dead, and some have just sat down by the line of march. They're out of water. The vermin take them. It's all grim news back there. We're losing the ones we've saved. For the god's sake, Trin Tain, can we let them camp down there? The priests ask. How soon will there be water?"

"Two days," he said. He lied. He had no idea whether they could make that speed to the tower, or what would happen, or how long they would be encamped and under siege from the heavens once the hammer came down. "A storm's coming. There's no chance up here. The Keran will establish their tents down below." He added, calmly, "Your mother and your wife and your aunts have gone down with Keran tribesmen to watch them. Aigyan's in charge, below. Get yourself under shelter once you get there and then set up tents to welcome in those that have just come down. Then give them the same word, everything calm, but push as hard as you can to get canvas up. We will lose lives. The hammer is coming down. It's on its way now. I don't know what may happen next."

"It's coming."

"It's coming," Marak said. He grew calmer in saying it aloud, to a man who understood him. "There's no other consideration."

"The Ila wishes to talk to you, once we're down there."

"I'll come when I can," Marak said. The Ila was, at the moment, the least of his concerns. "Go down with her. Get off the cliff face. Give whatever orders make sense down there, and listen to Aigyan about the camp. I'll *be* there."

Memnanan left them, then, and all the while the sky weighed on their backs, heavy with disaster. The sunlight in a natural sunset had diminished to no more than a faint intimation of light, the sun long behind the western ridges. Below them the head of the column began to unload their tents, a little outward, but not that far from the cliffs, as he had said.

After Memnanan and his men the Haga began their descent: the trail was only wide enough for one at a time, one at a time, one at a time . . . for everyone alive in the world. For everyone who would survive.

The last of the Haga went down.

"Go down now," Marak said to Hati.

"You go," Hati said in a voice scarcely louder than the steady tramp of feet and the occasional complaint of beshti long on the trail and miserable with thirst. "Marak, come with me. Let's not both die here. What are you going to do? Leave Tofi in charge?"

There was an appalling thought, clever as the young man was. Tofi would not forgive him. Tofi would curse him to hell. Patya would not forgive him, for settling the Ila on her husband.

The vision leapt up, the rock and the sphere, only now it was true, and imminent: it filled the sky and the ground. He was somewhere above it all, and saw it coming.

"It's coming down," Hati said. "It's coming down. This is our chance. Please! Come with me!"

Marak, Marak, Marak, his voices said to him, and to Hati, perhaps . . . perhaps to all the mad in the world at once, for all he knew. And he did not want to go, following the voices. All his life he had resisted the voices.

"Get down there," he said to Hati. It was not yet. There was still time.

"You can't help anyone anymore up here. Get down yourself, or I'll stay here, too, I promise you. You're being a fool!"

He looked back at the throng of tribes, not even with a sight of the villages yet, the villages with all they held, all the lives, their whole way of life. The line seemed to go on forever in the dusk, and Memnanan had warned him of increasing desperation and decreasing strength back there. He feared far, far worse might be happening just beyond his view: if the horde at Pori had heard the whisper in the earth of so much movement, caught scent of so many helpless and dying among the dead. What did it take from the heavens, to kill them? The vermin sufficed.

And only the tribes had thrown away their extra weight. To villagers, to the dwellers in houses, everything was precious, everything was necessary. And he could not even pass the word to the first of them, to send sanity back through the line.

"They don't know," he said in despair. "They've no experience—"

Rock hit sphere, and the ring of fire went out and a fountain of cloud went up, and that sphere was lands and water and the sky where the sun was coming over the rim of vast water . . .

It hit. In the vision it hit. It was still coming. But in his foresight it had come down.

And there was such a silence . . .

Soon, Luz said to him, one clear word. Soon.

The beshti and the plodding thousands never heard, never felt, not being mad. The au'it, still with them, making the Ila's record, had written only what they said, in the last of the sunlight of an ordinary day.

"Listen to me," Hati said. "I know what you're doing. I know why you're still up here. But the rest *need* you to be down there, or it's just them, fighting each other. You can't stand up here like a fool waiting for the sky to fall on us. Come on. Come down."

He had made up his mind. He knew he had to admit it

was over, and go. But was it what he had wanted to hear, was it that he knew he wanted too much to listen, and save his own life?

"They're not all going to die up here, if they'll just toss the excess weight off the packs and walk the beshti down—"

"And some don't have the sense, and if we wait long enough, they'll slip off the trail and fall on us and damn the whole rest of the caravan! We can't help it!"

Osan wanted to move. He wanted to, and even knowing better, could not find a way to abandon his responsibility. He searched the rocks, the sand, the sky for an inspiration, and he saw the au'it still writing, by the last of all light in what might be the last day of all the world.

He saw the tall pillar of rock that marked the way down, and the au'it, and he rode close to her and took the ink-cake from her hand, and rode close to that rock. He spat on the ink-cake, dry-mouthed as he was, and drew a line on the rock as high as his chest, and spat again and wrote, as Osan fretted and jolted his writing: *No pack higher than this. Lead the beshti. Walk—*

The ink-cake, half-used, shattered and left fragments in his hand. The coming night would obscure his warning. But all through the night the villages would come to this edge, and the slowest, the less adept would still be coming to it at dawn, if the sun ever rose again, and if the wind delayed, and some of them would listen.

He rode over to a passing tribesman, and showed him the writing, such as it was.

"It marks the safe height of a pack. It says lead the beshti and walk down. Make this the rule! Tell the next tribe! Tell the villages! Leave anything but your tents and your food and water, whatever you have!"

"Yes, Marak-*omi*," the tribesman said, and looked up at the rock and the message, and rode and told another of his tribe. Among the villages, many read.

He had done all he could then. And knew it. He rode toward the gap, the start of the descent, and Hati and the au'it followed him as he rode down onto the trail.

But there, with tribes yet to come, with terror rushing at him in visions, he gripped sanity with both hands and followed his own just-made law, despite the others below him riding down the switchbacks. He slid down afoot, to lead Osan down, and Hati and the au'it dismounted, and so they walked the difficult, shadowed track, a trail only lit by the last glow in the sky.

Behind them the tribe was necessarily slowed in its descent. More, they dismounted and began to do the same, pride cast aside and prudence taking charge at this hazardous edge of night.

After all his worry and agony about the weak and the unskilled, it was that simple. If the tribes began to follow that one prudent example, the villagers would not be more daring or faster, and in the morning the sun would show those still to come the writing on the rock—surely the sun would come up, as surely as the fall of the hammer-stone had to make some change in the world.

Surely that would go on. And the line would come down as long as anyone could.

But it was as if his vision had cleared, as if all the self-made wall against Luz had broken down, and he heard the voices clearly, and he felt himself obeying the pull of the madness he had resisted—all the world seemed in motion again, and Luz was at last content. He walked, and walked with deliberation, thinking not what he could do, but sure now that he set the pace, and that he must not spread panic or make a misstep of his own.

At a turn of the trail he felt the earth shake and go on shaking. Small rocks slid past and quivered underfoot.

Then Osan threw up his head and struggled for footing as part of the trail slid and larger stones came loose. Marak did not attempt to walk for the first moments of that shaking, then decided he had its measure and led on, slowly, very slowly, not letting Osan have his way.

Hati was at his back. The au'it's besha could go no farther, and no faster, and the same with all those behind. Marak kept walking.

The shaking stopped.

Then a false dawn broke. A falling star shot past so close in the sky that the land leapt out in daylight clarity, and shadows traveled from dawn to zenith to set as if a sun had raced across the heavens.

Is that it? he wondered at first sight. Is that the hammer? Inured as they were to wonders, they could not help but watch as it crossed beyond the nighted plain, illumining the cluster of tents far out from the cliffs. Some of the tribesmen called out in alarm.

But it was not the star-fall they feared. His madness told him it was not, that it was still on its way, and he walked, the same as before. The dying star went beyond and lost itself in the distance of the eastern lowlands, where it became Luz's problem. But Luz went on talking to him, steadily now, showing him visions that half blinded him to his sight of the road.

"A star just fell," he said to Luz under his breath, feeling he possibly had her ear for the moment, at this time when Luz must want to know every detail of what transpired. "A star fell toward you. Did you see that? We're going slowly down the cliffs. If we go faster, we'll break our necks. Don't nag me. I need to see. It's dark. It's damned dark and bad ground, and the earth is shaking. I've told them camp close to the cliffs: if there's going to be a storm after this, I'm thinking the wind will carry the sand out, not down on us. Am I right?"

He got nothing but the ring of fire, twice repeated. Was that a wind? Was it fire? Was it anything he knew? He had no idea. He heard no answer. But he heard nothing from the voices, either, so perhaps that silence was Luz's sign that she was thinking about it. It was almost too late for thinking.

He knew that Norit was safe. He felt her presence. He felt, he thought, Lelie's. Tofi had gotten down and put the tent up.

Small stones slid past him, some striking his ankles, and the ground was loose under his feet, so that at the left edge the slide had bitten deeply into the trail. Panic wanted him to go on, ignore the hazard so long as he and Hati cleared it.

But he stopped. He squatted and methodically moved small stones until he hoped he had reinforced the eroded edge. He knew that tribesmen were behind him, and he hoped they would note that and maintain the trail under their own feet, to keep it fit for those that followed. He did the best he could, and when he had done what he could he got up and continued the downward course—no hurry, no haste, no risk he could avoid.

The earth shivered, and Osan, canny beast, simply sat down, quickly, and so the ones behind sat down, while rocks slid and bounced downslope, and gravel slides piled up against the beshti, not getting past them.

A commotion came down with a grating of rock, and a besha, sitting higher up, had simply had the trail give way under it, and slid down the gravel face of a switchback, slowly, ponderously fetching up against Hati's besha in the near dark. Hati's besha held its place, sitting and stable, and the fallen besha slid no farther. Its master came sliding after it, not by his own choice, it seemed. For a moment it seemed more of the trail might come down; but the slide stopped. The tribesmen above had to repair the damage to keep coming. It was their task, in their reach, not his. They did as they could.

Marak ordered Osan up, and in the pragmatic way of beshti, the besha pinned against the slide behind him made methodical efforts toward the open ground, dislodging more rock, while Hati's stubbornly sat fast, as beshti tended to do when they thoroughly had had enough of a situation. Marak seized the bridle and the mounting strap of the fallen besha, tugged in time with its efforts to free its legs, and it suddenly shoved forward, gained its feet, crowding him and crowding Hati.

The beast's embarrassed master reached a place where he could stand, and worked his way past the besha, which stood, barrier between the tribesman and a further slide.

"*Omi,*" the tribesman said, as shaken as a man of his kind was apt to appear, and Marak asked himself whether it was his repair which had given way up above.

But Hati was all right. She had her besha up, and the au'it did, by now. Marak could only keep going, with the tribesman between him and Hati now, the trail impossible for two abreast.

There had been shouting back and forth, the tribesman's kinsmen ascertaining he was alive, and now repairing the trail above them. On their own level, they moved carefully, beshti planting their feet gingerly on ground they no longer trusted, but going on, following those ahead as the gap widened. The instinct to go with the group overrode everything but immediate self-preservation, and Marak, with the bottom of the climb in view, let Osan set his own pace.

Three more sharp turns, three more sloping, rock-cluttered stretches of trail, and they began to go among projecting rocks, in places where they had to clear fallen stones from their way. They had lost sight of the men before, who had ridden down, who had been on lower courses when the shaking came: they were in the dark, now, and the rocks had cut off the view of anyone ahead.

But they came down past rocks Marak remembered from their last descent, and in the murk of the night, in a breathless hush of air, saw the tail of the tribe ahead of them, and tents promising shelter.

Now they could mount up and let the beshti go at their pace, but those still on the climb might take the same cue, and Marak refused. He walked Osan, leading him slowly, and came out onto the flat, where the tribesman who had fallen took his respectful leave and dropped back to join his kin, and where Hati and the au'it overtook him and walked beside him on the widening trail.

A rider came toward them, and then another and a third. The first proved to be Tofi, who had been watching the trail from a distance. In the starlight, under falling stars and on a tremulous earth, Marak saw more tents going up, the camp spreading out its canvas as fast as it could, bracing itself, waiting.

The second rider was Patya, the third, Norit, and they met

under the momentary flare of a falling star and a crash of ruin in the heavens.

Marak met them, touched hands, and Hati joined them, and the au'it, their own au'it, if there was justice at all. Norit stayed mounted, but Tofi and Patya jumped down to embrace them arm to arm. The beshti set to bawling and rumbling, rubbing necks and heads and snuffing familiar scents, as happy as the rest of them, weary as the creatures were, and deserving of rest.

"It's coming. It's coming," Norit said. "Get to shelter, those who can."

"Where's Lelie?" Now he missed her, in the distraction of a hundred thousand lives at risk behind him. But this one he felt, as he felt Norit, as he felt the danger rushing down at them. "Where is she?"

"Memnanan's wife has her," Patya said. "The Ila's in a fit. We've put the stakes down, deep, and we've braced the side canvas. Norit says the danger will come from the west, to dig in and put the webbings on. We hope we're dug in enough."

The ring of fire flashed across Marak's vision. For a moment he failed to know where he was, whether he was floating in the air or standing . . . as if, having stopped defying Luz, now he suffered all the pent-up visions, the impact, the ring of fire, and now a fountain of cloud, something going up and up, fire, or cloud, or water—he was not sure.

"Marak!" Hati cried. He reached out blindly for her, found her arm, held to her for a moment that the whole world seemed to turn and sway under them. Then he began to walk, urgently, desperately, toward the tents, and Hati stayed with him.

"Every tent," he said to those he met. "If you're done, help others. Fast as we can make it. Storm's coming. Eat. Drink."

"The water, *omi*," Tofi reminded him. "We're almost out of water. Even the Ila's out of water."

"Every man drink a sip, and eat a bite, and turn out to pitch tents as fast as they come in before the wind hits. Free and slave, the Ila's men, the tribes, all of us. We'll be doing it as long as we have time, all night and into the morning—in the calm or in whatever rolls in on us." He still could see nothing but the ring of fire, over and over again. He had held Luz at bay this long. He had ridden to Pori and back. Now Osan's strength was spent, and Osan would not kneel for him, so blind and half deaf to the world, he walked and walked, and tried to maintain his awareness of the world under feet gone all but numb.

He thought that Tofi and Patya had mounted up again, and he thought the au'it had lost her grip on her besha's rein and it had gone ahead of them toward the tents, but that was all right. The beshti all knew where their own herd was, and where their own tents were pitched.

Thirst had his mouth and throat all but incapable of swallowing: the air was dry as dust, and over the course of their walking, this close to safety, he offered Hati a sip of the water he personally carried, but, prudent, she had her own, and drank a sip. For himself, he drank the skin dry, the last bit, telling himself somehow there would be more, and somehow Luz would see them supplied, after all they had passed, but he was not through with his work. He had to wring more out of a body already exhausted, which needed water now, and no matter the thirst to come. He would not be through until every living survivor was down the cliffs and under canvas.

"The waters will rise up," Norit's voice cried behind him, thin and high, a voice divorced from reality. "The bitter waters will rise up like a wall and that wall will go out to overflow the edges of the world! It's coming down! It's already falling!"

Marak wished her quiet. He saw these things in his own mind when she said them. He had no idea what he was seeing until Norit named them, but she pulled the images into terrible clarity.

"The earth will crack! The bitter water pour in on the forge, and the heat of it will go up like a furnace, like water cast onto hot iron!"

It was the fountain he saw. He had thought it was cloud in the sky.

"The hammer will fall!" Norit shouted at the heavens, at

those behind them, at anyone near her who would listen. "The earth will ring like an anvil! The wind will come, stronger than any wind before!"

Marak turned, staggering in the giving sand. "When?" he shouted back at Norit. "How much time, woman? *Will it blow the sand over us? Are we too close to the cliffs?*"

But Norit was not sane enough for that reckoning, and continued to shout about cracks in the earth and pools of fire in a voice that broke, ragged with thirst.

He turned back. He walked. They walked, almost at the tents, and when they looked back, the line of those still coming toward them went on back into the dark, in the starlight, as far as the cliffs of the Lakht, on that trail where the tribes still descended and where the villagers—the foremost of the villagers—had yet even to reach the cliffs.

The weak almost certainly could not do it. There would be falls. Fatalities.

There remained nothing—nothing at all Marak found to do for them, once he reached their own tent.

"Death comes down on us!" Norit shouted in his distant hearing, distracted, gone wandering, disturbing other hearers, and Marak moved to stop her, but Hati held his arm and tugged at him.

"Let her go. She'll know when to go to cover, more than the rest of us, she'll know. Luz won't let her die. She moves everyone to work. We all have to do something when we hear that."

"We can't have panic. We're going to need every hand in camp. Every clear wit." Osan pulled at the reins, wanted his freedom, and his just reward, and Marak had not the strength left in him to unsaddle and care for him. He staggered to a stop.

Tofi took the rein from his hand without a word, and Patya took Hati's, as Tofi called Bosginde and Mogar to tend the beshti and get them unsaddled.

"I'll need another besha," Marak said hoarsely, "one that hasn't trekked to Pori and back. I'm too tired to walk, and I've got to talk to Aigyan. To Memnanan and Menditak."

"Then I need one, too," Hati said, exhausted as she was, and Marak said not a word to stop her, knowing he might need her to reason with Aigyan. The hush about the camp, the near-stifling stillness of the wind, warred with the chaos in his vision and the racket in his ears, warning, continually warning him, if he knew how to hear it, how short the time was . . . but only Norit had that burden, to take the message straight in and not to shut it out.

And Norit ran mad among the tents.

Sensible men around him, however . . . sensible men around them did sensible jobs, the only sort of thing they knew how to do. In astonishingly short order there were beshti saddled and even more precious water offered, and it took as much strength to refuse that as it needed for him to get into the saddle again.

Tofi got under him and, in undignified fashion, shoved, not asking if he needed help. Hati made it up mostly on her own, at the last with Mogar's help, and Marak reined off into the dark, threading through the little space there was, past the resting beshti, in among the Keran tents—Aigyan first, Aigyan, whose lead the tribes might follow.

And Menditak, the canny, the quick, the old man who had outlived most of his enemies . . . and befriended the greatest of them.

And somewhere amid it all, he searched for the Ila's captain.

24

Any tent, when the storm comes.
—Kerani proverb

Marak, the voices dinned in his hearing, voices thrumming with anxiety and disaster, while the dark and the open flat resounded with the sound of hammers and mallets.

Deep-stakes went down; and over all the commotion ranged the hoarse voices of tribesmen shouting orders, and arranging a storm camp, tents placed for best protection in the likelihood of a wind from the west . . . west had become the source of danger: Marak was sure of it in his own heart. West for danger, east for salvation.

Beshti complained in the lack of water and food. Children cried in the tents, weary and hungry and thirsty, but the very little little water there was, the tribes guarded closely and would not give up.

The Ila's tent was up and secure, staked deep in the stony sand. Lights shone inside it, making the canvas glow . . . because the Ila had lamp oil, carried along where water would have been far more useful.

There were instead, Marak recalled, all those books, the weight of which would have supplied the whole camp—

For what? For a day, on short rations? What was one day?

For those caught above the cliff, it was everything. It was the difference, for thousands, between getting off the Lakht to shelter—or not: but water could not give them time. Only the skies could give them that. Only his decisions, to camp, to move on, all the decisions during all the trek, could have given them that time—and those were his, balanced against this necessity and that and the strength of the villagers to keep moving. Those were his. He did not know whether they were the wisest decisions—the best economy of lives.

And when he thought how very many must still be up there on the cliffs, still making the perilous descent, still trapped between thirst and vermin, he could scarcely wrap his mind about the enormity of what he had told Luz he would do and what consequence every decision of his might have had.

He wielded a hammer himself in the dark, as camp after camp went up. Every tribe took their hammers and set the tents of all those that arrived, so that as fast as weary tribes reached the edge of the camp, the camp swallowed them up and gained workers.

Hati swung a hammer with him. Like others, like Tofi and Mogar and Bosginde, like Antag and his brothers, and every able man and woman, they wrapped their hands and worked and still bled . . . but in the mad, the makers swelled their hands with fever and activity. He and Hati healed as they bled, and as they exhausted themselves, strength came from somewhere. Villagers began to arrive, and young men and old, urged by the tribes, began to join the effort.

As for Norit, she wandered wherever she wandered in the camps, never quite out of their awareness, as the visions were constantly in their awareness.

Hammer, hammer, and hammer against the deep-irons, image of the hammer to come against the earth. Luz spoke to the mad, constantly, a nuisance that became, strangely, a reassurance that the tower still stood. They knew Luz was aware. They knew they were not forgotten, not yet, not now: death was coming, but the hammerblow was not yet on them.

Another tent rose, men and women pulling on the ropes, shouting together as the center poles came up and another canvas peak aimed at the uncertain heavens. Webbing went on, tied to the deep-irons, weighted with rocks where they could lay hands on them, to secure the frail canvas from billowing up in a gust.

The hammer-wielders advanced on another row of stakes, as women took another bundle cast from another packsaddle, and those villagers whose old and weak they had just scarcely sheltered joined them like the rest and took their efforts to another bundled tent, villagers unfurling canvas side by side with the tribes.

Another tent, and another. The camp spread and spread outward and sideways, onto every patch of sand that would take the stakes: the camp grew broader and deeper at a pace that had now the repetition of a machine, a pace that left the workers breathless, and a determination that continually sucked new workers into the frenzy. Any man, any woman who could unpack canvas or haul on rope surely became ashamed to sit still.

Still the new arrivals came down, and spread out, and kept spreading with that breathless speed—now and again a worker fell half-conscious on the sand, and lay with the weak, in a strange tent, cared for, given meager help, and two and three and four more newly arrived villagers took his place.

Hammer-sound echoed off the cliff face along a broad front, and beshti filed by, some laden with baggage, and riding beasts carrying the old and the young and led by the hale and fit: they worked through all this, and the earth shook, and shook again, and stars fell so near they lit the sky in untimely dawns, noons, and twilights, but they never ceased: men rested when they must, drove in stakes as they could regain their strength, as the villagers came down, staggering, some clinging to the beshti's mounting loops, scarcely able to point out their tents amid the baggage, and their water-starved beshti so anxious to sit down it was difficult to get the saddles off them.

Here was reason to keep working. Even the pragmatic tribesmen found reason to press their strength further, to provide minimal shelter, if not lifesaving water, and, in the way of the tribes in extremity, they pitched tents now in common, long constructions webbed down with whatever cordage they could manage, for villagers to pool resources and stay alive if they could.

But even men who had come in staggering with weakness managed to haul cord to shelter their families, and a few, the hardiest, having caught a little wind, joined the rest of them as they hammered and unpacked and spread canvas and snugged it down.

Here and there villages more prudent and better-led than the rest came in better condition, and some gave their water to strangers' children, because, one young idealist said, paradise was close and there would be no end of water.

Paradise was *not* close. The hammerfall was. *Marak, Marak,* the voices began to say, and while the cliffs cut all view of the Lakht, Marak could feel the fall like doom hanging over his shoulder. Closer, now, closer and closer.

Hati still worked with him. She placed the stakes and he hammered, and sometimes she directed villagers who grew confused in handling the ropes, an art she knew in her sleep, if she had had the strength left to manage it. Her hands bled. Marak's did.

Marak! the warning came to him. He saw the ring of fire, three times repeated. He saw the fall of stone on sphere, and it seemed he knew where Norit was, that she had found a besha and came desperately toward them.

Then he did see her: in the dark, mad as ever she was, Norit came riding toward him, but she came with Tofi, with Patya, and them leading beshti with them.

"The star is coming down," Norit said, Luz said. "Get to shelter *now!* Everyone get to shelter. It's coming. *It's coming down!*"

In his own vision he saw what he had always seen. But he believed her. He stopped his work and stood still, dazed, seeing all these men, tribesmen, who had come farther and farther from their tents and from safety . . . that was his first clear thought at the warning, that it was not only a question of his safety, and above that, Hati's, but of Tofi and all these other men.

But other men had heard the prophet. A panic began in that moment, even among the brave.

It tried to rise in him, the moment he gave it any room. "Hati," he said. "Spread the word. Then get home." *Home,* he said, like a villager fool, when Norit, their beacon, had come out here, so that in all this expanse of tents neither of them knew where that was.

But suddenly he did know. He knew, Norit knew, he thought Hati knew, and he thought strangely enough that, in the heart of all the world, a baby with the makers in her knew where the ones who loved her were standing at this very moment.

"Lelie's our beacon home," he said on a hoarse breath, and climbed to the saddle and took the offered rein. "Follow it! Spread the word: the storm's coming. Get to cover! *Now!*" He turned and waved and lifted his voice in the loudest shout he could make clear. "Hindmost tents, take in all comers! Spread the word! Spread the word! Get the beshti sheltered! Take in the stranger! Take in your worst enemy! In all the world, there's only us, and the storm!"

Men began shouting one to another, and what had been methodical work became hasty, then frantic effort, the last tents going up, the last webbing snugged down, the last-arrived wailing about their safety, their relatives, their belongings still without shelter.

Marak rode north, along the face of the camp, shouting at villagers just getting to shelter and at men still working. He heard the warning spreading up and down the rows, and back deep among the farther tents. *Take cover, take cover,* men shouted, when the night seemed as clear as any morning in the world, and not a breath of wind stirred.

But slowly, from the darkest dark of night, the detail of

ropes and irons began to seem clearer, and clearer, and he realized to his horror that the dawn was coming out of the west, not the east.

He looked back toward the cliffs and up, where climbers still labored downward . . . still they came, with shelter so close, and it was too late.

His voices clamored at him, and it might have been a moment, a heartbeat, the blink of an eye that he stared, but then he laid his quirt to the besha he rode and put the terror at his back.

Light sheeted above them, went on across the face of the world, throwing distant mountains into relief, showing them the whole world in a lightning stroke, leaving him nothing but the will to get the ones with him to shelter, where Lelie was—center of the world, that place, that refuge, that safety where Hati would go, and Norit. He saw tents around him, sitting beshti, exhausted, lifting their heads toward the strange dawn.

Marak tucked low, ready for quake or wind or whatever might come, rode and rode past tents and men straggling back to their own families, their own tribes, running now, desperately.

This light instead of fading only increased, and as he rode to the last tents, as he slid down to stand on the earth and looked up next to his own beshti, he saw a murky fire above the cliffs in the west, a fire shedding that unnatural glow in the sky above their heads.

He saw Norit and Hati arrive, and seized their reins, and helped them down. Tofi and Patya followed.

"The sea boils up!" Norit cried, her face turned up to that red-glowing sky. "A pillar of cloud goes up and burns with light, up and up and up, and the bitter water and heavens are overturned." She lifted up arms bare against that red, western dawn, and for a moment she seemed caught in that vision, spread against the sky, dyed in light.

Marak seized her, pulled her toward the tent.

The earth suddenly shook as if the world had broken. Beshti went down, some sitting down, one, Norit's, thrown down off its feet. Marak lost his footing, and protected Norit with his elbows. The tent and shelter was just next to them, while the shaking continued, and continued, and continued.

Then stopped. The whole world, lit red, caught its breath. The air was still. Marak moved, got a knee under him, got the other to bear and got up. Their tent was still standing. The au'it stood at the doorway, red-robed, expressionless recorder of all she saw.

Hati and Patya and Tofi tried to help him up, and he got up, hauled Norit to the doorway, used her body to brush the storm flap out of his path. Hati was at his back, all of them were there, and they tried to help him in the blind dark inside. It was all he could do, to carry Norit. His strength was flowing out of him fast; and when he reached what he thought was their place, their mats, he fell, trying to kneel, and bruised his knees in doing it.

He let Norit down from hands numb with swelling.

"Lelie," Norit said. "Lelie, Lelie, Lelie!"

She wanted her baby. Luz had left her. But Lelie was not his at the moment to give, and he knew at least Lelie was there, and Hati was. It was dark in the tent, while fire raced across the skies. He called for Patya, to be sure she was there, and Tofi; and hearing answers he fell down on the mat and lay there, only breathing, thinking of the beshti, still under saddle, and the people still on the road, and worst of all, caught on the cliffs with the storm still coming . . . since come it would.

They could still get behind rocks, at a last resort. He wished them to think of it, simply to snug down with whatever canvas they could secure against something strong—but he was powerless to help them, powerless in all events now. If the sky was burning—if the earth shook like that—what hope was there?

He shut his eyes, but the visions persisted. Stone had hit the sphere. The ring of fire had gone out, and that was what sheeted over them. He knew it now. He got up on a fevered, exhausted effort, and put his head out to see what he could.

There was as yet no sign of storm, only that unnatural glow in the sky, a glow enough now to cast a shadow.

The hammer of heaven had struck a spark to set the sky afire. But the wind—the wind was yet to come. A few more might straggle into the tents. A few more might live.

He knelt in the doorway of the tent, on knees numb with exhaustion, his arms and back afire with fever, and he felt Hati take his arm. He felt her presence, felt Norit's, Lelie's, continually. Norit and Lelie had found each other.

A new vision came: a pillar of cloud, lit red, spreading light across the heavens.

The bitter water, Norit had said. The hammer of heaven would come down in the bitter water, and the fountain would go up, and the earth would crack like a pot, pouring out fire.

Had they not felt the earth break?

"It shines like a lamp," Norit said. "The heat of it goes out and the ashes will fall and fall. The hammer is down."

If it were himself alone he might sit down in the doorway in a fit of shivering and watch what came next. As it was, he felt Hati's hand, and moved his hand to Hati's, felt her fingers, as swollen and rough and wounded as his own, and dragged his gaze away from the awful sky and toward the look she gave him.

"We're going to *live*," she said, and set her jaw in that way Hati had, and he loved her, he loved her so much in that moment he could look away from the sky.

But vision came, a vision of sky and dark, and it came, and it came, a ring of darkness behind the ring of fire.

Marak! the voices cried all at once.

He pulled the storm flap shut, worked with swollen fingers to lace it tight.

It was coming, it was coming, he said to himself, seeing the ring of fire and the ring of darkness again and again and again. Inside, Tofi told Mogar and Bosginde to pull the storm lines tight and hold on, back at the weather side of the tent, back where they had put their baggage: storm rigging—lines connected to the webbing above the canvas were anchored inside the tent, around the weight of the baggage. If anything held, those lines would hold, pressing the tent down harder the more the wind blew to lift it up.

They took their places inside, in the dark, with no lamp burning.

They braced. They sat ready. Marak joined those holding the lines. Hati did. Memnanan's wife and aunts and mother held one another, and Norit with Lelie and the au'it as well he thought had moved near them.

Thunder came first—and the ground shuddered with that thunder, a rhythmic beating like that of many footsteps: beshti from end to end of the camp bellowed alarm.

Wind hit like a fist, hit, and began to pull at the ropes, trying to lift the tent. The ropes began to vibrate, and hummed with the assault, and Marak gripped the rope, robbed of breath, as if the very strength of the air had been swept away around them. Ears congested; night-blind eyes seemed to swell in their sockets, and Marak shut his eyes tight, squinted down, to keep them from bursting, and pulled on the rope, and felt its vibration going through his arms, through his bones, and up from the sand under them. He might have shouted. Others might have. He was deaf, and his ears were bursting.

Debris hit the tent, a heart-stopping impact that hung and beat against them, threatening to destroy them. A wave of cold came. Still the wind beat at them, indistinguishable from earthquake. Marak bit his lip and hung on, and held on, feeling the line shake under the stress. Hearing had all but gone, but the vibration in his bones had a voice, the wind's voice. Distanced by the congestion in his ears, it had voices wherever it found a chink, an inlet, and it wailed, it howled, it roared. *Marak,* his voices raged at him, but they were small against that voice. The visions showed him ruin and the ring of fire and the ring of darkness—and this was it, he thought, this surely must be the worst.

His hands gripping the rope were beyond pain: cord met raw flesh, and he would not let go, would not give up their tent to the wind. They were the outermost of the crescent of tents: they were the ones exposed to the greatest force of that wind coming off the cliffs, with no shelter at all but the tents behind them, and if their position was wrong, they were dead, but the sand was going past them . . . was going *over* their heads, in a wind greater than any wind that had ever blown.

A second object hit the back tent wall, something huge that flapped about and rumbled over the top of them with indistinct sound: it might have been a tent blown loose, its people dead in an instant in this wind, its goods carried away on the storm front. The seams of the tent strained, and sand rubbing against the canvas was a force that could wear away the threads, secure an opening, and if there began to be an opening, the wind could tear it wide.

Marak held on. He had for days denied the voices, and now, like a penitent thief, he hoped for some answer from Luz: in extremity and fear for all their lives he begged for a voice, contritely, obediently, ready to surrender to his voices if only they would tell him what to do.

He held, and the wind that came now was not the slight coolth and strange smell of deep sands overturned. This wind stank with a stench that raised the fine hairs on his nape, an indescribable mix of scents, things that never have been carried into the light, the depth of the destruction of Pori, and Oburan, and the overthrow of the bitter water itself. It smelled like a forge confounded with a graveyard, it smelled of the wind off the high mountains and the rotting bottom of a garden. It was all these things, and the wind grew louder, and louder, and louder and his ears more and more congested, until he thought his head must burst in the next instant.

Then, like an immense weight on their shoulders, the storm began to let them go, and passed them with a roar so deep the ground seemed again to thump in its going.

Someone wept. Lelie set up a wail drowned by the wind.

Then a woman's voice came clear in a sharp, gasping cry for help, and he began to realize that it was Memnanan's wife.

"It's now!" the lady cried, breathless, terrified, and then Marak understood the commotion and dismay. Her baby was on its way, in the dark, in the storm, in the noise that drowned everything but the loudest shouts.

Even so, the wind was falling. The ache in his ears subsided. He had no knowledge of birthing babies, but he knew beshti, and he knew the storm that had rolled over them might have brought it on. His ears might clear, but the woman had no such relief. The birth pangs were not likely to stop, once started, no matter what the storm did, no matter the things that could go terribly wrong if the baby was not ready to come.

He heard a commotion among the women. Lelie, apparently shunted aside in the confusion and the dark, wailed her distress and her fear in the dark, but he thought Norit had her. The women asked each other advice, gathered about Memnanan's wife: Norit had birthed a child. Memnanan's mother assuredly had.

"What can we do?" he heard Tofi ask, and he heard Patya and Hati and then even Bosginde talking to Memnanan's mother, their voices even so smothered by the wind and the racket of the canvas, and by the bubbles that seemed lodged painfully inside his ears.

Memnanan was out of reach. It was folly to try to bring him: their tent had stopped trying to fly away, but it still shuddered to gusts strong enough for any storm. The sand would be too thick to breathe out there.

Marak cautiously released the rope he had held, forced locked, swollen fingers to move. His mouth was so dry his throat felt coated with dust. He rubbed at a coating of fine, dry dust on his face and about his eyes, and made matters worse. He hardly had strength left to lift his arms.

"Can we get a light?" Memnanan's mother pleaded.

They had a lamp, the most basic sort of lamp, as every tent had, in their dwindling store of supplies. It was something men could do. Feeling their way in the raucous dark, he and Tofi and the slaves got the elements together from their baggage.

Then it was another lengthy and doubtful process to light it while the wind ripped and battered at the canvas. Mogar carried a small flintwheel, that most elementary of firestarters in a desert night, but drafts through the tent lacings quenched the sparks they raised.

They lacked quick-fire, or any other element to make it easy. Bosginde, however, said he could do it, and they were able, finally, to bring fire to a dry nest of fibers and what seemed strands of Bosginde's hair, and then to a piece of oil-soaked wick. All the while the tent shook under the gusts, and they used their bodies for a windbreak.

The fibers in the cut end of the cord glowed minutely. It was a race between their fire going out and the wick taking light, and Marak yanked out a loop of his own hair to keep the little flame going; Tofi did, and the fire still went out, the middle of the hair loops burning through too quickly.

But the wick had just caught, and in their deep dark and the overthrow of the world, it cast comforting light on worried men's faces—it reached up and illumined tent canvas that quivered under the steady onslaught of the wind, and it reached aside to the women's circle.

Carefully, carefully, shielding the light all the way, Marak turned and gave it to Hati. It lit female faces, the lady's, the mother, the aunts, and Hati and Patya and Norit—and, distressed and tremulous of lip, Lelie. The au'it, too, was there, frowning and without advice—the Ila's virgin servant.

In the violence of a sudden gust the lady screamed, but the wind drowned the most of it, and Marak sat unhappily listening to a pain he could not help. It would be what it was. If there was anyone to intervene, the women knew, the women would.

"It's her first," Marak said to Tofi with a shake of his head. "It's a month early. It's the storm. I hope that baby is brave enough to be born."

"They don't ever change their minds, do they?" Tofi asked.

"Not often. Not when it's this far." Excluding some wisdom of the an'i Keran that he had never heard, the birth was in progress. Not to the good of the mother would the baby change its mind now.

The au'it, incredibly, spread her book and wrote, slanting

it to the little light there was. The record resumed. The world went on. Marak drew a wider breath.

Tofi even dared take a brief look outside, through the lacings.

"They're alive out there," he reported of the beshti. "I don't know how."

They sat, waterless, without easy rest. The wind blew. The labor went on and on, until at last the women clearly despaired of what they saw, and roused the lady up and supported her from either side in a walk about the tent, around and around and around, while Bosginde sheltered the lamp for them.

The lady lay down again. Got up again.

"Is it any closer?" Marak asked Hati.

"No," Hati said. "No. It isn't."

There was yet another circuit of the tent, but the lady failed and collapsed in the women's arms, screaming in misery none of them could help, crying for her husband, her own mother, people none of them could find. Lelie began to cry, and the wind howled, never less than storm force.

"She wants her husband," Marak said. "If she wants her husband, he's not that far."

"*Omi*," Tofi began to protest, but his voice trailed off under a series of gasping cries from the lady.

"If I can see the tent, I'll make it."

"Take a rope," Tofi pleaded with him, Tofi, who had lost a father and brothers to an ill-advised venture out in a storm less than this one.

He had no need of a rope: he could find Hati blind and across the width of the Lakht . . . he had become convinced of that. But Tofi gave him a coil of cord otherwise set aside for repair, and he gave one end to Tofi to hold.

Then he took a tight wrap of his aifad, unlaced the storm flap and escaped the pain and anguish inside the tent into a hell on earth outside.

It had begun to be daylight. The air outside was all red dust, beshti half-buried and with windburn so bad the wounds were caked and plastered with the same red as the air. He had lied. He could *not* see the Ila's tent, but he remembered where it had been when they set up camp; he ached with the need to do something more than sit waiting—and if it were Hati, he knew he would want to know; and there were debts, to the lady, to Memnanan. There were debts that asked a risk. There was, below it all, a need to know what the state of affairs was in the camp, a need to reach someone outside their tightly clenched world and reassure himself there were other living souls.

He walked out from the lee of the tent, staggering in the gusts—there was the hard part, maintaining his orientation when he was blown half off his feet and blinded by dust, but the wind itself was a direction marker, and he walked, with the wind battering his left shoulder.

He counted two intervening tents, the Ila's servants or her guards had crowded up their tents between: he had not marked *who* was in the tents, but he had remembered they were there.

He made his way past two groups of beshti in no better and no worse condition than their own, sandy, wind-scoured ghosts in the red murk that passed for daylight.

Now the way was straight out of that wind-shadow across a narrow gap of blowing sand, and to the Ila's tent, with two others pitched up against it.

He was blind for a moment, then found the ropes, and followed the side of the main tent around to the sheltered east end, where the storm flap was laced tight. The wind gusted: canvas shook to a wind so hard and sand-edged it abraded his exposed hands. He saw fraying on a taut edge of the canvas itself, and bones—*bones,* scoured white, that had blown up against the tent wall, along with minute scraps of cloth tattered to rags, buried in sand.

"Memnanan!" he called out. "Captain!"

He could cut his way in, ruining precious cordage, risking the tent, but he waited at the door, and shouted twice more before a voice answered him and someone began to work at the lacings inside. In a moment more the storm flap lifted slightly, and one of the Ila's servants looked at him, wide-eyed at the apparition that came to them out of the storm.

The servant did not release the flap or widen the opening. Marak thrust his arm in, to prevent the servant sealing it up again.

"I'm Marak Trin," he said, pulling the aifad down, "and I'm here for Memnanan. His wife's in labor. Bring him."

"Stay there!" the servant told him, and disappeared.

Stay outside, in a storm that burned the skin, by bones the wind had scoured and dropped at the door.

Marak shoved the flap wider, tearing at the lacings he could reach, and widened it enough to step inside, into a canvas foyer lit with a brass lamp. He had brought the last of his cord-coil in with him, his link with Tofi. He cast it down there, brushed off enough sand from his robes to leave a haze on the figured carpet, and waited, fighting a dry cough and a mouth so dusty his tongue had stopped sticking to his teeth.

Memnanan came through to meet him, Memnanan—clean, well fed, showing none of the desperate condition of the rest of the camp, no more than the servant.

"Your wife," Marak began, and coughed with the dryness of his throat: his voice shredded with it. "Your wife is in labor. She's having some difficulty. I've rigged a guide rope. You can follow it over there."

Memnanan's worry was evident, but he made no move toward the door, rather had his hand on the curtain through which he had entered, as if at any instant he would go back to his duty. "I can't," Memnanan said. "I can't go. Go back!"

Go back. A man dismissed his wife's possible death with that *go back.* A man stood with his hand on that curtain as if it concealed the secrets of heaven and earth.

Something was wrong in this tent. Something was damned wrong, give or take a man's natural embarrassment at having water enough, and food enough.

"Is something the matter with the Ila?" he asked.

"For your own safety—" Memnanan's voice dropped. "*Go.*"

He was ready to. He believed the captain. He had no reason to doubt Memnanan's loyalty to the Ila had just met the edge of his personal debt, and Memnanan warned him the Ila was in no good mood.

But he stood there . . . on the edge of his own debt to this man, even to the Ila, he hesitated to wonder what *was* behind Memnanan's refusal.

And it was one heartbeat too long. An au'it brushed aside the curtain the captain held: the au'it, with her book, stopped, looking steadily at Memnanan, and retreated.

"She'll tell the Ila I'm here," Marak said. "She'll tell the Ila we talked. But the Ila doesn't care, man. Get to your wife, while you have a wife!"

"Get out," Memnanan said to him. "Go. Now."

They had survived the hammerfall. They had not yet survived the storm, and the Ila kept secrets, or the Ila's staff did. Memnanan was afraid of something here besides the sky that roared destruction against the tent walls.

And suddenly came a sound of a tent wide curtain singing back on its rings.

"Get out!" Memnanan repeated.

Their own parted in the same abrupt way and opened the tent all the way to where the Ila sat. A man stood by her, a man indistinct of origin, aifad wrapped up to the eyes, neither quite tribesman, not quite villager in what he wore.

But Marak stood stock-still, with no attention to the Ila, seated on her chair: his vision was all the man beside her, that figure dislocated from here and the Ila's presence in memory of his own home, his own hearth. That man, that same figure, identical in the wrap of the aifad and the pitch of the shoulders, the stance of the feet . . . could not possibly be his father. It could not be, standing by the Ila, before the aui'it, free, and armed.

But the companion reached up a hand and pulled down the aifad; and it *was* his father's face. It was Tain, armed, and free, and in the Ila's close company.

"Father," Marak said. His thoughts skittered this way and that, helpless between surmise that the Ila was a prisoner and surmise that this improbable conjunction was a vision, like

the star-fall, like the ring of fire and the pillar of cloud—or
that the Ila had no idea who this man was.

"I said I might take a husband," the Ila said with a wave of
her hand. "Have I offended you, Marak Trin? Do you object?"

He pulled down his own aifad, and tried to find any advantage, even any sanity, on either side of this maneuver.

"You're both mad," he said, *he* said . . . the madman, in the
presence of Tain Trin Tain, the arbiter of sanity.

"He has all your advantages," the Ila said, "a leader, and
desert-wise, and one more. He's *not* Luz's creature."

"Whatever you say to me," he reminded the Ila, appalled,
thinking even then that the Ila might damn them all, "Luz
knows."

"Oh, I know she knows. But you don't know as much as
you think. Neither does she." The Ila rose from her chair and
stood, red-robed, not a tall woman, a figure of flame red silk,
with that white, white skin unmarred by the desert. "*Memnanan* has a new commander."

There had been the instant in which thought simply
failed him. But rational thought came back, began to assess
the ground, the conditions, the hazards. There were curtains
to either side of the Ila's chair. He knew the configuration of
the Ila's tent from outside, how servants' tents abutted. He
knew his father's tactics, he knew that curtain might never
have gone back if his father was unwilling to have this confrontation, even if the Ila willed it.

There might be ten, twenty men behind those side curtains. Or aui'it. Or simply servants.

Go back, Memnanan had warned him with all his might,
and that had said everything about Memnanan's situation . . .
and the danger.

"My mother would warn you against your choice," he said
to the Ila, with all possible meaning. "You're being a fool."

Did that score on his father? Tain's face, image of his own
as it might someday be, held no expression for an enemy,
and he had become that. Kaptai's son, the madman, the embarrassment, had necessarily become the enemy.

"More," he said, chasing whatever quarry he might have started in the Ila's mind, "did I mention that he'd killed four *other* Haga? Did he mention Menditak and Aigyan have sworn water peace on his account, and mean to kill him? Your ally brings you every tribesman alive for enemies."

"I'm aware of their opinion," the Ila said. "But you take Luz's orders. Is that better? You can take his orders, now . . . or you can decide not to. Luz may have other intentions. What will those be?"

Prudence told him to lie, but the business between him and his father said his father would never believe a soft answer. "Common sense says he's a dead man. And he knows it. He won't say a word to me, will he? *Will he?*"

There was, in fact, only a stony stare, a stony, unpleasant stare; and he knew what his father had come to do, and what his father had *had* to accept, and the conditions he had had to take . . . the Ila's outrageous offer: *life,* and the unlikeliest, most fragile alliance.

"He's *ashamed*. He's disgraced himself with Kais Tain, he's alienated the tribes, he's sold out his own village, and he's sold himself to you to seal the bargain because he has nowhere else to go. Like *me,* like *me,* father, just the same. Don't tell me otherwise."

The curtains at either hand stirred. He was not surprised. He assailed Tain and four more of Tain's men showed up, men whose names he knew, every one: killers, men with *machai* in their hands—able to kill the Ila, but bent instead on silencing an unpleasant, unwelcome voice.

And was Tain stronger for their backing? Marak looked his father in the eyes, and they both knew the truth.

"Give up," Marak said. "The Haga won't trust you. And I won't. There *is* no bargaining."

Tain drew his pistol, wanting to make him flinch: Marak knew the moment, knew the gesture, knew when his father had done that to other men, knew his father wanted, *needed* that moment of fear before he pulled the trigger.

Marak jumped for the wind-stretched side of the tent and the shot burned through his side and through the tent wall as he moved, letting loose a shriek of wind—and off that wall, he lunged not at the men who drew knives, but beyond them, through them, at Tain himself, and his gun.

A *machai* caught in his coat and raked his ribs. Another sliced across his back as he seized hold of his father's left sleeve and wrestled for a grip on the trigger hand.

The gun went off. Went off twice and three times as they struggled for grip and balance: a man swung a *machai* at his back and he swung his father into the glancing blade as a fourth shot creased his shoulder. He grasped the gun in Tain's hand and tried to force his finger into the trigger guard. Fifth shot: it hit something metal and fragile, and he would not turn his back to his father's men, would not give up, no matter his father had one hand on his face, trying to get a thumb into his eye or a grip on his ear, trying to swing his back to his allies. They had fought a thousand mock fights; they had fought mock fights that turned real, fights he had to lose or have his father's spite; but not this fight, not this one, not now.

They staggered together into an obstacle, a tent pole, and Tain tried to bash his hand off the gun, tried to break his finger in the process, and kneed him and brought a foot down on his instep, all of which he gave back with a blow to Tain's head—where his father's men were in this, what they waited for, he had no idea: he turned, jerked Tain around, looking for enemies in the process.

Tain fell and dragged him down, leaving Marak's back exposed. Marak rolled, put himself underneath and in the process gave Tain the heel of his hand under his chin with everything he had in his arm. He saw Tain dazed for a moment. Men hacked at the rolling knot of their bodies, and in one moment a *machai* hacked down into his back, but he had a deathlock on the gun and meant to batter Tain loose from the one weapon that equalized the odds.

"Marak!" someone shouted, a shot exploded near his ear, two shots that had not come from the pistol. In the same moment Tain butted him in the face, but he regarded neither—got his best grip on the gun and twisted, and rolled, turning Tain's arm under him, seeing in his blurred vision that Tain could *not* let go the gun, but had no command of it either. He had a leverage: he had a hand free: he seized Tain's wrist and rolled loose.

He gained his feet, soaked in blood. He faced his father, half-winded, with the contested gun in hand.

Then he saw Memnanan with a rifle, and three of his father's men down, and the fourth wounded. The Ila sat on her chair amid all of it, in the most incredible attitude of calm.

The fourth man broke and ran. Marak stared dead-on at Tain and Tain at him. The truth he tried not to betray was that his trigger finger was too mangled to function: maintaining that stare, he changed to a two-handed grip, and Tain returned him that *hell with you* glare that he turned on any infraction against his authority . . . that old, old implication of threat and disdain for the odds.

Not beaten, not Tain. Not until he was dead. And it was on him to do it.

"Get out of here!" he yelled at Tain, last chance, last try. "*Get out of here!*"

He knew he was a fool when he gave Tain the chance. Tain's expression changed to that cocksure confidence his enemies dreaded. Tain backed a step and turned.

Memnanan fired, and took Tain dead in the middle, and twice more to be sure. Tain died at his feet, and he stood there, numb.

And after that it was themselves, and the aui'it, and the red-robed Ila, who sat on her throne with her hand pressed to her side and dark blood leaking over her fingers.

The Ila looked over the corpses of Tain and three of his men, and then at him and Memnanan. "I still rule this camp," she said.

A shot had hit her in the stomach. She was still sitting upright. She was still on her throne. The aui'it clustered around her as if they foresaw and dreaded her fall.

What was there for them to say? That the Ila was the one name that tribes and villages alike knew as authority?

That no one outside these canvas walls knew what had transpired in this tent?

His own blood was leaking fast from a dozen wounds. The fever was coming on him, the healing fever. He wanted to go lie down. He wanted Hati, and to lie still under a friendly roof and let the makers work, if they could heal so many wounds, with such scant resources left.

Marak, Marak, Marak, his voices said: and they *wanted* the Ila, they *wanted* her life as they wanted the east.

Memnanan had made his own choice, and stood now with the rifle aimed at the floor, deaf to voices, not knowing now what to do.

"Go to your wife," Marak said. "*She* needs you. You have an obligation."

Memnanan hesitated, perhaps weighing his choices, and asking himself where right was, or what he intended. Memnanan to this hour had not left the Ila, had not left the authority he had served, and defended, and obeyed all his life. And the storm still raged beyond the walls.

"Tell him to go," Marak said to the Ila. "His wife is in labor. She needs him. There's a guide rope still at the door." Came a crash in the heavens, and a battering blast beat against the tent. "Ila, tell him that. The sky's getting worse. Send him! You owe him that!"

The Ila lifted her hand, red glove stained dark with blood, signaled Memnanan's dismissal. That was all. The hand fell.

A breath more Memnanan hesitated, then turned and, hesitating for a last look, went back to the outer door.

Marak, the voices said. *Marak.*

And Marak reached down and drew the Ila to her feet and into his embrace, close, closer, body against body, blood into blood. He knew what the voices wanted. He knew what he had done with Lelie, and why Lelie had lived.

The Ila, no fool, must know. They stood that way for a long time, they stood there while the fever came, and the blood beat in Marak's ears.

"This is war," the Ila said in their long standing there, so that only he could hear. "This is *war,* Trin Tain." Her lips met his and opened, and her mouth was moist, water-rich as his was dry. Blood mixed. Incredibly, there was passion in the kiss.

Aui'it and servants moved around them, and *Marak,* his voices said, *Marak, Marak.* It *was* war. His hands and arms and back took fever-fire. Pain enveloped him, enveloped her, a shared environment, and the ache in his side and his skull fed her hurts.

If the makers in his blood bred and multiplied to heal him, he thought they must exist in hordes and clots by now, his whole body become a furnace of healing.

And they met the Ila's makers, and hers met his.

Marak, his voices said, thrumming in his head, *Marak.*

It might be his imagination, but the voices seemed perilously fainter, perhaps failing him—or appeased at last by what he had done, or perhaps just preoccupied.

He felt the ground. He had gone down on one knee and dragged the Ila with him, locked in his arms. He heard Norit in that moment as if she were right beside him. He was aware of Hati, and Patya and Tofi being near her.

Hati knew what had happened: she knew about the fight, about his father. Norit did. Memnanan told them. Memnanan, for some reason, was dripping wet; and when he wondered he knew what Hati saw, looking out, knew that that crack was lightning, that, outside their struggle, water poured down in sheets and blew in veils. They welcomed Memnanan into the tent. They besieged him with questions that made no sense.

Marak, his voices said, but he made no sense of what followed.

The water kept coming on the roof, and made pools and puddles. He heard it. The Ila did.

Luz knew. Luz told them.

The fever built in him, threatening to sweep everything away. Hati was running, alone, through the cold wet, and then Patya and Tofi had overtaken her, and they sprinted, soaked as they were, through a murky grayness and a grayed red of puddles. Norit came after, holding Lelie, all of them drenched.

Marak, his voices said, and he was aware of the Ila's limbs, fever-hot, and the war they fought, each holding the other up.

"Why take up my father?" he asked, and, for his pride's sake: "How long?"

The Ila laughed, not a pleasant laugh, near his ear. "During your search, *my* men found him. I've always taken alternatives. Always alternatives. He was in and out of my tent, from time to time. He followed, outside the column, in a Haga's robes. I'm tired. Lie down with me. See which of us wins."

It was easier to sink down, both on their knees, then on the carpet, twined together. After a time he saw them lying there like the dead, two bloody figures locked in embrace. He saw, and knew he looked from outside himself, and that it was a vision of sorts, Luz's vision, what Luz saw of him, but he had no idea how she saw.

Then Norit came and touched his forehead ever so gently. His wives and his sister Patya and his brother-in-law Tofi all came to that bloody place, and sat down near him and waited, and waited. They expected—they feared, perhaps, for him to lose consciousness in fever, or to die. The Ila's servants moved about them. The aui'it were there, perhaps their own au'it as well.

A moment of darkness. "Marak," a voice said then, asking his attention, and someone lifted his head and gave him water, an abundance of water, as many drinks as he wanted. He was fever-hot. Heat swept through him then like a furnace, as if water were all the makers had waited to have.

Thunder walked overhead. Water dripped somewhere. It sounded like a fountain, dripping and gurgling like the Ila's Mercy—water, the universal condition of life, had become that abundant.

Someone came at that point, someone who wanted Hati, and Norit, wanted them urgently. He thought it was Patya. He dreamed it was Patya, who bent and kissed him before she took away all his help, all his protection, leaving him entirely alone with the Ila.

But shadows immediately came and peered down at him, a handful of veiled, armed shadows, who had no possible reason for being where they were, in the Ila's tent.

They retreated and sat, with their weapons, and they watched ... Keran, he was sure. But were those Haga, sitting with them?

"Your helpers," the Ila said to him, faintly, wryly, from beside him, in this makeshift bed they shared, of pillows and blankets and blood-soaked carpet. "I made a good throw, didn't I? Now, one way or the other, *we* become allies ... and what will we *do* with Luz, do you think? Or what will Luz do with you and me? —Or what, do you suppose, will we *all* do with the *ondat*?"

"I don't know," he said, in pain, not knowing where to take the Ila's words, or how to answer. The fever produced unbearable headache, and swelled the flesh around the wounds. He had nothing to do with the Ila's questions. The makers were at work. He had to endure it.

And the way he had held Lelie, and shed makers into her blood, he had pressed his wounds to the Ila's wounds, and hers to his—both of them, makers shared. Makers at all-out war not only with the wounds ... but with each other, live or die, win or lose.

He understood the Ila's dealing with Tain, when she caught him. What else was she to use for weapons, when her makers had consistently lost their battles with Luz's makers?

What else was she to use, when Tain fell into her hands?

Tain, being Tain, to be sure, meant to seize power for himself ... he had not made his move yet, but that had been his intention, and surely the Ila knew it, being old as the world and still alive.

But Tain was also her weakness: Tain had *not* known how far Memnanan had allegiances elsewhere. Tain had not known how much a man could love a wife, that a man could have a friend against his own interests. *There* was Tain's downfall, in every canny truth he thought he knew, in every lesson he had tried to teach his son about the world.

Kaptai, against all odds, had taught him otherwise.

His head throbbed. Pain shot through his ears and eyes. It might have been a skirmish his makers had just won. Or lost.

One au'it among the lot of aui'it, perhaps their own, wrote and wrote. He was aware of the movement. The drip of water. The rumble of thunder.

And he became aware of Hati, of Hati and Norit, near Memnanan, and he saw a vision, Tofi struggling to heat a pan of water.

Hati's impatience came through. And Norit's.

They were not in his war. They had *Luz's* makers in them. And he heard them, saw them.

They shoved Tofi sharply aside.

"Push," the women cried together. "Push! Now! Now, woman!"

Came a woman's shout, then, and cries from the others, and then from the men.

A newborn baby cried protest, newly arrived, as the heavens poured.

"A boy!" *Memnanan's mother cried above a crack of thunder. "My son has a son!"*

25

Things change. That is what I arrange to happen. In a limited system, in an alien environment, that means frequent intervention, with only my returning nanoceles to report on the local health of the system. That means I am the living template, and in my own cells I assure a standard. Whenever I am tempted to create a match for myself, I ask myself whose would be the standard then? And would they understand at all what I have done, and why I have done it, even if I told them?
—The Book of the Ila

Visions ceased, the providers of visions grown exhausted, and resting. The dark lost all feature except a red glow that pulsed, more and less, more and less, like the fire that burned through his veins.

Marak lay still, measuring his breaths until the pain became bearable. He heard thunder. The rush of wind.

But the tent ropes held. The canvas did.

Marak, the voices whispered, wanting his attention, and visions claimed him.

It seemed the stars came out in this vision. Then a strange thing appeared in the night, white, and looking like a village from a distance.

He drifted closer.

It glittered with lights, some that blinked, others that lit its walls.

And this place, above all visions he had seen, was ominous to him. He had no trust in Luz, that the vision would prove harmless.

Ondat, his voices said to him.

"Do you see it?" he asked Luz in a whisper, and then, thinking that someone else, perhaps Hati, was close to him. "Do you see a village in the night sky?"

"I see something white," Hati said, and a hand rested on his shoulder, comforting him. "It could be a village. But its towers go off in every direction."

"Like the tower," Norit said, from behind her. "It's a tower in the sky."

Luz warned them: the *ondat* were here. Somehow the *ondat* had established a village that had no ground under it, and Luz showed them this sight to amaze them.

"What does it mean?" he asked Luz in that absence of other questions. "What are they? Where are they?"

Up, that strange sense of direction told him, as it had at other times told him *east.* This time it was *up, up, up,* when he knew there could be nothing up there but the sky and the stars.

Perhaps the *ondat* had breached their treaty and taken over.

Perhaps after all they would destroy Luz and her tower, and with Luz, their refuge, and all of them would die.

Perhaps their real safety, now that the hammer had fallen, was not the tower, but to scatter into the low desert, and hide in caves, hoping to live in whatever circumstances they could.

"What do you want us to do?" he asked Luz in a whisper, as he always had to speak to Luz aloud to be heard.

He only felt a direction, and that direction was what it had been. *East. East.*

East.

He felt someone rest a hand on his shoulder. Tofi was there. The tent above him seemed far less fine. Daylight came only from an open flap. There were no lamps lit.

"We're in danger of drowning," Tofi said. "We're going to move the camp."

"East," he said. The vision of the tower in the stars broke apart, became irretrievable, something beyond imagination.

"East," Tofi said, and that satisfied him. Satisfied Luz.

It dawned on him the plain tent above him was his own, and that Hati and Norit were on his other side, with Lelie, and that there were, unaccountably, more points of contact than the three of them. Four, one in this tent, largely unaware, asleep. *Five,* the last at a little remove from him.

That one was aware, and in pain. It was the Ila.

"We're going to have to pack the tents wet," Hati said to him, businesslike. "We have to move. There's water just flowing through, washing out some of the tents. It's become the one thing we're not short of."

"I probably could ride."

"Probably you could," Hati said. "But you're not going to."

He shut his eyes.

Eventually they moved him onto a litter, and wrapped him in two blankets and a piece of canvas, and carried him out into the light.

The world had changed its coat. It had been all blowing sand. Now it was murky grays, sandy mud, and a dull sheen of reflections off rain-pocked water. It was as if a well had overflowed. Some water-au'it had not been doing her job.

He shut his eyes. They balanced the litter on two bundles of baggage. Hati bent and kissed him. He heard a small baby crying. Then Lelie set up a howl. A new baby had come out of nowhere and cried, taking attention, and Lelie, he thought, was jealous, and angry.

He went to sleep again. When he waked, he saw tribesmen carrying the litter, tribesmen afoot and walking. He found that curious and went back to sleep.

Mostly he slept, and waked again, once as the earth shivered, then again at a change of bearers.

Then, a distant whisper, he heard his voices. *Marak,* they said. *Marak, Marak.*

Calmly. A part of the world. Contact, with Luz.

He drew a wider breath, ignoring the pain in his ribs. He reached up an unwounded finger, pulled down the stiff canvas that covered him above the chin, and gave a critical eye to the world.

It was unremitting gray overhead. The sun went veiled. He ventured more of his hand into the sunlight, and realized then something strange about his hand, as if it was suddenly someone else's. It lacked the killing-marks. He extracted it completely from the canvas, held it up to the light, and saw only the reddened trace of the marks that had existed on his fingers.

A part of him, a part of his former life, was wiped out.

He shoved the canvas farther back, blankets and all as the bearers carried him, heedless, and he looked at the skin of his chest, which showed only the faintest trace of the abjori mark, as his hands showed the redness of healing cuts, and the wound in his side was sealed, swollen, painful.

"Lie still," Hati said from the lofty height of her saddle. Her besha moved with lordly ease beside the struggling bearers. "Don't make trouble."

"What happened to the Ila?" he asked, but once he asked, he knew, he *knew* her location, as he knew Hati's, Norit's, Lelie's, at every moment he was near them. And the new one.

"You beat her," Norit said, also from above. She was riding on his other side, with Lelie on her saddle. "She's with the priests. Memnanan's gone to see to her. We *know* where she is. Always."

So did he. She was behind him in the line. As weak and sick as he was, he thought, and with the remnant of a hellish headache.

He lay back and drew up the blankets against the chill in the air. He slept again, slept until they camped and raised the tents.

By then the rain had stopped, but a nearby pan had become a pool of water, safe, at least, for the beshti; and the tents went up with the lighter stakes this time, a quicker job.

Hati offered him a drink of sweet water, and he drank, and slept—and waked in the enclosed dark of the tent as the earth shook.

The baby born in the storm—Memnanan's son—let out an infant cry of disturbance. That point of awareness was active. Then the Ila waked, elsewhere. Hati and Norit were much closer.

Thunder rumbled. The whole world felt strange, the air choked and thick with damp.

Marak rubbed his ears, rubbed his eyes, decided he could sit up, and did. Hati set her hand on his arm.

He moved that arm, embraced her shoulder, drew her close. They sat that way a while, one leaning on the other. Norit slept with Lelie across her lap.

He felt exhausted, drained of all the strength he had ever had.

Marak, Marak, Marak, the voices said. Luz said. Or whatever it was that droned on that way. The world had reached a sort of exhausted peace. He saw Norit wake, and he put out a hand and caressed Norit's knee without resistance. Norit set her hand on his, looked at him, for the most part sane.

They rested that way until the light crept back, slowly, sullenly. He decided finally that it was morning enough, and that today he would get on his feet and get into the saddle again.

It took two tries to get on his feet. Hati braced herself and pulled and he made it up, and walked, and passed the tent flap to the outside, into what passed for a dawn.

The air was cold, bitter cold. The sand was wet. He wrapped his coat about him, and saw others stirring out of their tents. He walked past the edge of the tent and looked around the camp, all around, seeing tents as far as he could see. After the wind that had blown over them, after seeing the scoured bone that had landed at the edge of the Ila's tent, he had feared far worse was the case. Beshti, some of them, bore cuts and gashes. Some were burned over part of their skin, the hair simply gone. They were a sad-looking lot, and some might have died.

Tofi came out of the tent. Patya did. "You're all right," Patya said.

"Well enough," Marak said, and heard the voices to distraction: Luz was nagging him. Luz wanted something that did not involve the east, rather *north. North. Not far.*

He looked, saw the Ila's tent, and walked that way without a word to anyone. Hati and Norit went with him, perhaps under the same instruction, hearing the same voice. The au'it was not with them. He had no idea whether the au'it still attended them. Or whether the Ila, on second thought, *needed* an au'it with them any longer.

They went into the Ila's tent, and inside, Memnanan was there, just putting on his belt. With him in crowded circumstances, in the tent foyer, were three of his men, an au'it, and two tribesmen, one Haga, one Keran—neither Aigyan nor Menditak, it seemed, had left anything to chance, or to the Ila's goodwill. They had slept there, and had just begun to prepare for the day.

"Marak Tain," Memnanan said, looking at him as a man might look at the risen dead.

"Alive," Marak said. And added: "Grateful."

Memnanan nodded slightly, acknowledgment.

Hati said darkly. "My husband saved the Ila's life. But I doubt she's grateful. She's awake. I think we need to see her."

Memnanan indicated the way, the curtain. "My men take my orders. The priests . . . have come here. They've been about. I haven't let them in—waiting *your* orders, *omi*."

The priests: a reservoir of the Ila's own makers, a source, like a well, of her former independence.

But there was, he suspected, no renewal there: if they were overcome in her. Luz's would win, every time, now, and every priest who took in the Ila's makers would now take in Luz's. That was the truth his own body told him. That was the answer the world had, from now on.

He pushed the curtain back. The Ila's servants, rising up to bar the way, saw him and hesitated. He simply walked through with Hati and Norit, in Memnanan's witness, and the tribesmen's, and flung back the last curtain.

The Ila, aware of them as they were of her, sat in her chair, waiting for them. Aui'it attended her. Her white skin, the red robes—those were the same. But bones stood out in her hands as they did in his. They both had given up substance to the struggle.

Hati and Norit stopped one on a side of him. They were alike now, all together, all part of a set.

The Ila moved her hand, and the aui'it settled on the mats on either side of her and opened their books.

"You've had your way," the Ila said. "You think you've won."

"*Luz* has won," Marak said, but he was unwilling, himself, to concede that without limits. He added, for himself: "So far."

"So far." The Ila's voice was weak, but edged. "I gave you your freedom. I gave everyone in the world their *freedom*, such as we had, so long as it lasted. Now there's one way, one blood, and one tribe in the world, and *we've* joined it." She drew breath, and her eyes held the old fire. "So let the *ondat* worry about *that.*"

"So you have secrets," Norit said. "You change your makers at will. You're trying to change them now, but so far, it's not working, is it? We'll understand how you do that. Sooner or later, *we'll* know."

"Luz."

"Yes?" the answer came.

The Ila smiled ... smiled with chilling serenity. "We'll see. Granted we have an immediate problem ... still, we'll talk."

"We *are* pragmatists," Luz said from Norit's lips. "You can't feed this mass of people, or shelter them. We can. You think you can change my makers, given a hundred years, or two hundred, or three. *Try.*"

"I assure you, I'll try."

"We should go," Marak said to his wives, and took them each by an arm and walked.

He had seen enough to satisfy himself the Ila was alive and that she had become one of the mad. But she was not content to be that—she never would be content. She meant to change the order of the world, and now meant to do it from inside their ranks.

Luz then would change it back, and so it would go, by degrees as tiny as the makers themselves. Now there were two gods on the earth, and neither one was, or would be, perhaps for all time to come, completely in power over the other.

There might be gods in the heavens, too, the *ondat*, watching to see how it all came out: he believed his vision of the tower in the stars.

But the *ondat* could scarcely observe a war of makers, carried on in the veins of two determined women.

Himself, he had done with gods, and had no desire to contend with makers. He put an arm about his wives, one on either hand, and went out through the curtain, taking one combatant out of speaking range, at least for now. It might be a while before the Ila heard the voices he heard, if she ever did.

He gave Memnanan a passing courtesy, and went out into the morning. An au'it followed them, and took up her duty.

They packed up and they rode, a long, weary line of riders.

They went in a kind of twilight, the air cold, the sun thickly shrouded in slate gray cloud.

But the light was enough, finally, to show them a strange, upthrust shape on the horizon.

It was the tower on its hill, on the rim of the land they could see.

"We're almost there," Marak said, and pointed it out to his wives, who already knew.

26

Another year is gone, as much as that means.
—Marak's Book

The air was cold and clear, breath of man and beast frosting on the wind . . . it was noon, though anyone who remembered the sky as it had been would never know it. Snow had fallen in the morning, and lay all about . . . more boded in the west, out of which all weather came, but Marak Trin had seen the stars scream down from the heavens. That was hazard. He had seen the deep snows. That was hardship. This little spit of snow failed to daunt him.

More, he was on his way home, and going home, in a logic that defied the tower's careful teaching, all distances were shorter.

Once a month at least he saddled up Osan and rode out as far as the cliffs of the Lakht.

Once a month he surveyed the lakes and the pools below the rim, gathered samples . . . and came back again, surrendered himself and Osan to Ian's examination. Luz wanted to be sure he had picked up nothing new and unplanned in his blood.

He had that examination ahead of him, a small price for his freedom. And he was as interested as Ian and Luz in the quality and persistence of the makers. That his so ably survived reassured the *ondat* in their sky perch—the *ondat*, who were coming to understand the Ila's methods themselves, and who therefore might feel less threatened by the wide expanse of . . . all Luz said existed out there among the stars.

His own travels were to the rim and back. That was enough. Sometimes Hati came with him. Sometimes Norit joined them both. They had seen the whole world change, and skies darken, and the snows pile up.

Then they had seen them melt.

The tribes had spread a few tents outside now, weary of the confinement, and there were a few structures outside, these days, outposts from which trained observers watched the changes in the world. But it was the tents that the tribes longed to see. Aigyan and Menditak talked about establishing outlying camps, and seeing what living could be made out there, given adequate supplies, but Luz said it was too early, that they had yet to release the living things they had engineered . . . that was their word for it: *engineered*. Everything would fit together. The tribes would have their livelihood. There would be a place in the world for them.

There was no sign of vermin. Nothing grew, but a handful of small things that had greatly interested Luz . . . he had brought those back years ago.

But of larger life, nothing moved.

He argued for making the trek up to Pori, such as remained of it, if anything remained on the Lakht. He found it hard even yet to think that nothing at all had survived. Luz sent her fliers up there, and they found nothing different than what was below, but Marak thought a man might see more, do more, find out more.

The *ondat* remained suspicious. He knew about them. He knew about other worlds. He knew how the Ila's people had pushed too fast in their own investigations of territory, antagonized the *ondat* and fought a war with makers—the details were disputed, and the Ila claimed that never was the case, but Luz thought otherwise, and the *ondat* seemed to.

He knew how the Ila had come here and done everything she could to survive, fearing Luz's kind as much as she feared the *ondat*—which argued that the Ila had known there was a wrong, and justice for it.

He knew very many more things about the world he owned than he had ever suspected. He knew that they were allowed to live here, that Luz had made some arrangement with the *ondat,* that, in a sense, they were as observed as Luz's specimens in the lab, to see what the makers in them would do, and to see how the world recovered.

The hammer had come down in the sea, and the shock had rung around the world until it melted the rocks of the eastern ocean, and cracked the world, as Norit had put it, like a broken pot. The earth poured out floods of molten rock, and went on shaking, and sent up smoke to darken the sun—but Luz showed the villagers how to build walls that would not fall in earthquake, and promised the tribes new tents that, with very little effort, could keep out the cold.

It was all what people had done once before, the Ila said, disdainful of their effort. And she would have shown them those things if they had needed them.

They knew. They had put together all the books that reached the tower, and there were no secrets. Deep in the tower depths now was the record of everything that had been erased off the earth. He was written there. So were all of them, every bearer of every book, and all they had done. So were things written there that the *ondat* might not like to know—he had no idea: certain books he knew Luz and Ian and the Ila kept to themselves. He knew various things, being what he was, that those three might wish kept quiet, but he had no disposition to talk about them, and no one cared, outside, anyway. All the excitement these days was about the outposts, and the beshti that were being let out.

There had been a time breathing the air outside had burned a man's chest, a time when even beshti could not thrive above ground. In those days they had gone out with masks and machines.

But Luz said the sea survived. Luz had already loosed makers into the creatures he brought back, to be released again. And he had dug down under thin patches of new snow and sowed seeds as far as the cliffs . . . being born a villager, he found himself doing what a villager did, and planting crops, of a sort, whatever might come of them.

The Ila said they had done all that before, too, and with a great deal more work, too, except they had had the vermin to carry the makers. She and Luz held long, long discussions.

So, well, he scattered seeds. With no vermin in the world to eat them, they would wait. Seeds were good at waiting.

By midday he rode into clear view of the tower, over a remembered last rise in the land.

He was surprised. He saw tents, white tents far outlying the walls they were building, a stubborn little clump of them well out from the tower. He would all but wager those were the an'i Keran. And that other one, equally separated, in an opposite direction—those might well be Haga.

It was spring. He supposed Luz herself might have encouraged this sudden flowering into the open, if it had not been a spontaneous rebellion. The tribes were getting restless under a solid roof.

It was a very good sight, those tents. But the tribes would have to devise a way to signal their differences, some badge of color and pattern. He was sure they would find it.

He crossed the last flat before the tower hill, leaving solitary tracks in the snow behind him, seeing a pattern of tracks going out to the tents. There were beshti out there, on either hand.

And being the only traveler out of the west, and having all that activity outside the tower, he was not surprised to be noticed.

He was not surprised to hear voices, *Marak, Marak, Marak*—and not surprised to feel that increasing warmth in the world that defined home, wherever it was.

His wives knew now he was coming. They were paying attention.

They came out from the tower to meet him as he rode up toward the doors, Norit anxious to welcome him home, Hati eager to ask what he had seen.

The children came running out, too, Lelie's daughter's youngsters, and his and Hati's great-grandchildren running across the light coating of snow . . . that young-looking man that had come out was Memnanan's tall son Memnanet, father to several generations himself, with Lelie.

They were a tribe, themselves. They had gotten to be . . . and a handful of all of them did not age, and healed of their wounds—templates, Luz called them, not their word for it. Memnanan had become one: the three who ruled their lives counted him necessary. And for that reason Memnanan knew he was back, as he knew exactly where Memnanan was, out in the tents, arguing with Aigyan on issues he could almost guess.

But of all the rest, passing the clamorous rush of small children, it was Hati who came running out to meet him, Hati, forever young, braids and veils flying, bracelets flashing gold under the leaden sky.

He slid down from the besha's saddle and opened his arms.

But, almost within his reach, she stopped and looked up, light touching her, and the tower, and the astonished children, who gazed skyward half in fear.

Marak looked up, too, at a long-forgotten power in the heavens.

Sunlight, if only for an instant, found its way through the clouds.

We hope you've enjoyed this Eos book. As part of our mission to give readers the best science fiction and fantasy being written today, the following pages contain a glimpse into the fascinating worlds of a select group of Eos authors.

Join us as acclaimed sf great C.J. Cherryh unveils a brand new universe where two interstellar empires, scarred by nanotechnology, are poised for battle on a distant desert planet. As Ben Weaver takes us on an action-packed adventure into an intergalactic civil war, and James Alan Gardner visits the most dangerous and mysterious planet in the Expendable universe—Earth itself. As Anne McCaffrey and Elizabeth Ann Scarborough reveal the latest adventure of Acorna, the beloved unicorn girl, and her fight to save her homeworld. And as Stephen R. Lawhead concludes the sweeping historical saga of faith, magic, and mystery—Celtic Crusades.

FALL 2002 AT EOS. OUT OF THIS WORLD.

HAMMERFALL

C.J. Cherryh

August 2002

Imagine first a web of stars. Imagine it spread wide and wider. Ships shuttle across it. Information flows.

A star lies at the heart of this web, its center, heart, and mind.

This is the Commonwealth.

Imagine then a single strand of stars in a vast darkness, a beckoning pathway away from the web, a path down which ships can travel.

Beyond lies a treasure, a small lake of G5 suns, a near circle of perfect stars all in reach of one another.

This way, that strand says. After so hard a voyage, reward. Wealth. Resources.

But a whisper comes back down that thread of stars, a ghost of a whisper, an illusion of a whisper.

The web of stars has heard the like before. Others are out there, very far, very faint, irrelevant to our affairs.

Should we have listened?
—The Book of the Landing.

DISTANCE DECEIVED THE EYE IN THE LAKHT, THAT wide, red land of the First Descended, where legend said the ships had come down.

At high noon, with the sun reflecting off the plateau, the chimera of a city floated in the haze, appearing as a line of light just below the red, saw-toothed ridge of the Qarain, that upthrust that divided the Lakht from the Anlakht, the true land of death.

The city was both mirage and truth; it appeared always a day before its true self. Marak knew it, walking, walking end-lessly beside the beshti, the beasts on which their guards rode.

The long-legged beasts were not deceived. They moved no faster. The guards likewise made no haste.

"The holy city," some of the damned shouted, some in re-lief, some in fear, knowing it was both the end of their tor-ment and the end of their lives. "Oburan and the Ila's court!"

"Walk faster, walk faster," the guards taunted them lazily, sitting supreme over the column. The lank, curve-necked beasts that carried them plodded at an unchangeable rate. They were patient creatures, splay-footed, towering above most predators of the Lakht, enduring the long trek between wells with scant food and no water. A long, long line of them stretched behind, bringing the tents, the other appurte-nances of their journey.

"Oburan!" the fools still cried. "The tower, the tower!"

"Run to it! Run!" the junior guards encouraged their pris-oners. "You'll be there before the night, drinking and eating before us."

It was a lie, and some knew better, and warned the rest. The wife of a down-country farmer, walking among them, set up a wail when the word went out that the vision was only the shadow of a city, and that an end was a day and more away.

"It can't be!" she cried. "It's there! I see it! Don't the rest of you see it?"

But the rest had given up both hope and fear of an end to this journey, and walked in the rising sun at the same pace as they had walked all this journey.

Marak was different than the rest. He bore across his heart the tattoo of the abjori, the fighters from rocks and hills. His garments, the long shirt, the trousers, the aifad wrapped about his head against the hellish glare, were all the dye and the weave of Kais Tain, of his own mother's hand. Those patterns alone would have damned him in the days of the war. The tattoos on the backs of his fingers, six, were the number of the Ila's guards he had personally sent down to the shadows. The Ila's men knew it, and watched with special care for any look of rebellion. He had a reputation in the lowlands and on the Lakht itself, a fighter as elusive as the mirage and as fast-moving as the sunrise wind.

He had ridden with his father to this very plain, and for three years had seen the walls of the holy city as a prize for the taking. He and his father had laid their grandiose plans to end the Ila's reign: they had fought. They had had their victories.

Now he stumbled in the ruin of boots made for riding.

His life was thirty summers on this earth and not likely to be longer. His own father had delivered him up to the Ila's men.

The others all had their stories. The caravan was full of the cursed, the doomed, the rejected. Villages had tolerated them as long as they dared. In Kais Tain long before this, Tain had issued a pogrom to cleanse his province of the mad, ten years ago; but the god laughed at him. Now his own son and heir proved tainted. Tain of Kais Tain had successfully rebelled against the Ila and the Lakht, undefeated for ten years, and had all the west under his hand. But his own son had a secret, and betrayed himself in increasing silences, in looks of abstraction, in crying out in his sleep. He had been mad all along. His father had begun to suspect, perhaps, years ago, and denied it; but lately, after their return from the war, the voices had grown too persistent, too consuming to keep the secret any longer. His father had found him out.

And when shortly afterward his father heard the Ila's men were looking for the mad, his father had sent to the Ila's men . . . had given him up, his defiance of the Ila's rule broken by the truth.

REBELS IN ARMS

BEN WEAVER

SEPTEMBER 2002

PART ONE: CAMPAIGN EXETER

From my seat on the dais, I looked over the crowd of cadets about to graduate from South Point Academy. Could they really listen to a middle-aged soldier like me drone on about the challenges of being an officer? After all, the commandant, a war vet himself, was already at the lectern and boring them to death with that speech. In fact, when the commandant had asked me to speak, I had panicked because I knew those kids needed something more than elevated diction and fancy turns of phrase. But what?

The commandant glanced over his shoulder and nodded at me. "And now ladies and gentlemen, at this time I'd like to introduce a man whose Special Ops Tactical Manual is required reading here at the academy, a man whose treatise on Racinian conditioning transformed that entire program. Ladies and gentlemen, I give you Colonel Scott St. Andrew, Chief of the Alliance Security Council."

Applause I had expected, but a standing ovation? Or maybe those cadets were just overjoyed that the commandant was leaving the podium. I dragged myself up, wincing over all the metal surgeons had jammed into me after the nanotech regeneration had failed. Unless you were really looking for it, you wouldn't notice my limp. I tugged at the hems of my dress tunic, raised my shoulders, and took a deep breath before starting forward. The kids continued with their applause, their eyes wide and brimming with naïveté.

"Thank you. Please . . ." I gestured for them to sit, then waited for the rumble to subside. "First, let me extend my gratitude to the commandant for allowing me to be here today." I tipped my head toward the man, who winked. "As all of you know, we are living in some very turbulent times. The treaties we signed at the end of the war are now being violated. Rumors of yet another civil war pervade. But let me assure you that we at the security council are doing everything we can to resolve these conflicts. Now then. I didn't come here to talk about current events. I came here to tell you what you want to hear—a war story—not because it's entertaining, but because it's something you *need* to hear . . ."

I lay in my quarters aboard the *SSGC Auspex,* cushioned tightly in my gelrack and in the middle of a disturbing dream. My name wasn't Scott St. Andrew; I wasn't an eighteen-year-old captain and company commander in the Seventeen System Guard Corps, in charge of one-hundred and sixty-two lives; and my cheek no longer bore the cross-shaped birthmark that revealed I had a genetic defect and came from poor colonial stock.

In the dream I was a real Terran, born in New York, and about to download my entire college education through a cerebro. I sat in a classroom with about fifty other privileged young people who would never need to join the military as a way to escape from their stratified society. I looked down at the c-shaped device sitting on the desk in front of me. I need only slide it onto my head and learn.

But I couldn't. I was afraid I might forget who I was, forget that my father, an overworked, underpaid company geologist had tried his best to raise me and my brother Jarrett, since my mother had left us when we were small. Jarrett and I had entered South Point Academy just when the war had begun, and Jarrett had died in an accident during a "conditioning process" developed by an ancient alien race we called the "Racinians." The conditioning, which involved the introduction into our brains of "mnemosyne,"—a species of eidetic parasite found aboard Racinian spacecraft,—enhanced our physical and mental capabilities, and aged us at an accelerated rate.

No, I couldn't forget. I needed to remember what I had become, because I sensed even then that if just one person could learn something from my story, from my mistakes, then the universe might forgive me of my sins.

They were many.

TRAPPED

James Alan Gardner

October 2002

It was a creamy tube of light, glinting with colors like the Aurora Borealis. Green. Gold. Purple. As it shimmered in the darkness, I could see the stars behind: the tube was like glowing milky smoke. It stretched so high it disappeared into the blackness as if it soared beyond our planet's atmosphere—but that was just as terrifying as if the thing were simply a ghost. A ghost could only go, "Boo!" Mysteries from outer space could cause *real* trouble.

I couldn't help thinking of Opal's story. A Spark Lord. A Lucifer. An Explorer from the galaxy at large.

The upper body of the tube flapped and fluttered like a banner in a stiff wind, but the bottom seemed rooted in place. Though the trees blocked our view, I knew the spectral tube had attached itself to Death Hotel. I could imagine it like a phantom lamprey, mouth spread and locked onto the building's ugly dome; or perhaps the tube was a pipeline that fed ethereally into the sealed-up interior, and even as we watched, it was pumping down a horde of aliens. Or spirits. Or worse.

"Oh look," said Pelinor, pointing at the tube. "Isn't that pretty." Pause. "What is it?"

Nobody answered. The horses stopped one by one, either reined in by their riders or halting of their own accord as they saw the tube twinkling in the sky. The thing fluttered in silence—the whole world had hushed, as if even the horses were holding their breaths. Then, without a whisper, the ghostly tube snapped free of the mausoleum like a broken kite string, and in the blink of an eye it slithered up into the night.

Deep dark quiet. Then, beneath me, Ibn gave a snort that filled the cool air with horse steam. The other horses snorted too, perhaps trying to decide if they should worry or just shrug off what they'd seen. In front of me, Myoko cleared her throat . . . but before she could speak, an ear-shattering <BOOM> ripped the silence.

I had an instant to register that the noise came from the hotel: like a cannon being fired. Then there was no more time for thinking, as Ibn went wild with fear.

ACORNA'S SEARCH

Anne McCaffrey and
Elizabeth Ann Scarborough

December 2002

Acorna said, I will take first watch."

"Watch?" Maati asked. "Watch *what*? This planet can't sustain sentient life. I thought we'd established that. Well, except for these jungly plants and that scuttling thing and—I guess I see your point."

"I will watch, also," Aari said. "It may be best to do so in pairs for now."

"I might as well watch with you also," Thariinye said, "because I cannot imagine that I will sleep a wink in this place." But he did, and almost immediately.

Acorna and Aari sat, relaxed, each with one knee drawn up to their chins, each with one leg dangling over the side of the largish rock on which they perched. They gazed toward the jungle growth slightly above them, instead of back in the direction from which they had flown. The leaves and fronds of the strange forest were not outlined black against the night, as they might have expected, but instead glowed in the darkness with a greenish iridescence. A small wind stirred the leaves. Otherwise all was silent.

Acorna almost expected to hear a birdcall, or the snuffle of some smaller creature in the woods around them. Neeva had told her once of the endearing furred creatures that lived in the forests of Vhiliinyar before the Khleevi came—but they were no longer here, and the jungle was nothing but mutated weeds and brush grown very tall. The creatures of old Vhiliinyar sang in lovely voices and delighted all who heard. Their beautiful forms entranced all who saw them. Acorna wondered—had *aagroni* Iirtye managed to save specimens of all those creatures, or even samples of their cells to clone them from later on? What a wrenching loss it must be to have known such creatures well, and to lose them, along with all of the other wonders this planet had held when it was beautiful and whole.

Absorbed in her thoughts, it took Acorna a moment to realize she was hearing a noise, a soft snuffling sound, from beside her. Trails of tears ran down Aari's face.

She took his hand. (Penny for your thoughts, or was I broadcasting, and you were responding to mine?)

He sniffed again and turned a chiseled manly countenance to her. (What is a penny?)

(A primitive coin used by one of the nations of humankind before it became so devaluated it was not worth the materials needed to create it.)

He gave a short laugh. (Ah, a coin worthy of my present thoughts, indeed. Which are that we would have a better chance of re-forming narhii-Vhiliinyar into a semblance of Vhiliinyar than we have to return Vhiliinyar to its former state, as the *aagroni* wishes. Who would have thought even the Khleevi could so mutilate the landscape that its own people could not recognize it? I was wondering where the mountains were, where the lake was, and the waterfall. I see nothing here that resembles them.)

(And yet they are here. I sense the iron and granite of the mountain, and the plateau—the bones of that formation run beneath us and all through the area. Also the waters of the lake and cascade are here, though there are elements of sulfur and mercury and other contaminants in them. I do not think it will destroy our horns to purify that water. But there is something worrying about those plants . . .)

They heard something then: the thump of paws jumping

down and a scattering of small stones beneath soft footpads, the movement of a dark plumed tail hovering at the edge of the plants. RK, Acorna realized, had to relieve himself and he was not happy about the only available cover.

In a moment he disappeared from sight and the Linyaari couple concluded he had found what he was looking for.

Then an earsplitting yowl burst from the greenery several yards to the left of the campsite.

Acorna and Aari jumped to their feet, stumbling over the rocks in the dark. Acorna fell heavily and scraped the skin from her right arm and knee. Aari turned back to her, his horn lowered to help with the healing, but Acorna waved him on urgently.

(This will keep. See to RK. Help him!) she insisted above the cat's caterwauling as she climbed painfully to her feet. (That does not sound like a cat bellyache to me.) She brushed her wounded arm over her horn but the cat screamed before she could touch her leg. Her wound could wait. Something was very wrong with RK. She moved as fast as she could toward the noise. Sounds of thrashing and howling, snarling and more shrieks and screams rang through the night as she limped forward to see one of the tall plants whipping a furry tail back and forth in the air. Nothing remained evident of RK but his furious cries and his tail. A huge green bulbous protuberance on the plant concealed the rest of the cat.

Aari leapt for the lashing tail but it whipped out of his grasp.

They had no weapons handy, no implements or utensils that would be useful in destroying the plant. And RK's cries were growing weaker, strangled, more pitiful. They had to do something . . . now!

THE MYSTIC ROSE:
Book 3 of the Celtic Crusades

Stephen R. Lawhead

December 2002

The younger man lowered himself to his seat, and Caitriona proceeded to the table, remaining behind de Bracineaux and out of his sight. She placed the tray on the table, and made to step away, her right hand reaching for the hilt of the slender dagger at her back.

As her fingers tightened on the braided grip, the Templar cast a hasty glance over his shoulder. She saw his lowered brow and the set of his jaw, and feared the worst.

Silently, she slipped the dagger from its sheath, ready to strike. But the light of recognition failed to illumine his eyes. "Well?" he demanded. "Get to your work, now. Light the lamps and leave us."

Cait hesitated, waiting for him to settle back in his chair. When she did not move, the Templar turned on her. "Do as I say, girl, and be quick about it!"

Startled, Cait stepped back a pace, almost losing her grip on the weapon.

"Peace, Renaud," said his companion. Reaching out, he took the Templar's sleeve and tugged him around. "Come, I have poured the wine." He raised his cup and took a long, deep draft.

De Bracineaux swung back to the table, picked up his cup

and, tilting his head back, let the wine run down his gullet. *Now!* thought Cait, rising onto the balls of her feet. *Do it now!*

Her hand freed the knife and she moved forward. At that instant, without warning, the door burst open and a thick-set, bull-necked Templar strode into the room behind her. Cait whipped the dagger out of sight, and backed away.

"Ah, here is Gislebert now!" said d'Anjou loudly.

The Templar paused as he passed, regarding Cait with dull suspicion. She ducked her head humbly, and quickly retreated into the darkened room.

"Come, sergeant," called the fair-haired man, "raise a cup and give us the good news. Are we away to Jerusalem at last?"

"My lord, baron," said Gislebert, turning his attention to the others. "Good to see you, sir. You had a pleasant journey, I trust."

As the men began talking once more, Cait was forgotten—her chance ruined. She might cut one or even two men before they could react, but never three. And the sergeant was armed.

Still, she was close. The opportunity might never come again.

Reluctant to give up, she busied herself in the adjoining room, steeling herself for another attempt. Fetching some straw from the corner of the hearth, she stooped and lit it from the pile of embers. There was a lamp on the table, two candles in a double sconce on the wall by the bed, and a candletree in the corner. She lit the candles first, taking her time, hoping that Gislebert would leave.

She moved to the table and, as she touched the last of the straw to the lamp wick, became aware that someone was watching her from the doorway. Fearing she had been discovered at last, she took a deep breath, steadied herself and cast a furtive glance over her shoulder.

She did not see him at first. Her eyes went to the men who were still at the table on the balcony, cups in hand, their voices a murmur of intimate conversation. They were no longer heeding her. But, as she bent once more to the task at hand, she caught a movement in a darkened corner of the room and turned just as a man stepped from the shadows.

She stifled a gasp.

Dressed in the long white robe of a priest, he held up his hand, palm outward in an attitude of blessing—or to hold her in her place. Perhaps both, she thought. A man of youthful appearance, his hair and beard were black without a trace of gray and the curls clipped like the shorn pelt of a sheep. His eyes, though set deep beneath a dark and heavy brow, were bright and his glance was keen. He stepped forward into the doorway, placing himself between Cait and the men.

When he moved she felt a shudder in the air, as if a gust of wind had swept in through the open door; but the candles did not so much as quiver. At the same time, she smelled the fresh, clean scent of the heathered hills after a storm has passed.

"Do not be afraid," said the man, his voice calm and low. "I merely wish to speak to you."

Cait glanced nervously beyond him to where the Templar and his companions sat at their wine.

"Blind guides," he said, indicating the men. "They have neither eyes to see, nor ears to hear."

"Who are you?" As she asked the question, she glanced again at de Bracineaux and his companions; now laughing heartily, they appeared oblivious to both her and the stranger.

"Call me Brother Andrew," he said.

At the name, Cait felt her throat tighten. She gulped down a breath of air, "I know about you," she said, struggling to keep her voice steady. "My father told me."

"Your family has been in my service for a long time. That is why I have come—to ask if you will renew the vow of your father and grandfather."

"What vow is that?"

"I asked young Murdo to build me a kingdom where my sheep could safely graze . . ."

"Build it far, far away from the ambitions of small-souled men and their ceaseless striving," Cait said, repeating the